DREAM OPERATIVE

GARY WESTFAL

Copyright © 2013 by Westfal Publishing & Graphics, LLC

All rights reserved. No part of this book may be reproduced, scanned, or distributed in any printed or electronic form without permission. Please do not participate in or encourage piracy of copyrighted materials in violation of the author's rights. Purchase only authorized editions.

ISBN: 10-061570073X

ISBN-13: 978-0615700731

BOOK DESIGN BY: Westfal Publishing & Graphics, LLC

Scott Grinnell, Graphic Artist

This is a work of fiction. Names, characters, places, and incidents either are the product of the author's imagination or are used fictitiously. Any resemblance to actual persons, living or dead, businesses, companies, entities, events, or locales is entirely coincidental and does not imply an endorsement of any kind.

All image permissions have been secured and/or released for use by their originator or rightful owner and documentation is on file with the publisher.

DEDICATION

This book is dedicated to my wife, Janeen, who encouraged me to write about my dreams. Never in my wildest imagination did I ever think doing so would ignite an unquenchable passion for writing.

ACKNOWLEDGMENTS

This book would not be possible if not for the men and women who unselfishly serve our country in the quiet and humble capacity of their profession of arms through government service. Peace through strength and the unending devotion to the cause of freedom. I salute you!

To those who inspired me, encouraged me, and provided critical reviews that kept the drive of my desires going through many a long night's toil, I thank you all.

To my editors, specifically, the Amazon CreateSpace team, for their guidance and insight, helping to make this book the very best it can be.

To Mrs. Jan Waddy—for taking the time to find and correct distracting inconsistencies and punctuation oversights, in the kind and gentle manner that kept me smiling throughout the arduous process.

1

Two men stood guard outside the door at the end of a darkened hallway of a rundown building in the heart of the city. Much like the city of New York, there are over eight million people in Tehran. So finding an abandoned building was the easy part. Keeping it secure from thugs and curious outsiders was a different matter altogether.

Two more men, posted across a narrow street, kept an eye on sparse activity out front. All were armed to the teeth. All were prepared to die to protect the occupant of the room.

The red light on the video camera came on. The room was dark and dingy but provided just the obscurity he needed to get the message across and confuse the analysts, who would attempt to dissect the clues to decipher his location.

"This is a warning to the enemies of Allah and to all who support the misguided causes of the West..."

The man seated in front of the camera was obscured for deception and anonymity while he delivered his message. There was no mistaking his identity, however. Like Bin Laden himself, he had become a most highly sought-after terrorist and served as the architect of some of the world's most lethal activities since the attacks of 9/11.

He was elusive, well-protected, and connected to a network of supporters loyal to his radical rhetoric and calls to war against the West and virtually everyone associated with them.

"We will begin striking you with the full force of our might until we see a withdrawal of forces and occupation from our sovereign lands, a release of all political prisoners, and the lifting of sanctions against the people of

Iran. This must commence within twenty-four hours, or you will begin to experience the horrors of the Jihad, serving as an example of what is to come in cities across the globe."

Khalid Abdul-Hakim was dangerous, unpredictable, and always a step ahead of his pursuers. He had been second only to Bin laden, until SEAL Team Six took care of that problem. Now he was number one—a distinction he took seriously and with the full intent of proving himself worthy of the promotion.

He rose to his feet. The cameraman turned off the device. Both men looked at each other with concern when they heard a distinctive sound just outside the door. The cameraman drew his weapon and called out to the guards.

"Hamad, is the exit secure?"

Silence.

"Sir, I humbly implore you to stand back," warned the cameraman.

He cautiously opened the door and carefully peered into the dark hallway. Blood spatters painted the empty hallway wall across from the room. He looked over his shoulder to check on Hakim, and a bullet pierced his right temple that sent his body crashing to the floor.

Hakim drew his weapon and slowly backed into a dark corner of the room.

Two men charged the entryway, preceded by the crimson laser beams of their silenced weapons. The first one entered the room and was the recipient of the same welcome the cameraman received—a single bullet to the temple. Hakim was an expert marksman. The second pursuer hesitated outside the doorway just long enough for Hakim to determine his location. Hakim fired two shots, one into the back of his head, the other into his neck. Both shots were fired with precision through the thin plaster walls of the room. The man's limp body slumped to the floor with a definitive thud.

Hakim grabbed the video disc, stuffed it into his shirt pocket, and quickly made his way toward the front of the building. He looked out the door and saw a taxi parked down the street about a half block away on the left side of the road. He placed his weapon in the waistline of his pants at the small of his back and boldly stepped out from the building, casually making his way toward the taxi. Tires screeched behind him. He turned to see a late-model Mercedes aggressively headed toward him, the two men inside brandishing weapons. Hakim simply smiled and pressed a detonator inside his pocket that sent the luxury automobile into the air in a ball of fire. It was enough of a diversion to allow him to get to the taxi undetected.

He climbed into the driver's seat, reached up to the visor to retrieve a key, and disappeared into the city.

Joey G. Weston nearly rolled completely out of the hammock as he clumsily reached for his cell phone. Catching his balance, he managed *not* to knock over the Captain and Coke ™ sitting on the table next to him. His head was swimming from the emotion of his dream and an eclectic mix of too much sun and slightly more than a few drinks.

Like most of his dreams, this one made little sense, but it was filled with the vivid details and sordid emotions that provided the elements of intrigue he'd come to expect.

"G," as he was commonly referred to by most who knew him well, pressed the "record" button and began randomly reciting the various emotions of his dream, followed closely by the fleeting details he could recollect.

"Anxiety, pleasure...trepidation, euphoria, welcomed distraction..." he paused to mentally capture the images incited by each of the emotions.

"Water, wind, heat...an explosion...and a tall, attractive brunette with big, beautiful...eyes."

There was something about the woman he dreamed of that dominated most of his focus. The thought of her *demanded* his attention—consumed him, in fact.

Joey G Weston was a twenty-seven-year-old clinical psychologist with a passion for oneirology, or the study and analysis of dreams. It was the major theme of his doctoral thesis and, to him, a logical platform focus to his professional aspirations of self-discovery and a deeper understanding of human psychology.

G was a frequent dreamer. He couldn't really recall a time when he *didn't* dream. He was determined to explore the boundaries of the science by using himself as a central subject. After all, who better to truly capture every vivid detail than himself? G possessed a desire to gather an even deeper level of understanding through dream interpretation and, if possible, manipulation. The more he learned, the stronger his passions grew, and the more his mind discovered things most humans never truly *see*, much less comprehend.

He enjoyed evaluating dreams—his own and those of others. It was his passion, an intriguing obsession, really. He was determined to unlock the *secrets* of oneirology and focused on ways in which to control, and ultimately manipulate, dreams inasmuch as any human could control and manipulate reality. As a post-graduate research student and PhD candidate, it was his life's mission. The fact he enjoyed it as much as he did was a bonus.

The complex, less glamorous aspects of the science involved alter conscious induction, electromagnetic impulses, brainwave activity, and sleep patterns—all of which were scientific elements that supported his deep desire to discover new horizons in the alter conscious domain. His status as a student didn't affect the fact that he was already well-known as one of the best in the small pool of experts studying the science.

On vacation in Belize, he frequented the BOHICA Bar and Grill, owned by Frank Waddy, a former USAF Special Operations pilot. Retired Colonel "Ox" Waddy was a known cigar-smoking hell-raiser who had no intention of spending his "afterlife" anywhere north of the Tropic of Cancer. So he signed on with the *Agency* as a contract pilot to feed his adrenaline and his ego and to maintain a steady stream of income—as if the six-figure, retired air force colonel's pay wasn't *already* enough to live on in Belize.

Ox had purchased the small beachfront plot outright and helped build the shanty biminis bar himself. He hired some locals to keep it operating in the black and to provide a legitimate reason for living in the area. The true allure of the place was the awesome view and the cheap drinks, not to mention the friendly staff and peaceful, unassuming local atmosphere.

G first found the BOHICA in '02, when he and some close friends ventured away from the typical crowded destinations on one of their college spring breaks. They traveled to Belize, where they discovered the breeze, the sunsets, the rum, and the hospitality of Ox Waddy and the BOHICA.

G enjoyed Belize for everything it offered. It provided his mind a sanctuary to truly unwind and offered a place where he could vividly "go deeper" into his dreams and awaken with a clearer memory of the details and a connection to alter consciousness he couldn't quite explain beyond theories and hypotheses.

G graduated summa cum laude from both his undergraduate *and* graduate classes—a savant of sorts, at least considered as such by some. To him, things were just *easy*. The simplicity of it all often gave G's mind too much idle time, so he would often find creative ways to keep busy that invited

Dream Operative

drama and excitement into his life—normally induced by the consumption of his favorite beverage, alcohol.

He wrote a graduate psychological editorial once, under the influence of alcohol, in which he described, in detail, the office layout of the mayor of New York City. The editorial made its way to the New York Times, where it received more than its fair share of readers. Independent investigation later revealed the *amazing accuracy* of his account and went so far as to accuse him of having "eyes on the inside" or of actually having visited the mayor's office; neither of which was ever proven true. G simply attributed his account to having been "present," in an alter-conscious dream state, in the mayor's office in one of his early attempts at "controlled" dreams.

He enjoyed talking about his research and would often lecture on the subject when he had a captive audience, whether it was an audience of one at a bar or one hundred in a lecture hall. He was passionate and determined to perfect the art behind the science.

G's alter-conscious abilities were met with reverence, admiration, and skepticism. He was sometimes referred to as a magician in a popular sarcastic or cultic sense; and he'd often be asked if he could see the future or whether or not his "powers" allowed him to see through walls. He took each question and skeptic in stride but would file their questions away in his mind in a databank of possibilities he could use later as postulates for further research. The pinnacle of his goal was to be able to *manipulate* the *type* of dream he entered and, once present, control various aspects and movement abilities within the altered state of consciousness of each plane. He often wondered if the elements of a dream could have a direct effect on reality in such a way as to manipulate, affect, or predict *future* human behavior. He had no idea just how the science was about to affect his life and the manner in which he was accustomed to living it.

―――♒―――

Hakim had just finished a Quaran lecture to a small group of students.

His knowledge of the Quran was especially keen, as he had been formally educated in the best of Middle Eastern schools and was believed to be predestined to study the teachings by virtue of his royal ancestral lineage. His name translated to "Eternal Servant of the Wise One." Abdul-Hakim was indeed wise, even beyond the expectations of his royal lineage. He was a master of several languages, well-respected among elder religious leaders, and well-connected in political circles.

The man known to the public in the Middle East was everything one would expect of someone from the royal bloodline. The man known to the Agency, however, was one of cunning, deceit, explosives mastery, and terror.

A man of thirty-seven years, he was considered young, by Middle Eastern cultural standards, to hold his position of power and influence; yet he was certainly old enough to have learned how to be extremely dangerous. He was a master of disguises and was often referred to in US clandestine circles as *the faceless man.*

As he was gathering his belongings and preparing to leave, Hakim was approached by one of the students, who handed him a small sealed envelope. The young man made the delivery without comment or eye contact, out of respect for the religious leader.

Hakim adjusted his glasses and opened the envelope to read its contents. It was rudimentarily hand-written, and simply read, "عن بصرى" or "*Bosra.*" With that, he knew the actions he himself had initiated several months earlier were in motion, and his next destination would be an origin north of Bosra—Damascus, Syria, to be precise. The note was intentionally deceptive and was a covert confirmation that the location was "sterilized," or free of any imminent danger, at least for the time being. He would meet key followers, who would travel in from the world's crevasses to hear him offer encouragement, wisdom, and direction on the latest initiatives of the Jihad. He would leave right away.

Ox Waddy pushed the throttles forward on his Casa 212 aircraft. Looking out over the console, he was reminded of just how far he'd come since his infiltration and rescue flights of the Bosnian conflict between '92 and '95.

The coral-ridden, rutty airstrip he used provided a thrill for him as well as a reminder of how well-suited the Casa is to such less-than-ideal runway surfaces.

The twice-weekly supply run to embedded Special Operations Forces, or "SOF," in the jungles of South America gave him a purpose and kept him connected to a network of contacts that gave him liaison status between

Dream Operative

US operatives and the *ghosts* of Central and South America. He enjoyed flying the Casa 212, because it was a short-takeoff-and-landing workhorse capable of making it into, and out of, most destinations with less-than-ideal aeronautical conditions. It was also a rather inconspicuous aircraft, bearing unsuspecting military or government traits like that of other, higher-profile air frames.

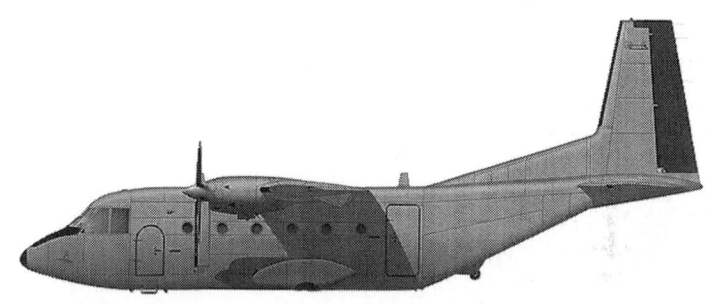

Sitting beside him on this trip as first officer was Ronaldo Torres, a young man from Honduras. Ronaldo was fluent in several dialects of Spanish and could shoot the back legs off an iguana from fifty yards with a 9 mm handgun, and do it in less time than it took to sneeze.

Ronaldo was new to Ox Waddy but no newcomer to the operations and region of Central and South America. But Ox trusted no one, even *if* the young Ronaldo came with the full confidence and endorsement of the Central Intelligence Agency. *This one you can trust without question*, claimed an Agency memo. *Hmmm, we'll see...* Ox thought, as he crumpled the memo and jammed it into his pocket.

Ox's eyes darted across the console, a last-minute check on the vitals. Looking up from the instrument panel to make one last scan of the airstrip ahead, he released the brakes that set the boxy craft in motion.

"Twenty knots...thirty...forty..." he called out to Ronaldo, in commanding fashion.

The airspeed indicator reached fifty knots when both men heard a loud *bang*, followed by a loss of groundspeed and a fire warning alarm.

"Brakes...pull it back to idle," shouted Ox.

Both men saw thick black smoke billowing from the starboard engine.

"Shut it down," commanded Ox.

Ronaldo was already ahead of him.

They managed to stop the aircraft quickly and taxi off the coral strip, where they shut down the remaining engine and disembarked with fire extinguishers in hand.

"Looks like *this* day is shot," said Ronaldo, looking for confirmation.

Ox remained silent and studied the engine, determined to discover the cause at first glance.

Arriving on the 6:17 P.M. flight, Abdul-Hakim was met by a non-descript man who drove him to his hotel in Damascus. The man said little but communicated reverently with his eyes.

Once checked into the five-star hotel, Hakim was left alone to pray and prepare for his lecture the following morning. He glanced at the clock and turned his gaze out the window.

The sun is setting, he thought. *Allah is great.* And at precisely 7:46 p.m., he answered the call to prayer heard throughout the city's loudspeakers.

After prayer, Hakim enjoyed a quiet meal and tuned the television to Al-Jazeera news. He kept the volume low. He preferred to hear the voice of God over all other voices, so his primary focus was ensuring all distractions in his life were kept to a minimum to remain in tune with his one true guide.

He sat at a table in front of a window with a picturesque view of the city. He could still see a hint of deep orange on the horizon as the sun yielded its last remaining grasp of the day. The city began to respond with the random twinkling of lights appearing in buildings across the skyline. He was no longer aware of the faint volume of the television in the background but was instead at peace and harmony with himself while enjoying the tranquility of the moment.

Mark Rubis opened a bottle of beer and settled in on the porch in an old wooden chair his father had built years ago.

As he sat there, images from his day raced through his mind, eventually making room for random philosophical thoughts of life. He heard the low rumble of a thunderstorm in the distance and smelled the moisture in the dense Florida air as the clouds grew darker. His life was hectic—always filled with something to do. But the approaching storm gave him pause as he took another sip from the bottle.

Mark's job required him to travel often, so downtime was rare. His job as intelligence analyst for the Agency required a lot of insight, interpretation, analysis, and thinking outside the lines of what's typically considered normal by more mainstream careers. He was in his fifties, and retirement was close enough to cautiously anticipate. But he was still in love with the game. Brief moments of quiet solitude such as this were welcome and seemed to recharge his thought processes. He watched the first few large drops of rain hit the porch railing as the ominous clouds grew darker overhead.

It's gonna be intense, he thought, *but it won't last long.* Ever the analyst...

By all accounts, and despite its fast pace, Mark's life was in perfect working order. He designed it that way. He lived in an affluent Florida community, populated by good people. No matter where his global travels took him, he was happiest here, at home with his wife Heather and two daughters.

The rain took on a steady pace. As he finished his beer, Mark's thoughts were interrupted by the mist from the showers that made its way to where he was sitting. His thinking turned to the briefing he would present to the staff in Maryland, so he casually made his way back inside to apply the finishing touches to the details of the brief.

Looking out the window of his home office, Mark paused to follow the lines of rain that now streaked across the window, his thoughts lost for a moment, wrapped up partly in a trancelike relaxation as he watched the artful nature of the rain patterns against the window. He enjoyed the view he had from his office. It was situated on the back corner of his house and gave him a tranquil view of a small lake. Native palm trees framed his view of the lake. When he was lucky, he'd catch a glimpse of a heron searching for fish in the shallows. The view was one of the primary reasons he and Heather had purchased the home.

Savoring the solace of the moment, Mark's mind was drawn to a particular pattern created by the rain collecting on the lower trough of the window sill. His analyst's mind was always at work, and this moment was no different. He resisted the temptation to discount the distraction and instead allowed his thoughts to be drawn in by the images it created. This was the way his mind worked best, and it typically yielded plausible results.

Mark was collecting data on some of the world's most elusive terrorists and was to brief his findings and recommendations to leaders at the National Security Agency (NSA) in the days ahead.

The movements are choreographed, Mark thought, as he continued to watch the rain.

Like the rain driven by the wind and the gravity outside his office, the latest movements of the primary tribe he was analyzing seemed to be taking on a choreographed nature. But the movement was one he couldn't yet clearly define or decipher. He had enough of a clue, however, to know that the latest developments were supported by a coordinated flow, much like the rain patterns on the window. His heart pounded as his mind ached for an answer.

"Give me a clue. Show me something," Mark quietly said, attempting to make sense of what his gut was telling him.

His thoughts and analysis were interrupted by the chirp of his phone. He looked at the caller ID. It simply read "Private." He answered. It was the station chief out of Damascus.

Dan Keppler's secretary was a witty government employee with ties that dated back to the Reagan administration. She was much more than a typical secretary, however. Janet knew the routine and ways of Washington. Dan counted on her more than he cared to admit and often consulted with her on matters of political considerations, decision implications, and national security protocol.

Dan arrived at the office and began mentally sorting his priorities, as he so often did, with the help of Janet's priority task list. Glancing through his calendar, he noticed his upcoming meeting with Mark.

It'll be good to see him, Dan thought, as he visualized the reunion with the highly competent analyst and close friend.

By all accounts, Dan was destined to be in a power position within the Agency. His background in air force special operations, coupled with the fact that he knew damn near everybody who was anybody in the SOF community, gave his credentials the extra boost they needed when he was brought on to lead the operations and analysis division as their newest director.

Dan had a way of finding favor with nearly everyone. He once served as the executive officer to Major General Silas Johnson Jr., in support of the US Military Training Mission and Foreign Military Sales in Saudi Arabia. The general had a soft spot for Dan and greased the wheels for him to meet the right people at the right time. That had eventually led to his current position with the Agency. A retired air force officer, Dan was now embedded into the fabric of operations and analysis for the NSA conducting "God's work," as he so often proudly proclaimed.

"Janet, please send me the latest Global Hawk images we have of the Khyber Pass," asked Dan.

"Already in your inbox on the SIPR computer," she replied.

"Should've looked there first," Dan quietly mumbled.

"Indeed you should have, sir," said Janet.

Dan wanted to know the latest on the movements of the insurgents in the region, so he would be prepared for Mark's analysis. Recent activity gave Dan reason for concern, as the Pakistanis were showing signs of weakness in their support of US pressure to maintain control of the region. That alone would've been enough to occupy his entire day. But, other parts of the world required the attention of the Agency and of the in-depth intelligence and collections analysis his department was known for.

Once logged on to the secret Internet protocol router—or SIPR, as it's more commonly called—Dan's mind came alive. This was *his* world. This is what he lived for.

When Dan read the daily situation reports from the field, his mind would transform the words into pictures and the pictures into investigative analysis. He was well-traveled and well-connected with highly competent agents placed strategically throughout the world. His reach was global, supported by a powerful and impenetrable net-centric system that few had access to. Not even the president of the United States had the tools he had at his immediate disposal.

As Dan read the latest reports, he too picked up on the subtlety of a coordinated movement that seemed to be drawing followers from various Middle Eastern origins to a centralized region of the Middle East. The movements seemed well-timed and were complicated by an overture of distraction from the Iranian government, as its rhetoric once again made its way into the mainstream media with headlines of significant nuclear advancements. Dan had intelligence on that issue and knew it to be a ruse—at least for the time being.

"Mark, I have information for you, can you go secure?"

Mark knew the station chief only as a familiar voice on the line, identified by a clearance code and the name "Grimes." He had been assigned to the Damascus bureau after proving himself in Kabul, Afghanistan during the early days of Operation Enduring Freedom and occupied a (rare) dual-hatted role, normally filled by the CIA, but was officially employed by the NSA. It was a position created at the behest of the president, designed to promote "collaborative cooperation" among and between clandestine agencies and the Office of Homeland Security. Whether or not the program was a success depended, in large part, on who spun the answer to the question.

Mark placed his phone in a cradle designed to scramble the signal and encrypt the message to speak securely with the station chief. When the device indicated the call was secure, he picked up the handset and reported in.

"I show *secret-secure* on this end," said Mark.

"Secret-secure on this end as well," said the chief.

"What have you got for me?"

"We have eyes-on confirmation that 'K. A. H.' is in country. We received intel that his destination was Bosra, but I assigned agents to several locations just to be sure," explained the chief. "He arrived this afternoon in Damascus and is currently residing at the Maaret Sednaya Hotel."

"Have you verified your source and made sure your guest has a shadow?" queried Mark.

"Affirmative…validated by a ghost agent and in accordance with current protocol. I have linked operatives watching his movements. I can have photos to you in an hour."

"Copy that, my friend. Send the photos to the Home Office. I'll be briefing there tomorrow. Timing couldn't be better on this. Oh, and use extreme caution; K.A.H. has his own eyes continually searching for company such as ours," Mark warned.

"Tell me about it. We have two dead double agents who thought they had him pinned down just outside of Tehran. Turns out they severely underestimated him and paid the ultimate price for the miscalculation."

2

Ox turned away from Ronaldo and walked several yards before pulling a cell phone from his hip holster and a cigar from his shirt pocket. He pressed a button and set circuits in motion that would connect him, via satellite, to an undisclosed recipient in Virginia. Once connected, he would relay the message that, for the time being, his mission would be delayed. He bit the end of his cigar and waited for the call to connect.

"Operator…"

"This is Ox Waddy, passcode x-ray, five-seventeen, golf. Unable to rendezvous with Rawhide due to maintenance. Expected delay unknown. Will advise."

As he disconnected the phone and replaced it in the holster, he looked back across the small airfield where he noticed a dust trail coming from an approaching vehicle, presumably on a mission to assist the now disabled crew and craft.

"You two OK?"

One of the local aircraft owners had seen the takeoff attempt and abort, accompanied by the smoke trail from the ailing engine cowl and was there to lend a hand or, at the very least, a ride back to the hangars. One of the local aircraft mechanics accompanied him.

"We're fine," replied Ox, "but I could use a ride back to the hangar."

Ox climbed into the Jeep and directed Ronaldo to remain with the aircraft until someone returned with a tow vehicle.

G had two days remaining in Belize before he was to return to the university, clinical research, and the routine of class lectures. After a morning bike ride and a quick swim to awaken the senses, he headed for his favorite spot at the BOHICA with his laptop stowed safely away in his backpack.

"Where's Lisa today?" he queried the bartender, as he headed for a table nearest the water.

"Out sick, but Athena will take good care of you, G."

The bartender vectored G's attention to a waitress he hadn't seen at the BOHICA, at least not yet. G couldn't break his gaze as he watched Athena work her assigned tables.

Damn, she stands out, he thought, studying her from behind.

He was captured by the way she moved gracefully between tables, the flow of her hair, and the near-perfect lines of her tall slender figure. The female staff at the BOHICA were notoriously attractive, yet G couldn't help but be unusually captured by Athena. Her shoulder-length hairstyle alone set her apart from the typical long-haired brunette local girls. Her multi-colored sarong, drawn low around her curvy hips, had an alluring contrast against her deeply tanned skin. Her pierced bellybutton stood out against the brown canvass of her tight, fit stomach.

She's gotta be a fitness buff with that body, he pondered.

He slowly shook his head in near disbelief and stole yet another glance while he removed his laptop from the backpack. He quickly glanced away when she turned to approach his table.

"Hi, I'm Athena; what can I get for you?"

Time suddenly slowed. G was helplessly captured by this beauty and drawn to one of the whitest smiles he'd ever seen. A smile is typically the *last* thing a man notices on a woman, but Athena's smile connected with a sensuality that demanded his attention—so much so that he found himself at a loss for words. Time returned to normal as he snapped out of his trance and tried desperately not to reveal his attraction by looking away. He nervously responded by ordering his usual Captain Morgan rum and Diet Coke.

"Got it," replied Athena. "And here's a menu, should you be hungry for anything else," she said, with a wink and a smile.

Their eyes connected when he reached for the menu, and he was suddenly overtaken with the *connection* and the visualization his mind created for him earlier in his dream. As he watched her leave to place his order with the bar, he found himself studying her once again: the sway of her hips, the flow of her hair, the color of her perfectly tanned skin, the small of her back, the balance of her fit body, and the lingering scent of her subtle perfume. His mind was in overdrive in an attempt to make the connection with the dream he had earlier.

Anxiety, pleasure, slight fear, euphoria, welcomed distraction...attractive brunette.

And what did she mean, if I should 'be hungry for anything else'?

Abdul-Hakim gradually became aware of himself, surrounded by unfamiliarity, as if he'd slowly appeared from nowhere and had awakened in a new place.

He was accompanied by a small, close group of followers. He didn't immediately recognize them but discerned that they were looking to him for guidance.

No one spoke. It was as if they were waiting on *him* to speak.

Despite his unfamiliar surroundings, he was at peace because he knew he had the protection of Allah. The traditional Arabian garment, covered with the *Jubba* overcoat and *Smagh* headgear, was noticeably absent. Instead, he found himself in typical western clothing and clean-shaven. He wondered for a moment whether or not he was wearing one of the many disguises he was known for.

He attempted to become more aware of his surroundings by examining the details of the experience. He knew he was in an altered state of consciousness. The experience was euphoric.

Can one know they are within a dream? he thought. *Perhaps one can know if Allah chooses for them to know.*

Attempting to pull meaning from his altered state of consciousness, he suddenly found himself facing an authority—a gatekeeper, perhaps. The gatekeeper queried him to determine the rite of passage he sought. Confused the gatekeeper didn't recognize him, he demanded passage.

"I represent the will of Allah," Hakim responded boldly. "You will let me through at once."

But the gatekeeper remained stoic. "Your credentials, sir," he demanded. "I must see your credentials."

As Hakim searched for the credentials, he mysteriously found a satchel at his feet. Despite being suspicious of the satchel, he searched it for the credentials required of him to gain access. While searching the satchel, it dawned on him that he was now surrounded by a large group of people busily going about their way, all seemingly wrapped up within their own worlds. The sounds of the crowd were low at first but gradually increased as they came into focus. He scanned the room, randomly glancing at faces in an effort to discover anything unusual when, there, across the crowded room, he noticed a man glance his way, hold his gaze for a moment, and disappear into the crowd.

Hakim's dream ended as he handed the gatekeeper a small document. But Hakim couldn't keep from concentrating on much beyond the man who he'd made a connection with in his dream.

Allah has revealed something important to me and I must discover its true meaning.

He was convinced that the origin of his dream was divine. He lived and breathed by his many survival tactics; among which was a knack for personal recognition and an innate skepticism of virtually everyone. He trusted no one and made a life-saving habit of focusing on a person's eyes as a centerpiece of their motive, intent, and personality traits. He was rarely wrong. He would recognize this man anywhere—he knew it.

The mechanics were busy repairing Ox's aircraft while he and Ronaldo got busy replanning their flight at the BOHICA.

"Assuming all repairs are made," said Ox, "we'll look for a takeoff time of seventeen hundred hours tomorrow. That'll put us over the rendezvous point just after sunset. I should hear from the mechanics by noon to make a call on go or no-go. I'll give you a call when I have something firm."

"Sounds good," replied Ronaldo. "I'm gonna grab something to eat and call it a day."

Ox noticed G sitting at a table, busily typing on his laptop, so he decided to pay the frequent patron a visit.

"What's goin' on, young man—thought you were heading back to the States."

"Hey, what's up, Ox? Headed back to the mainland in the morning… plan to catch an afternoon flight."

"I see…hey, what's wrong with this picture? Where's your usual Captain and Coke?" Ox asked.

"Oh, your lovely new waitress is all over it, my friend. Speaking of which, where *did* you find that dove?" G replied.

Ox could immediately tell his friend was smitten. He lit a cigar as he took a seat. "Actually haven't met her yet. I assume one of my managers hired her on recently."

"Well she sure is easy on the eyes," proclaimed G, " — enough to keep me coming back here, that's for sure."

Ox smiled. "And all this time, I thought it was my charming personality that kept you coming back."

The two men laughed as they watched Athena approach.

"Here ya go," said Athena, placing the Captain and Coke in front of him. "Can I get you anything else?"

"If you'd just keep 'em coming, I'd appreciate that, Athena," said G. "Oh, and you can tell me what time you get off work as well," he boldly added with his best and most sincere smile.

Athena returned the smile but didn't reply. She simply glanced over to Ox, then back at G, held her smile, and turned and walked away.

"Hmmm, well, that didn't go over too well," G murmured, forgetting that Ox was right there with him through the exchange.

He found himself studying her once again, staring actually, as she walked away and made her rounds. His concentration broke when he was interrupted by a firm slap on the back and a "Nice try, young man" from a laughing Ox. "You seriously think she'd reply to a cheesy line like that, with the boss sitting right here next to you? Besides, I hear she has a boyfriend twice your size, working for some special ops unit in the region. Hell, he could be here watching you right now, for all you know."

"Oh, don't say it's so, Ox. At least lie to me and let me run with the fantasy," G said.

He couldn't tell whether Ox was serious, half serious, or outright lying. Whatever the truth, G decided Athena was worth discovering. So he stayed and drank, continuously ordering from Athena until he decided to return to his bungalow for the evening, slightly inebriated, with a pleasing buzz that stimulated his creative side, giving him a bit of courage to boot. He left cash on the table for Athena, along with his phone number and e-mail address on a newly designed business card he had created himself. It was a simple card with a unique logo he was rather proud of.

Gary Westfal

Joey G. Weston
Professor of Psychology
Georgetown University
555-867-0000

g@gmail.com

The design was symbolic of real life and alter-consciousness intertwined in geometric shapes, with man in the center, draped by a black-and-white, counterbalanced background to indicate the stark contrasts of reality and alter-reality. He particularly liked the fact that his phone number ended with all zeros. To him, it was yet another implication of his profession: the unknown/untapped state of psychology and discovery of the mind. There was little doubt the logic was understood by the few big brains inside the profession. Those on the outside just thought it was cool.

G decided to retire with a purpose that evening. He'd make every attempt to place his entire focus on Athena to see where his dreams would take him. Despite the intense focus, however, the fate of his dreams took him elsewhere.

His mind had awakened to the sensation of falling when he became aware of his surroundings. He did his best to take control of his dream, as he was accustomed to doing, and began to analyze his surroundings. The speed of his descent began to slow as his awareness increased.

Dark...looking for a light, he thought. *I've arrested my fall, now where's the damn light?*

As soon as he finished the thought, the answer came to him: *Command the light.* Make *it light.*

Now, why didn't I think of that...I guess I just did, he thought, as the hint of a smile appeared on his face.

G pushed his mind to yet another level and began to see shapes forming around him. He heard murmuring voices of concern surrounding him. He struggled to hear an overarching voice announcement of some kind. He strained to listen closer to the words and was projected to the source. He found himself standing next to a middle-aged pilot making an announcement. The pilot was assuring the passengers that "everything was under control" and that soon, they would be safely on the ground.

Dream Operative

Although G knew how to manipulate the dream to find out *why* they had experienced such a wild ride, he decided against it. He closed his eyes and tried to project himself to the next phase of his dream, but it was beyond his ability. For now, he had to remain and observe his surroundings. He decided to walk through the cabin and take mental notes. Nothing immediately stood out. He was released to the next phase of his dream when the plane touched down onto the surface of the runway.

G suddenly found himself in an area crowded with people, oblivious to his presence and even that of each other to some extent; each wrapped up in their own world, busily moving about. He scanned his surroundings, analyzing various details of the journey. He could see light streaming from large windows above him, on his right. He concluded that he had transitioned to an airport customs gateway. His focus was diverted when he passed a processing room where a passenger was being questioned by a customs agent. He glanced toward the passenger, a man slightly his elder, and was surprised when the man returned the glance, made eye contact with him, and held his gaze.

G's heart began to beat heavily, trying to analyze the connection. There was an intuitive evil aura surrounding the man. G was consumed by the nature of the man with whom he'd made a definite connection. This was a first encounter of this kind for G. He tried to remain in place in an effort to further study the man, but the momentum of his dream continued to project him forward, beyond his control. He resisted, trying instead to take himself back to the room where the man had been, but he was unable to do so. He focused intently and made every attempt to remember as many details as he could about the man and the circumstances.

Once the man was out of sight, G's surroundings changed. His legs were submerged in water from the knees down. Traffic busily crossed a bridge above him. Despite being able to hear the calm lapping of water against the nearby shoreline, there was no ambient noise coming from the busy overhead traffic. Looking to his left, he noticed a small blue and white boat, occupied by two men fishing, about a hundred yards from his position. He heard them chatting but couldn't make out what they were saying. They seemed to be innocent enough and preoccupied with the business of fishing near the support pilings of the bridge.

G's cell phone started ringing. Reaching to answer it, he noticed it was at his feet, under water. Despite that, it was aglow and signaling audibly for him to answer. He didn't find it to be out of the ordinary. After all, in the dream world, anything was possible. When he picked up the phone, it was dry.

"Hello?"

"Hi, G, it's Athena."

"Rawhide, this is interior, how copy? Over..."

The unexpected radio call crackled in his earpiece.

"Loud and clear," answered the special tactics team leader, air force captain J. Booker.

The team was on scout maneuvers in the jungle, south of Bogotá, Colombia, when they got the radio call.

"Rawhide, be advised, scheduled rendezvous for Golf Lima Zulu is delayed. I say again, Golf Lima Zulu delayed. Expect update in twenty-four. Proceed to alternate, as briefed. Over."

"Rawhide copies," answered Captain Booker.

The radio call was designed to alert the six-man team to Ox's delay and direct them to their secondary extraction point. They were to meet with Ox at a predetermined landing zone, or "LZ," but for reasons unknown to the team, the scheduled rendezvous was canceled. They were trained for such occasions and well prepared for any inevitable delay or distraction. Their presence in the region was to assist the Colombian narcotics task force with counterdrug operations on little-known special operations directives designed to reduce the production of drugs, a large portion of which eventually made their way across US borders. They would expect an update in twenty-four hours or less.

G rubbed his eyes in an attempt to clear the dream from his mind. Reconnecting with reality, he realized he was actually on his cell phone, speaking with Athena.

"I'm sorry I woke you," said Athena.

"Nah, that's cool. I must have dozed off while I was reading. What time is it?" asked G, searching for his watch.

"It's twelve thirty. I just got off work and saw that you left your card with that generous tip. I thought it was really sweet of you, so I decided to take the risk and give you a call. I hope you don't mind. But I can call back tomorrow if it's too late."

"Absolutely not!" G said in a tone of desperation, realizing he was sounding a bit...desperate. "Would you like to stop by and chat for a while? I can put on some coffee."

"OK, that sounds nice if you're sure you don't mind. But I can't stay too long. I have to fill in for Lisa again tomorrow."

"Great, so I'll see you in about ten minutes or so."

"OK," said Athena with a cute chuckle, "but...can I have a clue as to where I'm headed, please, G?"

Man, she sounds so hot when she says my name, G thought. "Yeah, I guess that would help," he said, with his own uncomfortable chuckle. "So, take Coastline Road north, then west two blocks. I'm the third bungalow on the water...probably the *only* bungalow with the lights on this time of the day — or night."

"Got it. On my way now, G."

Holy shit. She did it again. I could listen to her say my name all night.

G was so engrossed with thoughts of Athena's pending visit that the details of his dream were starting to slip away from his memory. He made a habit of recording the details of his dream right away while the memories were fresh. He knew he should capture what he could, so he grabbed his cell phone and began reciting the snapshots his mind still held.

"Falling, flying, limited projection control, frustration..."

He tried recalling other details, but they were fast escaping his memory. Besides, Athena's pending visit kept distracting his focus. Then it hit him. "The encounter!" he said aloud, grabbing his recorder again. "Recognized by a man I've never met. Fear, sinister, confusion..."

The details of the dream were nearly gone when he remembered a few more seemingly insignificant details.

"The water, the bridge, the boat with the two men fishing, the traffic overhead, and the cell phone," said G, rattling off the memory flashes as fast as he could recall them.

He paused for a second to reflect about the cell phone and recorded one last detail.

"It's probably insignificant and indicative of my state of mind, but when I answered the cell phone...I was reconnected with conscious reality by a perfectly timed call from Athena. I'll attempt to analyze the connection, if any, at a later time."

He was satisfied he had captured enough of his dream to reconfigure the sequence for further analysis and put his cell phone aside to prepare for Athena's visit. He looked at his surroundings and realized he was nowhere near ready for visitors, much less someone he hoped to impress.

Holy shit, this place is a freaking mess, he thought. *Better get that coffee started.*

―⋙∫∭⋘―

Mark was up at 3:00 A.M. to prepare for the flight to Baltimore and to ensure he had everything he needed for his meeting with Dan. After going over his mental checklist several times, he kissed his wife, stopped at the doorway of his two children to look in on them, and headed for the car to begin his journey.

He enjoyed being up this early, driving the road alone. It was peaceful and offered a pace at which he could truly savor life. After clearing airport security, he stopped at a café and purchased a cup of coffee and newspaper. Upon arriving at his gate, Mark checked the status of his flight on the overhead marquis.

Good, still on time, he thought.

Mark had endured his share of delayed flights. Perusing the paper, he checked on the headlines and then the weather in the DC metro area. The forecast called for isolated afternoon showers; nothing to indicate that his flight from Atlanta, his first leg, would be affected. The local weather was supposed to get a little rough later in the day, but his flight was early enough to stay ahead of that, assuming an on-time departure.

The tightly packed regional jet taxied to the runway, and the pilot made his customary corporate announcement to Mark and his fellow passengers. "Uh, ladies and gentlemen, welcome aboard flight five-seventeen, nonstop to Atlanta. Our flight time to Atlanta this morning is one hour and twenty-eight minutes...should be a smooth ride most of the way, but weather in the Atlanta region is calling for some isolated thunderstorms. We'll do our best to keep you comfortable and get you there on time. If there's anything we can do to make your trip more enjoyable, please don't hesitate to let us know. Flight attendants, please prepare the cabin for departure."

Dream Operative

With that, the tiny craft revved its two jet engines and powerfully took to the air. Mark reclined his seat and settled in for the journey.

Hakim readied himself for the day ahead, while his mind was still preoccupied with the images of his dream. It had so affected him that he had difficulty focusing on the message he was going to deliver.

He tried setting aside the images and the distraction of their meaning while collecting the order and content of his speech, but his thoughts kept drifting to the dream. His mind persistently caught glimpses of the dream in between his agenda and the routine tasks it took to get ready for his address to the people. It was fast becoming an obsessed distraction he simply had to deal with and overcome.

The phone rang. It was the concierge.

"Sir, your transportation has arrived and is ready for you at your convenience."

"Thank you. I will be down momentarily," answered Hakim.

He placed the "Do Not Disturb" sign on his hotel room door and departed for the lobby. Hakim was greeted by a cheerful driver who offered to carry Hakim's only bag — a small leather satchel. He declined the gesture and indicated to the driver that he was ready to depart.

"Very well, sir," responded the driver, leading the way to the waiting limousine. Hakim would be driven a short distance to the Umayyad Mosque, where he would deliver his message.

"Subject is on the move," came a calm, quiet radio report from an observer drinking tea in the hotel lobby.

The announcement initiated a network of linked, clandestine observers who would keep an eye on Hakim as he made his way from the hotel to the mosque.

Hakim stepped toward the awaiting limo, casually conducting a visual sweep of his surroundings to determine if he perceived anything out of the ordinary. His goal was to see if he could identify any signs of security assigned to protect him. He couldn't. He found that to be reassuring, figuring that if *he* couldn't identify them, then others couldn't, either.

Meantime, high above the city, a CIA satellite was remotely engaged from the dungeons of the operations center at Langley, Virginia. The satellite's high-powered camera was affixed to the Sednaya Hotel and then onto a limousine uniquely identified with an infrared receptor in which Hakim was a passenger. Hakim was not aware of his "shadow" and focused primarily on his journey.

Doing his level best to tidy up the place in just under five minutes, G walked into the kitchen, stopped, and stared at the coffee maker AS if it were an alien from another planet.

Hell, I have no idea how to make coffee, he nervously thought.

He rarely drank the beverage, and when he did, it was normally purchased or prepared by someone else. He did the best he could, however, and successfully managed to find the power switch to get it started.

Man, I hope I didn't just screw that up.

He walked to the front door of the bungalow and turned on the porch light and decided to walk outside to see if he could see any signs of Athena. Outside, he could feel the thickness of the humid night air stick to his skin. The sky was clear, and the moon cast an illumination seldom seen in more populated areas of the world. He loved the scent of the salt air and, for a moment, found himself savoring life while soaking in the details of his surroundings.

G gazed down the street of his small, quiet neighborhood and watched as Athena appeared in the distance. Even as a silhouette, he knew it was her. Her very presence spoke to his core.

His pulse quicken as he anticipated seeing her again, alone. He stood there and patiently waited for her to arrive. As she got closer, he could see that awesome white smile when she spoke quietly out of respect for G's sleeping neighbors.

"Do you always stand in the middle of the street and greet your friends?"

G laughed. "Of course. You should see me try to pull it off in front of my apartment in Virginia."

They both laughed as he nervously offered her a friendly hug. It would be the first time he would touch her.

"Damn, you *are* fit," he said, shaking his head in disbelief. "Impressive… simply impressive."

Athena shyly thanked him for the compliment, and the two made their way inside G's bungalow. They could both smell the coffee, now brewing steadily from the kitchen.

"C'mon in. Sorry for the mess. Would you like something to drink?" he asked.

"The coffee smells good."

"Great," he said, and went into the kitchen, where he poured a cup. "Here you go. Hope you like it. I don't make it much," he said, as he rejoined her in the living room. "Would you like to sit out on the back porch?" he asked, hoping to lure her away from the clutter inside.

"Sure, that would be nice. Would you mind if I removed my sandals? My feet are killing me from standing most of the day."

"Not at all. Just toss 'em over there."

G motioned to a corner on the porch next to the stairs that led to a small dock where several other pairs of sandals, presumably left by other renters, were strewn about.

He watched as she bent over to remove her sandals. Her smooth brown skin and sensuous legs were alluring. The moonlight cast a captivating glow on her tanned skin that ignited his vivid imagination. She stood, glanced his way, and offered an innocent smile that nearly took his breath away.

G walked over to an old suspended swing on the back porch and waited for her to join him.

"I enjoy sitting in this swing. There's plenty of room for both of us if you'd like," said G, trying to gauge his limitations with her.

"Oh, that looks relaxing. I bet the view here during the day here is breathtaking. Wow, look at the moon tonight. It's just awesome," Athena commented, taking a seat on the padded swing next to him.

"Sure is. I can spend hours here alone sometimes. It's one of the main reasons I keep returning here as often as I can."

"Shame to have to enjoy that alone, G, but I understand how that can be liberating."

G tried to wrap his mind around Athena's comment.

What was she insinuating with that comment? he wondered. *And what's the real purpose of her visit? What does she see in me? Not that I really mind...I'm just a little overwhelmed. OK, calm down and enjoy the visit. I'm way overanalyzing this.*

His education and experience as a psychologist gave him good reason for pause, while simultaneously enjoying the moment and evaluating the encounter — and his own feelings. He knew enough about the psychological process to know that there are often hidden agendas buried deep within people that aren't always immediately evident. He had hoped this wasn't the case with Athena.

"Athena, I'm honored by your visit and am happy you stopped by, but what is it that has you here, especially at this unusual time of day, I mean night…uh, morning?"

G felt a conflicted mixture of emotions as he asked the question of Athena, but he knew an up-front approach was typically the best.

"Well, to be honest, I overheard you were leaving tomorrow, so I thought a personal visit would be better than an e-mail. Besides the fact that I find you to be so sweet, I asked around and just about everyone who knows you had good things to say about you…and I have a sense about such things," explained Athena.

"I see," said G, evaluating her answer.

"Besides, I was hoping you could help me save the world."

"I'm sorry…what did you say?" asked G.

Athena laughed. "I said, so…tell me more about G. Your card says you're a psychologist and a college professor. And I know you enjoy Captain Morgan and Coke. What else am I missing?" asked Athena, with a sultry curiosity enhancing her irresistible smile.

The flight attendant began her announcement: "Ladies and gentlemen, the captain has turned on the seatbelt sign to indicate our initial approach to the Atlanta airp—." her monologue was interrupted by moderate turbulence.

She made another attempt to complete the announcement. "Ladies and gentlemen, as you can see, we're experiencing some light turbulence, so I'll need everyone to remain seated for the remainder of the flight into Atlanta, please."

Mark glanced out the window and could tell by the size and shape of the clouds that the remainder of the ride into Atlanta would be interesting, to say the least—a bit rough, to be more precise. He'd traveled enough to realize the conditions they were likely to encounter. He tightened his seat belt as he mentally prepared for the remainder of the ride into Atlanta.

The flight attendants quickened their pace and secured everything likely to move or break loose. The cabin erupted violently, as if the bottom had fallen out of the sky. Screams and panicked moans could be heard throughout the cabin as the small craft fell uncontrollably. Mark

Dream Operative

gripped the arm rests of his seat and closed his eyes to brace himself for an inevitable crash. A loud *bang* thundered throughout the cabin when the aircraft hit the bottom of a large pocket of rough air. The aircraft violently rolled to the right. The cabin lights went out and left the out-of-control craft in an eerie darkness until the emergency lights came to life along the floor.

This can't be a good sign, Mark thought.

Flashes of his life sped through Mark's mind in short bursts as he thought of his family, his father who had long passed, his children...the reason he was on this flight in the first place.

The flight attendants did their best to calm the passengers, while the crew was doing all it could in the front to control the plane.

The pilot ultimately won the wrestling match with the aircraft and brought it back under control, despite the continuing bumpy ride that kept them all on the edge of their seats.

"Delta five-seventeen, this is Atlanta, is everything OK? I show a rapid descent on your transponder readout. Confirm altitude," the air traffic controller commanded.

"Uh, yeah, Atlanta, this is Delta five-seventeen...we just encountered a *severe* microburst. Looks like we lost about five thousand feet there pretty fast. Climbing back through one-five-thousand for flight level two-zero-zero," responded the pilot.

"Delta five-seventeen, Atlanta, maintain one-five-thousand, altimeter two-niner-eight-eight. Do you require any assistance?"

"Negative, sir. Would just like to get on the ground as soon as possible," replied the audibly-shaken pilot.

"Delta five-seventeen, roger, turn right heading two-five-zero, descend and maintain one-zero thousand."

"Delta five-seventeen, leaving one-five-thousand for one-zero-thousand."

"Better check in with the flight attendants and address the passengers," suggested the first officer.

"Agree," said the captain, pushing the call button to the flight attendants. "Everything OK back there?"

"Yes, Captain, no injuries, but we have some pretty shaken passengers. Are you planning an announcement?"

"Yeah, I'm gonna do that now. Please help me keep them calm. We're in position for final descent, but the weather's still pretty unpredictable.

I need you and the rest of the crew to remain strapped in, please." He then addressed the cabin over the PA system. "Ladies and gentlemen, this is the captain. What we just encountered together was a pretty severe microburst associated with the surrounding thunderstorms. I know you were all surprised by this, as were we here in the cockpit. I apologize for the rather rough ride. We believe this experience is behind us for the most part, but we may still encounter some turbulence, so kindly remain in your seats, securely strapped in; we'll have you safely on the ground in Atlanta real soon."

Mark was reassured by the announcement and calm demeanor of the pilot and prayed for a safe arrival into the busy airport. The remainder of the flight was uneventful. The silence among the passengers was noticeable as they were now focused on the safety of their recovery…or perhaps the mortality of their souls. When the plane ultimately touched down, some of the passengers applauded, while others remained still and quiet in their seats, trying to come to grips with the ordeal. Mark was one of the many passengers who made sure to thank the pilot on the way out for the outstanding manner in which he handled the fight against fate and nature.

3

The lead mechanic worked on Ox's crippled craft for a good part of the night. It was 6:30 a.m. when Ox received the call that his aircraft was ready to return to service.

"So what was the problem?" Ox asked curiously.

"You had a negative torque-sensing system malfunction that caused the engine to over-rev and, as a result, a fuel line burst. You're fortunate you didn't have a catastrophic incident."

"She's a tough bird," responded Ox, matter-of-factly. "So she's ready for flight then?"

"Gimme an hour to button her up. She should be ready for you then."

Ox called his new copilot.

"Yo, Ronaldo. Get your ass outta bed; we have a good airplane. I need you at the airport by noon to go over the flight plan and help me load some gear," ordered Ox.

"I've been up for two hours, Ox. Already ran a couple of miles, checked on the weather and our flight plan, cleaned my weapon, had some breakfast…would you like me to go on?"

Ox could visualize Ronaldo's cocky smirk on the other end of the line.

"OK, smartass, just show up on time. We have a schedule to keep."

Ox was used to the "expected" reverence he received from those he out-ranked in the Air Force, especially from young officers. The fact that Ronaldo was as cocky as he was indicated to Ox that Ronaldo was either trying to impress him or that he was in need of an "attitude adjustment." Either way, Ox would continue to press the young man for several reasons. If Ronaldo were to be a part of *his* operation, Ox expected only the highest quality of performance and an even higher level of loyalty. And Ox needed to know the limits of Ronaldo's ability to handle himself under pressure.

Hakim gently stroked his beard and glanced out the window to take in the view when the limo arrived at its destination. He was impressed by the number of people milling about the massive mosque.

The driver stopped the vehicle, exited, and made his way to open the door for his esteemed passenger. Hakim stepped from the vehicle and paused to examine the beautiful structure and to critically evaluate his surroundings, still searching suspiciously for anything out of the ordinary. No one made eye contact, which is not uncommon in that part of the world. Only when someone *does* make eye contact is it considered unusual.

The satellite overhead was now affixed on "the mark." Langley maneuvered the system to zoom in to get a better look. As Hakim paused outside the mosque, his image filled the frame of the camera, albeit the quality of which was still somewhat grainy and out of focus. Photos were taken for analysis and confirmation of his identity.

Hakim turned around and motioned to the driver, giving him permission to park the vehicle. He made his way inside the mosque, where he would be among his closest supporters.

"Subject has entered the mosque," announced an obscure radio call from an observer.

Standing US orders prevented any operations to be conducted in or against mosques and similar religious structures, much to the chagrin of the more creative intelligence collection and exploitation agencies.

When Hakim entered the mosque, he was greeted by one of his followers. Hakim removed some papers from his satchel and handed the empty leather carrier to the man.

"Go over every inch of this bag. Pull it apart, do whatever it takes to examine it completely, and let me know if you find anything that shouldn't be there," ordered Hakim.

"As you wish, sir." The man took the bag to a private room for examination.

Dream Operative

Mark's connecting flight from Atlanta to Baltimore-Washington airport was uneventful and had him there about twenty minutes ahead of schedule.

Grabbing his briefcase, Mark thought back to the harrowing flight. *I'm glad that's behind me. Looking forward to seeing Dan...need to find the limo service.*

He turned on his cell phone and waited to receive a signal. The phone chirped almost immediately. It was a voicemail from Janet, Dan's secretary. She told Mark that a car had been sent for him and explained where to connect with the driver. Mark made his way to the limo station, easily found the driver, and was on his way to the National Security Agency Headquarters within minutes.

"Please make yourself comfortable, sir," said the limo driver. "We should arrive in about fifteen minutes."

"Holy shit! Do you have any idea how long we've been talking?" asked G.

"Nope, guess I've been kinda wrapped up in the visit. I find you pretty fascinating, G," said Athena. "Especially your gift of dream analysis and, how did you put it...manipulation? You should be working for, like, the government or something."

"Why, so they can manipulate *me*?" G responded sarcastically. "Besides, I've found that most people are skeptics and can't exactly fathom what I do."

"Well, *I* think you have a gift," said Athena admiringly. "Look, I should go. I have to get some sleep before I report back to the BOHICA for my shift this afternoon. Is it OK if I e-mail you, G?"

Drawing a slow breath, G responded, "Of course, Athena. Is it too bold of me to ask for your number?" G walked Athena to the door where she stopped, turned suddenly, and gave him an inviting look.

He looked into her eyes as he approached her and gently touched the side of her smooth face. Their eyes remained locked as he brought his lips to hers and kissed her. She gently pulled back and shyly looked away for a moment. "I enjoyed spending time with you, G. I hope we get to meet up again sometime soon, perhaps when you return or back in the States somewhere."

"That would be awesome," he said, wearing a grin he wasn't aware of. He hugged her. The scent of her perfume made its way into the deepest part of his memory and connected with the vision he first had of her in his dreams. She turned and slipped away into the early morning darkness.

G closed the door and stood alone, silently, trying to savor the last remaining effects of the time he had enjoyed with what turned out to quite literally be the woman of his dreams.

Never in my wildest imagination would I ever believe I'd be kissing her, he thought. *Damn, that was nice. I better get my shit together so I can make it outta here on time...today.*

After packing a few things, G made his way to the porch swing, where he waited to catch one more glimpse of the spectacular Belize sunrise. It wasn't long before his eyes closed and brought him to a deep, pleasured sleep.

Ronaldo was waiting for Ox when he arrived at the hangar.

"We taking on company today, Ox?"

"Why do you ask, Sport?"

"Oh, so now I have a call sign? Nice," Ronaldo snapped right back at Ox and continued, "I ask because there are three *gentlemen,* and I use the term loosely, waiting to speak with you in the flight planning office."

"I don't have time for this. Who are they and what do they want?"

"Not sure. They said they'd only talk with you."

"I'll take care of it," said Ox.

He confidently strode into the flight planning office, determined to quickly erase the distraction of his visitors. He had little time or patience for such intrusions and was not known for pleasantries.

"Hi, I'm Ox. How can I help you fellas?"

"We know who you are, sir. We're here on official business. We have some equipment we need to put on your plane for your flight this evening," said one of the three men.

"Anyone wanna tell me who authorized you to even assume I'd allow that? And what *kind* of equipment I'll be carrying, and for whom?"

"All we can say is—"

Ox interrupted the man, "Look, son, I don't wanna hear *part* of your story or any half-truths. I've been around this op longer than you've been alive. And my clearance level is no doubt deep enough to bury you. Give me the 'no-bullshit' version, or nothing is going on my plane."

Two of the three men looked over at the third, expectantly.

"I was told to expect a rather colorful response from you, given this kind of intrusion," said the third man, who spoke from a subdued corner of the room, cigarette in hand, presumably the leader of the small team. "Look, we're on your side. Same team actually. I need to get this equipment on your aircraft for this evening, and I need to accompany the equipment so I can take some readings," he added, taking a rather long drag from his cigarette.

"Oh, now *you* need to be on plane too? Do you have any idea how that affects my mission?" Ox responded, nearly shouting at the man.

"I'll work with you as best I can," said the man, "But suffice it to say, it's in the best interest of our government and in all of our interests for me to be able to do my job. Once I get the equipment on board, I'll be happy to give you a cursory briefing on what I'm doing and what we hope to gain. My men and I can have the equipment installed and be out of your way in an hour and a half. You can verify our legitimacy with the home office, if you'd like."

"This better be damn important and not some experimental bullshit, because, as I said, I don't have time for this. I taxi out at seventeen hundred hours. Do what you have to do and be finished in an hour and a half so I can prep for *my own* mission," snapped Ox, storming out of the room.

One of the other two men spoke up and said with a grin, "I think he took that rather well, don't you?"

Ox checked with the operations center and discovered the group to be legit. Despite his reluctance, he decided to allow the hitchhiker to tag along, at least as far as the first leg would take them. He returned to the hangar, where Ronaldo was busy programming the flight management computer.

"Ronaldo, take a break for the next hour and a half and then be back here, ready to work. We'll be having one PAX on board with us this evening, playing with some equipment."

Ronaldo didn't push Ox for any more information. He could tell the boss was pissed enough already.

While waiting on his flight to the US, G updated the scientific world and his students with an entry to his online blog. He wrote about his time in Belize and recorded detailed elements of his dreams and offered cursory interpretations. He also gave his readers a chance to contribute by providing their own interpretations of various dreams and of the science in general.

He documented all of the elements he experienced to include his encounter with the man in his latest dream. Careful only to offer the facts, and not his own interpretations, G solicited input from his readers on what they thought of the connection. Hearing the call for boarding, he signed off and quickly shut down his laptop and stowed it into his backpack.

Mark placed his briefcase onto an X-ray conveyor and stepped through a metal detector as he made his way through security at NSA headquarters. Once cleared, he found his way to Dan's office.

Mark was greeted with a smile and warm greeting from Janet when she noticed him approaching the intelligence directorate's office.

"Well, hello, stranger," Janet proclaimed. "Welcome home. He's in his office and asked me to show you in as soon as you arrived. Can I get you a cup of coffee or a drink?"

"No thanks, Janet. It's very good to see you as well, dear," Mark responded politely.

Mark knocked once on the boss's door and was greeted with the sincerity and professional nature he'd come to expect of his close friend and of someone deeply involved with the interests of the country.

Dan was seated behind an old hand-carved teak desk he'd picked up while stationed on Guam back in the late eighties. Sky News was on a large flat panel TV in the corner of the spacious office, the volume barely audible. The walls were decorated with mementos Dan had collected across the globe, representing years of service to the country and accolades from the highlights of his illustrious career. The two exchanged pleasantries and initiated small talk to get reacquainted.

"How was the flight?" asked Dan.

"Ironic you should ask. We hit a nasty microburst that damn near had catastrophic results. In fact, I'm happy to be here having this conversation with you right now."

"Wow, you don't say...sorry to hear that. Things like that can really affect a man. I'm happy you're here as well, my friend. Hey, you hear about this shit yet?" asked Dan pointing to the television and the latest Sky News field report out of Washington, DC.

Dream Operative

"Seems someone was able to place explosives somewhere near the Arlington Memorial Bridge. That's right down the frigging street, brother." Dan said, shaking his head. He turned the volume up.

Mark listened as the reporter revealed the details:

What we now know is classified as an attempt to destroy or severely cripple the Arlington Memorial Bridge—a main thoroughfare in the city, in the very heart of the United States capitol region—has been foiled by a vigilant waterway inspection crew. This work, believed to come from embedded terrorist cells within the country and perhaps the city itself, is further proof that hatred for the United States is still widespread. No one has yet claimed responsibility for the attempt to destroy this heavily-used thoroughfare and national landmark. Stay tuned to Sky news for further details as we bring you fair and balanced reporting. I'm Jay Cooney in Washington, DC, Sky News.

"What do you make of this, Mark? I mean, who the hell would have the balls to hit us here?"

"How was the device discovered?"

"Routine check by the Harbor Patrol. One of their young troops actually spotted the device. Apparently, an LED was left uncovered and it was blinking its ass off when the young man noticed it and alerted his CO," explained Dan.

"So I take it the device has been disarmed and has been secured? Whose possession is it in now? Can we get to it, so I can take a look at it?" asked Mark, in a never-ending barrage of questions.

"Hold on, brother," said Dan. "Yes, I can get you in to take a look at it. In fact, I'm already on it. The device *has* been disarmed and is in the possession of the Department of Homeland Security. As I said, I already have some folks from this side as well as DHS working on access for us. From what I'm hearing, they discovered a shitload of explosives material. I was hoping you could provide me with some unbiased insight and analysis, so we can figure out whom it belongs to and perhaps send it back to them, if you get my drift."

Mark listened and nodded as Dan spoke.

"I'm postponing your briefing on the whereabouts of KAH so you can take this on for me. I'll need the file details of your presentation, though, so I can have the analysts pour over it. Is there anything you need me to know that's not covered in your brief?"

"It's mostly a movement analysis," said Mark. "But my gut tells me he's up to something, based on the very movements I'm detecting. It wouldn't surprise me if this Memorial Bridge incident is tied to him or his radical followers somehow."

"The gift of vision has been bestowed upon me by Allah himself," proclaimed Hakim, addressing a riveted audience of roughly one hundred followers.

Each represented various tribes or sects of every regional Islamic group. Most were devout followers of the Mullah for his teachings. No one dared challenge or question his claim of favoritism by Allah. Some were present merely to hear what he had to say in terms of teachings and divine interpretations. After all, Hakim had a reputation for being among a chosen few in the faith for his ability to discern and offer wisdom.

"I have been given the gift of insight and foresight. This is a *new* ability and one I assume with great humility, Insha'Allah" Hakim added.

He didn't elaborate in any great detail about his "visions" with the larger audience. Instead, he used the information as a support platform of empowerment and increased credibility.

After completing his sermon and dismissing the masses, Hakim asked his inner circle to join him for tea in a private room. As he made his way to the room, a man approached him and asked for a moment of his time. He was the same man whom Hakim had assigned to examine his leather satchel.

"Sir, I have something for you to see when you have a moment."

He brought Hakim to an adjacent room and showed him the now fully-dismantled satchel, barely recognizable.

"What did you discover?"

"Only this, Imam," responded the man.

In the palm of his hand he held a tiny circuit board with two soldered wires attached.

"Show me where you found this."

The man pointed to a tight seam he had pulled apart in the handle of the satchel. Hakim looked away for a moment without saying anything. The man stood quietly before him, his heart beating anxiously.

Hakim broke the silence calmly. "Well done. Find something inconspicuous to place this in and bring it to me. Ensure that the object is small. I expect it before I depart." He turned away to join his inner circle.

Dream Operative

Some twenty to thirty followers joined Hakim for his private session. He posted "sentries" at the door to ensure the highest privacy. Once inside the room, he addressed his most trusted followers.

"Gentlemen, we are at war. This you know. Your very souls are at risk... this, you may *not* know."

Hakim's tone grew sterner as he attempted to drive his point home with the group.

"We must never lose sight of the ultimate calling of Allah. To give one's life for the peace of Islam is the *highest* honor. Each of you must be ready to answer this call. Right now, throughout the world, your brethren are busy carrying out the will of God against the infidels," Hakim said with emphasis, as he began to look each one of them sternly in the eyes.

Scanning the crowd, he came across a man who gave him pause. "You," he called to the man. "Come forward."

The man obediently sprang to his feet and briskly walked toward Hakim, stopping a respectable arm's length from him. He was visibly nervous and concerned to have been called out by Hakim.

"This man is not convinced that what I say is at the behest of the *Highest One*. I am disappointed that there are those among you here in this esteemed group who doubt what I say is accurate or true."

He looked at the man with disgust and stared into his eyes with contempt as the man remained silent.

"Where are you from?"

"Damascus," responded the man humbly.

"Do you have a family?"

"Yes, Imam; a wife and two children."

"Do they enjoy all the freedoms you wish for them to enjoy?"

"No, sadly, Imam."

"Are you willing to die for them?"

"Yes, without question."

"Then die you will."

He turned to the group.

"I present to you our latest soldier of the Jihad who will boldly enter the streets of the Infidel and enter the kingdom of heaven gloriously by carrying out the will of Allah, faithfully and honorably. He is but one I have been called upon to choose from among you today to complete the will of Allah. His family will be well cared for, and his wife will taste the fruits of a new life as she remembers the sacrifices he has given for her and all of Islam."

The man was visibly shaken at the announcement, but he did not dare resist the Mullah.

Hakim continued, "Who among you is an expert in explosives that will prepare this soldier for his journey?"

G turned on his cell phone while the aircraft taxied to the Dallas–Fort Worth airport terminal. As soon as it picked up a signal, it alerted him of incoming e-traffic. Text messages filed in, one after the other, as did his e-mail and voicemail messages. The first text was from Athena.

Hope your journey is a safe and pleasant one. Keep in touch. A

He smiled as he read the message, realizing that, although she had *his* number, he had failed to get hers…until now.

Then he opened a second message from a trusted colleague. *Just checked your blog. OMG! Have you seen the news? Little room for interpretation….*

Text after text, e-mail after e-mail, contained similar messages.

Hmmm, better check the news, G thought. *Either I've been gone way too long, or something's up.*

G planted himself in front of the first television he could find to see what all the excitement was about. As luck would have it, a commercial was playing, so he checked the time, matched it against his connecting flight, and estimated he'd have enough time to make it to his gate if he could catch the news highlights to figure out what all the ruckus was about. His cell phone continued to chirp as the television commercials seemed to go on and on. One by one he read various text messages that centered on the account of his latest dream. He looked up at the monitor as the latest report replaced the litany of commercials.

This is a Sky News alert. Sources have confirmed finding enough high explosives designed to detonate and decimate the Arlington Memorial Bridge that connects Arlington, Virginia, to the heart of Washington, DC. The explosives were discovered early this morning on a routine security inspection of the waterways in the area. No one has claimed responsibility for the ordnance, and authorities have little to go on. If anyone has any information, they are encouraged to contact the FBI or DHS immediately. Jay Cooney reporting from Washington; Sky News.

Dream Operative

G sat stunned at what he witnessed on the news report. His heart quickened as he began to recollect the images of his dream. He was suddenly oblivious to his surroundings while he wrestled with his thoughts and tried to recount what he had dreamed less than twenty-four hours earlier, but he couldn't concentrate.

G had a renewed sense of urgency to get to his gate, so he could get to Washington and communicate with some of his closest collegiate colleagues to decipher and analyze the information against his dreams. He glanced at his ticket for the flight information, found a terminal monitor to verify his gate, and set out to make his connection, his cell phone chirping at his side the entire time.

"Sir, I have DHS on line one," Janet reported on Dan's intercom.

"Thanks, Janet, I'll take it," responded Dan, as he connected with his counterpart at the Department of Homeland Security. "What have you got for me, Jack?"

"What I've got is the FBI, the ATF, and everyone else who thinks they're an expert breathing down my neck for full control of the situation. On top of that, the White House is applying its usual political pressure tactics. If you're gonna get anywhere near this device, you better seize the moment. I'm doing everything I can to stall while our analysts pick it apart," responded the DHS Investigations Bureau Chief.

"Copy that. Listen, I have an analyst I'll be sending over. Man by the name of Mark Rubis. Please give him as much access as possible, so we can get a solid read on this."

Dan hung up the phone and gave Mark a look that placed the full trust of the Agency and the country in his analysis and investigative prowess. He dispatched Mark to an obscure location just outside the DC Beltway to analyze and collect information on the evidence. Mark was to examine the material at a predesignated EOD investigation site controlled by the DHS.

Thirty minutes later, upon arrival to the site, Mark's limo was met by an escort, who led him past security and into an obscure hallway. A single heavily armed sentry guarded a set of elevator doors at the end of the musty-smelling hallway. Mark assumed the sentry had been briefed on his arrival, because he made no move to acknowledge Mark or his escort. The doors opened immediately after the escort scanned his identification badge. The elevator ride took Mark and his escort on a slow descent but provided no visual indication on just how far down they would descend to reach their destination.

When the elevator stopped, the doors opened to a well-lit area, where several analysts were busy examining what at first appeared to be close to one hundred sandbags. The area was divided into smaller rooms; some were filled with chemical analysis equipment, computers, and technicians with gloves and masks. Other rooms contained computers, radios, and landline telephones. Most rooms were separated only by thick glass panes.

Mark was met by a man whom he assumed to be a supervisor. "Mr. Rubis, I'm Special Agent Mike Libby; please follow me."

Mike led Mark to an open room where several bags of explosives material were being examined by agents and specialists.

"Sir, what you have here is—"

"Ammonium Nitrate and Fuel Oil...ANFO," Mark interrupted.

"Exactly. So I assume you have a working knowledge of how potent this stuff can be?" asked Mike.

"Sure do. Same shit McVeigh used to slaughter innocent civilians at Oklahoma City in '95," Mark responded solemnly. "How much do you have here?"

"Fifteen hundred pounds. Enough to blow the entire bridge."

"And then some," added Mark. "I assume we have a detonation device somewhere?" he asked.

"We do. Follow me, and I'll show you what we've got."

Mike took Mark to a small shielded room where the devices were sitting atop a well-lit examination table. A technician was analyzing material in one corner of the room.

"We've been waiting for someone to analyze this for us," commented Mike, as he directed Mark's attention toward the devices. "We're trying to determine the origin. The markings appear to be foreign..."

"Where are the blasting caps?" asked Mark, rather nervously.

"They're in another room," said Mike.

"Separate from the explosives, I hope," stressed Mark.

"They're still being collected and separated," said Mike.

"Give me some assurance that the activation devices have been removed from the caps," said Mark.

Mike's brows tightened as he returned a look of concerned uncertainty. "We're double-checking that...I'm certain they have been," he said nervously, his words trailing off as both men noticed one of the circuits on the table light up. The room holding the ANFO exploded, bringing both of their worlds and the surrounding infrastructure violently crashing down around them.

Ox drove up to the Casa 212 as it was being refueled. Ronaldo was supervising the fuel truck operation and conducting a pre-flight walk-around inspection.

"Any sign of the three stooges?" asked Ox curiously.

Ronaldo shot him a look, tilted his head toward the aircraft, and said sarcastically, "One of them is already onboard, playing video games with his computers."

Ox rolled his eyes and turned to enter the aircraft where he found the lone operative sitting in the aft section of the plane facing forward and busily tapping on a computer keyboard.

"We start engines in twenty minutes," Ox noted nonchalantly.

The man glanced at his watch and commented, "Running a little late are we?"

Ox stopped in his tracks but didn't turn around to answer the man. What he felt like doing was ripping him apart or throwing him off the aircraft, but he thought better of it and decided to proceed to the cockpit for his instrumentation check.

A senior member of the group attending Hakim's private chat stood to be recognized.

"Teacher, there are two among us who have a highly experienced network of explosives experts willing to support the cause for Jihad and Islam. Several of these men have supported operations against US and Russian forces successfully on the battlefield."

Hakim took interest in knowing his efforts would be supported by such a competent and experienced network. "Your services are recognized," responded Hakim. "Prepare our soldier for success with your resources. I hold you and your team personally accountable for the successful completion of his mission. You will also ensure his family is well cared for when he has completed the ultimate call of Allah."

Hakim continued his dialogue on the importance of defeating the infidels and western ideology.

"The West has eroded our way of life. They defile the sanctity of our beliefs and believe they can impose a western governmental infrastructure and belief system upon us. They spit upon us and support those who occupy our lands, such as Israel. They attempt to convince Islamic political leadership that a democratic society is superior to that which we have known for centuries."

Hakim paused for effect and emphasis.

"We have spilled blood on our streets and on our land in defense of our way of life. These acts of unselfish loyalty by those who have gone before you must never be forgotten." He pounded his fist onto a nearby podium. "They must be honored. Therefore, we must exploit the vulnerabilities of the West, particularly that of Great Britain and the United States. We must integrate ourselves into the very fabric of their societies.

"I will personally supervise, fund, and facilitate the birth of the first 'society cell' within the countries of our enemies. This cell will serve as a model for the composition of what I expect in terms of integration, activity, and objective. I will be traveling to the United Kingdom and the United States soon. I will be operating under cover to conduct my own investigation of vulnerable vital centers of interest and will meet with trusted insiders to capitalize on the weakness of our enemies. I will contact you in the near future to arrange another meeting, where I will expect relevant findings from each of you.

"As for our soldier, I will meet him in London, where I will provide him with further guidance on his assignment. When he has completed his calling, I will honor him by ensuring prosperity to his family."

4

"Sir, there's a Mr. Jeff Hines here from Central who wishes to speak with you. He doesn't have an appointment but says it's urgent," Janet said, as she broke through on Dan's office intercom.

"Send him in, Janet."

"Jeff, how are you? To what do I owe the pleasure of your unexpected visit?"

"Good to see you, Dan. Are we secure?"

"One sec, Jeff," said Dan, holding up a finger in a silent gesture for Jeff to wait a minute. "Janet, we're going secure. Please hold my calls."

"OK, my friend, we're good. Whatcha got for me?"

"I know you guys are working the Arlington Bridge situation, and all you've got is unexploded ordnance to work with, but what if I could throw you a bone that would put a witness on scene who could describe the idiots that set the device?"

"Well, I'd have to carefully consider the source and what they have to offer. You know the drill, Jeff. What are you getting at?"

"Look, I know this is gonna sound a bit…unorthodox, but take a look at this."

He handed Dan a folder marked "Top Secret," containing a transcript of G's blog and associated message traffic that clearly described the "visions" of his encounter and experience at the bridge in his dream.

"Whoa, wait a minute. You said you'd give me a witness who was on scene. You didn't mention anything about *psychological* presence. What do you make of this?" asked Dan skeptically. "Is this kid a psychic or something?

Because the last thing I need is another nutcase telling me what they *thought* they saw in some vision *after* the fact."

"I have to admit, those were my initial impressions as well, Dan. But after looking into the details on this kid, it seems he's for real. Or at least as *real* as it gets in his world. We've collected intelligence indicating that one of our field agents spent some time with him recently and was emphatic that someone should consider ways to use his 'abilities' to help us through situations like this. In fact, if this kid is for real, then he needs to be on the inside with us for sure. Imagine the possibilities."

Dan sat back in his chair in virtual silence, quietly contemplating the concept of Jeff's information.

Jeff broke the silence. "Oh, and check this out: he described a near fatal airline crash that occurred yesterday—*three days* before it happened. And if that isn't enough to pique your interest, this will be," said Jeff, showing Dan a transcript of G's encounter with the mysterious man he "connected with" in his dream.

Dan stared at Jeff for a moment, looking for any hint that what he was hearing and reading was bullshit. Jeff remained silent and returned the stare, hoping to solicit a response. It was Dan's move. Suddenly, Dan remembered his short conversation with Mark about how turbulence had rocked his first flight.

"Ya know Jeff, I actually *hate* this kind of thing. But humor me for a second. Can we get this kid in to have a chat and corroborate the details?"

"We're working that as we speak. He's actually on a plane en route to the DC area now. I can have some ground operatives extend a friendly invitation when he arrives."

Dan nodded. "OK, but let's not spook the kid. Keep me posted."

Jeff smiled. "When have you ever known me to spook anyone?"

Dan returned a sarcastic look, as if he could see right through Jeff's rhetoric.

"OK, forget I even asked that question," said Jeff.

G boarded his connecting flight. His mind was swimming in the thoughts and reality of all he had recently discovered. He found his seat as quickly as possible and grabbed the attention of a flight attendant, so he could purchase a drink.

Dream Operative

The perky attendant told him she would serve him once they were airborne. He strapped in, placed his headphones on, and closed his eyes. The headphones helped him focus and provided a barrier to any seatmate seeking to strike up an unwanted conversation.

G dozed off and began dreaming when the aircraft began its taxi to the runway. His first experience, ironically enough, was that of an aircraft aisle. He could hear the rush of air moving across the fuselage of the aircraft as it moved swiftly through the air.

Oh, great...another airplane dream, he thought. *Just hope I'm not here to experience more turbulence.*

As in most of his *typical* dreams, his presence among the passengers went undetected at first. He slowly moved through the aisle. Unsure of what he was looking for, he decided to allow the dream to take its course without an attempt to manipulate it. He would instead gather as much detail as possible and allow the dream to interpret itself.

He passed a young couple in first class, who seemed to be very close, judging from their behavior. They were writing notes on a napkin and giggling. His attention was diverted by a small child who was crying, clearly unhappy with flying. Her mother was doing her best to comfort her, while nearby passengers kept their patience in check. The mother picked up a napkin to wipe the child's nose. G looked over to see a flight attendant hand a drink to a passenger. In doing so, she dropped the napkin and bent down to pick it up. As she stood, she looked at the napkin curiously and slowly extended her arm to offer it to G without making eye contact. He looked at the napkin in her hand, and then he noticed all of the passengers were offering him napkins.

G squinted his eyes, trying to rationalize why he had suddenly become the focus. He felt an urge to leave the dream or project himself elsewhere when he noticed two men who weren't holding a napkin, but were engaged in evaluating something on their computer. Curious, he decided to project himself between them. They were reading a news article that described the terrorist activities at the Arlington Bridge. Innocent enough, or so he thought.

As he was about to leave the men, one of them quietly spoke. "Stupid imbeciles. I knew *we* should have been the ones to plant the devices. I wonder if they found all of the explosives."

The second man spoke in a calmer, quieter tone, "We'll find out soon. It doesn't appear they found the boat..."

G was abruptly awakened by a passing flight attendant on her way down the aisle to serve the passengers. He reached for his cell phone to record the details but remembered the rule prohibiting cell phone usage aboard airborne aircraft. So he grabbed a pen from his pocket and frantically looked for something to write on. The passenger next to him saw him searching for something, so he casually placed his napkin on G's armrest without making eye contact.

G looked down at the napkin. The memories of his dream flooded his mind like a raging tidal wave. The man nonchalantly turned away to look out the window. G rushed to scribble some details of the dream onto the napkin.

> More explosives? Possible future detonation? Return of more terrorists to the area to investigate? Where's the boat?

He thought back to the details of his first dream near the bridge.

The men were fishing…or were they? And who were the two men on the plane? How are they connected?

The sun was at mid-level on the horizon when Ox strapped into the cockpit and began his instrument checks. Ronaldo crawled into the right seat after securing the aircraft cabin doors and ensuring their passenger was safe and secure. He reached over and slid open a cockpit window.

"Damn, it's hot in here," said Ronaldo, to no one in particular.

"Ready for engine start on number one," commanded Ox. "Fuel pressure looks good. Hydraulics: check. Ready for taxi."

"Ready for taxi," responded Ronaldo, in true first officer form. Releasing the brakes simultaneously, they set the Casa 212 into motion on its first journey since the engine fire incident.

The Casa was positioned on the runway, prepared for takeoff, when Ronaldo turned his head around and stretched to tell his passenger they were ready for takeoff. The rider indicated he was as ready with a thumbs up. One last check of the airstrip ahead revealed the path ahead was clear. Ox barked out more commands.

"Throttles forward for run-up…RPM set…release brakes…now."

The boxy aircraft was once again set in motion as the propellers grabbed the humid air and clawed its way down the airstrip.

"Twenty knots…thirty…forty…" Ox continued calling out the speed.

Dream Operative

"Sixty...seventy...eighty...pulling back on the yoke...she's airborne. Retract the landing gear," Ox commanded.

Ronaldo set the switch to retract the gear and then alerted any and all aircraft in the area that the Casa was airborne and maneuvering to find its course. "Local traffic, this is Magic 36, airborne, climbing through one-thousand, five-hundred for six-thousand, five-hundred; southwest bound off Half Moon Cay, V-F-R."

"Call the company on secure net and inform them we expect to arrive at Delta Golf LZ at approximately twenty-fifteen," commanded Ox.

"Will do," responded Ronaldo.

G's flight ultimately made an uneventful landing. He hurriedly made his way to the terminal, hoping to find a quick exit to meet his colleagues and begin his analysis.

Unsure of whom to call first, he scrolled through his phone and called Athena to let her know he had arrived.

"Good to know you made it safe, G. I've been thinking a lot about everything we spoke about, especially your gift. Have you seen the news?"

"Yes, I have, Athena. There's so much I have to tell you..."

G thoughts drifted to the dream he experienced on the plane when he was distracted by a crying toddler being attended to by her mother. He scanned the room and saw the two familiar men from the plane departing through an adjacent exit. He quickly changed course to follow them.

"Are you there, G?"

The flight attendants were conducting a routine check and general light cleanup of the cabin when one of them came upon the notes G had scribbled on the napkin. He had inadvertently left it behind in his haste to exit the aircraft.

> More explosives? Possible future detonation? Return of terrorists to the area to investigate? Where's the boat?

After reading the notes, a flight attendant immediately alerted the captain, who alerted the airport authorities. Cross-checking and verifying the manifest, G's name was found and confirmed, and airport security was dispatched to find him.

Athena was still on the phone with G when she overheard the commotion of him attempting to follow the two men. She kept asking him why it sounded as if he was running and he said he would explain as soon as he could. Then she heard something else in the background that alerted her to the seriousness of his situation.

"Excuse me, sir. Stop right where you are and turn around slowly."

G turned around to see two airport police officers, accompanied by several FBI agents, with guns drawn. The last thing Athena heard was the disconnection of G's phone, followed by an attempt to redial her number. Known for thinking quickly, she ignored the incoming call and immediately made a call to alert her *real* employer in Fort Meade, Maryland.

G stopped in his tracks and looked over his shoulder, watching the two men move out of sight as two police cars pulled up out front to prevent *him* from going anywhere. He was handcuffed and led to an obscure room somewhere in the maze of the airport office infrastructure.

"This is Valerie Daniels, put me through to the operations directorate. My passcode is 8QC71N43," said Athena, using her given name, to the NSA switchboard operator.

She was taking a risk calling the boss, but knew she had to make the call. She knew her identity as a CIA *NOC* afforded her some of the deepest cover the government had to offer. Her *non-official cover* status made it easy for the Agency to disavow any connection it had to her, or those like her, in the event her identity or credibility were ever compromised.

No one really knows how many NOCs are on the government's payroll. Some will go as far as to admit that the Agency doesn't even know. Most don't work directly for the Agency and are typically paid well with foreign currency or in favors, access, or other forms of luxurious commodities such as homes, cars, sex, and so on.

"Yes, this is Victor Delta forty-three, request a secure line and a direct priority patch to the Operations Director, Mr. Dan Keppler."

―⋘⋙―

"What's this all about?" G demanded in an attempt to be bold, while his heart was nearly pounding out of his chest with anxiety.

The agents guarding him stood silent. They seemed to be waiting for something—or some*one*. G was seated in a cold room in a cold metal chair. One of the agents touched his earpiece and looked down. He turned away, leaving G with a lone agent to watch over him. G made an attempt to calm the situation by appealing to the agent's human side — if there indeed was one.

"Look, dude, I have no idea why I'm here, but do you think I'd be guilty of *anything* that would warrant this kind of treatment? I mean, look at me. I'm a frigging college professor, for God's sake."

The agent wasn't fazed and didn't make any attempt to return the conversation.

"Could you at least remove the handcuffs?"

After sitting in silence for nearly thirty minutes, the door opened. A man entered the room. He was large in stature and had the beginnings of a graying hairline. He wore a badge on his belt on his left hip that G could see when his sport coat occasionally revealed it. He walked over to G and unlocked his handcuffs. After removing the handcuffs, he placed his right hand on G's shoulder and asked if he would like anything to drink. G was under such stress that, as soon as the man's hand connected with G's shoulder, his mind went into an uncontrollable visionary state. He winced but didn't fight it. G knew enough about the mind to know that his was trying to reveal something to him. The new experience surprised him and was somewhat painful, given the sudden onset, voracity, and speed of the experience.

Rapid, random, lucid visions of the man sped their way through G's mind. He felt the man's emotions, knew his drinking habits, the brand of cigar he last smoked, the mistress he had sex with that morning, and…the conversation he had with one of the men G was attempting to chase down in the airport.

The experienced subsided as the speed of the images in G's mind slowed. Things suddenly turned dark and cold. He could hear movement of ahead of him but still couldn't see anything. He could smell what he thought was gunpowder, followed by an awful, overpowering, putrid smell he'd never before encountered. He began to cough uncontrollably and immediately took control by manipulating his surroundings in the same manner as he had learned while in a dream. But this experience was different than a dream. He just wasn't sure how to categorize it yet. He found himself in a *conscious* state of mind, experiencing *subconscious* brain activity. He began to doubt himself, his theories, and…his abilities. His clinical mind searched for a plausible explanation. Could he be experiencing…*schizophrenia*? He agonized over the thought of it.

G struggled to find a way to escape the experience. It wasn't working. He felt trapped, alone, and afraid. Something was wrong. He called out in attempt to identify the source of the movement he heard; then he sat quietly, awaiting a response. As he was regaining full consciousness, he heard a faint response. *I'm here...over here...*

"Hey, I'm talking to you!" said the man, as G regained his conscious senses. "You want something to drink?"

His mind continued to race as he attempted to put the pieces together while trying to formulate a normal response to the question.

"Yeah...water," he said softly.

The man motioned to an agent, who quickly responded by leaving the room. G stared at the man he was getting to know through his visionary analysis and physical encounter.

"Tell me about your plan to subvert the US government by planting explosives in the capitol region," he said.

G sat silently, offering only a blank stare in return.

"Look, I have ways to break you, so don't *fuck with me!*" sternly warned the man, raising his voice.

G tried to figure out the best way to deal with the arrogant prick. "I... have no idea what you're talking about," he finally said in a quiet, exasperated tone.

The agent calmly slid the napkin across the table that G had used to scribble his notes while on the aircraft. G examined the napkin containing his own handwritten notes, thinking, *Finally...something I can work with.* It was his first clue as to why he was being held.

How could I have been so careless, he thought. *How could I have been so stupid? This is not happening. I am so screwed.*

"Mr. Keppler, this is operator sixteen, I have a secure priority voice call for you," reported the NSA switchboard operator.

"Copy," said Dan. "Push it through at once, please."

Dan heard the switchover and confirmed the security of the call.

"This is Delta Kilo Zero One..."

"Sir, Victor Delta forty-three, are we secure?"

"Affirmative, Valerie, how can I help you?"

Dream Operative

Valerie gave Dan the short version of the details surrounding her encounter with Joey-G and her attempts to cultivate a trusting relationship with him. She explained the details surrounding his unique abilities and attempted to offer a convincing argument on how G's abilities could help the Agency and the interests of the US government.

"You're not the only person to tell me about this young man, Valerie, but I get the impression you have a deeper reason for making this call instead of filing your periodic report through customary channels."

"Yes sir," Valerie said with slight hesitation. "I just got off the phone with him, and it seems he has fallen into the hands of our overeager brothers at the Bureau."

"So you're telling me he's in FBI custody? What did he do to piss *them* off?"

Valerie gave Dan a short explanation of what she had heard transpire at the airport and was in the middle of providing the details when the phone call was abruptly disconnected.

Dan's office lights flickered and his computer screen briefly went blank but powered back on again quickly with the aid of the back-up power system. He attempted to contact the switchboard but couldn't get through. Assuming the building had experienced a power bump, he walked out of his office to ask Janet to re-connect his call with the switchboard operator. When he approached Janet, he could tell by the look on her face that what he experienced was no ordinary power bump.

"Talk to me, Janet. What's going on?"

"There's been an explosion, sir. We're not yet sure of the source, but it was pretty huge…a couple of blocks away, perhaps."

"Son of a bitch," said Dan, as his blood ran cold. "Janet, assemble the team. My office, ASAP! Get a hold of Mark Rubis. And for God's sake, find the source of that blast!"

Dan assembled his crisis action team, or CAT, composed of experts from across the spectrum of special operations, emergency response, communications, engineering, and intelligence—all experts and leaders in their respective fields, empowered with the full authority to make decisions on matters of grave danger to the nation. The CAT had exercised many times, but was not assembled with such urgency since the attacks of 9/11.

Captain Booker directed one of his men to provide an estimate of their arrival to the designated LZ that would rendezvous his team with Ox.

The Casa 212 was the team's quickest and safest way out of the jungle. Once safely extracted, the team would be flown to Howard Field in Panama for a quick stopover and then on to the United States for repatriation.

The Colombian jungle was thick and especially humid as night began to cast itself upon the landscape. The LZ was designated a safe extraction zone, but Captain Booker's responsibility was to make *sure* it was safe for both him and his team and for Ox as well.

"What's our estimate to the LZ?" asked Booker to one of his teammates.

"Nineteen-forty-five hours, sir," responded the young special tactics troop.

"That puts us about two hours out. OK, let's roll," said Booker. "Jones, take the point at thirty yards ahead, and from here on out, no one breaks radio silence without my permission. Don your NVGs at official sunset, which I show to be nineteen hundred hours. Keep your eyes peeled for unfriendly."

The team made its way through the thick jungle canopy on a course to the designated extraction site.

G Picked up the napkin from the table and examined his handwritten notes. He could clearly see how the words implicated him, allowing others to draw conclusions about the panic now present in the nation's capitol region.

"Things aren't always what they seem," he said quietly, barely understanding the meaning of his own words.

"Why don't you give it a try, and explain the reality of it all to me then, Mr. Weston," said the agent.

G didn't like this imposter. The visions he had of him provided insight into his hidden motive and intent. G felt a surge of courage well from within that he didn't know he had.

"Nicaraguan Maduro," said G, while coldly staring into the eyes of his captor.

"Is that some kind of code I'm supposed to figure out?" asked the agent sarcastically.

G calmly replied. "Nope...it's the brand of cigar you smoked this morning."

The agent was clearly taken off guard with G's comment and stared at him for a moment, giving himself time to figure out this complex riddle.

"Well aren't you just a fucking magician. Give the man a prize. He guessed that I smoked a stogie," he said laughing. "You probably smell it on my breath. Do you like cigar breath?"

G started to enjoy the game and pushed one more time, with a defiant, sinister grin painted across his face. "Tell me, how does your wife feel about your girlfriend? Does she even know about her?"

"Who are you? And who the *fuck* are you working for?" shouted the agent as he aggressively leaped from his chair to within an inch of G's face.

His heart nearly pounding from his chest, G summoned every ounce of courage he had left, gritted his teeth, and stared back at the agent defiantly. "I'm someone *you* clearly don't want to fuck with."

His comment sent the agent into a rage that ended with a surprise right cross that landed squarely on G's left cheek. And with that, he was knocked out cold.

"I'll find out just who you are, smartass," said the agent, rubbing his stinging knuckles.

"Let's pick up a heading of one-niner-zero, south-southwest," Ox said in an official tone to Ronaldo.

"One-niner-zero," responded Ronaldo, confirming the heading.

"Yo, can I ask a favor?" interrupted the passenger from the aft cabin.

Ox raised an eyebrow, pursed his lips and looked at Ronaldo, communicating his impatience. Ronaldo responded.

"How can we help you, sir?"

"Yeah, can I get a copy of our planned route of flight for this mission? I can use the data for my calculations," he said, while busily clicking away on one of his laptop computers.

Ronaldo offered Ox a quick glance, seeking his approval. Ox gave Ronaldo a less-than-enthusiastic nod that cleared the way for him to pass a copy of the flight plan to the passenger.

Examining the planned route of flight, the passenger spoke up. "I see we have a planned stop at Howard Field, but you have no route filed from there. Besides, wasn't that base deactivated in 1999?"

Ronaldo was about to answer when Ox responded, "Yeah, but we have a deal with the Panamanian government that allows us to stop over for things like gas and supplies. So we'll pick up some gas and lighten our load before we press forward on the remainder of our mission."

Ox had no intention of allowing the unwelcome passenger to continue to the final destination, but he kept that to himself for the time being. There was no sense in revealing too much information this early. The element of surprise would prevent Ox's decision from being overridden in the event things became contentious.

Athena (A.K.A. Valerie) tried several times to reconnect to her boss at the Agency, but each time she was met with an annoying busy signal.

Her frustration grew as her imagination drew obvious conclusions on how the feds may have been treating G, with their macho interrogation tactics. Finally, out of sheer desperation, she took matters into her own hands. If the Agency didn't approve, she could take the heat of her decision better than knowing she gave up and did nothing to help G. Her training and proactive nature compelled her to act.

Athena dialed her close friend and Agency "ghost," Todd *"T-Rock"* Jordan.

Jordan, an ex-Air Force administration specialist who found his way into the State Department on claims of "specialized computer skills" in the early 1990s, had become friends with Athena several years back when they served together on active duty. Although a bit of a stretch of the truth at the time, he managed to convince the State Department to invest in his self-proclaimed abilities and ultimately refined his computer skills to become one of the nation's premiere hackers. He jumped from one governmental agency to the next until he decided to opt for "free agency" and the ability to name his price, terms, and availability. He managed to break free from full-time service and pursued his passion of becoming a fledgling band promoter and gym owner just outside Manhattan. Those endeavors led to bigger and better things for Jordan—much bigger. He was now a successful promoter for several well-known artists and was in negotiations with willing philanthropists to start his own record label.

Dream Operative

Jordan's skills extended beyond the computer. He was still well-connected to sources buried deep inside government clandestine circles and held a solid reputation as a free agent among agents. He was also connected to characters who few would dare entwine themselves with. He had favors owed to him from top to bottom—the mayor's office, city hall, the streets, and back alley chop shops. He was several things to several people: a promoter, a con artist, an agent, a fund-raiser, a politician, and a businessman. But his favorite pastime activity was that of an "equalizer" for the right customer. He was loyal to his country and would never stray outside the lines of true patriotism. He had a particular penchant for doing bad things to bad people. He was good at choreographing an operation and eliminating evidence trails and often prided himself on predicting the moves of the enemy or adversary before even *they* had a clue. If time permitted, he would typically use his computer skills to learn everything he could about his "mark" and was known to destroy many with a few simple key strokes. He chose his opportunities carefully, however, and few had the direct access to him as Athena did.

"Yo, this is T-Rock, you're on the air..." Jordan's typical line when answering his phone. "...I'm sorry I can't get to the phone, but if you leave a message, I'll hit you back. Peace."

Athena had to leave an encoded message if she expected Todd to call her back with any sense of urgency.

"Todd, it's Athena," she said, with the seriousness she knew would grab his attention. "I need your services and would like to make a short-notice reservation."

She entered a discreet code and hung up, hoping for a lifeline of assistance from her highly capable friend. Within minutes, Athena's phone was ringing.

"What the hell are you doing?" asked an agent from behind the mirror.

The agent delivering the knockout blow turned to face the mirror. Almost forgetting he was being monitored, he looked at the ground and turned and walked out to find the men's room, leaving G's unconscious body lying on the cold, hard floor.

The agent watching from behind the two-way mirror picked up the phone.

"We have him in custody. What would you like for us to do with him?"

"Find out what he knows, *how* he knows it, and then eliminate the threat," responded the obscure voice on the other end of the line.

"I want to make sure I don't misunderstand you, sir. You want me to execute the man?"

5

Hakim made his way to the exit of the mosque, where he was approached by the man who found the tracking device in his briefcase. He handed over the briefcase, fully reconstructed, and reported that it was "clean." He also handed Hakim a plain black wallet that, he explained, now contained the tracking device. Hakim was impressed with the man's ingenuity.

"Well done. May you receive the full blessing of Allah from this day hence."

He looked to an elder and commanded the man's services to be recognized and his name added to the network of specialized members dedicated to their cause. He also left instructions for him to be well compensated for protecting Hakim's movements from watchful eyes, then made his way to the waiting limousine.

Hakim closed the door of the limousine and instructed the driver to take him to the center of Damascus. His plan was to blend in and lose his "tails" amid the chaos and irregularity of the 1.7 million inhabitants of the city.

After a short ride, he instructed the driver to stop in a crowded downtown shopping district, and he exited the vehicle.

"Subject has exited the vehicle," came an arbitrary report from an obscure observer.

"Does he still have the briefcase?"

"Affirmative."

"We're tracking the case. Maintain a safe distance and try not to lose sight of him."

Hakim knew the streets and infrastructure of Damascus better than most. He quickly made his way into a busy market section, where he stepped into the front and out the back of one store and into yet another. He expected to be followed; he counted on it.

Entering a smoke shop, Hakim made eye contact with a trusted connection, passed the wallet containing the tracking chip, and continued into a back room, where he was led by yet another contact to an obscure corridor. It was the last anyone would see of him in Damascus.

The signal from the tracking chip made its way throughout the city in the back pocket of Hakim's accomplice. Having lost sight of him, several agents were sent to the source of the signal emissions of the chip. While agents tracked the signal, Hakim was moving farther and farther away from his pursuers.

Hakim arrived at a safe house, where he assumed a new identity, using his masterful disguise skills. He transformed himself into a Turkish college professor, ensured he possessed all the right credentials for international travel, and boldly stepped back out into the streets of Damascus. He wore thick-rimmed eyeglasses, a trimmed goatee, and sported a graying ponytail. He dressed in a wrinkled, cream-colored linen sport coat and matching pants and walked with a cane. Hakim was very good at disguises; he had even devised a method for altering his fingerprints. He hailed a taxi to take him to the airport. His destination was set for New York City via London. Entering the taxicab, he even spoke the correct Turkish language with a perfect dialect.

"Şam havaalanına lütfen" [Damascus airport, please].

Dan responded to a knock at his door.

"Yes, come in."

It was Janet. Shock written all over her face, she confirmed Dan's biggest fears.

"Sir…the explosion came from DHS and the investigation site. There's been no word from Mr. Rubis. I've tried several times…" Janet explained, tears welling in her eyes.

Dan encouraged her to *dig deep* and to focus on how important her job had become.

Dream Operative

"I need all of your faculties focused, Janet," Dan said. "Keep trying to reach him...and let me know as soon as you hear from him. I need these phones back online. All I have is a computer, and its performance pretty much sucks right now. I want the CAT assembled, so if you have to dispatch a runner to alert the team, then grab anyone you can to help you."

"The team is ready, sir," said Janet, determined to overcome her emotions. "The communications director, Mr. Tom Herring, will be running slightly late, because he's working on getting the phones back up and said something about a camera issue you'll be briefed on during the CAT briefing."

"Thank you, Janet."

Dan walked briskly into the secure conference room and sat at the head of the table. As soon as he was seated, a young man rose to his feet, went to the front of the room, and began a briefing.

"Sir, our sources have confirmed that an explosion occurred underground in the vicinity of a DHS-occupied investigation site. This satellite image shows the location of the blast and is current as of ten minutes ago. It's the same site that housed the explosives found at the Arlington Bridge."

Dan interrupted and asked, "Do we know yet if there were any survivors?"

"Negative, sir."

"Negative what, young man?" asked Dan impatiently. "Negative, you don't know, or negative survivors?"

"Unknown survivors, sir. Crews are on scene, removing rubble and debris. The blast occurred some forty feet below the surface, so search and recovery will be on-going for quite some time. Our sources on scene report that the blast was pretty severe, however, and that survivability is unlikely."

Dan interrupted once again and said, "I realize that part of your job is to make predictions based on the facts young man, but when you render your next report to me, I'd appreciate it if you were to refrain from making survivability predictions until we account for everyone in the vicinity of ground zero—copy?"

"Roger that, sir."

"OK, so have we figured out how this happened yet, and do we have a clue on who's responsible?"

"There are some indications that the original explosives were constructed based on models and methods typically used by followers of Khalid

Abdul-Hakim. This information comes to us from initial reports filed by DHS investigators analyzing the material at ground zero before the blast. We don't expect to have detonation information until we get closer to the origin of the blast, sir."

"Can anyone tell me *when* we expect to be able to reach the epicenter of this incident?"

An older gentleman from engineering spoke up, "We're making decent headway now, sir. We're on track to clear five feet per hour, and I have fresh crews on standby, ready to provide relief in four hours."

The communications director walked into the briefing. "Sorry I'm late, Dan."

"What have you got for me, Tom?"

"I have a crew on scene, working with DHS and search-and-recovery teams. We've bored through most levels of rubble and have begun constructing a conduit large enough to drop an infrared camera and microphone. We'll be searching for any and all signs of life using these devices, once we break through...*if* we break through. This building is...was...a fortress. If anyone survived this blast, we'll find them."

"Well, I want to be on that first-to-know list, Tom. Good job. Who's keeping the media at bay?"

"We are sir," responded the Public Affairs deputy director. "We have a perimeter cordon established at two thousand yards that the media is *not* happy about. DHS has the lead on media interface and is doing an acceptable job at answering most of their inquiries at this time."

"Thank you. Final alibis, folks?" asked Dan, as he prepared to adjourn the meeting. "Good, no need for pep talks. Continue to do your job and be prepared to meet again in four hours. That'll be all."

"Janet, do I have a telephone yet?" asked Dan rather impatiently, as he returned to his office.

"Yes, sir, you're back in business."

"Thanks."

Dan returned to his office, shut the door, and collected his thoughts before dialing Mark's wife, Heather.

G's mind was thrust deeper into a realm of alter consciousness than he had ever experienced. The knockout blow delivered by the dubious agent provided a mechanism beyond the customary boundaries of REM sleep or even the occasional alcohol-induced state-of-mind he often used as a vehicle to alter consciousness.

In this state, his dream was accelerated and produced a lucidity that surpassed all of his previous experiences. He became more aware of his surroundings as he began to wrap his mind around the details surrounding his celestial body. This was more than a dream. This was alter consciousness at a level few, if any, would ever experience. Colors were more vibrant and seemed to have character and a noticeable distinction from life itself.

G could hear sounds from what seemed like miles away. Mental comprehension and learning were noticeably increased. As the experience accelerated, he closed his eyes to adjust his focus, thought briefly about Athena, and immediately picked up the scent of her perfume. When he opened his eyes, he found himself standing on the shoreline just outside the BOHICA, where she was working. The calm, warm waters lapping at his bare feet, the breeze moving through the palms, the sounds of gulls soaring overhead...it all felt like a high-definition version of reality.

The more G tried to analyze things, the sharper his mind became. His heart pounded when he caught a glimpse of Athena on the deck of the BOHICA; then, as soon as his mind could process the thought, he found himself standing next to her. She was unaware of his presence. He understood why, given the difference in their planes of consciousness. She was taking a drink order when he leaned in to smell her hair. He was pleasantly surprised to learn that not only could he smell her hair but he could also feel it blowing across his face as it flowed in the warm tropical breeze. He reached out to touch her shoulder and, when he made contact, caused her to turn suddenly, as if she was startled by something. G quickly backed off, puzzled by the experienced.

Did she feel that? he wondered. *Should this be something I should be careful about? What are the implications here? Is transference possible across conscious dimensions? How is all this happening?*

All of his questions produced answers that quickly overwhelmed the capacity of his mind to process it all. The one answer he was able to fully process was how he had gotten here in the first place. He remembered the confrontation with the agent and, as if in slow motion, was able to witness, from a third-person perspective, the encounter that triggered it all: the shouting, the comments, and the blow to the face that sent him to the floor and on his journey to deep alter consciousness through a state of unconsciousness. He was also able to see so many things at once, but didn't want to concentrate so hard that he lost the connection he established with Athena. He snapped back to see Athena answer her phone as she scurried off to find a private place to talk.

"Hello?" said Athena. "Hey, thanks for calling. Listen, I need your help, and I need it now."

G was listening but he could only hear one side of the conversation.

A man was on the other end of the line. Athena seemed to know him well.

"Yeah, this sounded urgent, so I hit you back as soon as I could," said Todd. "What's the situation?"

"I need a simple extraction with no casualties."

"How much time do I have?"

"Virtually none. I need this now. That's why I called *you*."

"Damn, woman…you love testing my abilities, don't ya?"

Todd listened while Athena explained the situation surrounding G's incarceration at the airport.

Mark's ears were ringing as he regained consciousness.

He could make out muffled sounds, but the ringing in his ears prevailed. He wasn't sure if he was blind or if the room around him was just plain dark. His survival training kicked in, and he began physically checking himself to assess whether or not he had sustained any injuries. Blood dripped from his left ear. Mark determined his eardrum had most likely been ruptured by the blast. His right ear seemed OK for now, despite some ringing. He had some trouble breathing but quickly determined that if he remained crouched close to the ground, he could avoid most of the caustic fumes hovering about two feet off the floor. Mark thought he heard movement, so he called out, "I'm here…over here…" but he didn't hear a reply.

Mark was determined to find a way out but knew he had to be careful. He began to feel his way in the dark for whatever he could find. His mind raced as he tried desperately to remember the layout of the room prior to the blast, so he could gain his bearings. He came across the first object—it was a man's shoe, a foot still in it.

"Shit!" he exclaimed. "Am I the only one left? I *know* I heard someone here earlier."

Again he shouted, "Hello! Can anyone hear me? Are you there?"

He continued his crawl, slowly feeling around in the dark in a desperate attempt to find something, anything that would connect him to an exit or the outside world. Then he remembered how far underground he was. His mind flashed back to the elevator ride that brought him to this dungeon.

How far down underground am I? he wondered.

His mind flashed back to Heather and the kids. The thought of them provided a deep determination to find a way out.

Surely by now they've been notified and are worried, he thought.

Mark felt something. It was another shoe. Only this one was attached to a lifeless body. He guessed it was that of Michael Libby, the young agent who was in the room with him at the time of the explosion. Dan felt for a pulse but couldn't find one. He remembered seeing Mike's cell phone on a holder on his hip and began to search for the device. Then he thought again about how far underground he was and wondered if the cell phone would receive a signal at all.

Feeling his way in the dark, he discovered Mike's fatal injury—a small steel beam of some sort that had pierced his chest. His clothes were soaked, presumably in his own blood. Despite his shock, Mark continued to search.

"Where's your phone, Mike? Where's that damn phone?"

It wasn't long before he found the phone, gripped tightly in Mike's hand. He pried it loose and turned it on. It provided the only light Mark had and was like a breath of fresh air. He immediately began using it as a dim flashlight to continue to search for a way out...if there even *was* a way out.

Booker's team came upon a clearing as the sun disappeared on the horizon; its orange rays the only evidence remaining of the day behind them. The point man halted the team and looked to Booker for instructions.

"We wait here for fifteen minutes, until the full cover of darkness," said Booker.

He sent two scouts out to scan the perimeter to determine safe passage across the clearing, which he estimated to be some two hundred yards across. The team could maintain cover by traveling the perimeter, but it would take too long, and they would miss their rendezvous with Ox. They rested and hydrated to prepare for the crossing.

The scouts returned, reporting no unfriendly forces in the area. As night fell, they set off across the clearing in teams of two. The first four men made it to the cover and safety of the other side and waited for Booker and Stokes, the remaining two teammates, to join up with them.

As Booker and his teammate set out to cross the open field, a single shot rang out from a position about one hundred fifty yards north of the team rendezvous point. The gunshot echoed across the clearing and sent roosting birds aloft from the tree line. Booker and Stokes immediately dove to the ground in a spread-eagle position in an attempt to avoid further fire. Stokes was ahead and to the right of Booker by approximately fifteen yards. The team remained silent while scanning the horizon for the source of the shot, using their night vision goggles (NVGs) and night scopes. There was no sign of the sniper, but the team knew they had to get Booker and their teammate out of the clearing and into the cover of the jungle.

Booker's dive to the ground knocked his NVGs from his face and cut the bridge of his nose. He quietly called out to his partner.

"Stokes, you OK?"

"Affirmative, sir."

"You still got your NVGs?"

"Affirmative, sir."

"OK, listen; my NVGs are *INOP* [broken]. I'll need you to lead when we cut loose. I've got you in sight right now, so when I call it, I'm gonna come and scoop you up by the back straps and lift you to your feet, and you're gonna lead us to the team...copy?"

Another shot rang out, coming amazingly close to the men. Booker actually saw the dirt explode next to Stokes and knew if they didn't move immediately, they would soon fall victim to the sniper. He rose to his feet, took off in the direction of Stokes, and forcefully grabbed the straps on his rucksack and heaved him to his feet with all his might. Stokes's feet were moving even before Booker managed to get to him, and the two were off and running. The team provided cover by shooting into the direction of incoming fire.

Booker could actually outrun everyone on the team, so he had to motivate Stokes to continue to give it all he had until making it to the safety of the other side of the clearing. Another shot rang out. The team watched Booker and Stokes hit the ground again about thirty yards in front of them. Booker slid low onto his belly, while Stokes fell awkwardly. Stokes was hit! Booker reacted quickly and rose to his feet, determined to get Stokes to the safety of the perimeter. Stokes's back straps still in hand, Booker dug in deep and dragged him along the ground toward the team. One of the team members ran out to assist Booker and helped drag Stokes to the safety and darkness of the perimeter of the jungle canopy.

The gunfire ceased, and all was quiet once again. The team assessed Stokes injuries. He had been hit in the foot. He would be fine, but he would slow them down. The team attempted one last radio call, hoping to reach Magic 23. The routine extraction was now a medical evacuation in a "hot LZ."

"Magic Two Three, this is Rawhide, over," called the radio operator attempting to reach Ox.

One of the team's very few reasons to break radio silence was unfolding before them — direct action involving small arms fire.

"Magic Two Three, this Rawhide, we are under fire, how copy?"

The team made the radio transmission "in the blind" hoping Ox would be close enough to hear their call on the predesignated, discreet frequency. They would make the call infrequently, in an effort not to reveal their position to the enemy.

"One more time," Booker said to the radio operator.

"Magic Two Three, this is Rawhide. Member injured, request top-cover assistance, over."

Dan hesitated before he allowed himself to dial the phone. It was a call he clearly didn't want to make.

Still uncertain, but hopeful on the fate of her husband, Dan knew he had to provide what information he could to get ahead of the media that would no doubt be knocking on the door of Mark and Heather's residence.

"Hello..." answered Heather.

"Hi, Heather, its Dan from Virginia, how are you?"

"Oh hi, Dan, doing well...getting dinner ready for the kids. Girls, please hold it down; Mommy's on the phone. Sorry, Dan...listen, if you're looking for Mark, he should've been in your neck of the woods by now..."

Heather was one of the most pleasant women Dan had ever met. This was gonna be tougher than he first thought. Dan got to the point.

"Listen, Heather, there's something I need to tell you…"

Heather let out a sigh and could hardly contain herself. She cut Dan off.

"Dan, what's happened? What's going on? Is Mark OK?"

"There's been an incident here in the city, and I'm afraid Mark has been caught in the middle of it all, Heather. He was assisting an investigation team by analyzing explosives, and—"

Dan tried to explain but was again cut off by Heather. "Dammit, Dan, don't sugarcoat this. Is Mark…*dead*?" Her question turned to crying.

The reality and blunt nature of Heather's question surprised Dan. "No!" he said, questioning his own answer. "I refuse to believe that, Heather," Dan reaffirmed forcefully. "I have the best rescue and recovery team in the United States on scene, and they *will* find him. I wanted you to know what's going on before the media gets to you. In fact, I have the local authorities on their way to you as we speak, so you're somewhat shielded from the chaos. This isn't going to be easy, Heather, but I need you to be strong while we look for Mark. You have my direct numbers. Call me if you need *anything* at all."

"You know I have no choice but to be strong, Dan…for the girls, I mean," Heather said softly.

"I'm doing everything possible here."

"Dan?"

"Yes, Heather?"

"Find my husband."

6

Ox had the airplane established on final approach to Howard Field when Ronaldo reported a faint radio call on the discreet frequency.

"Howard Tower, Magic Two Three, gear down, final-approach fix inbound, full-stop," reported Ox to the control tower.

"Hey Ox, I've got something on the discreet."

"If it's not urgent, we can get to it after landing," said Ox, managing the precarious phase of flight on final approach.

"We're below the mountains, so we'll need to execute a go-around to gain altitude so we can get better reception," requested Ronaldo.

"No can do, copilot. We need the gas, and we're on a schedule."

"Hey, I heard it too," yelled the passenger from the back of the plane. "In fact, I can play it back for you if you'd like," he added.

Ox didn't want to know how the passenger had recorded anything, much less a predesignated discreet frequency radio call.

"Great...now you've got the kid in the back seat all spun up about it as well. It can wait till we're on the ground," said Ox adamantly.

"Patch it through my headphones," said Ronaldo, determined to hear the radio call again.

"You got it."

Radio static in Ronaldo's headphones crackled with static as the broken radio recording playback was piped in from the passenger in the back.

"Magic Two Three this...Rawhide...under fire, how copy?"

"I knew it!" Ronaldo cried out.

Ox shot a look of anger as he was maneuvering the aircraft, now on short final.

"The team is under fire. We need to make contact to at least determine if they're safe or need immediate cover," pleaded Ronaldo.

"You better be damn certain what you heard was indeed what you thought you heard," said Ox, pushing the power throttles forward and lifting the nose of the aircraft while retracting the gear.

"Tower, Magic Two Three, we're going around. Request a suggested heading to the VFR holding point to assess a situation."

"Magic Two Three, turn left and hold east of the field. Suggest you maintain two thousand five hundred feet. Advise intentions when able," replied the tower.

"OK Jay, we're ready to air," said the cameraman, as he connected to the New York bureau.

This is a Sky News Alert. I'm Jay Cooney, reporting live from the Department of Homeland Security. There are reports coming in that give us reason to believe a large explosion has occurred in Ft. Meade, Maryland, in a warehouse outside the Baltimore-Washington Expressway. The explosion, said to be on a 'high order of magnitude' by intelligence sources, occurred approximately thirty minutes ago. The Department of Homeland Security has raised the terror threat level to RED or SEVERE—its highest level. DHS believes this explosion to have emanated from terrorists inside the country...or worse yet, inside the nation's capitol region. We'll have more from the site of the explosion as the story develops. Stay tuned to Sky News for continuing coverage. Reporting live from DHS Headquarters, I'm Jay Cooney, Sky News.

"And...you're off the air. Good job, Jay," said the Sky News producer in Jay's earpiece.

"OK, thanks...we're headed to the source of the explosion. I've got to get on scene. Besides, I don't want Geraldo to beat us there...or worse yet, anyone else from those other networks," said Jay.

"Go get the story, Jay," came the reply from the New York office.

"OK, you heard the boss. Let's go," said Jay, motivating his crew to get moving.

"Let me make a few calls, Athena," said Todd in reply to Athena's call for help. "I happen to be on a charter on my way up the east coast to N-Y-C. I'll have the pilot re-file, and we'll drop into Reagan National and see what's up. Meantime, chill, and if I need ya, I call ya."

"Thanks, Todd."

Athena felt a sense of nervous relief, knowing that Todd's methods could get a bit "ugly" for the recipients of his operations, but she knew he would do his best to respect her wishes for a "clean" extraction.

"Oh, I guess I should ask a few questions on what you'd like for me to do with this dude once I collect his ass from the Feds," asked Todd.

"Where did you say you were headed?"

"Oh, *hell* no, I ain't takin' him to NYC wit' me, woman! I've got a meeting with a huge recording artist that I've *got* to nail down, or I'm broke."

"Just get him outta there, Todd. Put him in your jet and make him comfortable, and I'll arrange to have someone meet you in New York," pleaded Athena.

"Whatever you say, Athena. I never questioned you before this, and I'm not gonna start any bad habits now," said Todd, conceding. "I know better. But I still don't like it. It has trouble trippin' all over it."

Athena hung up the phone and looked out onto the horizon to see a most spectacular Belize sun setting on the horizon. The moment caught her by surprise and gave her pause as she thought about G.

I'm not sure why I care so much about him, she thought. *But there's something about this that just feels right.*

G, still in a state of subconsciousness, sat next to her and enjoyed the moment.

With the sun's last rays upon the horizon, G stood, looked over his right shoulder, and felt a draw. He glanced back at Athena, now rising to her feet, sandals in hand, wind gently blowing through her hair. He smiled, then closed his eyes to examine where his mind would take him next.

Todd picked up the intercom and instructed the pilot to divert to Reagan National.

"*Monty*, how far out are we from DCA? We need to make a stop, and I'll need about two hours on the ground."

"We're about an hour and fifty five minutes from DCA," responded the pilot.

"Cool, make it happen and give me a shout when we're twenty minutes out."

Todd made a few phone calls for ground support and "assistance" from some of his sources in the DC Metro area. He knew the absolute best source to start with was Damian Bush. Damian was a kingpin of the DC underground mafia. A well-respected, nonviolent man, he was connected to everyone and anyone and could collect a team for Todd in a matter of minutes, which was pretty much all the time Todd had at that point.

"Yo, D, this is T-Rock. I need some special assistance and I need it pretty quick," he said, explaining the developing situation.

"I need an ID, airport access, a piece, a badge, and a *cleaner*. This should be a pretty simple extraction, given the proper amount of intimidation and convincing—gonna do things the ol' fashioned way. Gonna use my *'Jedi mind trick'* powers and charming personality," said Todd with a slight chuckle.

"How much time do I have?" asked Damian.

"Put your best on this one, D, cuz I ain't got much time, bro...like an hour."

"Shit, bro, this one's gonna cost you, but I think I can help. Good thing he's in a controlled environment."

"Well, with any luck we can bill the US Government for this one," said Todd.

"Well now, you shoulda mentioned that when we started this conversation," said Damian. "That makes a big difference in the level of service I can provide. I'll be in touch."

Dan turned on his office television to see if he could gather any information from the press he didn't already have in terms of actual video footage.

"Sir, I have a call for you from Tom," announced Janet.

Dan muted the television, but kept watching as one of the local networks reported on scene.

"What have you got for me, Tom?" asked Dan, urging Tom to get right to the point.

While Dan listened to Tom's report, he could hear the beeping of construction vehicles and alarms of emergency response vehicles in the background.

Dream Operative

"To be honest, Dan, this place is a mess. I'm staring at a one-hundred-yard crater where a good-sized warehouse used to sit. We've been able to run conduit through an adjacent A/C shaft, but we haven't made it very far — about fifteen feet so far. We estimate we have another twenty to thirty feet to go before we reach what was once the ground floor. We're hoping to break through at some point before we reach the bottom, but so far all we have is solid rubble," said Tom. "I've got crews setting up enough lighting to continue on through the night. Have you obtained any information on how many we're looking for?"

Shit. Dan thought. *All I've been focused on is Mark.*

"Negative, Tom," Dan replied. "That's been a slow process, but I'll re-engage. Can you tell me what your initial assessment is of survivability?"

"Not yet, Dan. But we're doing our best. To be honest, it doesn't look good."

As Hakim's taxi approached the Damascus airport, the driver asked if he had heard the news of the terrorist attack on US soil.

"The Americans have been attacked once again. It's the first since their infamous nine-eleven," said the driver. "It's all over the news."

Hakim listened and responded only with half a nod. Not having heard the news, he was understandably perplexed, yet he couldn't help but be initially intrigued by the news. The taxi stopped at the terminal, and he got out and thanked the driver.

"Teşekkürler."

He paid his fare in Lira, Turkish currency, and made his way to the departure gate of the airline that would take him to London.

"See if you can reach Rawhide on the discreet frequency," Ox ordered impatiently. "Make damn sure you don't compromise the team by asking their position in relation to the DZ. I don't want anyone finding them before we do."

Ronaldo shot Ox a look that, roughly translated, would equate to "DUH!"

"Rawhide, this is Magic Two Three, how copy, over…" called Ronaldo in an attempted to reach the team.

Ronaldo closed his eyes, tilted his head, and strained to listen for a response—any response.

"Hit 'em again," ordered Ox.

Before Ronaldo made his next transmission, their passenger spoke up from the back of the plane. "I may be able to help."

Ox had had enough and ordered the passenger to keep quiet. "Hey, sit down and shut the fuck up, or I'll throw you off this plane without a parachute."

"But I think I can reach the team with my equipment, if you'll just give me a fucking chance!"

Ronaldo jumped into the mix and ordered the two to stop shouting and to focus on the task at hand. "Ox, fly the damn plane and put us in a position to make a connection with the team," he snapped, surprising even himself with his newfound assertiveness.

Ox sat speechless, livid with the dialogue.

"OK, you, in the back...what's your name?" asked Ronaldo.

"Pat."

"OK, *Pat*, how can you help?"

G felt his celestial body surge, his mind accelerating through space and time. The experience was near indescribable. Never before had he actually felt such energy surrounding him.

Darkness and vertigo gave way to a faint amount of light and direction of movement that was relative to nothingness. His mind was soaked in the experience of it all while comprehending every detail at an amazing rate. In fact, speed seemed to be the predominant force of this experience. Movement continued to propel him in a constant direction, which, to the best of his knowledge, was forward in nature. Light began to wrap itself around him in a gentle manner while slowly transforming into kaleidoscopic color spectrums.

G reached out to touch the light, eliciting a magical response from his interaction and manipulation of its physical properties. Absolutely stunning blues mixed with the brightest yellows suddenly turned to the most gorgeous shades of green he had ever laid his eyes upon. He savored the vision and committed the experience to his deepest memory. He felt a sudden, rapid deceleration of that led to total stillness and silence. The silence gradually gave way to the most soothing sounds he had ever experienced. The sound wrapped itself around his very soul, grabbing his emotions and bringing them to extreme euphoria. He yielded to allow his mind and soul to fully absorb the totality of the experience as he continued to follow the colors surrounding him, slowly dancing to a metamorphosis of rhythm, light, and motion.

G began to hear the faint sounds of lapping water when he discerned he was approaching the threshold of a place unseen by outside eyes. The sound surrounding him changed and faded when he suddenly found himself in the company of others. He could sense their presence, yet he was unable to actually see anyone. He felt as if they could see *him*, however. He heard a collection of voices communicating softly among one another.

"What is this place?" he asked in a rhetorical whisper.

It is Nirvana, a voice answered in a soft confidence.

The voice he heard was that of an Authority that seemed to have come from within him.

It is that place which transcends reason. It is consciousness without feature; that place where knowledge and wisdom coequally reside, and it is evidenced by the luminescence of the mind.

"Why am I here? How did I get here?"

You are here because you chose to be. You arrived upon the energy of your desires.

"Is this a dream, or am I really here?" asked G to be certain.

Your true self resides within the sacred chambers of your soul. If your soul is present, you, therefore, are present as well, responded the Authority.

"Do I speak of this experience?" asked G.

You must, answered the Authority.

"How can I even begin to describe its depth, its beauty? And what am I do to do now?" asked G, humbly seeking guidance.

Use it for the greater good, as you are blessed with a gift.

"But—"

You must go now. Your conscious faculties will soon be required of you, warned the Authority.

G felt a force he had only come close to experiencing when taking off in a high-speed airliner, except this force was about five times greater. For the first time, G was conscious of the fact that he was returning to his physical body. When he regained consciousness and a connection to his physical body, he realized several things: he was still on the floor at the airport, his face was throbbing with pain from the fist of the agent, his head was pounding from an induced headache, and he could hear faint conversation outside the door.

Todd's intercom buzzed.

"Yeah, Monty, whatcha got?"

"We're twenty minutes out from Reagan National, Mr. Jordan."

"Thanks, Monty. Got a location on a parking spot yet?"

"Affirmative—west side, hangar two. We have a two-hour slot. I'll be refueled and ready to depart by then."

"Cool. I'll need the jet ready to roll, engines running. Copy?"

"Copy."

Todd picked up the phone and made a call to Damian to get an update on the support he requested.

"Yo, D, where we at on things?"

Damian had a way of coming through for his clients with more than they expected, which was typically a good thing, as *unexpected* situations were normally minimized or eliminated. As such, he could also be known to go a bit over the top in terms of flash.

"I've got two black Yukon SUVs scheduled to meet you when you pull into parking. I assume you'll be on the west side. Which hangar have you been assigned?"

"We'll be pulling up to hangar two. Listen, D, I hope these SUVs aren't the tricked-out version we use for our celebrity clients. I need official-looking, government style vehicles."

"I'm all over it, bro," Damian responded with a chuckle. "Hell, these are the real things, dog. A friend of mine 'borrowed' them from a friend of a friend."

"Cool. So how many assistants did you send? And what about the credentials I asked for?"

"It's all taken care of, T. Your driver is your 'locksmith' and will get you all the access you're gonna need. And I believe you'll approve of the assistants I've provided you with as well."

"Aight, I trust you, D. Listen, we're about to land. I gotta let you go. I'll contact you if I need anything else. Otherwise, I'll give you a shout once I'm back in the air with the mark."

Todd took a deep breath and reached for an energy drink from the refrigerator and downed it quickly to psych himself up for the "event." He quickly chased it with a shot of vodka.

7

The dim light provided by the cell phone gave Mark just enough illumination to find his way through the rubble, but he had no idea where he was headed or what he was looking for. Several questions raced through his mind as his survival senses guided him.

How stable is my environment? Do I have enough air? How long will I be here? Did all of the explosives detonate? If so, why am I still alive? Are they looking for survivors?

He had to re-engage the cell phone to keep the light illuminated. He looked up to see a layer of dust and smoke above his head and noticed that it had a slight movement to it.

"Airflow!" he said. "At least I have airflow...for now. I've got to stay low to keep my head out of that putrid air."

Looking at the cell phone battery indicator, he realized he had to conserve energy and use his light wisely, if he wanted it to last. He also noticed that reception was understandably nonexistent and questioned why anyone would even bring a cell phone into the building considering the lack of reception. Then he realized that Mike's phone was designed with a signal booster that allowed it to work outside the typical range of most cell phones. Encouraged, Mark scrolled through the phone to find anything official, held his breath, and hit "send."

"C'mon, connect, dammit!"

Listening for a signal, Mark was discouraged when the phone dimmed and didn't connect to the outside world.

"Son of a—" Mark caught himself as he was reminded to think positively and consider other alternatives that frustration would only blur.

It must be the building damage, he thought. *I can't just sit here and wait to be rescued. . I gotta move if I'm gonna get outta here. Maybe I can even find a spot where this thing will have some reception.*

Mark inched his way through the rubble, determined to see beyond the reach of the dim cell phone light. He stopped occasionally to listen for...anything, and would occasionally call out, hoping *someone* would hear him. Each time he could only hear the falling of debris or the settling of the structure around him.

Mark found the threshold of the room and illuminated the cell phone to catch a glimpse of the path ahead.

"Damn, this place is a mess," he said softly, then continued his crawl through the debris. Coughing from the dust, Mark paused to say a silent prayer and decided to go in the *opposite* direction of the dust movement above his head, hoping to find the source that was causing the airflow.

Hakim approached the airport security checkpoint with confidence and produced his passport and boarding pass.

"Good afternoon, Professor Celik," said the security guard.

Hakim replied with only a grin and a nod.

"Your papers are in order, sir; please remove your shoes and place them on the conveyor belt, along with your satchel, and have a good flight."

Hakim did as he was instructed. He was used to the routine. Making his way through security, he saw two government agents wearing business suits. There was something about the extra scrutiny they gave to their jobs, where traditional security lacked the personal attention. Hakim was trained to pick up on it and was careful not to treat the agents any differently than those he deemed "normal" by his standards.

Once through the security screening process, Hakim made his way to his departure gate. He was well aware of his surroundings and witnessed several armed military patrolling the airport. They didn't seem to be looking for anything or anyone in particular. He did notice a couple of suspected "spotters" on occasion who did seem to be on the lookout for out for something, or someone — perhaps even Hakim himself. He felt confident behind the genius of his disguise and stepped in line once his flight was called for boarding.

Dream Operative

Pat explained to Ronaldo that his equipment was designed with a satellite interface, connecting him to just about any and every government resource that supported intelligence, surveillance and reconnaissance. He had been "listening" since they departed Belize and had sent a message for unmanned aerial system support as soon as he heard the team make their radio call.

"So..." said Ronaldo. "You're actually ahead of us on this, aren't you?"

"I was told to stay out of your business and attend to my orders, but I can certainly justify *assistance* like this. So tell me what you need," offered Pat.

"Tell me what you've *got*," responded Ronaldo as Ox listened in.

"OK, I can verify the team's radio call as authentic. I even have it recorded, as I played it back for you earlier. I have a Predator Remotely Piloted Aircraft en route, but I don't have a fix on its position yet, so if you could provide the location coordinates for me, I can get eyes on the team and conduct a search for the gunfire that has them somewhat occupied at the moment. No promises, but these things have proven their mettle in situations like this."

Ronaldo gave Ox a look that solicited his permission to release the coordinates of the team to Pat. Ox was reluctantly realizing that his passengers were in fact starting to gel and work as a team in support of a common objective. He gave Ronaldo a nod and called the tower to tell them he would not be landing and would instead be proceeding with his mission.

"Tower, this is Magic Two Three, request to proceed VFR southbound. We will *not* be landing at Howard at this time."

"I recommend we make a radio call to the team once we're beyond that ridge line ahead," said Pat. "I should have an estimate for the Predator's arrival anytime now."

Ox pushed the throttles forward and climbed the aircraft as soon as he received clearance from the tower. He asked Ronaldo to calculate the fuel and to plan for alternate refueling sites once the team was safely extracted.

"I'm on it," replied Ronaldo.

Ox programmed the flight control system with the LZ coordinates and set a course for the landing zone as the orange hue of the sun receded to blue-black darkness.

"Finally," said Ox, as he removed his sunglasses and took in a focused breath that readied him for the "exciting" part of the journey.

Todd opened the door of the jet before it came to a complete stop.

The tarmac was still wet from an earlier rain. The reflection of the two black government SUVs were in full view when Todd stepped onto the extended steps of the jet. The door to the first SUV opened. A wiry young man walked to meet Todd halfway between the jet and the vehicle and extended his hand.

"Mr. Jordan, I'm Key, your locksmith—"

"You're shittin' me, right?" Todd said with a laugh and a warm smile. "I don't believe I'll have any trouble remembering *your* name, bro."

Key smiled and opened the back door to the SUV, where Todd found his lead "assistant," Stephanie. Todd and Stephanie were old friends, so he was understandably happy to see her again, albeit somewhat surprised by the encounter.

"Steph, what the hell are you doing here?" said Todd, the door closing behind him.

"Good to see you as well, TJ. Let's get reacquainted later, shall we? For now, as I understand it, you have a mission you need to accomplish?"

Todd paused for a beat and stared at her with raised eyebrows that pretty much relinquished temporary control as she briefed him on the details.

"Take off your clothes," she said.

"OK. Damn, woman, this is starting out on the fun side. But don't you think we should attend to business first?" said Todd, removing his shirt boldly in front of Stephanie. She stared at him, offered a sarcastic look of impatience and instructed him to don the official clothes she brought for his operation.

"I see you gained a little weight," said Stephanie, sarcastically.

"Yeah, I been workin' out," he responded with a smile.

"That's not the kind of weight I was referring to," she said, pointing to his midsection.

"Aw, girl, don't be hatin' on a brotha."

"OK, here are your credentials, your badge, and your gun. Your *mark* is likely in one of two known holding rooms in the airport security office. It'll be up to you to schmooze that info out of anyone who has knowledge. Key will get us past any security barriers."

"Why do I find that damn name so funny?" he said, laughing aloud once again.

"Are you listening to me, TJ?" asked Stephanie sternly. "You have to focus."

"I hear ya. What's *your* role?"

"I'm here to keep *you* outta trouble," quipped Stephanie.

"How you supposed to do that?"

"You drank an energy drink, didn't you? I can always tell."

"Maybe," said Todd, in a guilty tone.

"At least I know you'll be on your toes. I just hope you didn't spike it with your normal vodka chaser."

Todd turned to look out the window and thought about how well she knew him...still.

"OK, who's in the second SUV?" he asked.

"More support. They'll stay put, unless we require their services."

"How long you been working for Damian?"

Stephanie ignored his question and simply said, "We're here. You ready TJ?"

"Damn straight," he responded, suddenly taking on a more serious personality and official tone.

The two SUVs pulled up to the front of the airport and parked. Key got out and opened the door for Stephanie and Todd. All three stepped with confidence to the airport entrance. The driver of the second SUV got out of his vehicle and stood between both vehicles, waiting for airport security to arrive, which they did moments later. Once security was convinced their presence was *official,* they were expected to make a radio call to the airport central security office.

"Perfect," said Key, listening in on his earpiece, confirming their presence was preannounced. He looked at Stephanie and Todd. "They're expecting us."

Approaching the security checkpoint, Stephanie stepped forward and announced their presence as "Government Agents," flashed her badge, and demanded access to the main security office. They were challenged at the checkpoint by security personnel when Todd stepped forward and asked who was in charge. An overweight, middle-aged man spoke up.

"I'm shift supervisor and I'm in charge here. What's the nature of your business here?"

Todd gave him a look that made most men afraid they asked such a question.

"Yeah, I'm here on official government business, and I'm looking for someone who can make decisions. Is that you, or do you need to call someone?"

"Uh, I can help you, sir."

G was still trying to clear his head while he pushed himself up from the floor. He rubbed his temples and covered his eyes with his hand.

"I see someone has come to," said the agent who landed the knockout blow. "You feel like being honest with me yet?"

"I've *been* honest with you from the start, asshole!" said G. He was determined not to back down, even after taking the beating he had endured.

The agent walked over to G, grabbed him by the shirt collar, lifted him to his feet, and shoved him against the wall.

"I've just about had it with you. Don't you understand that *no one* is gonna keep me from beating *something* out of you, even if it's *not* the truth? Tell me who you're working with, or eat another one of these," said the agent, threatening G once again with a raised fist.

"Go fuck yourself," said G, bravely preparing for—in fact, anticipating—another right cross that would carry him back into alter consciousness.

G actually preferred to occupy unconsciousness, even if it meant getting there would amount to enduring pain on the way in…and undoubtedly on the way out as well. The thought did cross his mind on how he would actually get out of this predicament, but it was secondary to his current state of fear.

The agent drew back his fist to deliver another crushing blow, but he was interrupted by a second agent, who burst into the room.

"Sir, we have company."

The agent gripping G's collar dropped his fist and turned his head slowly toward the door. "Who is it?"

Shrugging his shoulders, the second agent simply responded, "Government."

The agent dragged G to the table and sat him in a chair.

"Keep him company while I take care of the 'government.' I'll be back in a minute to deal with this trash as soon as I get rid of the trash that's trying to crash our party," he said, glancing into the two-way mirror.

The agent behind the mirror glanced at his watch and picked up the phone.

"We have company. Word has it they're government. How do you want me to play this?"

"Whatever you do, don't compromise the operation. Maintain control of the situation and call me once they're gone," responded the obscure voice. "And don't allow the subject to get out of your sight."

The agent called the security supervisor and asked him to stall the visitors.

The airport security supervisor led Todd, Stephanie, and Key to a hallway door that required a cipher code to gain access. The security supervisor entered the code and opened the door. The door led to a dimly lit stairwell. He opened the door and held it for Todd's team to walk through first. Todd glanced at Key, who returned a disapproving look. Todd stopped in his tracks and looked at the supervisor.

"Do you think we're stupid? Do you? Why are you taking us *away* from the security offices, instead of *toward* them? Would you prefer I arrest you for obstruction of justice right here and find the office on my own? Stop jerking my chain!"

"Sorry sir, I was taking a shortcut," explained the security supervisor, nervously trying to escape a half-truth.

"OK, now *I'm* in charge," said Todd. "Surrender your radio. Give it to my deputy," he added pointing to Key.

"Sir, I can't surrender my radio. I—"

"I said surrender your radio. Key, take his radio."

As they made their way to the security offices, they were met by another airport security guard. Todd stopped and spoke with the guard.

"What's your name?"

The guard glanced at his supervisor to question Todd's authority and received a nod of approval from the supervisor.

"I'm Bruce," said the guard.

"Bruce, nice to meet you," said Todd with personality and a smile. "Bruce, I need you to take my deputy to your video control room, please. He needs to review some footage you have. How far back does your system take you?"

"Ninety-six hours, sir."

"Good. Key, go with Bruce and do...whatever it is you do. We'll be in touch when we need you," said Todd as he looked at the supervisor. "Now, where were we? Oh yeah, you were taking us to the security office."

The shift supervisor brought Todd to another door with a cipher lock and quickly entered the code that gave them access to a small waiting room. They were met by the rogue agent, who introduced himself to Todd and Stephanie as "Agent Smith."

"Agent Smith? Is that your real name?" asked Todd.

The agent looked surprised, puffed up his chest and said, "Of course it is. What kind of question is that?"

Todd smiled sarcastically at the agent, glanced at Stephanie, and turned back to glare at Agent Smith. Then Todd simply did what he did best. He punched Agent Smith square in the face and knocked him out cold with a "T-Rock" right cross to the bridge of his nose. Stephanie was stunned but moved quickly to subdue the supervisor. She pushed him to the floor and placed her knee in his back and used his own handcuffs to subdue him. He shouted out for help, so she clocked him in the back of the head with her fist to silence him. She looked at Todd with shock and a slight hint of admiration.

"Wanna tell me why you did that, TJ?"

"C'mon, Steph, the first thing he did was lie to me. I hate when people lie to me. You really think 'Smith' was his *real* name? I don't think so."

The agent remaining in the room with G heard the commotion outside. When he turned toward the door, G attempted to trip him, but he was no match for the experienced agent. A struggle ensued between G and the agent.

Todd and Stephanie looked at each other when they heard the struggle and burst into the room.

"Enough!" shouted Todd to both men. "Which one of you is G?"

"He is, sir," said the agent, struggling to catch his breath, pointing to G.

Dropping his head slightly and struggling to catch his breath, G simply responded, "Yeah, I'm G. Who the hell are you, and what do *you* want with me?"

Todd ignored G for the moment, realizing he had an armed agent to deal with first. He approached the agent calmly and asked to see his credentials. As the agent reached for his identification badge, he glanced around Todd to the open door of the room and saw his partner out cold on the floor. He quickly reached for his gun.

"Don't do that," said Todd. "Give me your piece, and everyone will walk outta here alive."

The agent looked at Todd and suddenly noticed that Stephanie already had her weapon trained on him, so he reluctantly surrendered to Todd.

"Cuff him, Steph."

G was confused by all the misdirection and dialogue and once again asked for someone to tell him what was going on. Stephanie holstered her weapon and placed handcuffs on the agent and sat him in the very chair previously occupied by G.

"Doesn't feel so good, does it, asshole?" said G with a sense of satisfaction.

G looked at Todd and asked, "Now what?"

"G, I'm here because you have friends in high places who wanted me to get you out of a 'situation.' You ready to roll?"

"Sure," said G. "Where are we *rolling* to?"

"All your questions will be answered soon," said Todd, leading G and Stephanie out of the room. They locked the remaining agent inside with his partner and security supervisor. "First, we gotta get you safely outta here. In order to do that, I need you to play along and do what I say. In other words, I need you to trust me," said Todd, looking squarely into G's eyes. "Can you do that?"

"Beats trusting these assholes," responded G with a grin.

"OK, then, I need you to put these handcuffs on your wrists."

"I can do that."

Hiding behind the two-way mirror, watching the entire encounter unfold, the lone agent chambered a round and remained quietly hidden. Instead of encountering G's newest friends, he opted for surveillance instead of engagement, where the odds were clearly against him.

Once G and the team were gone, the lone agent emerged from hiding with his weapon drawn. He placed a silencer on his handgun and quietly walked into the room holding the two agents and airport security manager. The agent handcuffed to the chair was relieved to see someone on his side.

"Whew, it's you," he said. "Gimme a hand and unlock these cuffs while we still have time to get those assholes.

He was confused to see the agent raise his weapon and point it at him. The last sound he heard was the suppressed sound of the handgun that put a bullet in his head.

The agent approached the unconscious Agent Smith and found his weapon. He removed the weapon and fired a single shot that sent a bullet into the head of the airport security guard. He wiped the weapon and placed it into the unconscious hand of Agent Smith, then put two bullets into him from the silenced weapon.

"I'm gonna need that security uniform, my friend," he said.

8

Athena made another attempt to contact Dan.

"Mr. Keppler, this is operator twenty-two. I have a secure voice call for you."

"Copy," said Dan. "Push it through, please."

Dan heard the switchover and confirmed the security of the call and recited his typical response. "This is Delta Kilo Zero One..." and waited for a response.

"Sir, Victor Delta forty-three, are we secure?"

"Affirmative, Valerie. Good to be reconnected."

"Sir, I understand you're very busy—"

"That's an understatement," interrupted Dan. "Valerie, if this can wait—"

"I'm sorry, sir, it simply cannot. You need to be aware of what's going on," said Valerie, as she drew a breath to prepare her dialogue for the boss.

Hearing her sigh, Dan prepared himself for what Valerie had to say. After providing the boss with as much detail as she could on her "operation," she waited for his response. She didn't have to wait long, as it came fast and furious.

"You did *what*?" exclaimed Dan. "On whose authority did you act? Who have you got supervising this op, *you*? What the *hell* were you thinking, Valerie?"

"Sir, given the circumstances, I *had* to act."

"No, you didn't. It was personal, and you felt *compelled* to act...on your own volition, I might add," said Dan angrily.

"With all due respect, Dan, I did attempt to get your buy-in on this. You trained me to think for myself. I did that. Please don't punish me for doing what I'm trained to do."

Dan collected his emotions and thought about what to do next.

"The last thing I need, Valerie, is an operative making these kinds of decisions without permission or top cover. This was clearly outside your lane," said Dan. "You wanna tell me your exit strategy?"

"That's why I called you, Dan. Here's what I need…"

Ronaldo reported that his calculations were complete.

"We have enough fuel to make it to the LZ, exfiltrate the team, and make it back over the southern border of Panama."

Ox returned a look of expectation, indicating he was waiting to hear more.

"That doesn't give me a warm fuzzy," said Ox. "I'm still waiting for you to tell me the part about where we refuel once the team is onboard, because I can see there's no way we're making it back to Howard."

Listening from the back, Pat spoke up, "If we can make it to Navagandi, I know of an airstrip we can use to safely land."

"And if we can't?" questioned Ox, with sarcasm.

Hearing no immediate response, Ox solicited an answer.

"Anyone?"

Ronaldo sat silently while contemplating alternatives, if there indeed *were* any. Pat remained focused on his computer and stayed busy, tapping the keys in an attempt to produce alternatives that would keep him and the team safe.

As Ox maneuvered the Casa across the southern border of Panama into Colombia, he paused for effect, then broke the silent tension.

"OK, if any of you brainiacs figure it out before I do, speak up. Meantime, we have a mission to accomplish. You ready for the excitement, kid?"

Ronaldo, not wanting to reveal the fact that he was a bit nervous, responded with a look of confidence followed by an affirmative thumbs-up as Ox instructed him to turn off the aircraft anti-collision lights and to don his NVGs. Once he and Ronaldo were prepared for "blacked-out" operations, Ox instructed everyone to prepare for a rapid descent. He pushed the nose of the Casa forward and accelerated into a steep dive to avoid radar detection. Pat sat nervously gripping the arms of his seat in the back, waiting for the aircraft to level off.

Ronaldo's body surged with adrenaline as he watched the terrain grow in front of him in the green hue of his NVGs. He glanced at Ox, now fully engaged in the skill and thrill of doing what he loved most. Ronaldo was mesmerized by the amazing detailed beauty of the earth below as Ox pulled back on the yoke to level the plane of the aircraft just above the tree line.

"Take the controls, copilot," commanded Ox.

Ronaldo was pleasantly surprised by the command and eagerly accepted the instruction.

"I have control," responded Ronaldo.

"You have control," answered Ox. "Now, just follow the terrain all the way to the LZ. And remember, we're in hostile airspace, so try not to bump into anything."

Booker's team had made their way to the fringe of the LZ when the lead scout signaled for the team to hold their position.

"Whatcha got?" whispered Booker.

"Not sure if it's a spotter or an innocent goat herder," whispered the scout, examining the LZ through night vision binoculars.

"Let's move to within forty yards of the LZ and stay upwind from the goat herder. Let me know if you see anyone else or anything that makes you flinch."

"How's Stokes?" Booker asked his medical specialist.

"Stable, sir. He'll be fine, as long as we get on that airplane."

"Oh, we'll get on that damn plane...don't you worry about that," responded Booker. "I just don't like knowing we have company on the LZ."

Booker checked in with his comm specialist. "Jones, you hear from Magic Two Three yet?"

"Negative, sir."

"Send a text query. Tell him we've arrived at the LZ but we have company," said Booker. "Send him our coordinates, and see if you can get his ETA."

"Will do, sir."

Key watched over the video surveillance screens from the airport security control room. He had managed to convince Bruce, the security guard, that he and his team were from the Department of Homeland Security on a mission to retrieve a high-risk terror suspect. He had also convinced Bruce that he would be officially commended for his support and professionalism for the safe transfer of the suspect.

"I could use your help, Bruce," said Key when he saw Todd and Stephanie escorting a "prisoner" on one of the video monitors.

"Sure, whatever you need."

"Awesome. I need you to ensure that nothing is on your recorded system that shows evidence that we were ever here. Erase all video surveillance and computer entries. Trust me on this, Bruce. You do *not* want to have evidence left anywhere on any of your systems. Can I count on you?"

"Absolutely."

"Cool. And what I'll do for you—just between us girls—is I'll make sure you're recommended for an interview with DHS because of your loyalty and professionalism. We're talkin' a huge pay raise, Bruce. But if even a trace of evidence remains…you won't like the consequences, and I won't be able to help you. Do you understand?"

"You can trust me."

"OK, get busy. Reboot your system, and someone will be in touch with you. Nice to have worked alongside of you, Bruce. I appreciate you, and your country appreciates you," said Key as he left the control room.

Key met the trio as they were walking down a hallway toward the airport exit.

"How we lookin', Key?" asked Todd.

"We're good."

"Where's that security guard you were with?" asked Stephanie.

"No worries. I have him convinced that he's our newest recruit and have ensured his full cooperation."

Stephanie raised an eyebrow and smiled as if to indicate she should have known not to even question Key's assigned objective results.

"Where's *your* security guard?" asked Key.

"He's takin' a nap," quipped Todd.

Key shrugged his shoulders, looked at G, and offered a simple greeting. "What's up?"

"OK team, on your toes, we're not outta this yet," said Todd, as they approached the main lobby of the airport.

Halfway to the exit, they were approached by a DC metro police officer.

"Excuse me folks, can someone tell me what's going on here? We weren't informed of your presence on the airport. May I see some credentials?"

Todd flashed his ID adorned with a bright gold badge. He approached the officer and examined his name tag. "Look, Officer...Beoletto, is it? Officer Beoletto, I can appreciate how seriously you take your job, but we simply can't accept any delays in transporting this suspect."

"And I can appreciate *that*, sir, but you're in *my* airport, and I run the show here," said Officer Beoletto. "I'm gonna have to call this in," he added.

Key stepped forward. "Tell you what, Officer Beoletto. We have the full cooperation of airport security and the airport manager. Check for yourself. In fact, if you let me use your radio..." said Key, as he politely grabbed the officer's radio.

Key quickly tuned the device to the discreet frequency of the video control room and connected with Bruce. "Airport security main office, this is Special Agent Key, how copy, over?"

Bruce was busy erasing all evidence when he heard the radio call.

"This is officer Henrich, loud and clear, sir," responded Bruce proudly.

"Yeah, Bruce, this is Key...uh, *Special Agent* Key...we've encountered an Officer Beoletto from the Metro Police Department who wishes to verify your knowledge of our presence. Would you mind speaking with him, so we can be on our way?" said Key in his most professional tone.

Todd and Stephanie looked at each other, wondering how Key was going to play the situation. Key turned up the radio speaker as Bruce responded.

"That's affirmative, sir, we're well aware of your presence. And may I say it was a pleasure working with you and your team on this operation," said Bruce, adding what he'd hope would be a clincher for a chance at a new job.

"You satisfied, Officer Beoletto?" asked Todd.

"Yes, sir, sorry to have held you up," responded the eager officer. "Have a nice evening."

Todd and the team made their way to the awaiting SUVs. He noticed they were blocked-in by three Metro Police cruisers, but before he could say anything, Officer Beoletto called out from behind them and waived off the cruisers, clearing the way for Todd and his team to depart.

Once inside the vehicles and behind the deeply tinted windows, Stephanie removed G's handcuffs. She looked at Todd approvingly. "I'd say that was one smooth operation, TJ. Nice going, Key," she said to Key, now driving them to the ramp and the awaiting jet.

"Yo, Monty, we ready to roll?" said Todd, calling in to his pilot.

"Waitin' on you, boss. How many passengers am I expecting?" asked Monty, who was running weight calculations.

Todd gave Stephanie a look, to which she responded, "I can't this time, TJ. Catch me when you come back through town, and we'll do lunch."

"Yeah," said Todd, disappointed. "I'll have my people call your people," he added sarcastically. "I'm bringin' one extra wit' me, Monty. See you soon."

"I still have no idea who you people are, but I take it I should be thanking you," said G, as he was trying his best to make sense out of his very long day.

"No worries," said Stephanie. "Todd will fill you in on what he can once you're in the air."

"In the air?" questioned G, surprised at the revelation that he would be leaving DC. "Like I said, I appreciate the rescue and all, but I need to stay in DC."

"My man, look, if I leave you here, we'll be doing this all over again," said Todd. "I think your life is gettin' ready to change, but it's clear you have no idea. I need you to get on my plane. You can go willingly, or I can force you," said Todd with a smile and an expectant look.

"OK, but I'd like some answers," said a reluctant G, as the SUVs pulled up to the jet. "Damn. Nice jet. Is that ours?"

"Uh, no, brah, it's *mine*," said Todd, with a cocky smile and a wink to Stephanie. "You just happen to have a first-class ticket on today's flight. Yo, Key, escort G onto the plane and make it look good for anyone watching our last moves. I'll be right there."

"Nice working with you, TJ," said Stephanie.

"You too, Steph. So you want me to strip again, or can I hang onto these official clothes?" said Todd, with a shit-eating grin.

"Get outta here, before Officer Beoletto catches on to our ruse, big guy."

"Love you, girl."

"Love you too, TJ. Fly safe, and don't be such a stranger."

Todd made his way toward the awaiting plane. As he approached the sleek jet, he picked up the scent of jet fuel, which he found to be rather pleasing for some reason. He called it one of the scents of success. He felt a surge of pride well within, knowing he had accomplished another successful mission by thinking on his feet and garnering the assistance of some of his closest friends.

Dream Operative

"Damn, what a fucking rush," he announced, as he stepped into the plush jet and turned to secure the door behind him. "Ladies and gentlemen, please turn off all cell phones and fasten your seatbelts," said Todd jokingly to his only passenger.

G was still attempting to wrap his earthly mind around the entire ordeal when Todd offered him a cocktail.

Watching their movements from a dark, obscure vantage point on the tarmac was the remaining agent. He managed to capture most details on the video feature of his cell phone. He recorded the plane's tail number, the license numbers of the two black SUVs, and grainy photographs of Todd and Stephanie.

Ronaldo closely followed the terrain along the preplanned route with the assistance of his NVGs and his flight management system, while Ox busily calculated landing and departure data with a mini flashlight clenched between his teeth.

"Hey, guys, the Predator is overhead the coordinates you provided," announced Pat over the intercom. "Is there any way you can capture the latest *exact* coordinates of the team for me?"

"Have your sensor operator use the infrared feature on that expensive camera system to find the team," said Ox, with the flashlight still in his mouth.

"Well, that wouldn't ordinarily be an issue…" said Pat with some hesitation.

Ox removed the flashlight from his mouth and keyed the intercom.

"What's the problem?"

"The *problem* is that I'm painting several heat signatures in the area of the team's last known location," said Pat. "You did say the team consists of only six members, correct? Well, I show about twenty-six in the area."

This wouldn't be the first time Ox executed an extraction with "company" in the area, but it was one of the rare times known hostiles were close enough to be an issue that raised the danger level. He felt a higher level of confidence, knowing they had a Predator overhead, but he knew he had to find the team's *exact* location if he wanted to mitigate the risk to the entire operation.

Ox checked his communications control workstation for any messages from the team. To his surprise, he found the team's latest text message.

"How the hell did we miss this?" he questioned to no one in particular.

Reading the team's short text message, Ox let everyone know the latest news over the intercom.

"Well, the team has arrived to the LZ, but they weren't specific as to their coordinates. They do report having company they're concerned with. I'll send a message requesting their specific coordinates."

Hakim sat in quiet solitude as his plane made an on-time arrival into Heathrow International Airport. His thought back to the meeting he conducted in Damascus, where he continued to sow the seeds of his deepest convictions among his followers.

His chosen one —the martyr— would meet him in London later that day for the details of his assignment.

Hakim casually made his way to customs and immigration. Although he was never really nervous, this was the most vulnerable part of his journey. He was always alert, but especially so during the transition through customs and immigration. There are typically very few exits or escape routes available in such areas.

"Good evening, sir. What is the nature of your visit to England?" asked the immigration officer.

"Leisure. I am on my way to the United States to lecture," said Hakim.

"I see," said the officer. "What is it you're lecturing?"

"Psychology and criminal behavior," said Hakim, looking straight into the officer's eyes.

"And you have just arrived from Damascus?" the officer inquired, while searching the database for information.

"Yes," responded Hakim.

"How long will you be staying in Great Britain, sir?"

"Forty-eight hours."

"Very well, sir. Have a pleasant stay," said the officer, handing Hakim's passport and paperwork back to him.

Hakim placed the passport into his shirt pocket and made his way toward the passenger pickup area, where he would meet his ride.

Dream Operative

"Excuse me, sir," called out the immigration officer.

Hakim's mind went into overdrive, his heart skipped a beat. Time slowed to a crawl as he turned to look back at the officer.

"You forgot your glasses."

"Indeed I did, young man…indeed I did. Thank you."

9

(6.4517N 75.5419W)

"Just received an update on the team's exact location," said Ox, jotting the coordinates down on paper. "Hey, Pat, any way you can produce a printout once you get a good view of the team in relation to the LZ?" he asked.

"Only if you start being nice to me," joked Pat.

Ronaldo broke his gaze from the terrain long enough to see a slight smile break across Ox's face in reaction to Pat's comment—albeit only for an instant. Pat was second-guessing his sarcasm as he waited through a seemingly long pause of silence following his response to Ox.

"OK, here are the coordinates," said Ox, breaking the silence.

Pat repeated the coordinates aloud to Ox to ensure he entered them correctly and, once he was certain, hit "send" on his keyboard. Now it was up to the sensor operator back at Creech AFB, Nevada, to find the team and identify any other "targets of interest" for Ox and his crew.

Dan could hardly believe his ears after hearing the risks Athena was taking to get this "G character" in to see him. There was clearly something about this young man he found fascinating, but wasn't yet convinced he could be used inside the Agency. After all, he was a civilian with virtually no training or operational background whatsoever.

"Tell me again what it is you need, Valerie?"

"Right now, I need your top cover and permission to complete the op."

"In other words, you need cash."

"Yeah, I need cash, and I need to get the hell out of Belize to run the op."

"You realize the reason I placed you in Belize in the first place was to keep a close eye on Colonel Waddy—"

"Yeah, Dan, I get it. I'm supposed to keep an eye on a man who bends the rules and gets a bit 'passionate' from time to time; a man, by the way, who has served his country in one form or another for most of his adult life and whose biggest thrill is driving his relic airplane and chasing skirts. C'mon, give this assignment to someone who *wants* to be bored…or to someone who surfs and dives. I've babysat this man for weeks and have found nothing out of the ordinary. You've practically replaced me anyway by placing Pat onboard with him. How much further up his ass can you actually get someone? Look, I don't give a shit how you run the show, as long as you let me back in to the ops world, where you *know* I can make a difference."

"Take a breath, Val. Damn. I can see you're passionate about this."

"We don't have time to debate it, Dan. I'm asking for your blessing. This is cutting-edge shit we're about to break in on, and I'm handing it to you on a silver frigging platter," said Valerie in one last attempt at convincing Dan. "At least I'm *trying* to. Open a funding line for me and give me a green light."

"All right, Valerie, I'll release you from your current assignment. But I'm putting you in a *temporary* position until you bring this guy in—which, by the way, you have seventy-two hours to do, or I'm cutting you *and* your funding line loose. Copy?"

"You won't be disappointed, Dan," said Valerie, now refocusing on her new assignment.

"It's pretty straightforward, Valerie, so I better *not* be disappointed. Reassume your NOC ID and contact me if you need anything. And don't be a hero. I've got all I can handle here right now with the crisis in DC, so I hope *not* to hear from you until you have your guest in custody and are ready for a meeting."

It was understood that Dan had the last word, so Athena simply hung up the phone, smiled like a schoolgirl who had gotten away with murder, and quickly sent a text to Todd to inquire about the status of his progress.

Todd picked up a phone next to a plush leather seat across from G.

"Yo, Monty, let's light this thing and get the hell outta Dodge. Set a course for NYC and gimme a shout when we're thirty minutes out."

"You got it, boss," said Monty, setting the Gulfstream in motion.

"So...*Todd*, is it? Well, Todd, when do you plan on giving me some details?" said G, "Because I'm still confused as hell."

"One sec, brah," said Todd, holding up an index finger. "I have to answer a text, and I'll find out how much I can tell you for now."

"Great," said G, with a bit of sarcasm. "Why do I suddenly feel like I'm wrapped up in some cheesy spy novel?"

"Package all secure. En route to NYC. What now? How much can I reveal?" Todd pushed "send" on his phone that would connect him with Athena to let her know the first part of her operation was complete.

While he awaited a response from Athena, he smiled at G and asked if he was comfortable.

"How's the drink? You want another one?"

"What I'd really like is some answers," said G, as patiently as he knew how. "But while you're figuring it all out, I *will* take another drink."

Todd looked at G, who was clearly exhausted, frustrated, and at his wit's end.

"Brah, I have no idea who you are, but I like you. And it's apparent that you're well-liked by some very good people in some very high places."

"Well, anyone who can snatch me from the jaws of the FBI and get away with it has *got* to have some power," said G.

"They weren't FBI, G. Those fucks may have been on the FBI *payroll*, but they weren't with the FBI *I* know."

G felt a familiar surge of power acting on his body as Monty powered the Gulfstream's jet engines and released the brakes to launch the aircraft down the runway. Todd reclined and smiled at G's reaction.

"Hang on to that drink, brah, cuz this bitch will set ya back."

"Sir we have contact from Magic Two Three," reported Jones.

"Do you have an ETA?" asked Booker.

"We do, sir. And there's a Predator UAS moving in above us that should be able to provide an IR feed to my laptop fairly soon. Magic Two Three will have the same picture as we do, so we'll all be operating from the same playbook. They estimate touchdown in thirty minutes."

"Cool. Perry, take KK with you and scout the perimeter of the LZ. Make sure all unfriendly are identified. Do *not* fire unless being fired upon. I don't want this shit to flare up on us."

"Hartman, be on the ready with your IR laser. I want the approach end of the LZ to be lit up like a Christmas tree for Magic Two Three when he arrives."

"Copy that, sir."

Mark activated the cell phone to look at his watch as he paused to catch his breath. He was discouraged to see that he had been trapped for only a few hours. It seemed a lot longer.

It'll be dark soon on the surface, he thought, wondering how long it would take to find a way out.

He continued to make slow progress through the debris, his mind firing away with random thoughts on ways to survive. He paused once again to study the path ahead and to assess his surroundings.

He remained still for a moment and contemplated his next move. He pressed his fingers into his ear to clear the dried blood that had pooled from the blast.

Using all of his senses to remain still and focused, he heard what he believed to be the faint sound of drilling followed by banging, but he couldn't pinpoint a direction. The sounds gave him some sense of reassurance, knowing that *someone* was making an effort to get to him. He could still smell the odor of the explosives and could see only the dimly illuminated path by what was left of the cell phone glow. He knew he had to find another source of light to navigate and ultimately survive. His mind carried thoughts of Heather and the girls, and he felt a surge of determination and motivation stir within him.

Crawling a few more feet over jagged debris, Mark came upon a door that was blocked by rebar and fallen concrete. He still had good airflow, so he decided to try to breach the doorway to see if there was anything behind it that could increase his chances for survival. He managed to clear enough of the doorway to expose the doorknob and was encouraged, until he attempted to turn the knob. It was locked.

"Shit, shit, shit!" he said aloud in frustration.

The cell phone gave up its last glow as the battery finally died. Taking a deep breath, he closed his eyes in the darkened chasm and calmed himself to think clearly and rationally.

Rescue workers on the surface were making progress, albeit slow and frustrating.

Tom stepped away to answer his cell phone. "Hey Dan, I assume you're looking for a progress check?"

"Yeah, Tom, but first I want you to know I made several phone calls and breached several phases of protocol to find out how many people you're looking for. I show eight total, including Mark," said Dan. "So tell me how you're coming with the rescue op."

"Copy, Dan—that's eight total," said Tom as he wrote the number on a scratch pad and handed it to a rescue coordinator. "We managed to push our conduit to twenty-five feet but still haven't broken through what we consider to be the bottom floor. All our drawings and layouts indicate we should've reached the bottom by now, so we're all a little frustrated."

"Listen Tom, stay the course. I can tell you that you and your team have about ten more feet to go. There's another level in that structure that was never included on the original drawings and schematics. Keep digging. And give me a call when you have any progress whatsoever to report."

"Will do, my friend."

Jay Cooney and his news crew arrived on scene at dusk as rescue crews were installing lighting units that would take the workers through the night.

"Let's set up a camera over there, and one over there as well," said Jay, directing his team to the best vantage points. "I'll see if I can find out who's in charge here, so we can get an exclusive."

Before he could get far, he was met by a plainclothes detective, who was manning an entry control point. "Excuse me, this is as far as anyone is allowed into the area," the detective said.

Jay flashed his press credentials and asked to speak with the on-scene commander.

The detective simply nodded. "I know who you are, sir. I've seen you several times on TV. I've been asked to send all reporters to the press station over there. You'll find your buddies from CNN and the local news there, as well as someone who will give you information on what's going on here."

"Damn, CNN is already here?" Jay asked, dismayed.

Jay and a handful of reporters were among the first to arrive on scene. He arrived in time to hear a spokesperson provide a cursory overview of the situation and cleverly provide cautious answers to questions posed by reporters—enough to provide fodder for an "interesting" report.

That wasn't good enough for Jay, however. When the briefing was complete, he approached the spokesperson and pretended to conduct a one-on-one interview and do his best to find out who was actually in charge of the operation.

It wasn't long before Jay had the name of Tom Herring, but he needed a way to get past the perimeter to get to the real story. His first field report was due to air. He decided to run with the information he had and insert a teaser at the end of his dialogue that would bring viewers back for the "rest of the story."

"This is a Sky News Alert. We go now to our man on the ground at the site of the explosion in Ft. Meade, Maryland. Jay Cooney, reporting live. Jay, what are the latest developments, and what have you learned so far?"

"Tracy, we're here at what used to be an ordinary warehouse just outside the Baltimore-Washington Expressway, where sources tell us that the explosion—said to be on a 'high order of magnitude'—totally decimated the building and its contents. DHS believes this explosion to have emanated from terrorists inside the country…or worse yet, inside the nation's capital region. The Department of Homeland Security has raised the terror threat level to RED or SEVERE; its highest level. Rescue workers are reportedly looking for up to eight workers as they dig through piles of debris left by the explosion. We expect to have an opportunity for an exclusive interview with the on-scene commander in our next report."

"Thanks, Jay. That's Jay Cooney, Sky News correspondent on the ground, live at the scene. Stay tuned as Sky News brings you continuing *clear and balanced* coverage on this developing story."

Mark sat on the ground, slightly dejected upon realizing the door before him was locked. Exhausted and out of breath, he collected his thoughts and contemplated ways he could get the door open.

Out of sheer frustration, he began to kick the door with both feet from his sitting position. It was no use. The door wasn't going to open without some kind of additional effort…or a key. Since the key option was out of the question, he thought of other solutions. He opened the cell phone once again in an attempt to get one more look at his surroundings. That, too, was no use. He needed another source of light, and he needed it now.

Mark took a breath, closed his eyes—as if that would help him concentrate in his dark surroundings—and slowly used his hands to search his immediate surroundings. He wasn't sure what he was looking for, but he knew he'd know it when he found it. He came across a small piece of metal at his fingertips that was shaped somewhat like a lever. He decided to give it a shot. He inserted the metal near the doorknob and, using his body weight, pried the door open.

"Thank you, Jesus!" he exclaimed, as he made his way into the small room.

He tried the cell phone again, hoping it would somehow produce some kind of light. The light dimmed for only an instant.

He extended his arms above his head to feel for obstacles and discovered that he was able to stand without any difficulty. He also found it easier to breathe inside the room. It felt good to stretch. He strained to see. The room was even darker than he imagined dark could be. He extended his arms ahead and took a cautious step forward, followed by another, until his hands made contact with a shelf.

Still unsure of where he was, he made certain to be extremely careful with his hand placement while feeling around for *anything* that could help him endure the conditions—and help him survive. He felt several items. Some of the items were easy to determine: a broom, some reams of paper, a box of pens, and some folders.

Are you kidding me? I'm in a frigging supply closet, he thought. *OK, what's in a supply closet that can actually be of use to me?*

His mind was in overdrive as he continued to try to use the "MacGyver" side of his brain to produce something…anything…that would help him to at least see. He reached back and closed the door, determined not to miss any space that would provide an item he could use.

10

"I've got a good lock on the team, using the Predator feed," said Pat from the back of the Casa, tapping on his keyboard.

"Awesome," responded Ox, unbuckling his seatbelt. "You got this, kid?"

"If you're asking if I can land this beast, then hell yeah, *I got this*."

Ox reminded Ronaldo to put the landing gear down and made his way to the back of the aircraft.

"I assume you can fire a weapon," said Ox to Pat.

"Uh, yeah, I can shoot."

"You any good at it?"

"Expert, why?"

"How's your accuracy while shooting from a moving airplane with NVGs strapped to your cranium?" said Ox rather sarcastically.

"Well now you're gonna have to *really* start being nice to me, if you want *that* kind of performance," responded Pat with a wink.

"Don't wink at me. It makes me uncomfortable," said Ox, tossing Pat a set of NVGs.

"Hang on to something, gents, we're starting our descent," shouted Ronaldo.

Ox slapped a fully loaded magazine into an M-4 assault rifle, cocked the weapon, checked the safety, and handed it to Pat.

"Don't fire this weapon unless you have to, or I order you to," commanded Ox, drawing his M9 sidearm, cocking the slide back, and checking the door of the aircraft. "You may want to tuck that toy of yours aside until our guests have boarded," he added, pointing to Pat's laptop.

"Five miles out," shouted Ronaldo.

"That landing gear down?" shouted Ox.

"Affirmative, gear down and locked."

Ox pulled out a handheld radio and made a call to the team.

"Rawhide this is Magic Two Three, we're at the corner of Broadway and Main, setting up for a drive-by. Is everyone ready for the party bus?"

"Magic Two Three, Rawhide is ready to rock 'n' roll. The lights are on, how copy?"

"Yo, kid, you pick up the IR strobes yet?"

"Got 'em," replied Ronaldo, all of his focus trained on the short landing zone.

"Rawhide, Magic Two Three, we see the porch light. Any ugly girls in the area?"

"Magic Two Three, none that we can see, but the bouncer is checkin' IDs, how copy?"

"Loud and clear, Magic Two Three out."

"We're cleared hot, kid. Put her on the ground and get ready to turn and burn," commanded Ox.

"WILCO," responded Ronaldo. He firmly set the aircraft on the rough terrain in total darkness.

As the Casa rolled out onto the rough LZ, Ronaldo pitched the propellers to reverse the thrust, revved the engine throttles fully forward, and practically stood on the brakes to bring the aircraft to a stop in as short a distance as possible. As the aircraft slowed, Ox released the door latch that set the rear hatch in motion to open, then donned his NVGs to acclimate his vision.

The aircraft now under a manageable speed, Ronaldo brought the engines to idle. Although this was their first mission together, he and Ox worked together like a well-oiled, choreographed machine. As he reached the end of the LZ, Ronaldo made a 180-degree turn to position the aircraft for a fast getaway. As soon as Ox knew they were in position, he jumped out of the aircraft onto the LZ in a crouched position and began to visually scan the area.

"Pat, get your ass out here and take a position to my right," shouted Ox, near the tail of the aircraft.

Pat took a position about twenty yards away from the portside, aft of the wing.

"Rawhide, this is Magic Two Three. Give me your position, so the bouncers can assure your safe arrival to the party, over," commanded Ox on the radio.

"Magic Two Three, this is Rawhide. We're approaching from the east, bearing two-four-zero at one hundred yards. There are five of us, with one straggler trailing at thirty yards to make sure we're alone," responded Booker, while he and Jones held onto the injured Stokes.

"Magic Two Three copies. We're looking for ya," said Ox. "Pat, lemme know when you spot 'em."

"Will do."

"I've got a party-crasher at two-niner-zero degrees," shouted Pat, as he spotted a lone figure running on the fringe of the LZ. "Looks like he's got a weapon…a rifle."

"Make damn sure he's not our straggler, Pat. We don't wanna shoot one of our own," said Ox.

"Copy."

A shot rang out across the clearing.

"OK, ladies, we have gunfire." shouted Ox. "Rawhide, Magic Two Three, you gents need to push it up. We have a hot LZ. I repeat—we have a *hot* LZ!"

"Rawhide copies. We're about forty yards from the party and have you in sight," said Booker.

Ox saw three men approaching from the shadows. Judging from the way they were helping the one in the middle, he determined it was Booker and two others.

"Got you in sight, Rawhide. Proceed to the front of the line." Ox searched for the remainder of the team.

"Firefly, this is Acrimony, how copy?" said Pat, attempting to make contact with the Predator overhead.

"Acrimony, this is Firefly. We have you loud and clear."

"Uh, roger Firefly, Acrimony requests ID assistance on a possible hostile at two-niner-zero for approximately forty yards from our position. Shots fired—the LZ is hot. Request assistance, over."

"Roger Acrimony. Firefly is searching…"

Ox made visual contact with two more members of Booker's team as he ran to assist Booker and Jones with Stokes.

"I have five accounted for, Pat. Stay engaged with your Pred—"

Another shot rang out across the LZ. The round struck the rear stabilizer of the Casa.

"Son of a bitch! Is that fire coming from your party crasher, Pat?"

Ox relieved Booker of his position helping Stokes, so Booker could help Pat assume a defensive fighting position. Jones and Ox made their way onto the aircraft. They strapped Stokes into a seat and administered an IV to help him replace fluids and quickly applied new dressing to his wounds.

Ox rushed to the cockpit to check on Ronaldo, who was crouched behind the control panel to shield himself from stray gunfire.

"I see you're doing OK up here," said Ox. "Need anything?"

"A cheeseburger, large fries, and a stiff drink...but I'd settle for a full payload, so we can get the *hell* outta here," responded Ronaldo sarcastically.

Ox shook his head in disbelief. "Nice. We're working on it, kid. Sit tight and don't go anywhere till I tell you to."

Perry and KK joined Booker and Pat near the aircraft.

"Perry, I need eyes on our party-crasher. Use your night-vision sniper scope and tell me what you see," commanded Booker.

Booker made a call to his last remaining teammate.

"Hartman, bring it in ASAP. You're all we need to complete the party bus."

Booker listened patiently for a reply he fully expected would come right away from Hartman, but there was nothing but radio silence.

"What's goin' on, Captain?" asked Ox.

"Something's not right. My last man isn't responding."

"Pat—" said Ox, as Pat interrupted his command.

"Already on it, boss...Firefly, this is Acrimony, request a wide-area search using *Blue Force Tracker*, priority code Alpha-867-Kilo-Hotel, over," said Pat as sternly as he knew how to ensure the Predator operator knew the seriousness of the situation they were facing.

"Acrimony, this is Firefly. We have a fix on your remaining member. Location: Two-Niner-Zero for thirty-eight yards, how copy?"

Pat cocked his head and looked at Ox curiously as he verified the location.

"Firefly, verify Two-Niner-Zero at *thirty-eight* yards? How many returns are you painting in that area, over?"

"Acrimony, this is Firefly...we show two, I repeat, *two* returns in that immediate area—one blue and one red, over."

"Gentlemen, we have a problem," said Pat.

"What's the problem?" said Ox and Booker almost simultaneously.

"We found your remaining man, but he's got an unfriendly right on top of him."

"That's why he's not responding," said Booker. "That tells me he's still concealed but he's close enough to be discovered if he answers. Perry, you got that hostile in clear sight?"

"Affirmative, sir."

"Acrimony, this is Firefly with a threat warning, over."

"Go ahead, Firefly."

"Acrimony, you have multiple targets encroaching from three sides of the LZ."

"Acrimony copies. How many targets are you painting?"

"Sir, we show three vehicles and *several* personnel, over."

"How much time do we have?" asked Pat in a slight panic.

"Less than three minutes, sir, how copy?"

"Acrimony copies. Gentlemen, we have several hostiles approaching the perimeter of the LZ from multiple directions," warned Pat to the group.

"Start turning those props, kid." said Ox to Ronaldo over the radio.

"I'm not leaving my last man," said Booker.

"Well we're not sacrificing the entire op for one man, Captain," said Ox. "You know the drill. You're welcome to stay, but I think we'll all be better off if we get airborne and figure it out from a safer position."

Booker looked at Perry and asked if he had a clean kill. Without taking his eyes off the target, Perry calmly nodded. "Affirmative, sir."

"Take the shot!" commanded Booker. "At least we can free him up to move till we can swing back around for an extraction."

Perry didn't hesitate. He squeezed the trigger, watched the target fall limp to the ground, and re-loaded the chamber of his rifle—calm and disciplined as any young Marine sniper would be expected to perform under such circumstances.

"Kill, sir," said Perry, in a quiet, matter-of-fact manner as he reached out to pick up the spent shell casing.

"Good job, Marine. On your feet. Get on board and strap in."

"Sir, request to remain behind to assist Hartman," said Perry with all the seriousness he could muster to a superior officer.

"Denied. Get on that aircraft, Marine."

Gunfire began to increase from several different directions as the team rushed to board the Casa, some of the bullets making contact with the aircraft fuselage. Ox and Booker were the last to board. Booker grabbed Ox by the arm and looked sternly into his eyes.

"Take care of the team and get 'em home safe."

Ox had expected Booker to remain to help his last team mate. He looked at Booker and nodded. "We'll be back for you ASAP. Take my NVG's."

"Thanks. Now, get the hell outta here."

Booker scurried off into the black of night and the Colombian jungle in search of his lone remaining teammate. Ox climbed aboard the aircraft and looked straight to the cockpit, where Ronaldo was turned in his seat, awaiting a signal. Ox gave him a thumbs-up, indicating everyone was on board and they were ready for departure. He pushed the hydraulic handle forward and the aft door closed. Perry rose to his feet and demanded to know why they were leaving without Booker. Ox stopped, placed his hand on Perry's shoulder and told him that Booker had decided it was best to remain behind. Perry was pissed. He demanded to be allowed off the aircraft.

"We can't leave them behind. Let me off this plane."

Ox did his best to explain reality to the young Marine. "I don't like this any more than you do, Marine. Fact is, your superior officer has the authority to make the call on that. And he wants you to make it home safely tonight. My job is to make sure you do just that."

"Ox, we're taking more gunfire!" shouted Ronaldo.

"Strap in, Marine, we're leaving," said Ox, making his way to the cockpit.

Pat was busy tapping away at his laptop, set on the dimmest possible setting, and listening to the Predator sensor operator on his headphones. Ronaldo maneuvered the Casa into a takeoff position as Ox strapped into his seat and began setting switches and reading dials. He searched his surroundings for his NVGs and realized he gave them to Booker.

"Pat, toss me your NVGs."

Pat tossed his NVGs to Ox, who quickly strapped them to his head and gave the takeoff command to Ronaldo.

"Push it up, kid, and let's get the hell outta here."

11

G sat stoically looking out the window of the jet while it climbed higher into the night sky.

"I think this might be yours," said Todd, handing G a cell phone.

"Where did you find that?" G asked, astonished he was even able to recover it.

"Dude I knocked out had it on him, so I figured it was either yours or his. Either way, one of us would be interested in it."

"Thank you."

"I'm sorry, what did you say?"

"I said…thanks."

"It's all good, brah. You hungry?"

G tried coming to grips with the overwhelming nature of his entire day. He shook his head slightly and asked Todd to repeat himself.

"I'm sorry, what?"

"I said, *are you hungry*? You know…food?" said Todd with a gesture and a chuckle. "Cuz if you're gonna continue to drink my alcohol then you should probably eat a lil' somethin'…I'm jes sayin'."

"Yeah, I could eat," said G. He was actually famished but didn't want to reveal that to Todd.

"Aight, cool. I'll go to the galley and see what I can find. Feel free to chill out, but I suggest you stay strapped in, since you've been drinking on an empty stomach."

Todd got up and made his way to a small galley in the back of the plane. G heard him rummaging through a cabinet and placing something into a warmer oven.

G scanned the inside of the jet. He saw a few framed pictures on the walls. He studied the one closest to him and noticed it was autographed. The picture was of Todd and a young man with shoulder-length hair and a goatee. He couldn't make out the signature, but he noticed that most of the pictures had some kind of autograph or signature on them.

"That's Chad Kroeger," said Todd making his way back to his seat with a tray of snacks. "You know, from the rock band Nickelback?"

G glanced at the picture again. Sure enough, he now recognized the lead singer of one of the hottest rock bands standing next to Todd in the picture.

"See that pic over there?" asked Todd, pointing to an 8x10 glossy photo capturing a group of four young, grungy-looking dudes.

"That's the group Creed."

"Awesome," said G. He reached for a snack, still gazing at the picture. "So why are you headed to New York City?"

"Meeting up with a new client. Maybe you've heard of him—Kid Rock."

G smiled, admitting he had heard of Kid, but found it difficult to believe that he could be a client of Todd's...even after seeing pictures of stars adorning the inside of the jet.

G grabbed another snack and took a sip of his drink and began to thumb through his phone. Starting to feel the effects of the altitude and his drinks, he was hoping to find a text message from Athena in his queue, but he could only find older messages that reminded him of her.

"Why don't you get some rest?" said Todd, turning down the cabin lights. "We got about an hour to go before we get to NYC. I'm sure you can use the rest after all you've been through today."

"Yeah, that sounds like a good idea."

"There's a footrest that'll kick out from underneath that seat, if you want to use it," said Todd with his signature smile.

G returned a hint of his own polite smile and extended the footrest, making himself as comfortable as possible. He couldn't wait to get to New York, where his phone would have a signal and he'd be able to call Athena. She was not going to believe the things he'd been through. He thought of how worried she must have been because of the way he last hung up with her during the airport ordeal. He took a slow sip of his cocktail and looked out the window, allowing his mind to relax and his thoughts to drift. He kept thinking of Athena and had hoped to find her once again in one of his dreams. He missed her and secretly wondered how he could be so easily enamored by a woman after such a short acquaintance.

Mark's frustration was growing. He couldn't find anything that was useful in providing a light source. Exasperated and exhausted, he lowered himself back down to the floor and took a breath.

He kneeled on the hard cement floor and continued to search the darkness with his outstretched hands in an attempt to find *something* that would provide the light he so desperately needed.

"I have a new appreciation for how the blind must feel," he said quietly.

His hands continuing to search, he came upon a metal ring in the corner of the room that seemed to be stuck to the floor.

Hmmm, this must be some sort of tie down, he thought.

Keeping one hand on the ring, he continued to feel his way around with his free hand. He reached out in an attempt to determine if it were possible for anything to be within reach that would connect with this ring. He stretched as far as he could. Suddenly, the ring gave way and began to lift from the floor. Mark's mind raced. Confused, he tried to determine, from a blind man's perspective, what was happening.

"It's a door! I found a door," he exclaimed aloud.

The rescue and recovery team finally broke through all subsurfaces of the site. As soon as they breached the lowest level, the crew could see and smell sulfur-like gases escaping from the breach.

"That can't be a good sign," said one of the workers.

"OK, let's get a conduit installed and get some fresh air into that space," Tom barked. "As soon as an airway is established, I want to be able to *see* inside that space, so we'll need the Explosives Ordnance Disposal team here with their cameras."

Tom and the surface crews managed to push an airway conduit all the way down to what was determined to be the bottom floor of the site. Despite the weariness of the surface crews, they were reinvigorated with their literal breakthrough, and the team took on a newfound determination to move to the next phase of the operation—camera search and communication with survivors. Tom called Dan to report their progress.

"Just a progress report, Dan...we've broken through to what we believe to be the bottom floor, where most of the personnel were when the explosives detonated. We've established an airway conduit, and we're busy pushing O2 in."

"Awesome, Tom. How soon will you have a camera down there to determine the situation?"

"EOD is on it as we speak. I can have a feed to you as soon as we connect to the computer."

"Great. I'm standing by. Give me a shout as soon as I can connect and follow this with you."

Joey G drifted off to sleep as he looked out the window at the flashing white strobe on the wingtip, his hand still wrapped around what remained of his third drink.

Man, I am feeling so frigging relaxed, he thought, as he slipped from consciousness straight to deep sleep. *Flying in style...has its...benefits...*

As he became aware and regained control of his thoughts, G began looking closely at his surroundings. He found himself in a dimly lit restaurant on an upper-level floor—a VIP section of some kind. His vitals were elevated. His breathing was labored, as if he had been running. And he was standing in a defensive position. Another quick visual scan of the room didn't reveal any immediate threat or chaos. Nonetheless, he sensed danger.

Purely by accident, he projected himself to a third-person state to gain a broader perspective.

This dream thing is unreal, he thought with a chuckle, realizing how that comment could've been taken by anyone outside looking in. *I can randomly choose any perspective I want...sweet!*

Looking back upon himself, he observed that he was wearing a dark, pin-striped suit and was armed with a shoulder harness holster and handgun. He was also accompanied by an ally, a male partner.

Dream Operative

He continued to scan the room, this time from a broader perspective, and detected danger just outside the restaurant. His intuition compelled him to pursue the danger, but he had to move quickly. His dream returned to a first-person perspective the instant he made a decisive move to pursue.

He and his partner drew their weapons and ran through the restaurant as fast as they could. G even jumped on a few tables, full of food, frightening patrons along the way, to find the shortest distance to the door. There was no verbal communication with his partner. Instead, it was all intuitive.

Outside the restaurant, G found himself in a courtyard with a large fountain, situated in a collecting pool, in the center between large buildings. People were milling about; some were enjoying lunch at outdoor tables. All were oblivious to him and his partner, each with weapons drawn.

G continued to observe his surroundings and tried to determine why he was even in this dream to begin with. The dream suddenly and unexpectedly placed him *in* the collecting pool of the fountain, in waist-deep water, with his weapon still drawn. The danger he sensed was still present. His partner sat casually at the edge of the fountain, trying to convince G that the danger had passed. Suddenly, fear gripped G. His adrenaline soared when he saw a man approaching his partner from behind. He tried to warn his partner, but the fear of the dream sequence prevented him from speaking or taking action. He watched helplessly as the man drew his weapon, placed it against his partner's head, and pulled the trigger. G, horrified in shock, watched as his partner's limp body fell forward into the fountain pool before him. G's heart pounded as the entire experience unfolded before him. He quickly looked up at the assailant and studied him.

G's mind became overwhelmed with details—fear, rage, emotion. The intensity of his fear kept him frozen and concealed while intense rage stirred within him. He moved slightly and was discovered by the man. Their eyes met, when suddenly, G realized he recognized him. G felt as if he was being analyzed by the assailant, trying to somehow penetrate his thoughts. He resisted. Consumed with confusion and sensory overload, G was unable to react quickly. Before he could process his thoughts, the man raised his weapon and pointed it directly at G.

*Son of a...*G thought, waiting for the bullet to exit the chamber of the man's gun.

Time slowed to a crawl.

What will it feel like? Will I even feel it at all? Is death even possible in a dream?

A shot rang out. It was the quietest gunshot G had ever heard. But it was not *he* who had been shot. It was the man standing before him. He took a bullet in the left shoulder by an unknown gunman. The man dropped his weapon, turned to see who had fired the shot, and ran away, leaving G in the blood-stained water from his partner's body.

Despite the fact that people were running about and screaming from the chaos, G heard only faint, muffled sounds. This was one of those vivid dreams, with all the details and lucidity *minus* the volume accustomed to daily reality. Given the situation, it was probably divinely designed that way on purpose.

As G approached the body of his partner, he noticed a woman approaching from the right periphery of his field of view. He turned, quickly drew his weapon, and took aim but didn't fire. The woman didn't flinch and quietly kept walking toward him.

"Leave him, get out of the pool, and come with me," she said. "Hurry… before they return."

G was thrust into a new phase of his dream—a hotel room with the woman who had saved his life. She handed him a towel and told him to dry himself. He watched her from behind as she removed her dress to reveal black lace undergarments; thigh-high stockings, heels, garter, bra, and panties. She wore a concealed gun belt on her right thigh, with a small-caliber weapon tucked neatly inside the holster. His eyes moved as he studied her slender body. Her blonde hair flowed to her shoulder blades. She motioned for him to come closer, and, when he took a step toward her, he felt a hand firmly land upon his left shoulder. Reacting on instinct, he grabbed the hand in an attempt to defend himself. He turned to see a man he didn't recognize and quickly reacted by grabbing him by the throat.

G violently awoke to Todd yelling at him. "Yo. What the fuck! Let go of me."

Realizing he had returned to conscious reality, he quickly let go of Todd and began to profusely apologize. "I am so sorry, Todd. I was dreaming."

"Yeah, I gather that," said Todd, rubbing his throat. "You're damn lucky I didn't kick your ass and knock you back into that dream of yours. Shit, brah, what the fuck?" added Todd once again for emphasis. "I was tryin' to wake your ass up to let you know we're about to land."

G rubbed his eyes, attempting to clear his mind from the fog of his dream. He grabbed his cell phone and, as a matter of routine, recorded the details of his latest dream. "High adrenaline, pursuit of an enemy, encounter with the enemy...familiarity with enemy..."

G paused to take a breath as his mind replayed the images of his encounter with the man in his dreams. He tried wrapping his thoughts around the familiarity of the man he encountered. It puzzled him. There was something about the man's sinister eyes that spoke to G's intuition. The eyes were cold, calculating, and unafraid. But there was more. It was as if he had seen this man before. The experience gave him a sense that he had encountered the devil himself.

"Cold-blooded murder," G continued, his emotions gripping him, remembering the vivid details of his unfamiliar partner falling into the pool before him. "Fear...expectation, confusion...saved by a woman."

G paused once again as he thought about the woman. Despite how alluring she was, he felt strongly about his growing feelings for Athena. Yet, admittedly, his intrigue for the woman's close resemblance to Athena had piqued his interest. Aside from a difference in hair color, the two could be related, if he tried hard enough to draw a parallel. His thoughts were interrupted by Todd, who had returned to the cabin to buckle into his seat across from him.

"You fully awake now, G-money?" said Todd, smiling and securing his lap belt.

Todd glanced out the window for a glimpse of the city.

"It never gets old, G. Comin' in to this town at night is as good as it gets...second only to Vegas in terms of nighttime beauty, but she's still my number one."

Dan sat down at his desk to make another call to Heather.

"Hello?" said Heather nervously.

"Heather, its Dan. Just calling to check on you—"

Heather interrupted his courteous dialogue.

"Have you found him, Dan? Is Mark OK? Is he...alive?" asked Heather, mustering as much courage as she had to ask such a question.

"We have no reason to believe otherwise, Heather," said Dan.

"Well, then, why are you calling me? Why aren't you busy looking for Mark and the rest of them?"

"I can assure you we're making progress, Heather. It's the reason I called. We've managed to penetrate the rubble and debris to a position where we believe Mark was when the blast occurred. It's a big breakthrough. And I figured it was time I updated you with some good news."

"I know, Dan. I apologize for being so short with you. It's just that the entire ordeal has been tough. And so far I've been able to protect the girls from knowing what's really going on. I haven't even decided whether or not to send them to school tomorrow."

"I understand."

"So what's next?" asked Heather, a bit calmer and more rational.

"We've begun to push fresh air into the cavities, and we'll be inserting a mini camera to help us search while we continue to remove rubble and debris. It'll help us reduce the chances of collapse and help pinpoint our efforts to rescue Mark and the others. I'll call you as soon as I have anything more to report to you."

"Please do that, Dan. And I want you to call me no matter what—good or…bad news. Do you understand?" said Heather, her voice breaking again.

"I will."

After hanging up the phone, Heather was met by her youngest daughter, who asked about her daddy.

"Mommy, were you talking to Daddy?"

"No, that was Daddy's friend, Mr. Dan."

"I wanna talk to Daddy to say good night. Can we call him?"

Heather nearly broke down, but she knew she had to be strong for the girls. Instead of refusing, she decided she would allow the girls to leave Mark a message on his cell phone.

"Well, Daddy is pretty busy tonight, but why don't we leave him a message on his cell phone that he can listen to when he's finished with his work?"

As soon as she suggested the idea to the girls, she knew it would be just as therapeutic for her. Heather nervously dialed the phone. When she heard the sound of Mark's voice on his voicemail, she nearly lost it, but she managed to keep it together for the girl's sake. The three of them left messages on Mark's phone, as if he were just a phone call away. The girls were satisfied and drifted off to sleep shortly thereafter. Heather retired to the solace of her bedroom to pray for her husband, whom she knew in her heart to be alive…and searching for a way back to civilization and his family.

Jay Cooney and a cameraman made their way to a construction and recovery crew tent to grab a cup of coffee, where they ran into Tom. Jay immediately noticed Tom's blue hardhat—different than the yellow or white hats most others wore. Tucking his press badge away to avoid spooking Tom, he approached.

"So, what's the status of the recovery now, boss?"

"We're making progress," said Tom rather nondescriptly. "What's your specialty?" added Tom directly, realizing he didn't immediately recognize the young reporter.

Jay figured he'd better not play games with him and risk being removed from the recovery site. "I'm Jay Cooney—Sky News," he said rather proudly, extending his hand in a warm gesture.

"Thought you looked familiar," said Tom, without returning the handshake.

"Sir, can I get a comment from you regarding the progress of the recovery?"

"Look, Mr. Cooney..."

"Please, call me Jay."

"Yeah, look...Jay, I don't typically make or release comments to the media. I have a job to do, and that keeps me plenty busy. If you'd be kind enough to ensure you and your crews don't get in the way, you'd be doing your part in helping to facilitate our efforts here. You can gather the latest developments from the media tent that's been set aside for you and the others over there. Rest assured they'll provide you with the latest information. That's the only comment I have for you."

"Mr. Herring, we have a video feed available, sir."

The announcement came across Tom's handheld radio as he grabbed his coffee and turned to leave.

"Would love to chat more, Mr. Cooney, but I have to run."

Jay never allowed an opportunity to slip through his hands easily, so he persisted. "Mr. Herring, how 'bout an exclusive?" he asked, in one last valiant attempt. "I won't transmit anything you don't personally approve. Can you at least tell me how many people you're looking for?"

"No can do," said Tom, his voice fading as he walked out the door.

Jay had just enough information to piece a few strands of a story together, so he called back to New York to provide an update and schedule his next on-air report.

"I'd love to find a way to tap into that video feed," he said aloud.

"Yeah the video would be nice, but we could still have an angle if we could tap that handheld radio of his," responded the cameraman.

Jay paused and gave him a look.

"Can you do that? Don't tease me, because if you can do that, then we'll be able to keep up with this entire operation from a perspective that *no one else has*."

"Not sure, but I believe I can. Depends on how secure that radio is."

Mark managed to get the door opened, which created another dark route for him to search for a way out of the dilapidated crypt. Despite his apprehension, he cautiously slipped into the hole in the floor. His foot found what he determined to be a ladder, which led him down to yet another darkened chasm. His mind continued to be his biggest hurdle.

Why do I seem to find ways to go further DOWN instead of UP? His thoughts raced. *Stay calm. Breathe. And for God's sake, be careful.*

Mark counted the rungs of the ladder as he descended. He reached the bottom after only ten rungs. He was able to stand upright. With a firm grip on the ladder, he breathed a sigh of relief and sarcastically jested, "OK, MacGyver, now what?"

The comment made him chuckle. Realizing he needed to move to make progress, Mark let go of the ladder and took a sliding step forward. He was on firm footing—concrete. He reached out in an attempt to feel his way forward and found the edge of a wall with his right hand. Taking two steps to his left, he found the left side. He determined he was in some kind of corridor. He continued to take careful steps forward, occasionally changing sides of the corridor so he wouldn't miss any openings or opportunities for discoveries. After what seemed like hours traveling in the blind, Mark came upon openings on both sides of the corridor.

Must be some kind of an intersection, he thought.

"Great, now what do I do?" said Mark aloud.

Frustrated, he decided to take a break and sat quietly on the floor. He was exhausted, and it wasn't long before he dozed off right there on the cold, hard concrete floor.

"Video feed should be on screen now, sir," a voice announced over Tom's handheld radio.

"Roger that, I have video. Hold that position while I make a phone call to the director."

"Whatcha got for me, Tom?"

"We have video. You should have a feed on the secure net."

"I see it, Tom, thanks. Tell me what we're lookin' at, please."

"My crew will narrate for us, Dan. Please stand by for audio." Tom then spoke to his crew. "OK, boys, let's take a look around," he instructed.

A voice from a lead agent came across the speaker. "We're at one hundred forty-five feet, which we believe to be the bottom floor of the structure."

Tom and Dan witnessed the effects of the chaotic destruction and debris and were both feeling pretty much the same as they watched the camera make its way over broken concrete, twisted rebar, and suspended dust illuminated by the bright light of the camera. The camera was maneuvered to conduct a slow pan of the immediate area.

"Switching to infrared," announced the camera operator.

The video feed took on a negative-like effect that indicated infrared, or IR, light was in use. IR was used to determine *hot spots*, or in this case, human life. Tom and Dan remained on the edge of their seats, hoping the IR would pick up on some kind of life to indicate survivors.

"No immediate indication of life," announced the camera operator. "Wait...switching back to normal view."

As the operator continued to maneuver the camera, he came upon the remains of two bodies.

"We have two victims, both male," announced the operator.

Dan peered intently at the video feed and quickly determined neither was the body of Mark.

The operator continued to maneuver the camera. "Moving in on what appears to be a shoe..."

Tom and Dan watched as the camera moved closer to a shoe, still attached to the severed leg of Mike Libby. The camera panned to reveal Mike's corpse slumped into the corner of the room.

"Victim number three," announced the operator.

"Hey, Tom, have the camera operator take a good look around that center room where Agent Libby is located. Mark should've been in the same room with Libby," said Dan.

"Roger that, boss."

"Give me a slow pan in IR mode in that area," instructed Tom. "We're looking for another person who should've been in the same room."

Dan and Tom watched while the camera slowly panned the entire dilapidated room, both studying every inch of footage.

"No signs of another person in this area, sir," said the camera operator. "And sir...that's as far as this device will take us into the structure. Recommend we keep removing debris to increase camera mobility."

"Copy that," said Tom. "Reel it in and continue to dig. We continue on the assumption that this is still a rescue op. Terminate the video feed.

"Hey, Dan, we need to continue to remove debris to provide more effective video."

"I understand, Tom," said Dan. "Send me a video recording of what we just saw, so I can have it analyzed. There's got to be something we missed that'll give us a clue on Mark's whereabouts...not to mention the others who may still be alive."

"I'll be here as long as it takes, boss."

Athena's flight touched down about an hour behind schedule. The flight attendant made the customary "welcome to Atlanta" announcement and authorized the passengers to use their cell phones.

Athena powered on her cell phone and checked her connecting flight information. Connecting to her next flight would be a challenge, but she figured she'd have enough time to make it to the gate before they closed the door. Knowing she'd be in a rush to make her connection, she quickly sent a text to Todd:

Arrived ATL. Hoping to make a tight connection. Will contact U as soon as I can. A

12

"Looks like you'll be hanging with me a bit longer than either of us expected, G," said Todd, after reading the latest text message from Athena.

G stared out the window of the jet as it executed a smooth landing at New York's JFK Airport. He had begun to expect the unexpected, given the circumstances. As the jet taxied off the active runway, G checked for a signal on his cell phone and made an attempt to contact Athena. He got Athena's voicemail greeting, so he left a short message and decided to follow up with a text message.

I know U must B worried but I wanna let U know that I'm OK. Please call me when U can. G

Todd unbuckled his lap belt when his cell phone started ringing with various ring tones.

"It never fails," he said with a chuckle. "Anytime I land here, it's like *they* know it before *I* do."

"Sounds like you're in pretty high demand."

"Sure as hell beats the alternative," said Todd sarcastically. "Maybe one day we'll have some time, and I can tell you how I went from being a poor airman in the US Air Force to where I am now," he went on, rather proudly. "I'm one of those people you hear about who makes more money than the president of the United States, but I don't have to put up with half the shit."

Athena retrieved G's text message and smiled, knowing Todd was doing a good job of keeping his mouth shut and not revealing too much information to G. She preferred to be the one to answer G's questions... no telling how he would handle things when confronted with the truth behind everything that had been happening to him. She checked her voicemail and also found G's latest voice message. Listening, however, she detected a series of clicks and tones that gave her pause. G's phone had been tapped! Someone was monitoring his texts and calls and could even be monitoring his conversations and spiking his smart phone. She needed to get that phone out of his hands. She quickly sent a short text to Todd:

Urgent! G's phone is dirty...remove and destroy ASAP.

Athena's connecting flight had begun the boarding process, so she grabbed her carry-on and boarded the flight that would take her to JFK airport, all while wondering who could be tracking G's movements.

G began to wonder why he had not heard back from Athena. He figured she'd at least be happy to hear from him, knowing he was no longer *in trouble* at the airport. He began to type out a second text in an effort to get her to respond.

Hello. Just checkin to see if U rec'd my last txt. In NYC...drop me a line when U can pls.

He added the "NYC" to the text in an attempt to get her curiosity up. Maybe that would prompt her to respond. The only problem with that was, Athena was no longer the only recipient of any messages his phone transmitted. Just before he pressed "send," Todd called out to him.

"Yo, G, you comin'? I know you like my airplane and all, but the limo is here to take us to the hotel."

G pressed the "send" button and placed the phone in his pocket.

Hakim checked into an airport hotel in London and was checking his e-mail when he received a special coded message.

Professor, Gateway 35 will be open in 48. Take exit 6 after 1800.

The message was sent by one of Hakim's stateside contacts on the "inside." Translated, the message broke down to the following coded elements:

The number 35 referred to the thirty-fifth president of the United States—John F. Kennedy—and served to indicate the "Gateway" or port of arrival was JFK Airport.

The "48" indicated that Hakim should make every attempt to arrive within forty-eight hours and to schedule his arrival as close to "1800," or 6:00 p.m., as possible.

Dream Operative

"Exit 6" referred to the best US Customs lane to use at that time. Hakim's inside contact was a man with many US connections, including lenient US Customs agents. He would ensure Hakim's passage was as uneventful as possible, given his loyalty to the movement and the subversion of the US Government, especially the current administration.

Hakim's travel to the US would facilitate a first meeting between the two men, despite a long-term, indirect working relationship inside the construct of Hakim's tightly controlled terror cell network. He erased the files, shut off his computer, and looked out the window of his hotel room at the city below.

Hakim's hotel phone rang. It was the front desk.

"Good evening, sir. Are you satisfied with the room?" asked the desk clerk.

"Yes, it's fine, thank you."

"Very good, sir. There is a message for you here at the desk. Shall I have it delivered?"

"That would be fine, thank you."

The cameras and lights were all set for Jay's next live report when the earth began to rumble beneath them.

"What the hell was that?" said Jay, looking at one of the cameramen. "Damn near lost my balance."

Looking around to gauge the reaction from other nearby reporters, he could tell he wasn't the only one who felt the tremor. Jay quickly dialed his cell phone to call back to New York. "Hey boss, this is Jay. I need a delay in my live report. We have new developments that I need to investigate before we go live."

"How long do you figure it'll take you? We don't want to lag too far behind the others in our report."

"Trust me, boss, I'm all over this, and I'll be ready for an immediate break-in broadcast once I get enough to piece a storyline together."

"OK, get on it then, and we'll continue with normal programming."

Jay hung up the phone and immediately went to his cameraman.

"Have you had any success breaking the code on that handheld radio? Because now would be a really good time to be listening."

"I'm in...or I should be, anyway," responded the cameraman.

Both listened patiently while Jay thought about how much time was being wasted listening to nothing. Then it happened…

"Somebody talk to me," Tom bellowed over the handheld radio. Hearing no immediate response, he emerged from his on-site office, conducted a quick scan of the area, and transmitted once again. "Hello. This is Tom Herring, and I want a report right now from somebody. What the hell shook this place so violently?"

"Sir, this is Russ Noble, civil engineering. We need you to come at once to recovery station two. We've had a catastrophic breach. The entire site just imploded."

"On my way," responded Tom. His heart and mind raced, thinking about Mark and the others still trapped somewhere in the debris.

Jay looked at his cameraman in disbelief at what they were hearing from the radio.

"I guess it worked," said the cameraman, surprising even himself.

"Uh, *hell yes,* it did," said Jay. "Stay on it and lemme know if you get any more details. Meantime, I'll get John to run a camera for our live broadcast and will let corporate know we're ready to roll. Good job."

Mark was awakened by the abrupt chaos of what seemed like an earthquake coming down upon him. Waking for the first time to total darkness had startled him and induced a state of confusion and fear that was compounded by the commotion surrounding him.

The walls and floor vibrated violently around him as he huddled on the floor with his arms covering his head for what he believed would be an inevitable collapse. Dust and debris rained down upon him, but his area remained intact, much to his surprise.

Mark was relieved that he decided to vacate his previous position for the one he now occupied, but he knew he had to keep moving if he was going to survive. Hunger pangs hit his stomach for the first time. He pushed the thought aside, knowing he had to find water soon, but a light source was still at the top of his priority list. He stood carefully, dusted himself off, and proceeded to slowly make his way forward again; his outstretched hands leading the way.

Todd smiled as he and G approached the limo.

"So, whatcha think, G?" asked Todd, referring to the tricked-out limousine, a stretch Cadillac Escalade with twenty-four-inch custom wheels.

G smirked and shook his head slowly. "Nice."

Todd chuckled. "Nice? Is that all you got, brah? Nice?" he said, laughing, as he and G climbed into the back of the limo.

"OK, what about the driver? You *had* to notice that badass driver who smiled at you as she shut the door for you. Or are you still sleeping?"

"Oh, I noticed. She was definitely hot."

"Oh, *hell yeah,* she was hot! The legs alone made me cry first time I set eyes on 'em. Damn, dude, we need to wake you up," said Todd, reaching into the icebox to retrieve a Red Bull ™ energy drink.

"OK, here's the deal…we're gonna stop and get you some clothes and then make our way to the hotel, where you're gonna get a couple of hours of rest while I take care of some business. Then I'm gonna take you out so you can meet some new people."

G stared at Todd, his mind still craving details on why he had suddenly become someone worth protecting.

"Look, you can take me to the hotel, but I'm not going anywhere else until you start giving me the details I asked for back in DC," said G defiantly.

Todd gave G a look, sizing up his remarks.

"Look, G, if I were in your shoes, I'd no doubt feel the same way. But you need to trust me for a little while longer. It'll all make sense when the answers come through for you. So, if you're not gonna get the answers you want until it's time, then why don't you allow me to play *Mr. Nice Guy* and enjoy the treatment? Let me run the show tonight. If you think about it, it's what I do best anyway. Look, I know your life has been totally jacked up and knocked on its heels today. But you need to take a breath. Your answers will come when they come. I'm not always gonna be this nice if you keep pushing me."

G wanted answers but knew he had to play his cards right. After all, he was no longer in a hostile situation with an angry agent sending him into alter-consciousness with a clenched fist. Besides, he kind of enjoyed the lifestyle he was being exposed to—even if it was temporary.

"OK, you're in charge tonight," said G, while checking his cell phone for some kind of response from Athena.

"Cool," said Todd. "But can I ask you a question?"

"Certainly."

"Why the hell you keep checkin' that damn cell phone? You lookin' at football scores, or are you communicating with some smokin' hot chick? I'm jes sayin'…it's gotta be one or the other, cuz I don't even check *my* phone as often as you do," said Todd laughing.

"Just waiting on a response from a friend."

"OK, then. So what's her name?"

"Athena," said G, looking down at his phone, as if it were providing the answer.

"Cool," responded Todd as nonchalantly as he knew how to, given the obvious connection he had with Athena. "What do ya say you put that thing aside for a bit while we check out some new clothes," he said, as the limo pulled in front of Neiman Marcus.

Reporters were busy clamoring for the latest news on the developments surrounding the aftershock at ground zero. They were demanding answers from the public affairs representative who offered cautious comments, careful not to divulge sensitive information. Meantime, Jay was preparing to air an exclusive insight on the cause.

"This is a Sky News Alert. We go live now to the man who's been on the scene from the beginning in Ft. Meade, Maryland, Jay Cooney. Jay, we understand there are new developments there on the scene. What's the latest?"

"That's right, Morgan, the press corps here was all set to receive the latest official briefing from DHS public affairs when, all of a sudden, the entire site erupted in an earthquake-like tremor. We literally felt the earth shaking and rumbling beneath us. It was a sensation we won't soon forget."

"Incredible, Jay. So what have you learned? Has anyone determined the source of the tremor? And have there been any new developments as far as rescue and recovery?"

"The details are sketchy at this time. But what we have learned through very reliable sources here, outside normal channels, is that some sort of 'catastrophic breach' has occurred within a section of the site itself. There have been no reports of additional casualties or injuries, but we will continue to update you on the latest as we have up-to-the-minute-details. What we *do* know is that officials are still considering this to be a rescue operation and not a recovery operation — meaning, officials still have hopes of finding someone alive, Morgan."

"Thank you, Jay. Please stay safe, my friend. Jay Cooney, reporting live from 'ground zero' in Ft. Meade, Maryland. Tonight, the President continues to monitor the situation in Ft. Meade from his vacation spot in…"

"And…we're off the air," said the cameraman.

"Thanks, John, good job."

Dan Keppler was studying the video recorded from the latest site penetration when he saw the live Sky News report from the scene appear on his office monitor. Turning up the volume, he learned of the latest developments before receiving a call from his on-scene commander, Tom Herring.

Dan's mind raced with images of what must now be the ill fate of his friend and colleague, Mark Rubis. He picked up the phone to dial Tom but knew he'd get little in terms of a more detailed update than the one he learned about from the news report. But having been trained not to believe everything the news reported, he made the call to verify the report and obtain any updates.

"Tom Herring…"

"Tom, Dan here. What's goin' on?"

"It's not good news, Dan," said Tom while receiving updates from the CE Chief, Russ Noble.

"Well, don't sugarcoat it, Tom. Give it to me straight. It's all over the news that there's been a breach of some kind."

"Damn press. I'm not sure just how that made it outside my network here, but I don't have time to run that down," responded Tom. "Look, I'm still learning things here, Dan. I hate to do this, but I have to call you back when I have a better report for you."

"I understand, my friend. Call me as soon as you have *anything* we can sink our teeth into, please."

"Count on it, Dan."

Hakim heard a knock at his door. Always cautious, he approached it slowly.

"Yes, who is it?"

"Bell clerk, sir. I have a message for you?"

Hakim peered through the view finder and saw a young man wearing a uniform. He opened the door and accepted the message. He closed the door, and then opened the envelope.

Sir, your brother wishes to meet with you while you're in London. If you can make it, kindly meet him in Saint James Park at the edge of the pond near the Changing of the Guard at sunset.

Hakim expected the note and knew it to be a coded message. Designed and written to inform Hakim on when and where to reconnect with his chosen martyr, it provided confirmation that things were progressing according to his instructions. He glanced out the window and noticed the sun beginning to set, so he prepared for his short journey to the park.

Todd handed his credit card to the cashier to pay for G's clothing purchase.

"Look, Todd, I really appreciate the gesture, but I think I can handle the purchase," said G.

Todd looked at G with raised eyebrows and a slight smile and took a yielding step back.

"That's cool, G, what was I thinkin'?"

G examined the receipt and nearly had a stroke when he found the bottom line total.

"Holy shit, I coulda bought a frigging Toyota for this price!"

Todd glanced at the cute cashier, a young woman in her early thirties, and smiled. "I believe this is his first time shopping here."

G pulled out his credit card and reluctantly paid for his purchase. "I'm ready to roll," he said humbly.

"Then let's roll, baby." responded Todd, with a hand on G's shoulder.

Todd poured two glasses of straight Vodka on ice for him and G once the limo was underway.

"Cheers, G," he said, handing a glass to G and raising his own in a toast.

G rolled down the window as the limo rounded a corner that brought it down Broadway.

"Ever been to New York before, G?"

"Nope, first time."

"Nothing like it," Todd said, as he too rolled down the window on his side of the limo.

"This place can get mad crazy, brah. But it's the epicenter of the land of opportunity. I thought I'd made it big, until I started makin' it here," said Todd, in a short version of a long story.

G pulled out his phone and snapped a random picture of the city lights.

"We're stayin' in one of the best places on Broadway—the Marriott Marquis," said Todd. "I've got you added on as a guest in my suite."

"You're makin' me stay with you in your room?" said G, disappointedly.

Todd laughed. "I don't think you *heard* me. I said you're staying in my *suite*. It's slightly bigger than a typical room. Somethin' tells me you'll be comfortable enough. Besides, unless you can afford to pay for your own room—"

"That's OK," interrupted G, thinking about the Neiman Marcus experience. "I'll check out your room...I mean, your *suite*."

He was beginning to learn quickly not to underestimate Todd's affinity for the finer things in life, as well as his ability to afford it all.

G's phone wasn't the only item that was "dirty" and being tracked. His credit cards were being traced and matched against his cell phone activity as well.

An agent tracking his moves suspected that G's protectors, if they were formidable, would soon discover the trace and take action to eliminate the tag. The agent knew G's whereabouts to be New York City and was merely awaiting a clue from G's activity to tip him off on an exact location before sending in a "shadow" to move in for a closer look. He spiked G's phone to capture a GPS location and hacked the video feature and discovered the photo G had taken.

"They're in Manhattan, staying in the Marriott Marquis on Broadway," reported the agent. "How do you want to play this?"

"Good job. Send in a shadow and have him maintain a standoff surveillance for now. I've got to check in with the boss on how he wishes to proceed before we attempt an extraction or...elimination."

The authority to watch or to "shadow" someone typically fell within the purview of a leadership position or a delegate. This was no ordinary operation, however, and it was being conducted with little or no knowledge whatsoever. Someone on the inside was acting on their own accord for their own agenda and knew how to manipulate and exploit the system.

G's value was becoming more apparent as word got out on his abilities to "see from the inside" unlike anyone else. His internment at the airport set off a notification process that permeated an underground, corrupt network that made its way all the way back to Khalid Abdul-Hakim himself. Exactly who was orchestrating the domestic events on Hakim's behest was still unknown.

13

Ronaldo released the brakes, and the two engines of the Casa roared like hungry lions, sending the loaded craft down the short airstrip straight into a line of approaching hostile forces.

"Hang on, Warriors," shouted Ox to his passengers.

Booker nervously watched from the fringe of the LZ as the craft, carrying most of his team, made its way down the airstrip. He could hear random gunfire in the distance but drew little comfort knowing they were firing indiscriminately in the dark of night. There was no way they could spot the Casa in the dark, unless they too were using NVGs.

Ox called out the airspeed to Ronaldo. "Fifty, sixty, seventy…eighty…ninety…one hundred. Pull that nose up, kid!"

"She's heavy, Ox. I need ten more knots!"

A random bullet hit the windshield on Ronaldo's side and left a bullet hole in the glass. Ox and Ronaldo both flinched but pressed through the chaos.

"You OK, kid? You hit?"

"No time to check, Ox. Help me get her airborne."

Ronaldo and Ox both pulled hard on the yoke, and the engines finally gave them the speed they needed to lift the loaded craft from the grasp of the earth in the humid, dense jungle air.

"She's airborne!" shouted Ox. "Retracting the gear…execute a firm climbing right turn," he added.

Booker watched as the tiny craft made an aggressive climbing right turn away from the hostile fire.

"Damn that was close." said Ronaldo, breathing a sigh of relief.

"Well?" questioned Ox.

"Well what?"

"Well I guess you weren't hit with that bullet, or you'd be complaining about it by now."

Ronaldo shrugged his shoulders. "Guess not. It seems the gods were with us for that escapade, huh?"

"Indeed. I just hope they stick around long enough for us to get to Navagandi."

"Or at least across that border," added Ronaldo.

Ox turned to check on the passengers and offered a thumbs-up.

"Pat, please come up front when you get a minute. And bring your headset," said Ox on the cabin loudspeakers.

Pat unbuckled his seatbelt, struggled a bit to keep his balance, and made his way to the cockpit. Perry stopped him before he reached the cockpit door. "We're not gonna leave them, are we?" he asked.

Pat looked at Perry, placing one hand on his shoulder for effect.

"Marine, we *never* leave anyone behind. We're working a plan now, and I'll keep you posted. But right now I have to talk with the boss about our next move."

Pat stuck his head inside the cockpit and touched Ox on the shoulder.

"Plug in so we can talk," said Ox pointing to a headset jack in the console.

Ox flipped a couple of switches that placed Pat's headset on a cockpit intercom system so he, Pat, and Ronaldo could communicate.

"We need to put our heads together," said Ox.

"The FMS, or Flight Management System, tells us we don't have enough fuel to reach Navagandi. I'm reasonably confident we can reach the border, considering our payload is a bit lighter than we had anticipated and the fact that we had to leave slightly earlier than we planned. But we're not confident on the Navagandi destination. I'm looking for some assistance, Pat. I need an alternate airport we can select that'll provide a refuel option between the border and Navagandi. I also need all known airports or landing strips between the border and Navagandi, in the event we have to make a forced landing. My plan is to take her as far north toward Navagandi as possible, but when she's outta gas, she's not happy, and it makes for a very bad day."

Pat listened, nodding affirmatively.

"I'd also like to know if there's any way your *Secret Squirrel* buddies can keep an eye on us from their Predator, in case we have to make a forced landing."

"I'm on it, Ox, but I can already tell you, there's absolutely nothing between the border and Navagandi," said Pat as honestly as he knew how.

"Great," said Ox, pondering the thought. "One more thing if you would, Pat," added Ox. "Let the troops know we're doing everything we can to track their teammates, and tell them we won't leave them behind."

"Already have," he said with a wink.

Pat unplugged his headset and returned to the cabin.

"I'm actually starting to like that guy," said Ox quietly.

Ronaldo gave him a look of disbelief and quietly returned to flying the aircraft.

Hakim made his way through the hotel lobby, en route to St. James Park. The bell clerk greeted him as he approached the exit.

"Good evening, sir. Do you require a taxi?"

"No thank you, young man. It is a nice crisp evening. Perfect for a stroll, don't you think?"

Hakim arrived at the park as the sun was making its final descent onto the western horizon. It was difficult not to be distracted by the picturesque beauty of his surroundings.

What a perfect setting to initiate the will of God, he thought.

Hakim found a set of benches by the water's edge and noticed a man sitting alone. Hakim casually approached the man and asked, "Pardon me, sir, would you happen to know the time?"

The man looked up at Hakim, stood reverently and offered a simple answer to his question.

"Teacher, the time is as you have directed and as God wills...and I am ready."

"Very well, young man."

Hakim handed the man a key and a small piece of paper containing the name of his next contact. The key would open a locker containing further instructions to carry out his mission. Hakim placed his hand on the young man's shoulder and looked him directly in the eyes.

"You will be remembered and rewarded richly. I've directed the elders to find a suitable husband for your wife and have deposited a handsome sum of money into her possession. You must forget her and focus instead on the calling of your mission."

Hakim turned and slowly departed. The young man slipped into the twilight, determined to fulfill his destiny in support of the Jihad.

"Don't we have to check in?" asked G, as he and Todd stepped past the guest counter in the hotel lobby.

"Good evening, Mr. Jordan," greeted the concierge with a smile.

"Sup, Terry," answered Todd.

Todd inserted his key card into a slot just above the lighted floor buttons and pressed "49," and looked at G and smiled.

"It's a hell of a climb to the top, G...but it's worth it," said Todd. He hoped G would understand the metaphor.

Todd pulled his cell phone from his pocket in an attempt to catch up on his latest messages. He laughed after reading one from Kid Rock inviting him to a *small informal* party scheduled for later that evening.

"Looks like we may be in for a hell of an evening. You better get some rest," said Todd, with a chuckle.

The smile quickly disappeared from his face, however, when he came across Athena's text, warning him of G's cell phone vulnerability. Todd pressed a button for the closest floor—the fortieth.

"Thought we were headed to forty-nine."

"We gotta step out here for a minute."

Todd put his hand on G's shoulder and led him out of the elevator.

"Give me your phone, G."

"Why?"

Todd gave him a serious look of impatience. G reluctantly surrendered his phone. Todd powered G's phone and examined it closely.

"Ya know I'm not real comfortable with you looking into the details of my phone, Todd."

"*Fuck me!* I shoulda suspected this. What the *fuck* was I thinkin'?" said Todd, ignoring G's concerns. "OK, where the fuck's the battery on this bitch?"

"I *need* that phone, Todd! What are you doing?" said G defiantly.

Dream Operative

"G, I don't think you realize the gravity of the situation here."

G felt strongly enough about his phone that he pushed back.

"If you'll give me some *goddamn* answers, maybe I *would* realize the gravity," said G, realizing he was starting to shout.

"OK, I'll give you *some* answers, but that phone needs to be disengaged. If you don't help me pull the battery, I'm gonna permanently disable it. And you won't like the way I go about that."

"OK. Here." G grabbed the phone and pulled the battery. "Now what?"

Todd took a deep breath and rubbed his forehead while contemplating his next move. He knew Athena would be out of touch until her flight landed, so he took matters into his own hands.

"Good question, G. Lemme think this through."

Todd scrolled through his own phone and dialed Damian.

"Yo, D, T-Rock," announced Todd.

"Sup, TJ? You make it back to NYC OK?"

"Yeah, but I got another favor to ask. I need some phone service…" said Todd, explaining the situation to Damian.

"No problem. Look, *I know a guy who knows a guy*," said Damian in a poor rendition of a New York Italian accent.

"Yo, D, I appreciate the humor and all, but this ain't the time, bro. I have real concerns here."

"OK, T, I get it. But I do know a guy who can hook you up. He's on *the inside*, and he's who I go to when I need a favor in NYC."

"Aight, cool. He better have 'game,' because this shit ain't for amateurs, bro. You got a name?"

"Yeah, brother by the name of Mario," Damian told him.

"*For real?*" exclaimed Todd. "Like, 'Super Mario'? You better be serious D, cuz I already told you, I don't have time for this."

"Yeah, dude…Mario knows everybody. In fact, he's a good contact for you to have in your hip pocket anyway."

"OK, so I assume you'll have this Mario cat contact *me* then? Standard protocol?"

"Yup, standard protocol, bro. You staying at the Marquis tonight?"

"Yeah, we'll be here, but we'll be out-and-about tonight."

"Perfect. I'll give you a call later so you and Mario can hook up."

"Sounds good, but what do I do with this phone in the meantime?"

"Beats me, brah. I'm not the technician—just the facilitator."

"Great," said Todd as he terminated the call.

Todd pressed the elevator button on the wall and looked at G. "I'm gonna hang on to the phone, G. I know you don't wanna hear that, but that's the way we're gonna play this right now."

G and Todd stepped back into the elevator, and Todd went through the entire key card process again to gain access to the top floor. "OK, Todd, but I need answers," G reminded him.

"I gotcha, G. Let's grab a drink and settle in, and we can chat for a few minutes. But I'm expecting company, so we won't be gettin' into any long-winded discussions."

"You mind if I ask what kind of company?" G asked boldly. "I'm just sayin'...if you're all spooked out about my cell phone, then maybe we shouldn't be entertaining."

Todd's smile returned. "First of all, *we* aren't entertaining. It's business. And it's *my* business. Don't worry, because once we're inside, I've gotcha covered with enough security to choke a frigging horse."

The elevator door opened directly into a penthouse foyer, which led to a suite that was adorned with a décor straight from the pages of *Architectural Digest*. G could barely take it all in. Everything was grand and professionally decorated. The floors were mostly marble, complemented by hardwoods that flowed into the penthouse suite as far as he could see. The walls were decorated with artwork bordered with ornate hand-carved frames. The rooms were furnished with inviting comfort and a classy style befitting royalty. And the place smelled great.

"So what do you think, G?"

"Impressive."

"Don't be too impressed, brah. Because in the end, *things* don't make a man. What matters most is whether anyone remembers you once you're gone. Besides, things aren't always what they seem. Remember that...it may save your life one day."

There was something insightful in Todd's comment. G was beginning to actually like the dude...even *if* he held his phone hostage.

A rather large man in a suit greeted the two men in a deep voice. "Good evening, Mr. Jordan."

"Sup Elliott." said Todd. "Elliott, this is G. He'll be our guest for a day or so. If he leaves, shoot him." Todd paused for effect and smiled.

"Just kidding...if he needs anything, please see that he gets it. But he doesn't leave here without me," said Todd, looking into G's eyes to ensure he understood the rules. "Let's grab that drink, G."

Todd's phone began to ring.

Athena made her way through the passenger terminal at JFK airport after a rare on-time landing. Scrolling through her cell phone, she could see that Todd had not yet responded to her urgent text concerning G's cell phone. She was understandably concerned, so calling Todd was her first priority.

"Yo, wasup," greeted Todd as he answered his phone.

"TJ, I *assume* you received my text message?" said Athena.

"Oh hey, *Crystal*," said Todd in an attempt to disguise Athena's identity from G, who was within hearing distance.

Athena knew the drill and asked about G. "Is he safe? Is he comfortable? Is he nervous? What about the phone?"

Todd found his way to a secluded room where he could talk openly. "Sounds to me like you may actually like this dude, A. Is that concern I detect in that raspy voice of yours?"

"We're getting off track, TJ. Have you secured his phone?"

"Yeah, but he ain't happy about it."

"I can imagine," said Athena. "He's been trying all day to contact me."

"So there *is* something between you two," said Todd attempting to connect the details.

"Yeah, I guess you could say that, but it's not what you think."

"I don't need the details, A. Just tell me how you wanna play this, so I can get back to my normal life."

"TJ, you don't *have* a normal life."

Todd laughed. "Yeah, you're right about that. OK, point taken. So what's the plan? You in NYC yet?"

"Yes, just landed. The plan? Well..."

"Don't tell me you don't have a plan, woman. You *always* have a plan."

"Yes, I do. Listen, we've gotta connect as soon as possible," said Athena. "You planning on being out and about tonight?"

"Yeah, as a matter of fact, I told G I'd take him to a small social event."

"TJ, you don't *do* small events...unless you're talking about your sexual escapades. And if you are, you can spare me the details on that."

"Nah, it's not like that, A," said Todd. "Look, lemme call you later wit' the details. G's phone is disengaged, we're gonna have a drink, and then I hope to convince him to get some sleep before we head out tonight. I'll call you when I have more details. Just have a plan by then."

Todd left the room to look for G. "Where's our guest?" he asked Elliott.

"He retired, sir."

"Retired, huh? Is that like *taking a nap*, Elliott? Cuz if so, I gotta teach you how to *just say* that," chuckled Todd.

"Shall I summon him, sir?" asked Elliott in a deep, respectful voice.

"Uh, nah Elliott. Let him sleep. He's gonna need the rest if I expect him to hang wit' me tonight. Besides, it'll give me time to take care of some business."

14

Hakim returned to his room. He kept the room dark to catch a better glimpse of the city, now adorned in lights. He was lost in thought as he stared out the window.

Looking skyward, he could see aircraft departing from the airport in the distance and thought about his upcoming journey to America. He lay down and slipped into a dream from a deep slumber. He began to feel a sensation of floating, surrounded by a sea of nothingness, gradually becoming aware of the surroundings of the alter-conscious dimension. Never had he had such intensely lucid experiences. He searched for something familiar but found only experiences he could describe as "spiritual" and determined he had once again found himself in the presence of Allah. He attempted to speak, but instead of words coming from his lips, they emanated from his mind.

Allah, is this experience from your hand?

The experience comes from within, replied a voice within his mind.

Is it a gift? questioned Hakim.

Indeed.

How am I to use it?

How you use the gift is up to you.

What are the limitations of this gift?

The limitations are naught, replied the voice.

The response empowered Hakim. What a gift he now had for the advancement of the Jihad movement. His followers would fall to their knees when they discovered the favor of he had received. Hakim projected his mind to see beyond his current surroundings and decided to travel.

He immediately felt a surge on his body that projected him through what seemed like several space continuums.

Realizing he had not set a destination, Hakim found himself randomly placed in a dream dimension where he was being pursued. He looked around to see that he was in an old-world style city. He had found a temporary hiding place from those who were pursuing him. His hand was wrapped around a small-caliber handgun. Checking the magazine, he counted seven rounds of ammunition.

Hakim struggled to come to terms with where his travels had taken him. He stood in the shadows of a large pillar in the center of the city as people walked by, oblivious to the fact that he held a weapon drawn at his side. His heart racing, he drew a breath and was about to take a step when he noticed two men running with weapons drawn.

These must be the men who are looking for me, he thought.

He stepped back into the shadows and watched as they stopped running and began looking around, high and low, in search of their target. Hakim wanted to know why or how they were fortunate enough to come this close to finding him. Never before had anyone been able to get so close.

He peered out from his hiding place just far enough to catch a glimpse of one of the men pursuing him. Channeling his thoughts, his mind immediately fell into a flood of sounds and images revealing the nature of the man and his connection to Hakim. Short, inexplicable visions flooded Hakim's mind, until he witnessed the man's past action as a US Marine sniper, taking a shot that would mortally wound Hakim's brother during the first Gulf War in Kuwait City.

Hakim became enraged at what he learned. He cocked his weapon, ensuring a round was chambered, and boldly emerged from the shadow of his hiding place. Standing tall and unafraid, Hakim never took his eyes off the man as he confidently approached him. The man had taken a seat at the edge of a fountain pool in the center of the city and was oblivious to Hakim's presence.

Time slowed as Hakim approached the man. Stopping at point-blank range, he pointed his gun at the back of the man's head and pulled the trigger, sending one round into the man's brain. He could barely hear the sound of the weapon, as his dream had suppressed it. He watched in slow motion as a shell casing ejected from his handgun and blood spattered while the man fell facedown, without resistance, into the pool before him. He replayed the sequence in his mind and could literally feel the transfer of rage as he pulled the trigger and felt the recoil of the weapon. The feeling was incredibly intense and the satisfaction overwhelming...empowering, in fact. He continued to watch as the fountain pool before him turned red from the blood of his victim.

He looked down at the blood-spattered cuffs of his white shirt. His face displayed an evil smile as he slowly looked up and around at the crowd of people who had become aware that something terrible had happened. He could see them running about but couldn't hear anything from them at all.

Suddenly, he became aware of someone in the pool beside his victim—someone in hiding, but somehow on the same level of thought and awareness as him. Hakim looked quickly at the man and began to analyze him. Time returned to normal speed. Hakim never hesitated...until now. Their gaze connected, his mind studied the man, finding him to be eerily familiar. He tried connecting with the man telepathically, as he had with his first victim, but was met with unusually strong resistance.

Hakim raised his weapon and took aim, realizing this was the second man in pursuit of him. He found him to be a far greater threat than the first, because he couldn't overcome the man's cognitive awareness and resistance. He had to be eliminated. His weapon trained on the man, he studied his eyes once again to ensure he remembered them. Just before he squeezed the trigger, he heard a shot ring out and felt immediate heat and intense pain enter his left shoulder. Dropping his weapon, he looked around to see a woman pointing a smoking gun at him. He quickly turned to run and projected himself out of the dream...anywhere but here. He was angry because he had hesitated. And he paid for it with a bullet to the shoulder. The pain was more intense than anything he had ever experienced.

Hakim awoke in a cold sweat, with his right hand covering his left shoulder and his heart racing. His dream was so real he had to turn on the light next to his bed to see whether or not he was actually bleeding. Hakim thought about the details while he checked his shoulder for evidence of any kind of injury. He found none and had to arrest the speed of his thoughts to bring himself back into reality and convince himself to erase the perceived pain. His mind was still freshly wrapped in the totality of his experience as he sat on the edge of his bed, thinking about the details. His dreams were becoming so vivid, he began to wonder how to separate them from reality.

Hakim was a deeply religious man, quick to give Allah praise for such experiences.

He had not formally studied dream phenomena and therefore had little knowledge of the scientific aspect of the experience. Instead, he prayed for interpretation from a religious point of view, hoping to discover a divine meaning and further guidance on how to handle the "gift." His thoughts drifted to his encounter with what his mind could only describe as Allah himself, or a divine messenger. He was emotionally overwhelmed. He fell to his knees and wept. He tried to come to terms with the fact that he was *chosen* to see such visions. He closed his eyes and bowed to the floor, his hands covering his head, praying a prayer of thanks and praise for the ability to escape the enemy. He also prayed for guidance on how to operate in the "other dimension," as he now referred to his dream state.

"I must learn the full capabilities of this dimension, my Lord..."

Booker's attention shifted to finding his lone teammate. Situated and camouflaged in the thickness of the surrounding canopy, Booker placed an earpiece into his ear and made the call.

"Rawhide three, this is Rawhide one, how copy, over?"

While listening for a response, Booker donned his NVGs and scanned the area for unfriendly. He could hear vehicles in the distance. He knew it wouldn't be long before the area would be swimming with unfriendly who would hinder his efforts to reconnect with Hartman. If he was going to be successful, he had to move fast, and he had to move now. Booker tried transmitting on alternate channels in an attempt to contact his teammate, and then he established contact with Ox.

"Magic two-three, this is Rawhide, how copy, over?"

"Rawhide, this is Magic two-three, loud and clear."

"Roger, Magic two-three, Rawhide one is tucked in and safe. Have not established contact with Rawhide three yet...still searching. Would you happen to have IR data that would help?"

"Rawhide one, affirmative. We show Rawhide three's last known location to be northeast of your position, bearing zero-one-zero, for one hundred five yards, over."

"Rawhide one copies. On the move," responded Booker, while gathering his rucksack and making his way toward the objective.

"What do you make of the radio silence from Rawhide three, Ox?" asked Ronaldo as he set new coordinates into the flight management system.

"These guys are trained *not* to respond for a number of reasons. He could have another unfriendly close enough to compromise his position if he were to respond."

"So, what's the plan to get those guys out?"

"Don't have one right now, chief. First thing on my mind is the safety of this crew. Speaking of which…Hey Pat, got any news for me?" asked Ox.

"Oh I have news, but it's not good," reported Pat. "My calculations tell me we're not gonna make it to Navagandi…not on these fumes with this payload. But I guess we've always known that."

"OK, what's your recommendation?"

"I recommend we take a direct heading to Yaviza, Panama. It's the closest thing between us and civilization on the north side of the border," said Pat.

"So we can make it Yaviza then?" said Ox with hopeful anticipation.

"I didn't say we could make it," said Pat. "In fact, I don't think we will. But the terrain north of the border en route to Yaviza is flat enough for us to put down in the likely event we're forced to set down someplace other than an actual landing strip."

Ox seemed to be lost in thought for a moment; then he looked at Ronaldo.

"Bring her about to a heading of three-six-zero, kid. Destination: Yaviza."

"Left to three-six-zero," responded Ronaldo.

G closed the door to his room and grabbed the remote control. He had full intentions of surfing through the channels to pass the time and perhaps get caught up on the latest news. But his body wouldn't allow it. He was wiped out, and in no time, he was out cold…fast asleep.

The excitement of the day's events carried through to G's altered state of consciousness and pushed him right into the fold of another dream.

While in this dream, G found that his manipulation prowess was at its highest. In fact, it seemed as though every new dream experience provided something new and exciting for him to learn or experience. It was as if his learning had been compounded upon the collective experiences of his prior dreams. The concept filled his mind with euphoria as he tried to comprehend it all. Little did he know he was being prepared for much bigger things.

With merely the slightest thought of anything entering into his mind, G found those things beginning to materialize or manifest themselves before him. So much so, in fact, that he now had to gain control of his thought processes to prevent anything "wrong" or unintentional from happening.

G began to think about the concept of time within a dream. He had learned to project himself from one aspect plane or *dream situation* to another, but those moves were typically *lateral* with regard to time. He still had questions, however. What about the aspect of time movements? Could he project himself forward or backward in time? And could he manipulate occurrences? After all, anything should be possible in a dream. And what about the fact that he now possessed the power of insight just by touching someone? G decided it was time to consult with what he came to know as *the Authority*.

Taking a moment to concentrate, G focused his thoughts upon the concept and question of time. He closed his eyes for a moment and, upon opening them, found himself sitting at a small table in a busy coffee shop. Looking around, he could tell this was not an ordinary Starbucks boutique. It was a small café, perhaps in a foreign land somewhere, but none he could easily recognize. The people milled about without regard to his presence. Uncertain why he would find himself in such a place, he sat quietly, remaining patient. He thought about how nice it would be to have a cup of coffee, a mocha latte specifically — his favorite.

G's dream awareness had progressed to the point where he could discern aroma, and while enjoying the aroma of freshly brewed coffee, he noticed a tall, blond young lady headed his way. Making eye contact with G, she smiled and, without opening her mouth, asked if she could join him. G smiled, stood, and offered her a seat, as any gentleman would. Taking his seat, he looked up to see some of the most gorgeous eyes. They were deep blue and danced upon the senses of his mind. The young lady had two cups of coffee in her hands and offered one to him.

This one's yours, she said, communicating directly to G's mind. *It's your favorite.*

"Who are you, and why are you here?" asked G.

The young lady smiled as she placed a finger gently against G's lips, explaining that he possessed the power to speak with his mind and encouraged him to try. Looking into her blue eyes, G summoned his thoughts and asked again, this time with his mind, *Who are you?*

Dream Operative

The young lady smiled. While taking a sip of coffee, she answered. *I'm Angel. I've been sent here by the Authority to offer you the answers you seek.*

So, you're an angel? asked G, in an attempt to make sense out of the encounter.

Angel smiled. *No, my name is Angel. I'm a messenger for the Authority… I'm your messenger.*

Why are you here, Angel?

I'm here because you asked for answers and…to bring you a message.

What's the message?

First, I'll give you the answers you seek. Once I deliver the message, you'll have a decision to make that'll determine the course of your life.

Great, **said G** sarcastically. *It seems to be apropos, given the changes my life has seen lately.*

Angel sat before him, listening and smiling.

OK, said G. *So, can time be altered or manipulated?*

It's a complicated answer, **said Angel.** "Manipulate" *is the operative word in your question, for manipulation is relative.*

Relative to what? **asked G.**

It is relative unto itself. Allow me to explain, **said Angel.** *Should something be destined to take place in a continuum of time, it will happen regardless of manipulation. Manipulation may in fact affect a situation for a given time, but it will merely alter the circumstances in which it will eventually take place.*

But it can be altered, is that correct? G responded inquisitively.

That can be correctly assumed, yes, **said Angel.** *But to do so is a delicate process.*

Can you show me?

I cannot show you per se, but I can provide an example for you to experience.

Angel took the time to explain to G the supernatural perspective of time. By figuring out how to view time as a *constant* moment rather than a *lateral continuum* of moments, she was able to show him how to mentally "fold" the space-time continuum and manipulate time sequences to occupy random, select spaces of time of his choosing. Most people consider time as a horizontal continuum, but Angel showed G how time is actually vertical. In other words, he discovered that time is essentially a "static" concept whereby the present "moment" is all there is.

G was overwhelmed with excitement at the possibilities—and dangers—of the concept. In a dream state, he discovered he could fold and essentially *compress* the time continuum and actually see or visit alternate spaces of time—present, past, and future. His ability to observe the *future* allowed him to occupy a vantage point in which to manipulate the present and affect a change in the future.

Does this concept have anything to do with the fact that I can sometimes consciously see things about people through a sense of touch? he asked.

It's a side effect. Side effects are random at first but can be harnessed with time and practice, if it's your desire to do so. Your conscious abilities are enhanced by your unconscious experiences. You'll find that your rate of comprehension will increase as a result of your introspection, or your ability to see within yourself. Sometimes, there are side effects that reveal themselves in a manner in which you have experienced, explained Angel.

So I'm not going crazy after all?

No, you're not going crazy. You're quite extraordinary, actually.

G was satisfied that Angel provided the insight he sought. She reassured him that he could call upon her whenever he needed the guidance, and she would be there for him.

Thank you, Angel. Now…you said you had a message for me?

Yes. Your message is that you have been chosen. Your life, as you have become used to it, will rapidly take on a new direction, and your gifts will be in demand by many. Some will seek to harm you, kill you in fact. You must continue to develop your abilities if you are to survive and assist others in doing the same. Does any of this make sense to you?

More than you know…but I have a lot of questions, said G.

Your questions will be answered in time, said Angel.

In time for what?

In time for the answers to be best served by you.

I see, said G reverently.

Do you accept this responsibility?

I do.

Good. Then we begin at once.

Angel suddenly disappeared, and G began to awaken from his dream, his mind still tightly wrapped in the experience of his encounter with his newfound friend and guide.

Mark stopped to listen to his surroundings. Despite the fact that he was still wapped in total darkness, he still had other senses he could rely upon.

He had never felt so isolated. Here he was, in total darkness, in a labyrinth of unknown proportion. Feeling his way through the darkness, he kept quietly repeating a passage of scripture from Psalm 23 that brought him comfort. "Yea though I walk through the valley of the shadow of death, I will fear no evil."

Mark paused when he thought he heard the sound of trickling water. His caution began to wane, and his hope began to rise. He set out with new determination to find the source. He stopped every few feet to remind himself not to allow his excitement and thirst turn to carelessness. The sound gradually became distorted.

Alright, slow down and think about this, he thought. *Which way is that sound coming from?*

Mark picked up a trace scent moisture and wet concrete, so he knew he was close. The opening he approached gave him pause on which direction to take. He decided not to turn from the path he was on. Instead, he would forge ahead.

The scent of moisture continued to get stronger and was encouraging him, as he believed he was getting closer. Feeling his way through the darkness, he noticed the concrete walls becoming cooler to the touch.

I've got to be close, he thought.

His hands came in contact with a wooden barrier of some kind. He could hear the water just beyond the barrier and could smell the moisture in the air. Mark searched for a latch of some kind that would help him get through the barrier. No latch, no handle. And it wouldn't budge. He tried kicking it and even ramming it with the full force of his body, all to no avail. He grew more frustrated.

"Shit!"

He had no choice but to turn around and attempt an alternate path, hoping it wouldn't lead him away from the water. He painstakingly retraced his steps back to the last intersection. When he reached it, Mark paused again to determine the best course. He began to realize how his other senses were starting to compensate for his inability to see. He could still hear the water, although the scent of moisture had faded. He could also feel the rhythm of his heart beating as his anxiety increased. He was determined to get to the water source as soon as he could, because he knew his body needed it if he were to survive the night.

Mark felt an opening to his right and, with arms stretched out, took several steps in his new chosen direction. Feeling his way along the wall, his hands came upon a railing. He stopped, cautiously realizing that if there was a railing, it was there for a reason. His path began a gradual decline, and Mark pressed ahead on blind vision and faith that action was better than the alternative.

Continuing his gradual descent, he picked up the scent of water again. He walked several more steps after the path leveled and came to the end of the railing. Stepping forward cautiously, he came upon yet another barrier—a metal door. Mark could feel that it had a moderate-sized window in the middle, about chin high. He attempted to open the door, but it, too, was locked.

It was time for Mark to use his ingenuity and what adrenaline he had left. He had noticed on the way down that one of the sections of railing leading to the area was loose. So he went back and broke that section loose and returned to the door, determined where the window was, closed his eyes, and swung the railing section into the glass, shattering it after several strikes.

He removed his shirt and wrapped his hand to clear the remaining glass shards from the window frame. He reached through the window, unlocked the door, and made his way into the room. He was relieved to have made the breach but anxious about what he was up against on the other side.

Mark stepped confidently into the room and walked directly into a table. Stopping to regain his bearings, the scent of water filled his nostrils. This time the scent was mixed with the smell of various chemicals. He began to carefully feel around for objects he could use as a light source. His hands led the way along the walls where he eventually came across a light switch. He flipped the switch several times hoping for some kind of light, but to no avail.

He stretched his arms across the table in an attempt to find something that would help him and discovered a Bunsen burner igniter. He manipulated the igniter and produced a spark. He was elated. Although it was a mere spark, it was the first light he'd seen since the cell phone lost power. He almost cried at the very sight of a mere spark. Mark knew he was in some kind of lab, and that would require some caution, given the potential flammability of the contents of the room. He could still hear the trickle of water and attempted to locate the source while he tried to find a way to produce light.

Dream Operative

The sound of running water became louder as he walked further into the room. He was so thirsty; he was ready to lick the walls if he found they contained enough moisture. His anticipation was mixed with frustration. The anxiety was unlike anything he had ever felt before. The entire ordeal was an exercise of the mind.

15

"Hey, Pat," called Ox from the cockpit. "Any way you can place a call to 'Mother' to have her keep an eye on us from the heavens?"

Ox loved using clandestine slang, often mixed with his own cowboy jargon, to iterate a point or command. Pat wanted to make sure he understood Ox's request, so he confirmed it with his own translation.

"I'll make the call to see if home station can pick us up on satellite and track us," responded Pat, hoping he got the translation correct, then he made the call.

"Firefly, this is Acrimony, how copy, over."

"Acrimony, this is Firefly, loud and clear."

"Roger, Firefly. Acrimony requests an 'Eagle-Eye' escort of our team en route back to base."

"Acrimony, what is your relative position, over?"

"Acrimony is approximately one-hundred fifty kilometers southeast of Yaviza, Panama, bearing one-six-zero degrees," said Pat, realizing it would be the most vulnerable communication he would be required to transmit.

"Firefly is searching...please stand by."

"Acrimony, this is Firefly, we show *three* targets in your general vicinity and are unable to track you at this time. We're dispatching an asset to fly overhead for a better look. Expect a thirty-minute delay, over."

"Acrimony copies, out."

"Hey, Ox, when you have a minute," said Pat.

"Go ahead, Pat. You get the assistance I asked for?"

"Our request is in, Ox, but we apparently have company in the air nearby, and our Eagle-Eye is unable to distinguish us at this time."

"Copy. Keep me posted," said Ox, with a bit of concern in his voice as he peered through the cockpit windows into the black, early morning sky in search of other targets.

Todd knocked on the door to G's room.

"Yo, G, you awake?"

"Yeah, c'mon in," answered G, rubbing his tired eyes, followed by a yawn.

"Hope you got some sleep, cuz we're gettin' ready to *hit* it, brah. Grab a shower then get Elliott to make you a drink."

As he lay in one of the nicest beds he'd ever slept in, G began to soak in the events of his life. Rising to his feet, he walked over to a rudimentary pencil drawing hanging on the wall. It was framed, as if royalty had drawn it. G tried reading the signature and could barely make out the words *Picasso*. He shook his head in near disbelief and made his way to the bathroom. As he walked in, he was not surprised to find it to be one of the nicest bathrooms he'd ever seen. He had no problem indulging himself in an oversized shower fitted with multiple shower heads.

"Damn, so this is how the wealthy live. I could get used to this."

You will get used to this.

"Who said that?" asked G, rather startled.

It's me.

"Angel?"

Yes.

"OK, you're kinda creepin' me out. Can you see me? After all, I *am* taking a shower."

You already know the answer. I can see everything.

"Great..." said G, realizing his guide was with him now, whether he liked it or not.

He rushed through his shower, all the while looking around, as if he might catch a glimpse of someone. He finished changing and donned his pricey new clothes.

"Now *that's* what I'm talkin' about, G!" said Todd when G emerged from his room, sporting his new clothes—True Religion Jeans, a Seven

Diamonds button-down shirt, black leather woven belt, and matching black Italian shoes.

"Lookin' good, Dawg," added Todd.

"Feelin' good, TJ," said G, using one of Todd's many nicknames for the first time.

"Damn, you *must* have gotten some good sleep, G. That's the first time you've felt comfortable enough to use a call sign...I mean a nickname," said Todd chuckling. "Yo, Elliott, have the limo meet us downstairs, please," he added.

Elliott handed the two their drinks.

Todd announced, "Let's roll, G."

"I really could use my phone'" said G, as he and Todd descended in the elevator.

"I know it's a bitch, brah, but—" said Todd.

G reached up and hit the stop button on the elevator.

Todd shot him an intimidating look. "What the fuck, G? Get your hand off that button!"

"We're not going anywhere until you give me some answers, Todd. You 'rescue' me..." said G, using air quote hand gestures, "...you stuff me into a limo with people I don't even know. You ask me to *trust* you. You insist I get into your jet...not that I'm an ungrateful son of a bitch, mind you...but then you take my *phone* away from me and keep promising me answers. None of this shit makes sense, Todd. It's time for answers," said G, with his own intimidating look.

"G, I don't wanna have to get all ugly up inside this elevator, but if you force my hand—"

G took a deep breath and looked at Todd as sternly as he could. Suddenly, the elevator lights sparked and went dark. Then, the elevator jerked and brought both men back to reality.

"Alright G, you win," exclaimed Todd. "Put this box back in motion, and you'll get your answers in the limo. That's the best I got," conceded Todd.

"I'm not sure what the hell just happened, but I've got to get the hell out before we fall to our deaths," said a nervous Todd.

G released the emergency stop button and set the elevator back into motion. He too was as curious as Todd as to what caused the elevator to shudder as it had. Both men remained silent the remainder of the way down to the lobby.

Todd and G walked directly out of the hotel lobby toward an awaiting black stretch Cadillac Deville limousine. Tucked safely inside the car, G shot Todd a look of expectation. "OK, TJ…the details," he demanded.

"Yo, driver, take us to the *Boom Boom Room* on Washington Street."

"I know it well, sir," responded the driver.

Todd looked suspiciously out the rear window of the limousine as the car pulled away from the hotel.

"Now what?" asked G, thinking his information request was to be slow-rolled yet again.

"We have a shadow," said Todd. "Not to worry, though. He's in *my* town so I can take care of it."

"You mean someone is following us?"

"Yeah, that's what I mean. I need to make a call to see if we can get some assistance with this, G. Then, I promise, we'll have our chat."

"Great. It's always something isn't it?"

Todd made a call to Damian to see if he could enlist the help of his NYC contacts. "Yo, D, I need to chat with this Mario cat…like right now, brah."

"He hasn't called you yet? Dude, lemme connect with him, and I'll hit you back."

"Make it quick, D. I need some local assistance, like *right now*."

"Call you back, TJ."

Todd typed out a quick text message to Athena to let her know that he and G were on their way to the Boom Boom Room but to be cautious and on the lookout for a shadow. Athena answered with a text saying that she would be in the area and would rendezvous with him and G there.

Todd's phone rang…*Unknown*.

"Yo, this is T-Rock—"

"You have what we want. Have your driver take the next exit, and I won't kill you."

Todd heard his call-waiting signal and knew Damian was supposed to be calling in so he had to think quickly if he wanted to avoid a nasty situation.

"I hear ya, we'll take the next exit," said Todd, in an attempt to appease the caller.

He immediately switched over to his second line to answer Damian. "Yo, D, the situation here is going south quick—" began Todd when he was interrupted by another unfamiliar voice.

"Todd, this is Mario. I understand you may need a favor."

"Holy shit dude, you have a gift for calling at the right time. But I'm not sure you'll be able to help," said Todd with concern in his voice.

Todd's call-waiting signal began to alert him once again.

"Shit, Mario, I've got unwanted company, and they're calling me again. They want us to pull off onto the next exit. They sound like they mean business."

"Go ahead and pull off the exit, then, Todd. We're right behind your shadow. Have been since you left the hotel," said Mario in a calm manner.

"You're shittin' me. How the hell…aw, never mind. I'm just relieved to know we're not alone."

"Answer the call and let me know what your instructions are. We'll be ready for any surprises," said Mario.

"Yo, Todd, what the *fuck* is goin' on?" pressed G, as he witnessed Todd's behavior and ensuing phone dialogue.

"G, I'm trying to save your ass *again*, my friend. This time it's *my* ass, too. You need to be patient with me and do *exactly* what I say. You got that?"

"I got it," responded G reluctantly.

"This is T-Rock," said Todd, answering his phone to the unknown caller.

"Take the Washington street exit," instructed the caller, followed by a disconnection.

"We can do that, but—damn, that was rude. Son of a bitch hung up on me."

"G, see if the driver has a cell phone we can use."

"If I had *my* cell phone we could use that," said G sarcastically.

Todd gave him a look that pretty much said he was close to kicking his ass. Todd had G by fifteen to twenty pounds. All muscle. He had enough size to intimidate G into thinking twice about a challenge. So G calmed down a bit, spoke with the driver, and was able to deliver his cell phone to Todd.

Todd used the driver's phone to text Athena to let her know they would be arriving to the club with a "shadow" in tow. He also told her about enlisting Mario's assistance.

Sounds like things have heated up 4u this evening, responded Athena. *I'm prepared for your arrival.*

Tom Herring called Dan to offer an updated assessment of the scene at ground zero.

"It's not good, Dan. I've got the best guys on this led by the best civil engineer in the business—Russ Noble. Russ is telling me that the entire thing is ugly. This guy calls it like it is, Dan. He's still assessing the area, but I'll tell you, my friend, the only hope for finding anyone alive has diminished with the collapse. We haven't given up, though, and will continue to push ourselves until we determine our efforts to be complete."

"It's complete when I say it is, Tom," said Dan. "If there's one ounce of hope that we find someone alive, then we continue the op."

"I agree, Dan. I just don't know what else to do."

"You're doing a good job, Tom. I need you to continue the course."

Jay Cooney's curiosity continued to get the best of him. He refused to believe that the entire sub-structure had given way, but he needed some perspective to be sure. His investigative instincts typically served him well and had shaped him to be the award-winning journalist he was. He and his cameraman set out to find Tom Herring to see if they could help in any way…and to see if there were clues on anything the other reporters were missing. They made their way to the public affairs tent and asked to see a copy of the building blueprints.

"They're classified," said a public affairs representative matter-of-factly.

"That's bullshit. Why are they classified? What kind of government operation is this, anyway? I demand to see Mr. Herring for comment," said Jay.

"Mr. Herring is busy with the recovery effort."

"Look, I just want to see *part* of the blueprints…so we have a better idea of the devastation. Do I have to cite the Freedom of Information Act to see the plans?"

"Let me clear it with Mr. Herring," said the public affairs representative reluctantly. "If he approves, then I'll share the info with you. If not, then there's nothing I can do."

Jay flipped open his cell phone and made a call back to the home office to talk with the producer and explained his efforts. "Can you see if you can grease the skids for us to obtain a copy of those blueprints?"

"Sure can," said the producer. "Let me make a couple of phone calls to see what I can come up with."

It wasn't long before Jay's phone rang. It was his producer. "I'm sending you a gift. Check your e-mail."

"Thanks," said Jay. "Sweet." said Jay, opening an e-mail from his producer with an attachment labeled "blueprint." "Hey John, are you any good at reading these things?"

"Certainly, but it's of no use unless we can get an enlarged version. There's way too much detail to read on your phone."

"OK, let's think about this. Where can we download this to get a full-sized print?"

John shrugged his shoulders and simply said, "I don't know…Kinkos?"

"Brilliant," said Jay. "Let's go find a Kinkos to run a printout and grab a cup of coffee. There's not much going on around here right now anyway."

"You serious?" said John. "Because I was just joking about the whole Kinkos thing."

Booker maneuvered his way through the thick jungle canopy, focused on getting to Hartman as soon as he could.

Knowing he was getting close to Hartman's last known position, Booker made sure to reduce his noise footprint and slowed his pace as he inched his way toward the expected rendezvous point on his belly. He could see the tree used earlier as a perch by the sniper and was close enough to see the bloodstained tree trunk left by Perry's expert placement of a 7.62mm round that brought the sniper to a quick death.

Booker came upon a clearing and stopped to gain his bearings and assess his surroundings. The jungle air was thick and provided a haven for the aggressive mosquitoes. He noticed a rise in the lay of the land to his right, about thirty yards away. It was high enough to give him a better perspective of his surroundings than his current position offered, so he made his way toward the ridge. He rose from his crawling position and quickened his pace in a protected crouched position to avoid detection and to get there as soon as he could. He was sweating from the dense night jungle air and had to stop along the way to clear the sweat from his eyes.

Perched upon the ridge, Booker peered through his NVGs to take stock of his surroundings. To his discouragement, all he could see was thick jungle canopy. It was late and dark, but Booker was trained not to give up. He would persist all night if he had to, in order to find his teammate. Any delay could mean the difference between finding Hartman and losing him for good. Booker could hear voices and machinery in the distance but found the immediate area to be clear of danger…or so he thought.

Making his way down from the ridge, Booker stopped suddenly after hearing voices close by. He had been in the region long enough to determine that the voices were speaking Spanish but couldn't quite make out what they were saying. As he got closer, Booker could finally make out the words: "¡Levante! ¡Levante!" which means, "Get up! Get up!" Booker figured the voices he heard were about twenty yards off to his left so he quietly made his way toward the source.

"Your team has left you behind, Gringo," said a Hispanic man, laughing. "You are alone, outnumbered, and will not live to see the sunrise. Now tell me how many more of you there are in the area and the reason you're in my country."

"Go *fuck* yourself," responded Hartman in a low, raspy voice of defiance.

Booker picked up the scent of smoke. Slowly peering through the dense, dark jungle with the help of his NVGs, he could see that part of the jungle was aglow with what he suspected to be a campfire. He quietly made his way toward the area. Anytime he or his team was this close to unfriendly forces, they were trained to be extra vigilant for perimeter defenses. The unfriendly hadn't been in the area long enough to set traps but were smart enough to post perimeter sentries in case anyone like him should show up. He needed to get a good look at the situation to know what he was up against. Sunrise would occur in about three hours, so time was *not* on his side. He'd have to figure this out quick, if he wanted to use the element of surprise to get Hartman out alive. He stopped suddenly when he heard the disturbance of the underbrush nearby. Slowly turning his head to his right he saw an armed unfriendly taking a leak in the jungle and smoking a cigarette. Booker could plainly make him out in the green glow of the night vision goggles but was uncertain if he himself was far enough away to remain undetected. Instead of trying to move, Booker remained stone still while he watched the unfriendly finish his business and turn and walk back toward camp, with his semiautomatic weapon slung over his shoulder. Booker's heart pounded as he studied the man's path. Taking careful, quiet steps, Booker followed.

Russ Noble called tom Herring to provide an update on the breach.

"Whatcha got, Russ?"

"Hey, Tom, my guys have managed to find a route to the lower levels with little debris. So we've cleared a path and have already sent the camera down to take a look around."

"Awesome. So what did you find?"

"It's pretty bad down there, but I think I can get a better assessment if I could send a man down to take a look."

"I don't like the sound of that, Russ. It's still too unstable. Tell you what, send me the video footage so I can take a look at it, and I'll get back to you on it ASAP."

"I can certainly do that, Tom…but as you know, time is of the essence on this."

"I understand that all too well, my friend. Tell me, who you plan on sending down that hole? We can't afford to lose anyone else on this operation."

"That's why I've decided to go myself, Tom," said Russ.

"Well that gives me even *more* pause, Russ. But I suspect there's no one more experienced than you for this kind of operation. Send me that video so I can decide whether to support you on this or not."

"Right away, Tom."

Jay Cooney and his cameraman were able to download and print the file of the building plans.

"Looks like an ordinary warehouse to me," said Jay, doing his best to examine the blueprints.

"Can't figure out why anyone would want to blow up a building that looks like it shoulda been on the demolition schedule anyway," said the cameraman.

The two men continued to examine the drawings.

"Hey, take a look at this," said John.

Pointing to one of the last few pages that were printed, John discovered a series of rooms and corridors that were part of the lower levels of the structure.

"What do you make of it?" asked Jay.

"Well, it looks like there are, or *were*, additional areas within the structure that were not part of the original design or layout of the building."

"How do you know that?"

"Look, right here," said John, pointing to the lower right section of the layout where the legend is located.

"There's typically a legend here that identifies the drawing. It should have the name of the structure, the date, the architect's name and few other details. But there's nothing in there but a code I don't recognize," explained John.

"Dude, I don't mean to sound like such a dumbass, but what are you saying?" asked Jay.

"I'm saying that this part of the structure was never meant to be known or discovered, as it was never officially registered with any public records department."

John looked up from the drawings and directly at Jay. They communicated without words for a moment.

"We gotta get this info to Tom Herring," said Jay. "There could still be people down there *he* doesn't even know about."

"But what if he *does* know about it?" asked John, as if they had discovered a conspiracy.

"It's our duty to discover the truth and to report it," said Jay. "We don't have much of a choice. Besides, we're not the only ones with these plans now."

16

Athena arrived at the club just before Todd and G. She was loosely disguised in a short blond wig, wearing a knit top covered with a cropped Louis Vuitton black leather jacket that conveniently concealed her Kimber 9 mm snub-nosed pistol. She also sported a matching short black leather skirt, accompanied by a wide snakeskin belt that rode low on her hips. She topped it all off with an oversized Prada handbag packed with a few backup weapons in case she needed them; among them was a silencer for her handgun. To say she was armed to the teeth would be an understatement.

Athena typically had no difficulty making it past security into any nightclub. Most door guards were more enamored by her sheer sex appeal than their concern for security. The more hot women they could get into the club, the better the reputation and overall business...and bottom line.

Athena conducted a quick assessment of the building to determine her exit strategy and eventually made her way to the bar, where she waited for Todd and G to arrive.

The limo took the exit off the freeway and traveled down Washington Street. Todd's phone rang.

"Yo."

"Take the next right and stop in the alleyway," instructed the voice on the other end.

"Uh, I don't think we can do that right now, but we appreciate the invite," said Todd sarcastically as the limo slowly pulled up to the Boom Boom Room.

"You'll regret your decision if you don't comply with our instructions."

"Yeah, OK, listen...gotta go now. Nice talkin' to ya, said Todd, hanging up the cell phone. "We're here. Let's go, G. Keep your eyes open and watch your back."

G answered with a look of concern.

Exiting the limo, Todd and G's heads were on a swivel, searching for anything that looked out of place. They quickly became overwhelmed by the sea of people gathered outside the club. G looked at Todd expectantly and asked if he had the clout to "cut in line."

"I don't do lines, G. But even *I* have a tough time gettin' in here sometimes. Depends on who's in the club on any given night. All we can do is try."

They tried making their way toward the door but found themselves in back of a heavy crowd of people, vying to be noticed to get into the club.

"Looks like the word is out that *Kid* will be here tonight," shouted Todd.

"What's that?" said G, straining to hear Todd above the noise.

Todd's phone rang while he and G waited.

"I really don't need this shit," said Todd, expecting to be pestered again by the threatening caller. "Yo, this is T-Rock," he said, pressing the phone against his ear with his left hand while covering his open ear with his right.

"Todd, this is Mario. I need you to raise your hand and wave at the gentleman at the door, so he can pick you out of the crowd."

Todd looked around as if he expected to see someone else on a cell phone. Looking back toward the door of the club, Todd raised his hand as he was told and waived at the doorman. All of a sudden, the crowd of people parted like Moses and the Red Sea, and two large, bodybuilder-looking doormen approached him and welcomed him to the club.

"Mr. Jordan?"

"That's me," said Todd.

"Right this way, sir. You and the gentleman can follow us."

Todd looked at G, shrugged his shoulders and smiled. "They think you're a gentleman, G."

They made their way past a sea of people hoping to get into the club sometime that night. Todd and G were met at the door by a young lady, who escorted them to a private table.

"Can I get you gentlemen anything?"

Todd looked at G and smiled.

Dream Operative

"The 'gentleman' is drinking Captain and *Diet* Coke. Bring him the entire bottle of Captain. Make it a 750. You can bring *me* a bottle of Grey Goose, 750 as well, please—oh and two Acid Blondie cigars as well," said Todd, sitting back in a plush leather lounge chair.

"This is gonna be one hell of a night, G. Soak it in, brah, cuz it's about to get all crazy up in here," said Todd with a chuckle and a huge grin pasted across his face.

G tried to enjoy the experience, but he kept thinking of Athena and was still struggling over the reasons he was here in the first place. And what the hell was all the commotion about in the limo? The music began to play as the lights grew dim, and a kaleidoscope of sight and sound began to fill the room.

Athena watched Todd and G walk right past her and make their way into the club and into the VIP room. Her emotions grabbed her as she laid eyes on G for the first time since their brief encounter in Belize. She was impressed with how good he looked in his new clothes. He was even more attractive than she was prepared for.

Todd's phone began to light up with interaction. His first text was Mario.
U should B safe inside. I have U under watchful eyes
The second text message came shortly thereafter. It was from Kid Rock.
Yo, TJ, U at the BB yet? — Kid
Todd responded, *Sure am, brah. Get your ass here. We're in the VIP*
Todd decided he would text Athena, but his phone lit up with yet another unexpected text message.
You made a fatal mistake. We will get what we're after and you will lose
Todd looked around the room, glanced at G who was pouring drinks, and then back at his phone. He considered sending an answer but decided against it. Instead, he forwarded the text to Athena.

G stood and excused himself.

"Be right back, TJ. I gotta pee."

"Watch your back, bro," said Todd. "And you already know what I'm talkin' about."

"Gotcha."

As G made his way to the men's room, he couldn't help but notice a cell phone sitting on a nearby table. He quickly glanced around the room and considered *borrowing* it to call Athena. His thoughts and follow-through were interrupted when a young lady picked it up to answer a text message.

What am I thinking? G thought, continuing his walk toward the restroom. *I need to get a grip.*

After examining the video footage of the damage, Tom Decided it was worth the risk of sending a man down to gain a live perspective.

Tom placed a quick call to Dan. "Our plan is to send Russ Noble down for a hands-on look, Dan."

"What are the risks, Tom?"

"The ultimate risk is that the entire thing caves in on him. But we've done everything to prevent that. And Russ is the best in the business. He knows how to handle himself in such situations. He knows structure and has a long history of firefighting and engineering. I wouldn't send anyone else."

"OK, Tom, but I don't want him down there any longer than he has to be."

"I don't, either."

"Let me know as soon as he's back safe and keep me posted on what he finds."

"Will do, boss."

Tom placed a call to Russ and gave him the go-ahead. "You're cleared hot, Russ. You have the complete trust, faith, and prayers of everyone here. I want a camera accompanying you and a clear exit strategy in case you get into a jam down there."

"Got all that covered, Tom," said Russ. "My guys are fully briefed should they need to get me outta there in a hurry. I'll also be wearing a radio, so I should have two-way comm the whole time."

Russ was outfitted with a breathing apparatus, harness, two-way radio headset, gloves, safety goggles, first-aid pack, and rappelling helmet. Intense safety lights shone brightly down the shaft constructed by the rescue engineers. Above the opening was a crane, outfitted with a cable that would lower Russ to search for any signs of survivors. One of the engineers handed Russ a high-powered light as others were attaching his harness to the cable.

"Test one, two…how do you hear me?" said Russ, testing his radio.

"Loud and clear, Russ," responded the comm operator with a thumbs-up.

"OK, ladies, we ready to do this?"

Dream Operative

Jay found his way straight to Tom Herring's on-site trailer without being stopped. He had to tell him what he and John had discovered.

Both men walked right into Tom's trailer. Tom was looking at his computer. He immediately recognized them. "How the hell did you get in here?" shouted Tom. "Get the hell outta here before I call security."

"Listen, Mr. Herring," Jay pleaded. "We have information for you that *no one* else has. We're bringing it to you first. Take a look at it, and if it's not useful, then John and I are outta here and will park our asses back in the press tent," Jay continued. "I came in here with *no* camera and *no* agenda other than to get this information to you."

Tom stood with his arms crossed, a stern look of disgust painted on his face, while Jay nervously awaited his reaction. After a very brief moment, Tom decided to give the two their one and only chance at redemption. "Whatever you have better be good, because I don't have time for bullshit. If you waste my time, I'll have you kicked off this site and prosecuted for interfering with a federal operation," warned Tom. "So what's so important that you have to show me now?"

Jay was initially stunned that Tom would allow him the time to share the blueprints. His reporter's mind wanted to ask questions, but he knew that would get him nowhere fast.

"Take a look at this," said Jay, spreading the blueprints across a large table in the room. "John, tell him how you see this."

"Uh, yes sir, Mr. Herring, these are the plans for the building—"

"I *know* what plans look like, son. Get to your point, fast." John looked at Jay, who gave him an encouraging look to continue.

"Yes, sir, these are the main plans to the building that was destroyed, originally drafted in nineteen-seventy-four," explained John. "But these last few pages aren't part of the original design. Here...these are dated *ten years* earlier and are part of an entirely different structure. What we don't know is whether the two structures are connected."

"If they *are* connected," said Tom, "that would provide an exit for anyone who knew about it..."

"Or anyone who may have discovered it," added Jay.

Tom paused and placed a hand on his chin to help him think of the possibilities.

17

Dan decided to spend the night in his office, given the current state of affairs. He was tired but hungry. Making his way to the break room to search for something to eat, he ran into Jeff Hines.

"How's goes it, Dan?"

"Rough day, Jeff."

"I'll say…you're still here. You spending the night?"

"Actually, I am. Too many activities going on to be away from the office."

"Man, last time I saw you here this late was just after nine-eleven. Anything I can do to help?"

"No thanks, Jeff. You're here after hours as well. What brings you around this time of night?"

"I came in to read the SITREPs on a case my folks are working."

Dan nodded his head as he continued into the break room.

"Oh, hey Jeff, were your DC agents able to interview the kid you were telling me about? You know…the one with *unusual abilities*?"

Jeff was caught off guard with the question but shrugged it off and put on his best "liar's face." "Damn agents royally screwed that one up, I'll tell ya. Seems they grabbed the wrong guy at the gate. I mean, how damn simple is it to follow directions?"

Dan's hunger distracted his ability to apply a full focus to Jeff's explanation, so he offered a simple courteous nod as he grabbed a small Tupperware container, removed the lid, and placed it into a microwave oven. Two minutes on the timer.

The Boom Boom Room was a temporary sanctuary for G and his new friend. Todd felt good, knowing that Mario and his gang were there, along with Athena, incognito. He and g were there to have a good time and he was determined to show his new friend how the well-connected party.

G returned from the restroom to a room full of beautiful company sitting around Todd.

"Hey, ladies, this is my good friend, G," said Todd, raising his cocktail glass. "G, say hello to the girls."

"Hi," said G, a bit taken off guard, but with a smile clearly painted across his face.

One of the lovely ladies in the room handed G his drink and invited him to sit next to her on a couch, next to where Todd was seated. When she turned around to walk back to the couch, he conducted the customary visual scan to determine whether her invitation was worth the acceptance. She was certainly cute enough; medium height, brunette with a short stylish haircut, well-balanced figure, and a form-fitting outfit that accentuated her best assets from every conceivable angle a man would approve of. He accepted the drink and the invitation and decided to relax and enjoy the moment…despite the excitement and confusion of the evening.

Todd proposed a toast. "Here's to life, lust, and living on the motherfuckin' edge."

G cautiously raised his glass and took a big gulp of his Captain and Coke. The young lovely sitting next to him did the same and made an obvious move by placing her hand on G's thigh. G's mind was elsewhere, however. As much as he tried, he couldn't get beyond the fact that he was sitting in a VIP room somewhere in New York City, when he *should've* been in his apartment in Washington, DC. Why was he here? Where was Athena? What would be next?

The club lights changed from dim to dark as the music grew louder. G could feel the bass of the house speakers echo through the room and through his body.

"Do you dance, G?" asked the young lady with her hand now gently stroking the inside of G's thigh. G raised his glass slightly.

"I do after enough of these."

She smiled and pulled him closer so she could look directly into his eyes.

"Well, drink up big daddy, because tonight I want you on the dance floor and *then* I want you in my bed," she said seductively.

G smiled but didn't offer much more of a response than that. Then he poured another drink.

The number of people in the club grew to a point that Athena could no longer keep an unobstructed eye on the VIP room, so she decided it was time to make an appearance. She told the bartended she would be in the VIP, and he winked and nodded in a cheesy attempt to be cool and acknowledge her.

G's attention was immediately diverted to Athena as she walked into the room. He subconsciously rose to his feet out of respect; something his father taught him when he was a young man. He was told that women not only deserve the respect but they also appreciate the gesture, and that *he* would stand out among most men by doing so.

Athena was dressed in a perfect balance of class and sensuality. She had removed her jacket, so her knit top draped slightly over her short, form-fitting skirt. The entire ensemble was topped off with a gorgeous pair of metallic high heels that made her long legs look good enough to eat right then and there.

She was like a work of art. Her high heels drew his gaze involuntarily up her long, luscious legs to the hem of her short skirt. He studied the lines of her body as if it were an exotic sculpture only few could afford to enjoy. The lines of her hips arrested his attention and caused his heart to quicken. He became aroused as his gaze made its way to her breasts, where he could see just a hint of revealing cleavage. He slowly glanced up to make eye contact with her and was captivated by her eyes, matched only by those of Athena's, and strangely similar.

Not expecting Athena, G's mind convinced him that this was a cruel trick of déjà vu. So he decided to enjoy the ride and the sensual experience of arousal this woman offered. He took another sip of his drink without breaking his gaze and was drawn in, as if he had no choice but to give in to the seduction of her attraction. Locked onto those gorgeous eyes of hers… it seemed as if time stood still for the occasion. She returned a glance along with a smile. Ah, that smile…*wait!*

G took a step toward her but was distracted by a tug on his shirt by the young lady desperately attempting to win his attention. "Hello. Hey, what the hell? Pay attention to *me*."

G shot her a look that pretty much indicated he was *not* interested. She returned a look of disappointment and disdain and reluctantly took her seat in a huff. The entire club began to cheer at the announcement that Kid Rock had entered the club.

Athena stood still; slightly overwhelmed by the direct contact with G, a glance from Todd that indicated he wasn't expecting her, and the entrance of a rock star celebrity. Athena vanished into the growing, consuming crowd.

As G was studying Athena, the young lady he was with secretly spiked his drink with a double dose of Rohypnol—the date rape drug. She made one last attempt to win him over before making a decision to *punish* him by allowing him to consume the drink.

"So G, why don't we get outta here?"

"Can't do that, babe," said G, without making eye contact.

He was cut off by the entrance of Kid Rock into the VIP area. The celebrity was accompanied by a man who appeared to be a bodyguard. Standing a minimum of six feet five inches, the black mountain of a man wore a serious expression and was very alert.

"What's happenin', Kid?" said Todd, moving in for a man-hug with the rock star. The two exchanged pleasantries and were laughing at private comments that couldn't be heard over the noise.

The rock star wore his trademark hat and sported the bad-boy goatee he was famously known for. G could hardly believe he was in the presence of the *Detroit Badass*. It was all kind of euphoric, actually.

"Yo, Kid, I want to introduce you to my friend, G. G, this is Kid Rock."

The menacing bodyguard took a step forward. G stopped. Todd laughed.

"It's cool, *Brutus*, or whatever your name is," laughed Todd.

"G, huh? Does that stand for something, or did your parents run out of vowels?" said Kid, laughing at his own wit.

Todd and Kid laughed hysterically. G stood there, smiling, taking it all in, despite the fact that he was the brunt of the jokes. After all, a famous rock star was actually *talking* about him.

Todd raised his glass. "Put 'em up, ladies. This is a toast to my good friend, *Kid motherfuckin' Rock*, the baddest cat on the planet...besides me, that is," said Todd as he tipped his glass back. The room erupted with cheers and more noise.

G picked up his drink and did the same. The young lady stood and raised her glass and offered a private, silent toast and clanked glasses to force G to take yet another sip. He turned away from her, and she slipped out of the crowd to avoid the wrath of her deception.

G looked around the room to find the woman he'd seen earlier before the commotion. He searched for the short blonde hair between the masses of people. He focused intently, squinting his eyes to find her. Suddenly, he spotted her and set out to catch up with her.

"Yo, G, where you headed now?" shouted Todd.

G turned toward Todd when he heard his name and stumbled slightly. He looked at Todd and tried to focus. His vision began to blur, shaking his head slightly in an attempt to clear the cobwebs. Staggering, he took two steps toward Todd and stumbled again. Unable to stand anymore, G felt himself falling toward the floor. His brain was shutting down, and he was losing control fast. Todd, realizing the seriousness, sprang from his seat in an attempt to catch his new friend or break his fall, but G was on his way down fast.

G was just conscious enough to know he was bumping into people as the floor rapidly approached his face. He closed his eyes just before impact and felt only the percussion of his head and body making contact with the floor. Todd rushed over and demanded the crowd provide room and shouted at the crowd. Girls could be heard screaming in fear of what was taking place.

"Somebody call 9-1-1. Now, dammit!"

Athena heard the commotion and rushed to Todd's side. A crowd of people gathered. Some people asked "What happened?" One of the spectators turned to make a call on his cell.

"He's out. Good job."

G blinked. He tried to regain his bearings and determine why he had not yet felt the impact of the floor. Instead, his fall continued into alter consciousness, where he was surrounded by nothingness.

He made a conscious effort to arrest his fall as he often had in his dreams.

This attempt failed.

He tried concentrating harder.

Nothing.

His fall accelerated. He found himself anticipating yet another impact of some kind. Would it be fatal? Was he in fact *dying*? Was this a fall of death? He was aware only that he was falling.

Just as suddenly as he was falling, he stopped...suspended actually. His body was awkwardly positioned and floating until he felt himself gently come to rest. He looked down to see he was standing on firm ground. He picked up a scent of salt air. Nothingness continued to surround him.

As his field of view increased, he could see that he was standing on a rough-cut boardwalk, commonly found at a beach. He felt a presence. Looking ahead, he could see the boardwalk stretch for miles. Looking behind, he could see only darkness. The air was thick and humid. He stepped forward. As he did, the path behind him disappeared into nothingness. He still had no control of this dream, and it bothered him. He made an attempt to project himself out of the uncomfortable dimension but could not.

He saw something in the distance on the path that piqued his curiosity. As soon as he processed the thought, he came upon it. There before him was a thick, colorful snake. He marveled at its beauty—about six feet long, adorned with brilliant colors of fiery orange, deep cobalt blue, reflective gold and silver tones, deep red, and luscious greens laid out in a pattern only the finest artist could imagine. Although not particularly fond of snakes, G was attracted to it. The snake darted its tongue quickly and picked up G's presence. It slowly turned and tilted its head to make eye contact with G with its dark, empty eyes. Then it spoke to him in a raspy, but attractive whisper.

"Hello. I've been waiting for you." Its voice was alluring and erotic.

G's thoughts preceded his ability to speak.

What is this place?

"Do you think I'm attractive?" asked the snake, ignoring his question. "Don't you want to touch me?"

Not sure if I should, responded G.

"What's the harm? Come closer."

G was skeptical and suspected there would be a penalty for his curiosity. So he declined.

I'm fine right here where I am.

"What's wrong? Don't you love me? Don't you *want* to love me?"

I don't even know you.

"Au contraire. We've met before. I recognize you," said the snake in a calm and confident manner.

I don't believe we've met, said G confidently.

The snake slowly transformed before G's eyes and took on the appearance of a beautiful woman. She was perfect in every imaginable way. Her hair was deep red, long and flowing. It magically floated just off her shoulders. Her eyes were dark, and she didn't smile. Her lips were luscious and red.

She was tall, sensuous, and completely naked. A tattoo of a snake adorned her body wrapping itself from her right thigh, across her stomach and left breast, over her left shoulder onto her back, and over her right shoulder. The tattoo depicted the very same snake she transformed from. She was surrounded with an alluring aura G had never experienced. It attracted every fiber of his being.

"Would you like to touch me *now*?"

G sensed danger, yet his desire to engage grew stronger. He tried to break the spell she seemed to have on him. Each attempt to gain control over his mind and attraction was met with futility. His senses were fully enveloped and captivated by the woman.

"Where does this path take me? And may I please pass by?" said G in an audible attempt to dissuade her and to gain passage.

"You may do so as soon as you touch me," responded the woman. "Or…would you prefer to *kiss* me instead?"

G stood silent and contemplated his options. He considered jumping back into the nothingness behind him but was unsure of the implications of that option. He looked around her and could see nothing but a continuing path that lay beyond the woman that disappeared into the distance. At the termination point of the distance, he could see a large tree. He took a deep breath and looked squarely into the eyes of the woman. He tried to concentrate but was unable. There was something blocking his thought processes. He became frustrated.

"Stop it!" shouted G.

"Your thoughts, abilities and freedoms will be released once you touch me. And you will be free to pass," said the woman.

G remained silent and stood his ground.

"What do you wish for? Abundance? Prosperity? Health? Clarity? Sex? I can give it *all* to you," said the woman. "I can even give you the one thing you do not yet have," she added.

G remained silent. He knew the one thing he didn't have was Athena. He grew angry.

"All you have to do is show me some affection. Touch me," said the woman as she peered deep into G's eyes.

G tried to mentally justify the risk. He continued to struggle. There was something just as alluring with the woman's voice that dangerously drew him in. He dropped to both knees and stared directly downward. He took another deep breath and looked up. He saw a dark, ominous, gray ceiling of unending stillness. Somehow, he summoned every ounce of courage and ability he had. Only one option came to mind.

"*Angel!*" cried G.

Angel dutifully appeared and was positioned on the other side of the woman. She seemed different here. It was as if she were surrounded by her own unique aura of protection. It appeared to provide a source of strength for her. She appeared to be floating a few inches above the boardwalk and was dressed in a deep blue flowing wrap befitting a spiritual warrior. She smiled at him without breaking her gaze.

G rose to his feet and looked into her eyes for answers. He tried communicating with her in every way but he was unable. He gave her a look that pleaded for her direction. She narrowed her eyes and slowly lifted her right arm and pointed in the direction behind him. Looking back over his shoulder, he saw a door, partially opened. Without rationalizing or hesitating, he burst through the door and fell into the dark abyss that lay beyond the threshold. His mind went blank as he fell into nothingness once again.

18

Mark had a renewed sense of optimism after he found the igniter. He decided to search the room for something he could actually ignite that would provide a steady source of light.

The spark gave off an immediate and intense burst of light. Mark would have to decipher his surroundings in the split-second assistance it provided. The light was so intense, Mark could see spots and images burned into his retinas well after the spark had surrendered to the darkness. It wasn't comfortable, but it was all he had. He extended his arms full length and shielded the most intense part of the spark with one hand while holding the igniter in his other. He struck the igniter again. The method helped. He could see slightly better without the intense burn-in.

He activated the igniter over the table.

Strike one—a weak spark. He remembered seeing the outline of bottles and test tubes scattered about the table. He leaned closer to the table and used his sense of smell to determine any presence of gas.

Nothing.

Strike two—good spark. A good amount of light was cast over the table. Chemistry ensemble confirmed. There should be something there to help him. One more try. This time he would zero in on something useful.

Strike three–good spark. There, in the right hand corner of the table, was a Bunsen burner bottle. He reached for it and nearly knocked it off the table before getting a firm grip on it.

"Whew, that was close."

He replayed the images of the tabletop contents in his mind. He remembered something toward the middle of the table that would be useful.

One more strike oughta do it, he thought.

Strike four—shitty spark. Not worth a damn.

Strike five—bingo. Good spark and just enough light to reveal a bottle cap with a wick inserted through it.

"Yes! Now all I need is a fuel source," said Mark aloud.

Breathing a sigh of relief and feeling some sense of progress, Mark stood still, igniter and Bunsen burner ensemble in his hands. He focused on the senses that would lead him in the right direction from this point.

I need water, and I need a fuel source, he thought.

Saying a prayer, Mark asked for guidance.

"It's just *You* and me down here, God. Show me the way."

The crane slowly lowered Russ into the fragmented cavern. He was careful to look in all directions on his way to the floor of the site. Russ listened carefully to the boom operator lowering him into the dark shaft.

"Passing ten feet…twenty…twenty-five. How ya doin', Russ?"

"Doing ok. This place is a mess," responded Russ, scanning his high-powered light in all directions.

He could hear the creaking noise of stress on the thick cable attached to the bucket. Pointing his light downward from time to time to check the clearance below, he couldn't yet see the bottom. He was completely enveloped in darkness, aside from the strong beam of his light.

"Thirty-five feet. Slowing for the last five to ten feet," called the crane operator.

Russ pointed the light downward once again. *Finally,* he thought.

"I have the bottom in sight," said Russ, as he called out the final few feet.

"Five…four…three…two…one," he said, inching closer to his destination.

"I've arrived. Climbing out now," said Russ, maneuvering himself out of the basket and onto the floor of the epicenter of the blast.

Pointing his hi-intensity beam in all directions, Russ could see the results of a horrible blast that left twisted metal and broken concrete in a chaotic disarray of horror. He called out to see if anyone could hear him.

"Hello," he shouted. "Can anyone hear me?"

He thought about the damage the percussion would've caused to any human eardrum and decided to step into the wreckage as far as he safely could.

"Stepping forward to conduct initial recon," said Russ, reporting his progress over the radio.

Russ strained to see past the suspended dust that still hovered after the blast. Turning to check his distance from the basket, he could determine that he was about twenty yards into the scene. He scanned his beam across the basket and awakened two red reflectors attached to the side.

Hmm, didn't know those were there, he thought. *Glad there're people who think of the details.*

Russ stopped to listen to his surroundings. He could hear the faint sound of the motor of the crane on the surface. He called out once again, hoping to hear some kind of response.

"Hello! Can anybody hear me?"

Determined to find something of value, he forged ahead then stopped suddenly when he heard the sound of debris falling to his right. He quickly turned his light toward the area and saw some small pieces of concrete falling. More dust rose and obscured his flashlight beam. He knew he was taking a risk just being there. But he had to determine if anyone was alive. He lowered himself to get under a fallen beam and checked his footing to ensure he was on safe ground. He scanned his light back to the basket. The only thing that revealed his origin was the two red reflectors. He was about forty yards into the site.

"Comm check. How do you hear me, Russ?" came the radio check from above.

"Loud and clear," answered Russ, grunting slightly in an attempt to maneuver through the debris.

Stepping very carefully around the twisted metal and broken concrete, he came upon what appeared to be a segregated room. Surprisingly, most of the glass surrounding the room was still somewhat intact but severely stressed and cracked. He determined it to be bullet proof or blast resistant. The door to the room was open and off of one hinge. He scanned the light inside. First high…nothing. Then low…his first fatality discovery. He moved close to the body, felt for a pulse and determined him to be dead. He searched for identification, found his wallet, and pulled his driver's license. It was Mike Libby, the young explosives expert.

"First victim discovered. A Mr. Mike Libby," reported Russ to the team.

Russ checked the room once again for any clues he could use to find anyone else. Scanning the floor, he noticed what appeared to be drag marks along the floor. He followed the marks with the beam of his light. He traversed an obstacle course that only a determined person would take to find a way out. The marks eventually led him to a dead end where debris must have fallen on top of a victim with the second breach.

Turning to find the red reflectors of the basket, he was surprised to see that the path had distracted him long enough to become disoriented for a moment. Retracing his steps, he found his way once again and made his way back slowly toward the basket. The amount of dust and suspended debris frustrated Russ, but he kept going.

He stopped about thirty yards from the basket on his way back. His light picked up the glint of something shiny in a debris pile. He carefully made his way toward the object. He stopped suddenly when he felt the floor give way slightly about six feet from the object. He knelt down and wiped his visor to get a better look at it. He inched forward. He heard the floor creak under the weight of his body. He reached out and quickly grabbed the item and slowly moved back along the floor on his knees until he determined it was safe enough to stand and return to the safety of his basket. He clenched the item in his hands and returned to the basket, where he called for the crane operator to lift him out of the dark, crypt-like cavern.

"Russ Noble, all secure. Ready for liftoff," reported Russ to the crane operator.

Russ felt a sense of relief to feel the basket break away from the floor of the site. He slid to the bottom of the basket and opened his hand to reveal a shiny security badge, number 3557990. It was enough to help determine who it had been issued to. A badge-wearer himself, he felt a sincere sadness for whoever last wore the emblem of authority. Looking up, Russ could see the lights of the crews above him drawing closer.

"He's not responding," said the emergency medical technician.

Athena looked up at Todd with tears in her eyes.

"Do something, Todd. Don't let him die."

The emergency techs lifted G's limp body onto the gurney, placed an oxygen mask onto his face, and began pumping his chest feverishly. Todd looked at Athena with concern written all over his face. They followed the emergency med techs out of the club.

"Yo, A...stay on your toes. This is just the kind of shit someone would pull to get to him."

Athena climbed into the back of the ambulance with G and a med tech while Todd summoned the limo driver to follow. Todd quickly sent a text to Mario.

G is down. Headed to Mt. Sinai hosp. I'm in the limo following the ambulance.

Todd slid into the back of the limo and shouted at the driver.

"Follow that ambulance."

Todd suddenly realized he had company in the back of the limo. A rather big man. The kind of man who shops at the big and tall stores, only slightly fatter. He was wearing a black suit and did a good job of blending in with the black leather seats and the dark interior of the limo.

"Who the fuck are you?" demanded Todd.

"We told you not to fuck with us," said the man.

The driver's window slid open. "Where to, sir?"

"I said follow the goddamned ambulance!" shouted Todd.

The driver looked at the man seated near Todd for instructions. The man nodded, and the driver closed the window and pressed the accelerator.

"What the *fuck* is goin' on here?" shouted Todd.

"Calm down, Mr. Jordan."

All Todd could think of was the safety of his friends. The limo sped ahead to catch up with the ambulance. His mind raced as he tried to figure out a way to handle the piece of shit who had pirated his limo. What happened to his driver? Was he all right?

"Smoke?"

"No."

"Mind if *I* do?"

"Of course I mind, you *fuck*."

The man simply raised his eyebrows and reached into his coat pocket for his lighter. Todd could see the outline of a holster strapped to the inside of the man's rib cage so he knew he was armed. It presented an entirely different set of options if Todd were to consider overtaking him by force. Still, his mind stirred with ideas and emotion.

Todd still had his phone in his hand and did his best to conceal it. He remembered his last phone call was to Mario, so he did his best to press "dial" on the phone in an effort to create an open line with Mario. The best he could hope for was that Mario would be smart enough to listen and figure out the situation.

"Speak to me, TJ," said Mario when he picked up the call.

"So I see you're armed, you prick. What are you gonna do, shoot me?"

"We're right behind an ambulance, so you should have no problem getting medical attention," said the man, in a poor attempt to be funny.

The limo slowed.

"Why are we slowing?" shouted the man to the driver.

"The ambulance is slowing, sir."

The limo came to a sudden complete stop.

"Now what?" asked the man impatiently.

Gunfire erupted outside the vehicle. Muzzle flashes illuminated the driver's section of the vehicle. Todd reacted with lightning speed and lunged forward as soon as he saw the flashes. He put his forearm into the throat of the man and his knee into his groin. The man was stunned by Todd's speed and resolve. Todd leaned in harder until the man passed out; a trail of smoke escaped his lungs from the last drag on his cigarette. Todd took the man's weapon and aimed it at the door in anticipation of another assault from whoever just greased the driver.

His mind raced while he waited. He could feel his heart pounding. Determination chiseled into his face, he held the aim of the gun on the passenger door.

Todd's phone lit up.

"You OK?" It was Mario.

"Yeah, but I'm stuck inside the limo and unsure of who's waiting for me outside."

"Relax, we're the ones outside. Come out slowly."

Todd opened the door of the limo, raising his hands, one of which still had the small-caliber handgun in it.

"Drop the weapon."

"I will when I know my ass is safe," said Todd.

"It's me, Mario. Drop the weapon, TJ."

Todd threw the weapon on the asphalt. Two armed men rushed in to pick him up and quickly carried him to a dark SUV off to the right side of the road. Todd looked around to see another SUV pulled in front of the limo, blocking it in.

A young African American man approached Todd, extended his hand, and smiled. There was something about Mario that made Todd feel safe. A politician of sorts, but nonetheless a man in control. "I'm Mario. Come with me. I'll get you to the hospital."

"What about this mess?" questioned Todd.

"It'll all disappear, bro. My guys are on it, and there'll be no trace of anything. C'mon, we gotta move quickly."

Todd nodded and climbed into the back of the SUV with Mario. As they drove past the limo, Todd heard a single gunshot and looked at Mario.

"It's OK, dawg, they're just making sure there's no trace or chance of anyone coming back to life and haunting us," said Mario stoically.

"He's in de-fib," shouted the emergency med tech tending to G. "Hang on buddy."

"We're arriving now," said the ambulance driver.

Tears streamed down Athena's face as she struggled with the fact that G was fading fast.

19

The light of the morning dawn had yet to reveal itself when Hakim made his way through the hotel lobby toward an awaiting airport limo. The lobby was devoid of life, other than the desk clerk working the last of the graveyard shift. Hakim walked past the counter, unnoticed and unacknowledged. The electronic doors responded on cue to his approach. He could feel the damp London air against his face. The driver offered a tired greeting and grabbed Hakim's bag and placed it into the trunk. Hakim took a casual cautious look around, as he always did, and entered the limo.

Arriving to an awakening airport, Hakim retrieved his bag, tipped the driver, stepped onto the sidewalk leading into the airport, and made his way toward the security checkpoint.

Hakim checked his watch: 5:11 a.m. His flight was scheduled to depart at 6:50 a.m. He had plenty of time.

"Good morning, sir. Headed to JFK today?" asked the gate agent.

"That's correct."

"Aisle or window, sir?"

"Aisle, please."

"Very well. Seat twenty-two B, gate twenty-three. Have a good flight."

Hakim couldn't help but feel something was amiss with the gate agent. It wasn't anything overt. More of a feeling, actually. Hakim had a sense for these things. He became acutely more aware of his surroundings as he made his way toward security. Was he being watched? His eyes darted randomly throughout the area. After all, things are not always what they seem.

"Please place all jackets and shoes on the conveyor belt and remove your laptop computers from the cases," announced the security agent somewhere toward the front of a small line formed at the checkpoint.

"Please have your boarding pass and passports available for the agent as you approach the checkpoint," came yet another announcement.

Hakim put on his best act, hobbled toward the security agent and presented his papers and boarding pass. The agent examined Hakim's passport and looked up to verify the photo against the holder.

"Any liquids, creams, or gels with you in your carry-on bags today, sir?"

"No."

"Enjoy your flight, sir," said the security agent, clearing the way for Hakim's safe passage to the interior of the airport.

Safely past the most vulnerable point in his departure phase, Hakim casually gathered his belongings and ventured into the airport duty-free mall, where employees were busy opening storefronts and people were beginning to show for the day's flights. Most people were gathered outside small cafés, drinking hot tea or coffee.

Hakim glanced at his watch. Sort of an involuntary gesture, actually. It was 5:28 a.m. Plenty of time.

He scanned his surroundings to take stock of those around him while slowly moving toward his departure gate.

Security guard to the left. No threat. Not very alert. Passengers were routinely making their way to one point or another, most oblivious to their surroundings.

Hakim stopped for coffee and a newspaper, glanced at his watch, and paid the cashier in euro's. He casually looked around to see if he could pick up on anything suspicious. Nothing.

He found his gate and selected a seat in the waiting area with a perspective view. He glanced at his watch: 5:59 a.m. Plenty of time.

He opened the newspaper and began to pretend to read it. He peered over his paper to take stock of his surroundings once again and noticed a middle-aged man, medium build, wearing a dark suit. He could pick out an air marshal from any lineup or situation. Most were too proud or cocky to blend in appropriately. Hakim would keep an eye on him, but he wasn't overly concerned.

Hakim checked his watch: 6:04 a.m. The gate agent made her first announcement.

Dream Operative

"Those passengers awaiting boarding of Flight fifty-twenty-three non-stop service to New York's JFK Airport, please be advised that we will begin boarding approximately thirty minutes before scheduled departure."

Hakim checked his watch: 6:11 a.m. He was hopeful he would experience an on-time departure. He was anxious. He had good reason to be. At precisely 7:00 a.m. local time, his martyr would follow-through with instructions to sacrifice himself for the good of the Jihad in a very public, newsworthy place.

"Ladies and gentlemen, we will begin by boarding our first class passengers and those with small children or those requiring extra time to board. Once again, all first class passengers and those requiring extra time may board now through gate twenty-three," announced the gate agent.

Hakim glanced at his watch: 6:20 a.m. Boarding right on time.

It was a full flight. Hakim made his way to his seat. The last passengers were getting settled. One man was having difficulty getting his carry-on bag to fit in the overhead compartment. *There's always one.*

Hakim glanced at his watch. It was 6:42 a.m. His heart quickened as he hoped for an on-time departure. Any disruption on the scale he had planned would surely grind the city to a halt. That would no doubt include airport operations as well.

The boarding doors were closed when Hakim felt a nudge on the aircraft, indicating it was being pushed away from the gate by an airport vehicle. Hakim glanced at his watch: 6:51a.m. The engines began to whine as the aircraft powered forward to taxi to the runway.

"Uh, ladies and gentlemen, this is the captain. Welcome aboard. We're number two for departure today, so we should get off right on time for our seven-hour journey to JFK. Sit back and relax, and please let us know if you need anything at all. Flight attendants, prepare the cabin for departure."

Hakim watched through the tiny window as other aircraft roared down the runway. He could hear the engines of the aircraft power up as it taxied onto the runway. Hakim looked at his watch: 6:58 a.m. He closed his eyes and said a silent prayer as he anticipated the next two minutes.

The engines revved as the captain pushed the throttles forward and released the brakes. Hakim felt a surge of power against his body as the jumbo jet lurched forward. His eyes still closed, Hakim could feel the earth release its grip on the giant jet as it leapt into the air. He opened his eyes to glance at his watch. It was 7:00 a.m. Perfect timing.

The jumbo jet took an easy left turn to find its course and continued its aggressive climb. Hakim mentally visualized the destruction and chaos ensuing upon the inhabitants of London. It would be several hours before he was to know the details and extent of the damages. Hakim clutched his prayer beads and slid off into a light sleep.

A nondescript man entered the subway station outside the Apollo Victoria Theatre district, determined to board the Heathrow Express.

He wore blue jeans, tennis shoes, and a baggy blue sweatshirt. Strapped to his waist were enough explosives to kill anyone within forty feet — and, detonated inside a railcar, it was enough to derail an entire train. The explosives were enough to make a global statement that the Jihad was still alive and well in Europe.

The morning rush hour had begun its full flex, and the terminal was crowded with people busily moving about. The man slipped through a light security presence without a glance from anyone responsible for passenger safety.

The young man boarded the second car of a nine-car train. He positioned himself in a seat that was located above a forward axle of the railcar, as specifically instructed by the engineer who designed the explosive device. He glanced at his watch: 6:51 a.m. He sat in a seat and looked at the floor beneath his feet. He thought about his wife and family. Emotion welled within. He thought about Hakim and his words. Doubt welled within. He was careful not to make eye contact with anyone. Determination replaced the doubt.

The train filled to near capacity. The doors closed. He looked at his watch: 6:52 a.m. The train began to move forward. His heart raced. Eight minutes to live.

The train reached its first stop. Time: 6:55 a.m. More people crowded the railcar. He stood and grabbed an overhead railing with one arm extended over his head. The car doors slid shut, and the train pulled out of the station. It quickly picked up speed as it raced toward Heathrow.

He glanced to his left long enough to see a young lady make eye contact and offer a smile he didn't return. The car gently rocked back and forth on the rail as the air streamed around the bullet-like shape of the exterior. It was moving near one-hundred miles per hour — a feature often bragged about in advertising campaigns to allure passengers.

Dream Operative

The man glanced at his watch: 6:59 a.m. He had reached the pinnacle of his calling. He armed the device with a flip of a switch under his baggy sweatshirt. A man beside him placed his hand on his waist in a polite gesture to move past him to a nearby handrail. He felt the explosives wrapped tight against his body and looked at him with shock, curiosity, and fear. The martyr grabbed the man by his necktie, looked deep into his eyes and shouted, "I'm really sorry to have to do this. *Allahu Akbar!*"

The train jumped from the tracks as the explosion ripped the front half of the railcar apart from its axle. A terrible crash ensued, and the sound of scraping metal against concrete reverberated under the streets of London like an earthquake. The trailing cars absorbed the impact like a collapsing accordion.

Those who survived the initial impact of the crash were trapped in twisted metal, caustic air, and darkness. Electrical grids went dead. Traffic signals on the surface above were inoperative. Smoke billowed from nearby stairwells and manhole covers. The entire London transportation grid came to a grinding halt as the city became paralyzed in the grip of terror.

G awoke surrounded by darkness. He was sitting in three inches of water.

"Angel? Are you there, Angel?"

G heard the faint sound of water dripping. He stood quickly and banged his head against a low ceiling.

"Ouch. Dammit."

Crouched low, G felt his way forward and came to a slightly brighter area. It was open and wide. He was able to stand and take in his surroundings. He looked up and saw light penetrating the edges of what seemed to be a cover of some kind. The only issue was that the opening was some twenty feet above him. There were ladder rungs protruding from the wall about six feet above his head.

Just out of reach.

He thought of ways he could reach the ladder but couldn't see any immediate way to get to it. He decided to venture back into the darkness to see if he could find anything useful to help him.

Traveling some thirty yards from the lighted area, he stopped suddenly when he heard something. It sounded like footsteps in the shallow water. G's heart raced. Could it be Angel? Could it be someone he needed to be concerned about? G crouched lower and tried to blend into the darkness. The footsteps stopped. Did they see him? Did they hear him? Seconds passed. G inched forward and came into another dimly-lit opening and froze in his tracks when he saw it—a dark silhouette of a man carrying something in his hand.

"Please don't shoot," said G nervously.

"I don't have a gun," answered the man, just as nervously.

"Who are you, and what are you doing here?" said G.

"I could ask you the same question."

"I don't actually know how I got here, but I think I know a way out," said G.

The man seemed grateful to be talking to someone, like he had been alone awhile. "You know a way out? Which way? Do you have any water?"

"This way," said G, turning to lead the way. "Watch your head. The ceiling gets pretty low."

G led the man to the illuminated area he had found. "Over here. We're gonna have to work together to make this work," said G, as he disappeared from the man's view.

"Wait! Hey, where did you go? What's your name? Are you there?"

Todd met Athena in the emergency room waiting area. She rushed into his arms and held him tight.

"Oh, Todd, tell me he'll make it," cried Athena.

"He'll make it, A...he'll make it. We've come too far for him not to make it," assured Todd.

"We've got a heartbeat," reported a nurse.

"Good. Stabilize him and let's get those nasty drugs out of his system," ordered the attending physician. "I'll go notify his friends."

Todd and Athena were seated, consoling each other quietly, when the doctor walked into the waiting area. They looked at the doctor expectantly.

"You've got a tough friend. He's gonna be a little sick until we flush the drugs from his system, but he's gonna pull through," reported the doctor.

"Oh, thank you so much," said Athena. "When can we see him?"

"It'll be about an hour. My staff is still attending to him, and they've started to pump his stomach. Someone will notify you when he's moved into recovery."

"Thank you again, Doctor," said Athena.

Mark stopped in his tracks when he heard the sound. He thought about striking the igniter but decided instead to remain still and calm.

He thought he heard the sound of human footsteps. He thought about crouching down in a protected position but decided instead to remain still and quiet. He could always strike the igniter if it were an animal. That would surely scare it away. Mark could hear the footsteps once again and braced himself for whatever it was that was approaching him.

"Please don't shoot," came a voice from the dark.

"I don't have a gun," replied Mark rather nervously.

"Who are you and what are you doing here?"

"I could ask you the same question," said Mark.

"I don't actually know how I got here, but I think I know a way out."

Mark's heart raced, becoming encouraged for the first time since the blast. Not only was he actually talking with someone, that someone was helping him.

"You know a way out? Which way? Do you have any *water*?" pleaded Mark.

"This way," came the response as it drifted deeper into the darkness. "Watch your head. The ceiling gets pretty low."

"Wait! Hey, where did you go? What's your name? Are you there?" said Mark, frantically trying to keep up.

Mark kept his head low as instructed and could see the tunnel getting brighter as he made his way forward. He came to an opening that was lit by a partially covered shaft about twenty feet above him. The light appeared to be artificial, like from a lamp or streetlight. He studied the shaft and saw ladder rungs positioned about five or six feet above his head. He looked around for his "friend," who had led him here.

"Hello? Hey! Where did you go? I need your help!"

20

Hartman sat at the base of a tree with his hands tied behind his back. He hung his head in a feeble attempt to get some sleep. His thoughts drifted to his team and the sound of the Casa lifting off safely from the airfield. He was relieved to know his team made it out. It allowed him to focus on himself and his own situation. He was trained to look for opportunity — any opportunity to exploit the situation to gain an edge over his captors. He was beaten and bruised, but he still had his mental faculties. He knew he needed rest if he was to outmaneuver his captors.

Booker removed his rucksack and grabbed a small bundle of parachute chord, checked to make sure he still had his knife, secured the silencer on his sidearm, and tightened his boot laces. He quickly applied dark camouflage paint to his sweating face and hid his rucksack in the jungle canopy. Taking stock of his surroundings, he found a tree nearby that he could climb to give him better situational awareness, or what is commonly referred to as "SA." He found a good high spot and donned his NVGs. He positioned himself to see what he could of the campsite. His night vision goggles cast a green hue that permitted him to clearly make out obstacles at night. He counted five men: two standing on a makeshift perimeter on opposite sides of the camp, two huddled around a small campfire, and one sitting nearest...Hartman!

Hartman rubbed his face on his shoulder to ward off the mosquitoes. He opened his eyes slightly and noticed the man next to him struggling to stay awake. Opportunity was slowly revealing itself. He maneuvered his hands in an attempt to determine the quality of the knot binding his hands. It was pretty secure. He studied the knot binding his feet. He figured he could untie his feet pretty quickly, if his hands were free. His mind calculated the options as he studied his surroundings for anything that would help him break free. He knew enough about the jungle to know he could survive the elements and evade his captors, if he could just find a way out of his current situation. He looked up slightly and conducted a slow count of his captors. Five total that he could count, including the thug sleeping next to him.

Booker removed his NVGs, quietly slid down the tree, and set off on his stomach in a slow crawl toward the camp. He was determined *not* to leave without his teammate and would eliminate anything that had the misfortune of getting in the way of that goal. He would have to employ every ounce of rescue and assault training he had learned. And he had to be patient.

The night had matured, and Booker figured that as long as Hartman wasn't moved, he had some time on his side to be careful and calculating. He could see the warm glow of the campfire through the underbrush. He could feel the adrenaline surge as he inched closer to the campsite. He stopped to listen and allowed his mind to recount the positions of his enemies. He could hear the two men closest to the campfire talking but couldn't hear anyone else. He carefully made his way toward the perimeter guard closest to him. The guard wasn't very alert and had his back toward him. Booker was about three feet away when he removed his knife from its sheath and slowly stood to his feet. The guard never saw it coming. Booker covered the guard's mouth with his left hand and drove his knife into his throat with his right. The guard immediately fell limp into Booker's arms and was carefully placed onto the ground to avoid alerting the others.

With the one perimeter guard out of the way, Booker had a clear path to Hartman. The only problem facing him was how to deal with the chump sitting next to him. He returned to a crawling position and slowly made his way toward the tree where Hartman was positioned. He hoped Hartman wouldn't be startled when he took out the man next to him.

Booker hid in the underbrush behind the tree and heard the two men near the campfire laughing. He stood to his feet and slowly peered around the tree to get a good idea of their position. They hadn't moved. In fact, it appeared they were drinking something from a bottle, and it didn't appear to be water. If it was tequila, that would be an advantage to Booker.

Booker removed his knife from its sheath, wiped the blade with his gloved fingers, crouched down, reached around the tree and with a quick movement, sliced the throat of Hartman's guard. The execution was so swift, Hartman almost missed it…but he didn't. He cracked a hint of a smile, knowing he had friendly company. He raised his head very slightly and looked for a reaction from the two men near the fire.

Too drunk to notice.

Hartman searched for the remaining perimeter guard and couldn't locate him.

"You OK?" whispered Booker.

"Affirmative," answered Hartman in a whisper, looking straight ahead.

"Can you move?"

"Negative. My hands and feet are bound."

"Copy. Slowly maneuver so I can cut your hands loose," instructed Booker.

Hartman did his best *not* to attract the attention of the two men. It took some time, but he was able to get into a position that allowed Booker to free his hands. He felt the snap of the rope binding his hands when Booker sliced through the restraints. His shoulders and wrists were sore from being bound behind his back. He remained still until Booker placed his knife into his hands.

"Here, take this. Give me time to take out that last perimeter guard. I'll signal you when to cut your feet free. Once you do, proceed northwest for three clicks and stay put," said Booker in very specific terms and very quietly.

Hartman raised his head in silent acknowledgment. Booker didn't even wait for the acknowledgment, because he knew his teammate would follow his instructions to the letter.

Booker set out to find the remaining perimeter guard. He was uncertain if there were any more unfriendly in the area, so he had to make sure not to accidentally run into someone he didn't count on. He donned his NVGs and scanned the jungle for his foe. He heard something close by and froze in his tracks. He slowly looked up and to his left and saw a South American jaguar perched on a ledge staring straight at him from about twenty yards away. He heard the low purr of the big cat's growl. His heart pounded fiercely as he slowly crouched to a lying position. The big cat growled once again and took a calculated step toward him. Booker slowly pulled his sidearm from its holster; silencer still attached, and took aim on the cat. It growled again. Attack was inevitable. The cat took another careful step toward Booker and was ready to pounce when Booker heard the shot ring out.

The perimeter guard had also seen the cat and had him in his sights. Booker breathed a sigh of relief followed quickly by an adrenaline rush. He knew the two men back at the campsite would notice the shot and begin to take stock of their surroundings. He had to act quickly. He leapt to his feet, looked up and saw the surprised guard begin to take aim directly at him. His weapon drawn, Booker reacted and fired one bullet into the bridge of the man's nose.

Hartman heard the shots and reacted swiftly by slicing the rope around his boots. He looked up to see the two men scrambling for their weapons. He rolled to his right to get behind the tree and rolled into the body of the man who was guarding him—now dead. He searched for a gun but couldn't find one. He quickly stood to his feet behind the tree, the knife his only weapon. They would be coming after him, for sure. After all, he was their prisoner. He thought of the few defensive options available.

One of the men ran quickly around the left side of the tree. Hartman reacted swiftly by turning and crouching simultaneously, driving the knife into the man's abdomen then pulling back to ensure a good tear. Hartman grabbed the man's weapon and rolled into the jungle anticipating the next man not to be too far behind in pursuit. He was right. Shots were fired. Hartman lay still in the underbrush, his heart beating, silently waiting. He mentally checked to determine if he was hit. No pain. His assailant was as blind as he was in the dark jungle. All he had was his sense of hearing. He listened intently. Another shot rang out. Then silence.

"Yo, Athena, maybe you should make that call to your boss now," suggested Todd.

"You're right, Todd," said Athena. "We're up against our deadline as it is. He's probably waiting on my call."

Athena asked Todd to keep an eye on G's movement within the hospital and made her way outside to place the call to her boss. She found a dark, isolated spot in the parking garage on the street level and connected to the Agency switchboard.

"This is Valerie Daniels, put me through to the operations directorate, my passcode is 8QC71N43," said Athena using her *real* name when she connected with the NSA switchboard operator.

"One moment, ma'am," responded the operator.

"Mr. Keppler, this is operator twenty-two. I have a secure voice call for you."

"Copy, push it through please."

After a series of beeps and clicks, Athena heard Dan pick up the phone.

"This is Delta Kilo Zero One…"

"Sir, Victor Delta forty-three; are we secure?"

"Affirmative, Valerie, been waiting to hear from you. How are things?"

"Remind me to give you the exciting details one day over several beers. Suffice it to say, however, that we have secured the mark and will be ready to transport in about three hours."

"Why three hours, Valerie?"

"We're at the hospital. Like I said, it's been a long night," explained Valerie.

"Copy. You alone other than the mark?"

"Negative, sir. Have company—friendly. Todd Jordan. You may know of him?"

Athena knew that Dan would be running Todd's name through the database as they spoke and she knew Dan would find that Todd's clearance and need-to-know would reassure him that things were in capable hands.

"I'll dispatch a team to pick you up in three hours. Have the mark ready to transport. Call if you need anything else," said Dan.

"Will do, boss."

"Valerie."

"Yes, Dan?"

"Good job."

Dan terminated the call as abruptly as Athena was used to.

Athena pulled the SIM card and battery from her phone to destroy any chance of a trace, then inserted an alternate card and the original battery. She looked around to see if she was being watched and then casually made her way back inside the hospital.

"Any changes, Todd?"

"Negative. You get through?"

Athena responded with a nod and a look. Todd knew the look meant more drama was possible. Taking a deep breath, he let out a long sigh and cocked his head slightly, indicating that he half-expected it not to be an easy night…or by this time, an early morning.

"Are we safe here?" asked Athena.

"It's cool, A. Mario's boys are outside, keepin' an eye on things," said Todd, confidently.

"No they're not, TJ. If they were, I'd have seen them. I pride myself on surveillance, and there wasn't anyone to be found...at least outside where I was located," said Athena with a bit of trepidation in her voice.

"Son of a bitch," responded Todd. "Lemme give Mario a call before we go gettin' all panicked up in here. Meantime, *you* find the doc and *demand* your way to G's side."

Athena nodded and purposefully turned away, determined to find G and not leave his side. She placed her right hand on her leg, checking to make sure her small-caliber pistol was still strapped to her thigh. She hoped she wouldn't need it but was determined to protect G at all costs. The only mission now was to find him, fast.

"Excuse me," said Athena to a floor nurse. "Can you please tell me which room is Mr. Weston's?"

"Sure, but the doctor has ordered that he not...hold on a minute," said the nurse as she scanned the patient roster. "I'm sorry, ma'am. Someone should've notified you. He's been moved to a room already."

"Which room?" said Athena rather abruptly. "When?"

"Fourth floor, E-wing, room four...hey Beth, which room was Mr. Weston transferred to? Oh, here it is—room four-sixty-seven."

Athena turned away quickly, determined to find G and room four-sixty-seven. She burst into the waiting area and shouted for Todd. He was nowhere to be found. She sent a short text to Todd.

G was moved. Don't know where. I'm on the hunt. A

Slight panic set in as she collected herself and put her skills to work. She found a building map on a wall and determined E-wing to be just down the hall, one wing south of her position. She set off on a quick trot, turned into a narrow corridor and saw a wall marker indicating *E-wing*. She came upon an elevator and pushed the slow doors aside as they opened. She pressed "3." Her training had taught her that if anyone was watching the elevator, they would be ready for her on the fourth floor as she exited.

Getting to the third floor seemed like it took forever. She checked her weapon again to ensure she had easy access and allowed the elevator doors to open fully before she cautiously peeked outside the threshold to make sure no one was waiting for her. The halls were empty, given the early morning hour. She stepped into the hallway and made her way down a long corridor of closed offices.

"Three-forty-four, three-forty-five..." she counted the third floor office numbers until she knew she was positioned just below the area of floor G was reportedly taken to. Then she found a stairwell and cautiously entered it. She drew a handgun from her purse. It was the one with a silencer attached. She ascended the stairs slowly until she came to a closed door to the fourth floor. The door had a window that was frosted over. She couldn't make out any movement or hear any sound coming from the other side, so she put her hand on the door handle and pulled it open, placing her foot in the threshold to prop it open enough to take a peek before committing to a full entry. She saw nothing, so she boldly stepped into the corridor and looked down the hall.

"May I help you, ma'am?" came a voice from behind her.

She quickly turned and smartly covered her weapon. She saw a man in a white lab coat approaching her.

"Oh. Hi. I'm looking for a friend of mine, who was transferred up here from the emergency room," explained Athena. "Could you tell me where he's located?"

"Yes. But I can probably help you faster if I have a name?" responded the man with a smile.

"I'm sorry, Mr. Weston...*Joey G Weston?*"

"Why don't you come with me, and I'll help you find him," he offered, motioning for Athena to follow him.

He turned his back and began to walk away from Athena. She tucked her handgun into her purse carefully. Something didn't feel right, so she made sure to keep the gun accessible. This area of the hospital seemed to be unusually vacant. Athena noticed random ceiling tiles missing, as if someone were rewiring or installing some kind of conduit or network cables in this section of the building. She looked up at a hallway mirror and could see two other people nearby who were in the area.

"You guys doing some work here?" asked Athena.

The man leading the way stopped and gave her a curious look. Athena responded by looking up at one of the tiles, which provided a clue as to what she was referring to.

"Oh, yeah, I think they're working on the sprinkler system."

The man led Athena to a room and opened the door for her. "He's in here, ma'am. We're keeping an eye on him but he's doing really well now. I can only allow you to stay for a few minutes."

Athena had no intentions of leaving him.

Jeff knocked on Dan's door, slightly winded from the quick pace he had taken to get there.

"What is it, Jeff?"

"You're gonna want to see this."

"Come in. Whatcha got?"

"This just came off the wire. It's a report of a bombing taking place in the London subway about an hour ago. It's ugly, Dan."

As Jeff was showing the report to Dan, they both looked at the television to see the reports of the bombing coming through.

"Any initial INTEL on this, Jeff?"

"Not much to go on yet, but we're already hearing claims emanating from followers of KAH, or Khalid Abdul-Hakim."

"Anybody have a fix on where Mr. Hakim is *currently* located?"

"Negative. He was last seen in Damascus on the run after he spotted one of our agents. He could be anywhere," said Jeff. "As you know, he's a master at disguises and would blend in easily in Damascus."

"Thanks for the info, Jeff. Keep me posted on any new findings. I'll contact our field office in England for more information. You around all night?"

"Negative. I'm on the road tonight on a short trip to the Big Apple. Gonna meet up with a contact that may be of some help on another case."

"Staying busy as usual, I see," responded Dan.

"You got that right, buddy. Good luck on things and let me know if I can help at all."

"I will. Be safe."

Confusion set in as G tried to come to grips with his latest dream.

Where had his journey taken him? Whom did he encounter—and had he been enough help to the man he saw? Analysis was difficult because of his drug-induced state of mind. The trauma to his body had taken a toll, and he was slipping in and out of consciousness.

G awoke when he felt a light touch on his hand. He looked up to see a woman staring at him. He did not yet fully trust his conscious mind and returned a questioning glance to her. Then she smiled, and G's heart nearly leapt from his chest! It was all starting to come back to him. He caught a fleeting glimpse of that smile in the VIP room at the club...or did he? He struggled to speak and literally willed one word from his heart.

"Athena?" said G with a look that simultaneously painted confusion and joy across his face.

The woman of his dreams, literally, had come to be at his side. She looked different for some reason, but G couldn't determine why or how. All he *knew* was that it was her.

"*Shhh*, you need your rest, G," said Athena softly, tears welling up in her eyes. She had never become so personally involved and now questioned her ability to remain loyal to the Agency. She knew she ran the risk of ruining the relationship that was taking shape between her and G by putting the Agency first. But she knew in her heart that G had the ability to be an asset to the Agency and to his country and that remained the driving factor in her determination to follow through.

"Don't leave me, Athena," said G, drifting off once more, struggling against a tide of sleep that seemed to come in waves.

"I'm not going anywhere, sweetie," said Athena. "No one is gonna make me go anywhere," she added in a determined whisper.

Athena looked around the room. There was a clock on the wall. It was 3:45 a.m. G's IV dripped steadily. Athena's instinct warned her that they would be under surveillance. She carefully slid her phone out of her purse concealed in a tissue and wiped G's face. Pulling the cell phone back into her hands, she typed a quick note to Todd.

Need backup. Room 467. Found G.

21

Hakim awoke to the flight attendants talking about how they were fortunate to be able to depart just before "the bombing" in London. One of the senior flight attendants noticed that Hakim had awakened and stopped to see if he needed anything.

"Hello, sir, I'm Colette. Is there anything I can get for you?"

"Yes, would you have some hot tea?"

"Certainly, would you like a snack as well?"

"No, thank you."

Colette made her way to the galley.

"How's the flight seem to you, Colette?" asked one of the junior flight attendants.

"Fine, considering the shutdown we all just barely avoided. The captain has asked all of us to keep a close eye on the passengers, however, in case anyone gets emotional in any way. Watch for everything," cautioned Colette.

Colette returned with Hakim's tea and placed it on the tray extended before him.

"Here you go, sir. Please let me know if there's anything else I can get for you."

"Thank you once again."

Hakim gently sipped his hot tea and allowed his thoughts to drift. He visualized the destruction that lay at the feet of the British. They would surely get the message to stay away from a support role to the United States. If not, he would mastermind yet another attack and drive the point home. He looked forward to meeting with his network of contacts on US soil to plot an attack that would threaten the American way of life. He visualized his gate at JFK, mentally rehearsed his words for US Customs, and envisioned meeting up with his longtime US contact.

Athena continued to study her surroundings and quietly slipped into the bathroom.

The room was connected to an adjacent room. She tried turning the handle, but it was locked from the other side. Something still didn't feel right.

Where are you, Todd? she wondered.

Athena heard someone in the room, so she flushed the toilet and returned to the room.

"Oh, hello ma'am, I'm Dr. Pierce," explained an attractive woman in her mid-thirties. She wore a lab coat, black mid-height heels, and sheer nylons with a black tint. She had short blonde hair, attractively styled, and wore tiny black pearl earrings.

"So how is he doing, Doctor?" asked Athena, studying the response and personal mannerisms of the young lady.

"Oh, he'll be fine. He needs more rest. We'll probably release him tomorrow. As for you, though…visiting hours are over, and I'm afraid you're gonna have to leave shortly," said the young woman, with a sincere smile.

"I was afraid you were going to say that," said Athena. "Do you think you can do me a favor just this one time and allow me to stay with my friend? I really think we'll all be much happier if I could."

"Well, I'm not really supposed to…but I can check with the senior floor nurse and see if I can convince her. She owes me a favor anyway," she added with a wink.

"That would be so awesome," said Athena, with a convincing smile of her own.

The young lady turned to walk out of the room, seemingly unbothered by the request, when Athena interrupted her stride with another question.

"Doctor?"

"Yes?"

Those are gorgeous earrings. Where can I find a pair?"

The young lady smiled and involuntarily pushed back her hair just enough to reveal the earring and said something about Bloomingdale's but expressed that they were pricey. Then she walked out of the room.

Athena knew they were not in a good situation. When the young lady pushed her hair back, she revealed the cord of an earpiece, common among agents…or worse yet, agents who were not necessarily on the same team as she was. She didn't have time to contemplate who the agents were working for or where they were from. Her only goal was to get G out safely. She grabbed her cell phone and quickly pushed a text to Todd.

Situation HOSTILE! Use extreme caution.

She made several attempts to bring G to consciousness. She needed as much of his faculties as he could muster to get him out of there. She certainly wouldn't be able to carry him.

I need a diversion, Athena thought, trying to formulate her exit plan.

Athena unhooked G's IV and taped a bandage on his hand. The action awakened him once more. He struggled to keep his eyes open, trying hard to focus on Athena. She drew close and looked him in the eyes and whispered to him.

"G, we're in another bad situation. I'm gonna need you to trust me like you've *never* trusted anyone. Can you do that?"

G nodded his head and gave her an intent look of groggy determination.

"Good. How's your strength?"

"Pretty good, I think."

"OK, I want you to try to stand," said Athena, grabbing his arm and leading him to the side of the bed. "Hold on for a second," she added. "Lemme at least put some pants on you."

G allowed Athena to slip on the jeans. Then she helped him stand and zip and button his pants, then slipped on his shoes. While she was crouched, putting on his last shoe, she heard someone come in the room. It was the young doctor.

"Ma'am!" she exclaimed. "What do you think you're doing? You have to leave *right* now."

"We *are* leaving," answered Athena, without turning to look at her.

The young lady pressed her ear, as if she were listening to instructions. Athena turned and watched as she slowly reached behind her lab coat.

"You don't wanna do that!" warned Athena.

G watched the entire ordeal unfold before him. He shook his head as if to shake reality back into being. *I gotta stop these two before they start fighting,* was all he managed to think.

The young lady withdrew a snub-nosed Beretta 9 mm pistol from the back of the waistline of her open lab coat and swung around to take aim at Athena. She was far too slow and had a bullet in her head before she was able to make a full revolution. She fell limp to the floor with a light thud. Athena kept her weapon drawn, quickly moving it from side to side, aiming at potential points of entry for anyone else who decided to join the party.

G sat on the edge of the bed, mouth wide open in shock, as he looked at the body before him, bright red blood now pooling beside it.

"C'mon, G. On your feet!" commanded Athena, grabbing his arm firmly and lifting him with unbelievable strength.

She headed straight for the bathroom, pressed G against the wall, and looked into his eyes once again. "I need you to come around, G. And I need you to listen to me. I can't do this alone. Are you with me?"

G nodded.

Athena heard someone burst into the room they had just left. She also heard the person fall to the floor, apparently slipping on the bloody floor. Athena's mind was moving at lightning speed as she calculated her options. She had to move quickly.

Athena told G to cover his ears and then shot the lock of the other bathroom door followed by a swift kick to force it open. She grabbed G again and led him into the next room. It was empty. No patient, no bed…nothing. She positioned G against a wall and told him to remain still. She crouched next to the open bathroom door, took aim, and waited for their pursuer to appear. It didn't take long before she saw a small-caliber pistol in the grip of tall man who apparently knew little about pursuit. Athena put one bullet into the side of his skull and quickly moved toward the exit door. She cracked it open slowly to take a look outside.

Not detecting any immediate threats, she opened the door and put her hands outside, just beyond the threshold of the door while holding her weapon. She followed by poking her head out and quickly glancing both ways.

All clear.

She grabbed G and cautiously led him to the doorway. She stepped out the door, leading the way for G.

Just before G was fully exposed, she heard a loud command: *"Athena, get down!"*

Athena reacted quickly and instinctively. She shoved G back inside the room and fell to the ground. Two shots were fired. Athena looked up to see an armed man lying on the floor next to her. It was the man in the lab coat who had led her to the area. She looked in the opposite direction and saw her savior—Todd. He was smiling nervously, holding a smoking handgun. He ran up to Athena and extended a hand.

"I got your text," he said, rather nonchalantly, to break the tension.

"Yeah, I gather that now, TJ. Thanks," said Athena, slowly raising herself from the floor. She made her way into the room to attend to G, who was now crouched in a fetal position next to the body in the room.

"What the *fuck* is going on?" demanded G. He looked at Athena for the first time as if she were a stranger.

"And who *are* you?"

"It's me, G—Athena," she said compassionately. She slowly knelt by his side and removed her wig.

"You're not the Athena I know," he said, with disappointment and contempt.

The comment seared her heart, but she took it in stride, hoping he would see it differently in time. She turned to Todd and questioned his exit strategy. She was a professional first; and her profession demanded that she get her team out alive. All of them.

"Are there more we need to be concerned about, TJ?"

Todd hit a button on his cell phone.

"Yo, Mario, we're headed out, bro. East stairwell."

"East stairwell is clear," reported Mario.

"This way, folks," said Todd. "Let's go G," he added, helping Athena lift him to his feet.

"Take a look at this Ox," said Ronaldo, pointing to the fuel gauges. "I figure we got twenty minutes remaining at best."

Ox contemplated their options and checked the flight management system to determine their approximate position of fuel exhaustion. He decided to let Pat know so he could alert the passengers.

"Pat, come up front when you get a chance, please."

Pat unbuckled and made his way forward to the cockpit.

"Whatcha got, Ox?"

Ox explained their fuel situation and told Pat to get the passengers ready for a hard landing, considering the rugged terrain they were likely to encounter. He informed him that they would be well across the border but also well short of any kind of civilization.

"I'll make sure the team is ready, Ox. They're trained for survival, so as long as we get 'em safely on the ground, then we're in good hands," said Pat, placing his hand on Ox's shoulder in a reassuring gesture.

When Pat returned to the aft section, the team looked at him expectantly.

"What's the latest?" asked Perry.

Pat summoned the team's attention.

"Listen up! We have a low fuel situation. We're not gonna make it all the way to our nearest destination. We're searching for a place to set down on the best surface we can find. Only problem is, it's still dark, and even with NVGs, it'll be difficult to determine. So Ox has asked me to get you guys prepared for a rough landing. It could be really rough, if we don't get lucky. Our priority is getting on the ground safely. Then our priority is to take care of our injured. You guys are better trained than I ever hope to be, so I don't expect any questions from you. But I do expect to be a part of your team, so if you have a role for me, you're gonna have to tell me what you need." Pat took a breath, found his seat, and cinched his lap belt a little tighter than he typically would have otherwise.

Pat watched the team stow their gear and strap things down, chatting quietly with each other. They tended to their injured teammate and made sure he was secured tightly in his seat. Once everyone was settled, things got quiet. Except for the engine noise, no one spoke. Nothing more needed to be said.

Pat made another attempt to contact "Mother." No response. They were on their own...in the dark, somewhere north of the Colombian border, looking for safety.

"See anything promising through those lenses, Sport?" Ox asked Ronaldo.

"Just some pretty scary terrain—nothing that even resembles a flat surface. Damn, is there anything besides jungle down there?"

"Yeah, more jungle...and rocks," said Ox.

"What time is sunrise?" asked Ronaldo.

"Five-ten local time. About an hour after we're supposed to run out of fuel. We're gonna have to do this in the dark, kid," said Ox in a solemn tone. "Pat, any luck getting ahold of Mother?" he asked.

"Negative, Ox. Been trying. No contact."

Dream Operative

Ox looked at Ronaldo, who was doing everything he could to squeeze every last mile out of the fuel they had remaining. He grabbed a topographical chart and stuffed it into his shirt. He checked their altitude and looked outside the aircraft. It was pretty dark, with the exception of a crescent moon barely lighting the leading edges of the wings. Time seemed to barely move as he searched, waited, and hoped for a miracle.

"I think I may have something, Ox!" exclaimed Ronaldo, putting the plane in a fifteen-degree right bank followed by a slight drop in altitude. "I gotta check it though. I know I'm using valuable fuel, but if I'm right, we'll make it to some kind of flat surface."

Ox peered out the window attempting to spot what Ronaldo was seeing, but there was nothing but darkness. And then he noticed a reflection on the surface. As they got closer, Ox was able to make it out. The reflection he saw was the moon reflection off of water!

"Yo, kid, that's water!" exclaimed Ox.

"Yeah, I just figured that out. Seems to be a lake. No, wait…it's a river. Where does that put us on the map?" asked Ronaldo.

Ox quickly spread the chart and tried to pinpoint their location.

"Could be about anywhere along this route south of Yaviza," said Ox. "If our calculations are correct, we're right about here—"

Ox's comment was interrupted by the left engine failing and shutting down. Ronaldo diverted all fuel flow to the right engine, their only hope to land safely.

"So you haven't asked me what my plan is, Ox," said Ronaldo, maneuvering the one-engine craft over the lake.

"Well, kid, I look at it this way…you're either gonna set this thing down in the water, or you've got a better idea. Either way, we're not gonna be eatin' trees or a mountain. So I'm good," Ox said sarcastically while, he examined the chart.

"I'll tell you anyway, Ox," said Ronaldo as he made a low pass, looking out the side window to his right. "I saw a flat area we passed that appears to be just long enough to set this baby down."

"I hope you calculated the extra weight we have on board that'll increase our stopping distance."

"If we get in a jam, we can always have you jump out early," said Ronaldo, in an attempt to overcome the stress. He banked the aircraft hard left and brought it lower. Ox looked out the window on his side and could see the flat area Ronaldo had spoken of and was encouraged.

"Good eye, kid! Looks like a great place to set her down. Hey, Pat…you gents sit tight. We're landing."

Ox grabbed the yoke and assisted Ronaldo with the final and most critical phase of flight in a most critical situation. They leveled the aircraft and lowered the landing gear.

The right engine suddenly went silent. No more power.

The two could see mountainous terrain rise above the aircraft on both sides as they brought the rugged craft in for landing on a riverside gravel bed. Ox lowered the flaps as soon as the craft was positioned over the short landing zone. He and Ronaldo hit the brakes as they bounced hard along the gravel bed. The plane shook violently, gravel hitting the underside of the fuselage, while the two wrestled with the landing. They were ultimately able to execute a near-perfect landing without the assistance of power. Ox smelled smoke from the hot brakes, so he flipped a switch that activated the rear hatch and ordered the passengers to exit the plane in a precautionary move. Ronaldo unbuckled his seat harness and followed with a fire extinguisher in hand.

22

Jay and his cameraman waited patiently in silence while Tom studied the blueprints they brought to him. They had hoped they were able to provide something of value that could be used to help with the recovery effort. Tom eventually broke the silence.

"I'll need a copy of these drawings."

"Certainly. You can have those," said Jay, shrugging his shoulders.

"OK, so I assume you want something from *me* now?" asked Tom expectantly. "What can I do for you?"

Jay seized the opportunity, as any reporter worth his salt would do. "Can you give us an exclusive on the recovery operation? Do you have any comment or knowledge of whether this incident is related to the bombing in London?" Jay had plenty more questions, but he let up so he could gauge the amount and type of information Tom was willing to share.

"Look, you provided a piece of the puzzle we didn't know existed in the form of those drawings, so, tell you what I'll do. I'll provide information to you a full ten minutes before I provide it to anyone else. As for any connection to the London bombing, I have no knowledge of that. The latest on the recovery effort is that we put a man in the hole, and he didn't find anyone alive. This was a very big explosion, and people died. We don't have details yet on names, numbers, or anyone connected to the explosives."

"Do you personally believe the explosives were originally placed by terrorists embedded within the borders of the United States?"

Tom stood silent, quietly contemplating an answer. "Off the record — yes. But you'll never get me to admit that anywhere until we have clear proof. It's what the victims were actually trying determine when things went south. Now, I gotta ask you guys to return to the press area. I have a job to do."

"Can I report anything on the blueprints?" asked Jay rhetorically. He had every intention of reporting it but wanted to get Tom's reaction.

"At this point, it's conjecture and speculation, but you're welcome to report it. It'll be interesting to see how you spin it," said Tom with a slight smile.

Jay left the trailer with his cameraman, John. They went straight to their vehicle to set up for a news alert broadcast.

"So what do you make of that whole exchange?" asked John. "And why did you give him the drawings?"

Jay smiled. "No worries, brother. You don't think I'm stupid enough to give him *all* of the drawings, do you?" said Jay, pulling two pages from his coat pocket.

The two men laughed.

"I have a feeling Mr. Herring will be calling us when he discovers there are missing pieces," added Jay. "Let's get a jump on the others and get the latest out to the network."

Mario met Athena, Todd, and G in the east stairwell. He was accompanied by two large men who were heavily armed.

G's mind was euphoric as he tried to come to grips with the enormity of what he was wrapped up in. He still couldn't figure out why *he* seemed to be the focus of so many people. Mario led him and the others to a vehicle outside the hospital—the same SUV Todd had arrived in earlier. Todd helped him into the back seat and strapped him in. He took a cursory look around to make sure there were no stragglers coming after them and slammed the door shut. Athena entered the vehicle from the other side and sat next to G.

"You guys need a safe place for the remainder of the morning?" asked Mario.

"Negative, dawg, drive this beast on up to JFK. We gotta get Athena and G on a charter to DC," said Todd.

"What about your plane, TJ?" asked Athena.

"It's in for maintenance, A. Won't be ready in time for a quick departure."

Athena pressed a button on her cell phone. G could hear her talking quietly, but he could clearly make out most of what she was saying. She didn't appear to be hiding much at this point. She was talking with someone she clearly respected. G was struck by the irony of it all as he thought back to how he and Athena had first met. Was it all planned from the beginning? Was he a mere pawn in some government scheme? If so, he was ready to get off the ride.

"Sir, we had to leave the hospital sooner than we planned. We're on our way to JFK. Request a charter or a quick way to leave town. And we'll need a cleaner to go in and secure the hospital," explained Athena.

"Copy all. How many KIAs? How messy is it?"

"Three KIAs, sir. Three bullet holes and blood," said Athena, providing an exact account of her actions.

"Understand. No problem. There are no secure charters available to you on this short notice. I'll have two first-class tickets waiting for you on Delta's first flight out to Reagan National," explained Dan. "You'll have to go through the same security screening process as everyone else, so you know what that means."

"Yeah…no weapons," said Athena, realizing how vulnerable they would be.

"Ladies and gentlemen, in preparation for landing at JFK, we'll be making one more trip through the cabin to collect any items you may have to dispose of."

Colette made the announcement as Hakim's flight made its way toward the airport. It was a long journey, but he was excited to be returning to America. As Colette approached his seat, she stopped to check on him.

"Here are some customs forms for you, sir. Is this your first trip to America?"

"Yes," answered Hakim with a smile.

"Oh, great! Business or pleasure?"

"Business. I am to lecture on psychology and criminal behavior to university," said Hakim to stem further questions.

"Very nice. Should you require any assistance whatsoever on filling out the forms, please let one of us know. Oh, and if you could make certain your seatbelt is fastened, that would be appreciated as well."

Hakim lifted the shade on the window and could make out the contour of land below him. After an overwater journey, the sight of land was reassuring. He could feel the forces of the aircraft's approach maneuvers acting on his body as he buckled in for landing.

Athena hung up the phone and handed her weapon to Todd. Todd knew the rules of engagement. He also knew the risks of being without a weapon.

"How are you feeling, G?" asked Athena.

"Fine."

"Yo, dawg, there's water in the cooler back there. Make sure you grab one and keep drinkin'. You gotta stay hydrated, or you won't make it very far," said Mario.

"He's right, G. Keep drinking water," encouraged Athena.

Todd said little as they sped through the streets. He was lost in thought and busy surveying the streets for unexpected intrusions and was prepared to eliminate anything that impeded their journey to the airport. It had been a long night, and he was ready to put the excitement behind him.

"OK, folks, we're almost there. Which airline you takin' this morning, Athena?" asked Mario.

"Delta."

"Cool," said Mario, pulling the SUV to the passenger drop-off point. Todd and Athena exited the vehicle first and met outside G's door. Todd gave her a look and a wink of confidence.

"You did real well today, A."

"Thank you, TJ."

"Check in wit' me when things settle down."

"When you least expect it," Athena said with a slight smile.

Todd rolled his eyes and smiled.

Todd opened the door for G and grabbed his arm to help him out of the truck. He made sure G was able to stand on his own and put one hand on G's shoulder and looked him squarely in the eyes.

"G, I know you got a lot goin' on in that head of yours and still have a ton of questions. We never really had a chance to have that talk I kept promising you. But for now, you gotta *trust* this woman with your life. She's already saved it several times today alone. And give it some time to sink in, because there are a lot of good people lookin' out for you. Remember what I said about what really matters. In the end, *only people matter*."

Dream Operative

G listened to Todd and allowed his words to sink in, even past the reluctance. He knew he may never see his new friend again. Beyond that, he knew little else.

Todd looked at Athena one last time and gave her a nod of assurance. She grabbed G's arm and gently pulled him toward the terminal to find their departure gate. Todd returned to the SUV where Mario was waiting and never looked back.

Athena approached the ticket counter and handed over her and G's driver's licenses. The agent found the reservations without issue.

"Two for Reagan National this morning?" asked the agent.

"That's correct," said Athena, as she took a slow, cursory look around the airport at her surroundings. Nothing seemed out of place or suspicious.

"Any baggage for this trip?"

"No."

"Very well, then, here you go. Gate twenty-two C, to the right, just after airport security screening."

Hakim slowly made his way toward US Customs, taking care to ensure his pace matched that of someone in his disguise. He remembered the instructions he was given by his contact:

Professor, Gateway 35 will be open in 48. Take exit 6 after 0600. XX

Hakim knew he had to look for a customs station with a number 6. He rounded the corner and entered a corridor leading to customs and immigration and eventually entered a large processing room, where there were several people already forming several long lines. The longest lines were occupied by US citizens returning to their homeland. Hakim studied the station numbers and saw gate number 6. It was closed! He found a place to sit for a moment to contemplate his next move. He always had a plan, and this time was no different. He headed straight for a station designated for aircrew only and walked straight up to the customs agent.

"Young man, do you have a station number six?"

"Yes, but it's closed right now, sir. You'll have to get in line at one of the other stations," instructed the officer.

One of the other customs agents overheard the two men talking.

"Hey, Jack, I'm supposed to be on six, but I got diverted. Have him hop into my line, and I'll take care of him," said the agent, giving Hakim a look that gave him some reassurance.

Hakim turned toward the next station and was distracted by a familiar face passing by on the other side of customs and immigration. The two men exchanged glances as if they were drawn by a power bigger than either one of them…as if it were all predestined. Hakim stopped in his tracks and stared at the man as he passed before him, his mind racing to place how he knew him. He typically had an excellent memory, but he couldn't immediately place the man, even while trying to make a connection to the eyes. He never forgot the eyes…until now. He prided himself on not being recognized, so the encounter naturally disturbed him.

"Sir…you're next," shouted a customs agent.

Hakim's rhythm was clearly broken while he continued to struggle with where he had seen the familiar face.

"Sir, are you feeling OK?" asked the agent.

"Why, yes, I'm OK, young man. Why do you ask?"

"Well, aside from the fact that I've asked you more than once about the purpose of your visit, you seem to be preoccupied," said the agent. "Is there someone you need me to call?"

"No, thank you. It's been a long flight, that's all."

"I understand. So what is the purpose of your trip to the United States?"

"Business. I am here to lecture."

Do you have anything to declare?"

"No."

"OK, you're good to go," said the agent, as he stamped Hakim's passport.

"Thank you."

Hakim entered the lobby area where he had seen the man and considered taking the same direction, but he opted instead to find the exit and his awaiting contact.

G followed Athena past airport security adjacent to US Customs and immigration. He was lost in thought for the most part, but as he passed by customs, just beyond the bulletproof windows, G's attention was diverted.

He noticed an older man speaking with a customs agent when their eyes met. G was flooded with a sense of déjà vu as he studied the man. Time slowed as his mind was captivated by the encounter. He couldn't immediately place the man but felt the innate sensation that he was a threat. Chills drove their way through his body while his mind struggled to make sense of it all. He glanced ahead to find Athena walking toward their gate, occasionally glancing over her shoulder to make sure he was following. If he had his full strength, he'd turn around and chase down his curiosity. But he needed Athena.

"You OK, G?" asked Athena, turning to allow G to catch up. "You don't look too good. Let's stop and get some water."

"I'm fine. Just...thought I saw a ghost," said G quietly.

The two of them stopped at an airport kiosk and purchased water.

"Are you hungry, G?"

"No."

"OK here, drink this," said Athena, handing G a cold bottle of water. "Our gate is right over there. Let's find a place to sit."

Athena found two seats in the corner of the waiting area away from most other passengers. She helped G sit down by holding his arm on the way down.

"I'm fine, Athena...or whatever your name is."

Athena could feel the cold sting of G's pain but put up enough of a wall to protect her own emotions. She knew better than to feed or even try to quell the struggles he was dealing with.

"So where is it exactly you're taking me? Will I ever be able to return to my *normal* life?"

"All of your questions will be answered—"

"I know...all of my questions will be answered *in due time*," said G, making air quotes as he mimicked the line he'd heard more times than he cared to. "I've heard the line several times, Athena, so you can spare the rhetoric," said G.

Athena took a risk by extending her hand to gently touch G's chin to direct his focus to her eyes.

"Do you trust me?"

"No," answered G defiantly.

"I expected that answer, actually. And that's OK. But I *need* you to trust me *enough*. I need you to trust me enough to complete this journey. There's a helluva lot going on that you don't know about. I can't bring the answers to you, G. I have to bring *you* to the answers. That's what all this is about. I'm taking *you* to the answers, and you don't have to leave until you're satisfied. I hope that's fair enough for you. I think, in the end, you'll see we have your best interests in mind."

G looked at her stoically. His mind was returning to normal as the drugs wore off and time wore on.

G felt betrayed, but he couldn't figure out why. He didn't know whether to trust the woman he knew or suspect the woman he didn't. He *did* know that he needed answers, and Athena was quite possibly the best escort he could have for the final leg of this journey. And, for the first time, he actually heard her say *"we"* when she said, *"We have your best interests in mind."* He wondered who the "we" was that she referred to.

"I just need answers," said G, in exasperation.

G's mind drifted to thoughts of the man he saw in US Customs. The medication he was on was affecting his ability to focus. He grew more frustrated.

"Ladies and gentlemen, we're ready to begin our boarding process for flight fifteen-ninety nonstop service to Reagan National. Our first-class passengers may board at this time."

Athena grabbed G's hand and led him toward to the boarding door. G looked at Athena with curiosity.

"First class? Why do I *not* feel right about this?"

Athena thought it best not to respond. Instead, she led G to the ticket agent, presented the boarding passes, and casually looked around to see if she could sense any danger. Her instincts typically served her well. She felt no threat and proceeded to board. Once she and G were settled into their seats, they were greeted by a friendly male flight attendant, who welcomed them aboard and offered them something to drink.

"No thanks, I'm good. G? How 'bout you? Want anything to drink?"

"Orange juice, please," said G, adjusting himself into the plush leather seat next to the window.

Athena pulled her phone from her purse and sent a text to her boss.

On board. Secure. Last leg. A

23

The veins in his neck pulsated with the heavy beating of his heart as he strained to listen for evidence on the location of his pursuer. The familiar sounds of the jungle and the creatures that debut nightly filled the air. His attention piqued when he heard a familiar sound—the box whistle call of a whippoorwill. Hartman knew it was his teammate, Booker. He knew the sound, because the whippoorwill wasn't indigenous to the jungles of South America. Besides, Booker pretty much sucked at sending the call. It actually brought a smile to Hartman's face as he emerged from the jungle in a low crawl. Booker heard the movement of the underbrush and took aim while he watched through his NVGs. He could see Hartman emerge and scurry off to the predesignated rally point, exactly as ordered.

Booker arrived to the rally point a few moments later. "I take it you heard my bird call," he said, rather proudly.

"Yeah, I heard it. Knew it was you right away," Hartman replied, laughing.

"What's so funny?"

"Really? You think your bird call is really that good?" Hartman continued to laugh.

"Well, it's good to see you're in good spirits. Here, drink some water. You'll need it," said Booker, handing him his canteen.

"Thanks. Got anything to eat? My hosts weren't exactly hospitable."

Booker handed Hartman a protein bar and unwrapped one for himself.

"We don't have much time till daylight," said Booker. "We need to get as far from here as possible."

"Ready when you are. We headed to an LZ?"

"Not exactly," said Booker, as he examined a handheld GPS. "Something tells me we're gonna have to be here for a while. We need to blend back into the jungle and stay out of sight for a while. You really think my bird call was that bad?"

Hartman shook his head and didn't even bother to ask Booker about the details of their route. Safety was their first concern, and he was trained to follow the orders of his team leader without question. The two plotted their next move by examining the GPS and set out to cover as much ground as possible with what cover of night they had remaining. Booker handed Hartman a sidearm and a full magazine clip.

"Here, take this. I'm hoping we won't need it, but it'll be much easier to travel with than that relic rifle you confiscated. We head north-northwest. Look for a place that'll make a decent daytime hideout," instructed Booker.

Hakim made his way to the passenger reception area, where a well-dressed man was holding a sign that simply read "Celik."

"Good morning, young man. I'm Professor Celik," said Hakim.

The young man lowered his sign and offered to take Hakim's bag.

"No, thank you. Please show me the way to our transportation."

"Right this way, sir."

Hakim was led to the passenger transportation pick-up area outside the front of the airport, where he was taken to a large black Chevy Tahoe SUV with dark windows. The young man opened the rear door for Hakim and closed it behind him. Once he was situated inside, he was greeted by his contact.

"Could you be any more of a complete moron?" exclaimed Hakim. "What's the meaning of picking me up in a government vehicle?"

The agent was seated in the front passenger seat and didn't turn around to greet Hakim. He instead spoke in a very calm but firm tone. "Pleased to meet you as well, professor. Let's get one thing straight from the get-go, shall we? I'm the agent here, and you're a *guest* in my country. If I make a move, it's not because it wasn't calculated. The vehicle is so frigging *obvious*, it would *never* be suspected. We have much more important things to discuss. Now that we have *that* out of the way…" said the agent, slowly turning in his seat and extending his hand. "*As-Salāmu 'Alaykum*, Khalid, I'm Jeff

Hines. I have facilitated your entire journey and will continue to provide you with whatever you require to fulfill your destiny."

Hakim was livid, but the greeting calmed him. If it weren't for the fact that this agent had so much inside access, he would have eliminated him right then. Instead, he remained quiet and contemplated the higher calling of his presence in America. The agent was clearly attempting to establish his dominance, but Hakim knew the game and was much better at it than Mr. Hines. He was also wiser and knew the agent would eventually answer to him.

"*Wa alaykum as-salām,*" responded Hakim, looking the agent in the eyes while purposefully holding onto the handshake grip.

Jeff knew the traditional greeting in Hakim's native tongue would help to ease any tension he created with his dominant first move. He also knew well enough to be sure to establish that dominance, or he would be considered untrustworthy and weak. Jeff looked at the driver and nodded, indicating his permission to press ahead to Hakim's hotel.

The SUV pulled up and around to the side of the Chelsea Hotel, where Hakim was assisted to a discreet entrance. Jeff accompanied him to a narrow corridor leading to an elevator.

"Here is your key. You're on the tenth floor in a room reportedly once occupied by Sid Vicious," said Jeff, with a shit-eating grin and a wink.

Hakim could not care less who previously occupied the room. He needed a good room and a comfortable bed.

"Get some sleep. I'll see you later at the Blue Note," Jeff reminded him.

Hakim simply nodded and entered the elevator, anxious to get to his room, where he could settle in and adjust to the new time zone. Jeff turned and walked away before the doors began to close.

Hakim stood stoically and watched the sliding doors close. The slow ascent of the elevator gave way to an eventual stop at the tenth floor, where he cautiously exited in search of his room.

Hakim scanned his surroundings as he slowly walked the corridor leading to his room. The walls were decorated with original artwork from local artists. No surveillance cameras were evident, but he suspected they were hidden somewhere. He inserted the key to his room and pushed the door open to a quaint one-bedroom suite, adorned with elegant traditional classic styling befitting such a fine hotel. He set his bags down near an old handcarved desk positioned near a window. On the wall above it was an antique mirror, framed with what appeared to be a hand-carved classical frame. Hakim paused to examine his reflection and studied his worn disguise. It was time for the faceless man to don yet another disguise that better suited his purpose and intent. But he would have time for that later.

Hakim allowed his mind to rest as it momentarily slipped into nothingness. He drew a breath and turned to pull back the curtains on a window to his left. He gazed out onto the busy street in front of the hotel and studied the landscape before him. Dusk had given way to the night, and the neon city lights began their evening show. His mind drifted once again as he stared into the city. He casually closed the curtain and thought about getting some rest. He removed his shoes, laid out a small prayer mat, and quietly prayed before retiring for a short power nap.

Lying on top of the perfectly made bed, he examined the ornate ceiling tile. Exhausted by the length of his journey, combined with the difference in time zones, he quickly drifted off to a deep sleep.

Pat waited outside the aircraft for Ox and Ronaldo to join him and the team, now gathered about twenty yards aft of the crippled aircraft.

The sun was making its debut over a mountain ridge just east of their position about a mile away.

Ronaldo emerged from the Casa first, followed closely by Ox, who pulled a cigar from his shirt pocket as he walked out of the open aft hatch.

"OK, ladies, we got you this far; now it's your turn to navigate," said Ox, biting off the tip of his cigar.

"Anyone have comms established yet?" asked Ronaldo.

"We're not receiving a good satellite feed," said Perry.

"We're close to the mountain ridge," said Pat. "It's got to have something to do with this piss-poor reception."

"OK, we're not gonna get very far with an injured teammate," explained Ox. "Besides, I'm not leaving a perfectly good aircraft—"

"What's so perfect about it? It can't fly us outta here now, can it?" quipped Ronaldo.

Ox ignored the insolence. "Suggest two of you set out to higher ground and find some reception to call in some assistance. The rest of us stay put and wait on help," suggested Ox.

Dream Operative

"Sir, KK and I can handle the recon. We'll find a signal and send a relay for assistance," said Perry.

"Son, I gotta hand it to you. I now know why you're in this job. You're eager and just young enough *not* to appreciate the danger in what you do. But that's why God mints brave young Marines like you," said Ox. "Pat, Ronaldo, make sure these men are properly equipped and have the correct info and codes to get the message out."

Pat and Ronaldo helped gather the two special operators together and programmed their handheld devices for them to send encrypted relay messages to the right recipients on US soil. He made sure they had enough water and rations and sent them off to do their job.

"It's times like these that make a man proud to serve with such men," said Ox, casually taking a drag from his cigar while watching the two young men stride off into the distance. "OK, ladies, let's get settled in. It'll be plenty hot here before we know it. We're gonna need the shelter."

Dan checked his secure line and saw Athena's message. He knew they would be arriving in just over an hour. He glanced at his watch then placed a call to a small team of analysts embedded deep within the chasms of the agency.

"They're on their way. I want everything ready. Set up some food in the director's lounge. Keep the menu light. I want him to remain alert," Dan ordered an obscure agent on the other end of the line. He hung up the phone and headed for the NSA locker room to shower and prepare for their newest guest. He had no idea what he was in store for, and he had no idea how gifted G was. Nonetheless, he wanted to be as fresh as possible to fully analyze the situation as well as the man. He knew this could be a complete waste of time…or it could be a phenomenal breakthrough in psychological intelligence. Either way, he was determined to be there to observe it.

A small team of four highly capable, hand-selected agents gathered to complete the preparations for G's arrival as they assembled in an obscure room adjacent to an observation room, complete with one-way glass, cameras, bioanalysis detection, and enough computer power to make any technophile shudder with envy. The team scurried to complete electronic connections and conduct sound and camera checks as technicians positioned microphones and placed final touches to the lounge.

The lounge was atypical. Instead of the customary, cold table and two hard chairs found in an *interrogation room*, Dan had purposely directed that the room be set up as comfortable as possible, to help their guest relax and inspire trust. It would be the best chance they had to conduct an accurate initial analysis.

Dan arrived to find his analysts busy making connections and positioning cameras, testing equipment, and tapping on keyboards to start programs and recording software.

"How's everything coming along?" he asked.

"We're ready," answered one of the analysts.

"The room looks good. Just as I hoped," said Dan, looking through the one-way glass.

"Are you ready, Doctor Middleton?" asked Dan, turning to the clinical staff psychologist.

"I'll know in thirty seconds whether he's for real or not," responded a confident Dr. Middleton.

A well-respected psychologist and highly capable clandestine psychoanalyst, she was recruited to the Agency for her ability to analyze *and* manipulate the human psyche. She could control an interrogation unlike anyone else in the business.

"Good," said Dan. "I want to make sure we don't spook him. He's got to know we have his best interests in mind. We only have one shot at this."

"Certainly...I gather that's the reason you pretty much hired an interior decorator for the interrogation room?" said Dr. Middleton, with a hint of sarcasm.

"Sorry, doctor. No offense. I know you have the situation well in hand. That's why you're on this team. Besides, I wanted to make it less of an interrogation and more of an interview."

"No offense taken. Let's see where the young man takes us, shall we?"

Dan nodded and turned away and returned to his office.

—⁂—

Tom Herring pulled the handheld radio from his hip holster.

"Russ, you up comms? How do you hear me, over?"

"Affirmative Tom. Whatcha got?"

"Yeah, Russ, could you please report to the site office ASAP?"

"On my way."

Tom spread the pages of the blueprints on a large table to puzzle them together as best he could and stepped away to look for some tape to connect the pages. Russ walked in and closed the door behind him and looked at Tom expectantly.

"I don't have shit for supplies around here," said Tom, while rummaging through a drawer. "Whatever…hey, take a look at this, Russ."

Tom smoothed out the blueprints on the drafting table while Russ looked over the drawings.

"See anything here you recognize?"

"Sure. This looks like what used to be the building that collapsed here," responded Russ, pointing a finger at one section of the drawings. "Not sure I recognize this one though," said Russ, studying the drawings more carefully.

"That's why I called you here. And that's why I was looking for tape. Look at what happens when I put the two drawings together, side-by-side."

Russ looked on as Tom carefully lined up the edges of the blueprints.

"Holy shit…is that what I think it is?" asked Russ.

"Not sure," said Tom, shaking his head. "The plans are quite old. Only one way to find out," added Tom, looking at Russ, expecting him to read his mind.

"I'm ready when you are, Tom."

The light coming from the shaft above Mark's head began to change. It was dim at first and turned from an incandescent to a natural light. But he couldn't tell if he was hallucinating. All he knew at the moment was that he had to find a way out. He began to shout.

"Hello! Can anyone hear me? Hello! Anyone?"

Mark knew that if he kept yelling, he would sap what strength he had remaining, so he opted instead to see what he could discover that would help him reach that elusive first rung. He didn't relish the thought of going back into the dark tunnel, but he figured he had little choice. As he turned to head back into the tunnel he saw another passageway he hadn't noticed earlier. It was dimly lit by the ambient light seeping into the shaft from above him. Opting to move forward instead of returning to the darkness of the tunnel, he pulled a rock from his pocket and did his best to scrape an arrow into the moist wall to indicate his movement and stepped into the new passageway to see what he could find.

The passageway grew darker when he paused to look over his shoulder to check to see if his origin was still in sight. Mark took no more than a few blind steps before his feet hit an unexpected obstacle. He stumbled forward and fell onto stairs leading up. Unhurt, he pushed himself up from the stairs and took his first step. His mind began to draw the image of his journey when he remembered the igniter. Pausing, he drew it from his pocket and held it up to cast some light onto his path. He struck the igniter twice and saw what seemed to be a short set of stairs leading to a door.

Great, another door, he thought.

He placed the igniter back into his pocket and carefully ascended the few stairs until he came upon the doorway. He pushed against the door, fully expecting it to be locked, but instead, it opened easily. Encouraged, he stepped through the threshold without thinking to check the path ahead with his igniter. He took two steps through the doorway and fell through an old, dilapidated wooden platform that had rotted over the years.

Mark turned quickly and attempted to grab anything secure, but the momentum of his weight carried him into a single-story fall. His body came to a sudden stop; absorbed only by the broken boards and concrete floor that lay beneath him. His body hit so hard that it caused the alarm on his watch to activate. His breathing was labored, and his body was awkwardly positioned among broken boards and debris at the bottom of the dark space. Laboring to catch his breath, his hope sank when he realized the error he had just made. He focused on the fading sound of the beeping of his watch. His thoughts drifted to Heather and the girls while he fought to retain consciousness. His eyes grew heavy, and his thoughts drifted to prayer for the comfort of spiritual companionship.

God, what have I done? Don't let me die here...

24

The screeching sound of rubber making contact with the pavement was subdued by the standing water that had formed from an earlier rain. The airliner touched down on the wet runway just three minutes behind schedule. G and Athena were among the first to disembark from the MD-88 airliner. They were met in the reception area by two nondescript men who led them to an awaiting vehicle.

"So where are we headed?" asked G.

"Someplace safe."

G didn't respond. Instead, he looked out the dark-tinted windows of the black Chevrolet Tahoe into the dark evening. There wasn't much to see actually, just an occasional source of light from a passing car or nearby street lamp. The driver closed his door and sped off. Athena didn't offer any conversation. They hadn't traveled far when the vehicle came to a stop. The driver and front passenger got out of the vehicle and opened both rear doors almost simultaneously.

"Let's go, G," said Athena, turning to exit the truck.

"Of course," said G, making his way around the back of the vehicle to follow her.

G looked around to see that they had been driven to a private ramp at the airport, where a waiting helicopter was powering up its engines. G didn't bother trying to understand or make sense of things any more. He had resolved that sooner or later he would get the answers he was looking for. Having Athena close by gave him a strange sense of comfort, and for now, that was good enough. The driver of the limo opened the helicopter door and Athena climbed in first. G followed closely behind. The door was shut and latched as soon as his ass hit the seat.

"Strap in, G," said Athena, as she clicked her own seat harness, donned a headset, and plugged it into a console.

G fumbled a moment with the shoulder harness and lap belt but quickly figured things out, completing the task. Athena handed him a pair of headphones. He searched for a wire to plug in to the same console as hers but couldn't find one. He looked at Athena, who simply shook her head no. He would not be privy to the conversation or radio chatter that would obviously happen en route. He could see Athena holding the microphone boom close to her mouth as she spoke, but he couldn't read her lips or make out what she was saying. Soon after she made the gesture, the helicopter lifted from the ground and was airborne into the night sky. The ride was a first for G and was actually kind of cool, considering the circumstances.

The ground grew smaller beneath him. He could make out the enormity of the District of Columbia and the elegant manner in which it was lit. The pilot maneuvered the craft into a right bank to the northeast. He knew enough about the city to understand the direction they were traveling and began to guess their destination. Enough had happened that he began to put the pieces together. He figured he was in the hands of some kind of government Agency but couldn't yet determine which one.

The helicopter began a turning descent twelve minutes after it departed from Reagan National. G saw that they were approaching a rather large corporate-looking building, but they soon passed it by and landed in what appeared to be a parking lot about four-hundred yards away. The helicopter touched down, and G's door was opened immediately by a man wearing khaki cargo pants, a dark short-sleeved polo shirt, and hiking boots. G noticed right away that he was wearing a wired earpiece. The man led him and Athena to yet another government SUV, which was driven to the large building he had just over flown.

Dan watched as the SUV approached the northeast entrance of the NSA Headquarters building. He waited in a small lobby for the two to be escorted to him. He greeted G and Athena with a smile and a hearty handshake; one hand gripping G's right hand and the other hand grasping G's right shoulder in a warm, welcoming gesture.

"Mr. Weston, I'm Dan Keppler. We've heard a lot about you. Nice to finally meet you face to face."

G didn't say anything. He returned the handshake, nodded, glanced at Athena, and then looked around at his surroundings.

"C'mon in, there are some people I want you to meet. Are you hungry?"

"I could eat," said G, nodding.

"Me too," said Athena.

The three walked through a guarded metal detector. Dan went through first, followed by G. Athena walked through and activated the metal detector alarm. G turned to see Athena quickly raise some kind of credential to the guard while she kept walking.

"A fucking agent," G quietly mumbled.

"Yeah, but a damn capable one, wouldn't you say?" said Dan, as he turned and looked at G.

A bit embarrassed that Dan could hear what he said, G was both surprised and impressed. Dan led them to an elevator not too far down a central corridor. The elevator doors closed and opened once again after a short ride. G was led to a room he assumed to be a reception area for distinguished visitors. It was a comfortable room, warmly decorated and well lit. There were some snacks on the table.

"Can I get either of you something to drink?" asked Dan.

"Coffee for me, please," said Athena.

"Same for me," said G, to keep it simple.

Dan turned and made his way to an adjacent room and summoned an agent for the two coffee orders. He returned shortly with two hot coffees on a tray with creamer and sugar.

"Please, help yourself to something to eat, and make yourself comfortable," he told G.

G grabbed a small plate, loaded it with most of what was available on the table, and found a comfortable seat in a corner near a table with a lamp. He set his coffee on the table and proceeded to eat small bites of food.

"Now what?" asked G, shrugging his shoulders and looking at Dan and Athena.

"I like that," said Dan. "A man who gets straight to the point."

"Well, if you can actually *get* to that point you'd be the first one to do so since I somehow got wrapped up in all this...whatever *this* is," said G boldly.

"Fair enough, Mr. Weston. But for us to do that, I'm going to have to call the shots. I can assure you that if anyone can answer all of your questions, I'm *that* guy. If you'll trust that about me, I will provide you with whatever answers you seek. Fair enough?"

"On one condition," said G.

"What would that be?"

"You start by telling me who *she* is," said G, as he pointed to Athena without looking at her.

"She works for me. She saved your life. Nothing else matters."

"Well, see, there you go," said G sarcastically. "That doesn't sit well with me."

"We're not your enemies," said Dan.

"Then why the *hell* am I here?"

"If you'll allow me to give you that information, I plan on telling you everything," said Dan.

G could clearly see that he was not in charge of how things would go. He felt he was close to the truth he sought, so he took a deep breath and sat back in his chair.

"OK, how do we play this?" said G, as he stared straight into Dan's eyes.

"First, I'm going to ask that Athena leave us," said Dan without breaking his gaze from G.

"I'm OK with that...for now."

"Athena, would you please excuse us?"

"Certainly," responded Athena, as she rose to her feet, turned to look at G, and left the room.

G watched Athena leave the room. His attention was diverted when another woman strode into the room unannounced. G watched her as she walked across the room and took a seat directly across from him. She was an attractive woman in her forties, well dressed and well-manicured. G immediately stereotyped her as some kind of psychologist. Of course, he would recognize his own kind anywhere. There was something about those in his profession. They seemed to exude an air of confidence...or was it cockiness? Either way, he figured she was there for one purpose—to analyze him.

"Mr. Weston, this is Dr. Middleton. She's a clinical psychologist. Do you mind if she joins us?"

G shrugged and shook his head indicating that it didn't matter to him. He was used to working with psychologists, psychiatrists, psychoanalysts, neurologists, and the like. He wanted answers, and he figured he was very close to getting them.

"I'd just really like to get on with this if we could," said G.

"Great," said Dan. "I want to start out by saying that no one here is out to harm you. We fought hard to keep others from harming you, but *we* have your best interests in mind."

"By 'we,' I take it you mean the NSA?" asked G, fully realizing the answer.

"Yes."

"Mr. Weston, I've read your blog and have followed your accounts of your in-depth analysis on dream interpretation and manipulation. I have to admit, the subject is fascinating research and your theories are intriguing. And you have quite a following from what we can gather. It seems you've convinced a lot of people that you've had some serious breakthroughs in your study of oneirology," said Dr. Middleton.

"OK, look," interrupted G. "If you guys want to chat about my research, then why go through all the trouble to bring me here like this? Why all the drama and the killing? I mean, holy shit! Do either of you know what kind of life I've had the past couple of days?"

"We know a lot more than you'd probably give us credit for, Mr. Weston," said Dan.

"Well, whatever it is that makes me so important for the director and his top shrink to analyze me better be worth it. Look, I'm tired, let's cut to the chase shall we? *Why the hell am I here?*"

"You're here because we want to know if you're for real," said Dr. Middleton.

"We started analyzing your blog entries before you left for your vacation in Belize. Our analysis…and our interest in your abilities were piqued when you accurately described some of our findings concerning the Arlington Key Bridge bombing attempt," explained Dan.

"OK, now we're getting somewhere," said G, with a hint of relief in his voice. "So you assigned a female agent to manipulate me and 'recruit' me?" asked G.

"Not exactly," said Dan. "If you recall, it was *you* who pursued Athena. Despite what you may actually think of her, I can assure you, she genuinely cares about you. But that's beside the point."

"Really? How the *fuck* would you know? I mean that with all due respect, of course."

Dan figured it was time to push back a bit to effectively steer the conversation. "I *know* my agent. She's damn good and she never…let me repeat, *never* gets emotionally involved. She took risks with you...*for* you. She apparently sees something in you that I don't. At least, I don't see it yet. So let me be *perfectly clear* about something, Mr. Weston. The reason you're here and not hanging in some meat freezer in an obscure closet or at the bottom of the Potomac is due, in large part, to Athena's efforts to work through a lot of people and a helluva lot of bullshit to bring you here to me. This is where the story ends, Mr. Weston. And this is where the story can begin again. Whether it's a beginning or an ending is pretty much up to you. In the long run, it's me who will make that call. Are we clear on this?"

G listened to Dan's stern words without evidence of emotion. He simply nodded affirmatively.

"I hope some of the answers are starting to become clear. We have questions too, Mr. Weston. So we're hoping we can have an adult two-way conversation with you that yields results for both of us," said Dan. "Do you think we can help each other?"

"Yes," said G, as he took a breath, trying to relax and lower his guard a bit.

"Good. Would you *mind* if Dr. Middleton conducted the direction of our continued conversation?"

"Don't you mean 'evaluation'?" responded G.

Dan ignored the comment, rose to his feet, and turned to leave the room. He opened the door and turned to look at Dr. Middleton.

"He's all yours, Doc."

Hakim awakened to the sound of an alarm. He opened his eyes and struggled to determine where he was. It was dark, and he realized he was no longer in his hotel room.

He drew a breath and nearly choked on the putrid air. He could still hear the alarm. It was an annoying but familiar sound that would normally demand someone's attention, if they were able to control it. It didn't take him long to decipher the source as a timing device of some kind. His heart quickened as he thought of the dire possibilities he could be faced with. Could it be a timer on an explosive device? Hakim wasn't sure whether to pursue the source or run from it. He closed his eyes tightly and focused his attention on catching his breath. He calmed his mind and caught a breath and found a breathing rhythm that worked for him. When he opened his eyes, his subconscious mind revealed he was in a dream state. His awareness now in focus, he quickly willed the dark room to brighten to reveal the sound source. Off in the distance was a man trapped beneath a broken pile of boards and rubble. Hakim's eyes were quickly drawn to the man's exposed wrist, the alarm of his watch sending out its signal. He approached the man cautiously, careful not to startle or alert him to his presence.

The man *did* notice Hakim, however.

"Help me, please," he whispered from under the debris.

Hakim didn't respond. Instead, he stood there and studied his surroundings to try to determine where he was located and why he had found himself there. Looking up, he could see the broken platform that had given way. Hakim knelt down and cleared away a broken board to look the man in the eyes.

He reached for the man in an attempt to search for identification. When he touched the injured man, Hakim's mind was flooded with overwhelming images of an explosion, images that occurred before and immediately after the explosion, visions of the man's family, water, fire, depression, anxiety, emotion. The visions began slowly and accelerate through Hakim's altered conscious state of mind. Hakim quickly pulled back, reeling from the experience, and emerged with the man's wallet and a badge. The entire ordeal was a brand-new experience for Hakim. Shaking his head to make sense of the images in his mind, he stepped back and looked at the man once again. "NSA. You are a government agent. I cannot save you. Your fate is in the hands of God."

Hakim heard voices in the distance. They emanated from above where the platform had collapsed. He looked at the man lying before him and figured he wasn't going anywhere, so he projected himself to the doorway at the threshold of the dilapidated platform. Stepping through the doorway, he saw a set of stairs descending before him and could see beams of light in a small alcove at the base of the stairs.

He cautiously made his way to the base of the stairs and into the alcove. Once there, he looked up to discover a shaft that seemed to capture the attention of a group of people on the surface above his position. He thought the voices might be those of some kind of rescue team.

Hakim turned to ascend back up the stairs to finish off the agent. If he could accomplish an assassination in a dream, it would open an entirely new opportunity for the cause of the Jihad. His heart pounded with the excitement of the possibilities. He quickly ascended the stairs, but the door was closed at the top. He froze in his tracks as his mind raced to remember whether he had closed the door behind him when he first approached the stairs. He tried opening the door, but it was locked. He stepped back and attempted to force it open with his subconscious mind, but it wouldn't budge.

Hakim was suddenly faced with a new dilemma. He summoned all of his power to *force* the door open but was met by an even stronger resistance from the other side. He persisted and pushed as hard as he could until suddenly, the door burst open so hard it came loose from its hinges.

Hakim walked through the threshold with a purpose and stepped into a transition portal that brought him back to consciousness. Fighting to resist the transition, he was powerless against its pull.

25

The note was scribbled on the corner of a page that had been torn from a book. The page number, 152, was plainly visible near the corner of the note. It simply read, "*Meet me at the trailer ASAP,*" and was hand-delivered by a young man in a construction hard hat.

Jay shared the note with John, his cameraman, and the two quietly slipped from the press tent in search of Tom Herring's office.

"We got here as soon as we could," said Jay, breathing hard from the quick pace.

"Gentlemen, this is Russ Noble. He and I think you may be onto something. Since you were the ones who brought this to our attention, you get first rights of coverage. My only condition is that you respect certain sensitivities in your coverage and clear it through me, should we happen to discover anything requiring discretion. If we can agree, then we're ready for you to accompany us," explained Tom, looking at both men squarely in the eyes.

"Absolutely!" said Jay, nodding.

"Good. And because I'm *old school*, I believe that a man should honor an agreement with a handshake while looking him in the eye," added Tom to ensure complete understanding.

The men all shook hands, realizing the seriousness of their agreement. Tom led them to a white four-wheel drive Suburban parked outside the trailer. The men piled in and drove outside the perimeter established for the site of the explosion. They drove a block and a half before turning down an obscure side street. Russ was in the front passenger seat beside Tom, who was driving.

"Take a left here," said Russ.

"You sure?" asked Tom, as he slowed the vehicle.

"As sure as I can be, looking at thirty-year-old maps," quipped Russ sarcastically. "Wait! Stop!"

Before Tom could bring the vehicle to a complete stop, Russ opened the truck door. His work boot hit the pavement even before the vehicle came to a complete stop. Tom jammed the gearshift lever into park and turned off the vehicle as he watched Russ taking up a direction while holding the blueprints in his hand like a map. Tom turned and looked at his two passengers and shrugged his shoulders. "Let's see where this takes us."

Jay and John exited the rear of the vehicle simultaneously. Jay hesitated long enough to ensure that his cameraman had his gear intact. Grabbing a remote microphone, Jay nodded to John to activate the camera.

"Remember what I said, Jay," Tom reminded him.

"No worries, Tom, we're not live…just taking footage to document the discovery. You still have the release rights."

The camera lens captured Jay following the two men to a remote sight illuminated only by the rising sun on an eerily calm morning. Each man carried a high-powered flashlight to ensure they could see into any spaces they happened upon. Jay addressed the camera as he walked through the streets.

"What we're witnessing is the search for a possible connection between the sites of the explosion and that of a connecting building previously unknown. Building plans discovered by this reporter and his cameraman may provide a connection between two structures that could offer a lifeline escape for anyone fortunate enough to have discovered it before, during, or after the blast that has rocked this city." Russ stopped suddenly. He turned to Tom as if he were lost.

"What's the matter, Russ?" said Tom.

"Uh…you're not gonna believe this, but there seems to be a page missing," said Russ.

"What do you mean?" exclaimed Tom.

"Here, check it out. I believe we're located right here," said Russ, pointing to the drawings and then to a corner of a nearby building. "The next page I have doesn't make sense. I mean, I could take an educated guess, but we'd be shooting in the dark and wasting a helluva lot of time," added Russ.

Jay suddenly realizing what was going on, told John to turn off the camera then approached Tom and Russ.

"Gentlemen, I believe I may be able to help," said Jay with a slight look of guilt. He pulled two folded pages from his hip pocket. "I had to have insurance that you'd reciprocate on my gesture."

Tom wasn't happy, but he didn't say anything. He didn't have to. The look of disappointment on his face said enough. He unfolded the pages and handed them to Russ. Jay turned back to John.

"OK, turn the camera back on."

Russ was able to piece the drawings together and quickly got his bearings. The men followed him down an empty alleyway between two dilapidated old brick warehouse buildings. Russ stopped in the middle of the street.

"According to these plans, the two structures connect right about here… but I don't see any way they can, because there's no clear structural connection," explained Russ.

The three men stood there in the middle of the alleyway pondering the connection possibilities while studying the drawings. Tom's phone chirped. He checked the call. It was Dan Keppler.

"I have to take this call. You guys come up with something, or we take this back to the site to study."

Russ crouched to his knees and spread the drawings onto the alleyway to get a better look at the layout of the area.

"There's *got* to be something here we're not seeing," stressed Russ.

The humidity was rising as fast as the sun in the South American jungle. Booker and Hartman found an acceptable place to hide out near a small stream.

Both men were highly trained, so little needed to be said in terms of establishing an effective spot to rest. Hartman set out to establish a perimeter. He had four explosive charges remaining, so he set the devices at equal distances from the center of their site. Anyone who happened to be unlucky enough to walk near them would be seriously wounded, if not killed by the detonation. They would also serve as a warning to the two men should they have unexpected company approaching. Of course, the effect would be the same for any unfortunate animal, such as a jaguar or monkey.

Booker prepared the campsite by cutting small trees and creating a raised platform that would offer protection from jungle animals and provide a better perspective to scout from. They would protect themselves from the intense sun by building a thatched roof overhead. Booker lashed tree branches together using vines. The plan didn't call for the men to stay long, so the integrity of the structure was not as important as its completion.

Hartman returned from the perimeter with branches and palmetto leaves for the roof. Both men worked together to quickly establish a raised platform they could live with. Before they climbed into the temporary shelter, they both urinated around it. The tactic served to mark the territory and ward off most wild animals that would normally have a tendency to become a nuisance.

Booker tested the nearby stream water for purity and filled the canteens. He returned to the structure, handed a canteen to Hartman, and shared some fruit and a power bar that he had saved from an old military Meals Ready to Eat, or MRE. Hartman was happy to eat. Both men checked their weapons and ammunition and quietly discussed their exit strategy.

"We may find ourselves having to make the best of this for a few days," explained Booker. "How are you feeling?"

"I'm good. I'm glad we stopped, because I had to dry out my socks," said Hartman, removing his boots. "Have you checked the radio lately?"

"Negative on the radio. Plan to check in once we get some rest. Good call on the socks. I'll take first shift while you get some rest and your socks dry," said Booker.

Hartman hung his socks over the edge of the shabby structure and lay back against his rucksack while Booker took a sip from his canteen and listened to the chorus of the jungle.

Dr. Middleton sat stoically in front of G for a few moments before breaking the silence with a question. She casually crossed her legs as she studied the man in front of her.

"Why don't we start by getting to know each other, shall we?" offered Dr. Middleton.

"Is that the best you got, Doc? I mean, really? Because I really don't give a shit about pleasantries. Just tell me why I'm here and what you want from me," answered G, showing his impatience with the entire interrogation tactic.

"OK then, let's start by examining your so-called *gifts*, shall we? I know you proclaim to be an expert in the study of dreams. *Oneirology,* is it? That science is really in its infancy, is it not?"

G listened to the good doctor's diatribe and privately scoffed at her ignorance. She wasn't the only one conducting an evaluation. G arose from his chair and walked over to the table to pour himself a glass of water. He turned to face the two-way mirror, smiled and winked, and casually returned to his seat.

Dan was watching the entire ordeal from the observation room. "That son of a bitch is toying with us," he said.

"OK, Doc, what would you like to know? Or would you prefer I offer *proof* of, how did you put it...oh yeah, my *so-called gifts*?" questioned G, with sarcastic confidence.

Dr. Middleton immediately picked up on the overbearing attitude G was displaying and assumed it to be a psychological game of dominance. So she subtly pushed back with a reflective question.

"Do you *have* proof?"

"Do I *need* proof?"

The doctor quickly realized she was dealing with a professional in her own field and simply offered a truce in the interest of progress. "Look, Mr. Weston...may I call you G?"

"Nope."

Pausing slightly to take a breath, she prepared to lay out her offer.

G picked up on the pause and saw it as a weakness in her technique and a sign of frustration.

"Look, *Mr. Weston*, this will go a lot easier for both of us if we can just have a conversation. Can we do that?"

"Of course. Just don't pretend to be my friend while we're having the conversation."

"OK, I'll keep this as professional as possible, then. As a fellow professional, you're aware that, for me to effectively evaluate your abilities, I need to corroborate them with substantiation or evidence. Are you willing to allow me to conduct my evaluation while you're in a relaxed or hypnotic state?"

"I'm not real comfortable with you doing that right now," said G. "Why don't we stick to general questions?"

G picked up on the gesture Dr. Middleton was making but decided to play along. She would occasionally touch her right ear and pretend to adjust her earring. G suspected she was listening to someone from behind the mirror. The more they chatted, the more G became relaxed with the interrogation.

"How long have you been working for the Agency, Sibyl?" asked G. The question came as a complete surprise to Dr. Middleton.

"I don't recall telling you my first name," she said, with a look of suspicion.

"You didn't," said G, nonchalantly.

"Then how did you..." she began, then touched her right ear once again. "We'll get to that later."

"Why haven't you come right out and asked me the question you're dying to ask, Sibyl?"

"What question is that, Mr. Weston?"

"Wrong question, Sibyl—try again," said G, toying with the interrogator.

Dr. Middleton sat looking at G as she subconsciously placed her right elbow on the arm of the chair and her index finger onto her ear. Taking another breath, she made her statement. "What we discuss from here on out is classified. Our discussion in no way indicates that you are *read in* on any special operation conducted by *the Agency* or the United States government. You are given no provision of protection should you discuss this information outside this room. Do I make myself clear?"

G detected a change in the doctor's voice and demeanor. Her curiosity was replaced with seriousness. Her posture transitioned from a defensive gait to an offensive one. She took her job seriously, and it was something G could sink his teeth into. Now they were getting somewhere.

"Crystal clear. How can I help?"

"We have reason to believe a terrorist organization may be based in the US, specifically, the District of Columbia or surrounding area. You made a distinct connection with this activity on your blog recently when you wrote about your dream. Given the fact that your account was as accurate as it was, while you were known to be abroad in Belize, has piqued the interest of the Agency. We also understand that you have a degree of control while dreaming, and we'd like to help you explore ways in which to enhance those abilities."

"Of course, by *helping me*, you infer that I'm not the only one benefiting. Your offer to help me is suspicious, but I'll get to that in a moment. I can assure you I can do all of these things you describe and more. You have no idea, really. But before we talk about the Key Bridge incident, I have a question of my own for you."

"OK...what is that?"

"Wouldn't you *first* like to know where your agent is located?"

Dan was watching G and Dr. Middleton interact from the observation room on the other side of the mirror. Hearing about a *lost agent* nearly made him burst through the wall. He thought about terminating the interrogation but considered the risks and, instead, opted to sit still...for the moment. But to say his attention was captivated would be an understatement.

"Get him to give you more fidelity on the details. Ask about the agent, his name, appearance, how he knows these things...get as *much* info as possible, Doc," exclaimed Dan, nearly audible through the walls.

"What agent are you talking about?"

"Sibyl, do you *not* have a missing agent? You know, the one everyone thinks perished in the explosion? Why do you insist on playing games with all these questions? I thought we were going to have a civil, open conversation and help each other."

"That's it, he knows where Mark is," exclaimed Dan, storming out of the observation room.

Dan burst into the interrogation room and suddenly realized the manner in which he entered. He closed the door in a more controlled manner and turned to face G.

"OK, Mr. Weston, you have our attention. There's a lot going here that you can help us with," explained Dan. "If you know where my agent is and can help us find him, it would be a great start. You can continue your research, and we can fund it. Tell me where my agent is, so we can get him to safety," said Dan, almost pleading.

Dr. Middleton gave Dan a look of disapproval for the way he interrupted her analysis. Dan barely recognized her presence, much less her demeanor.

G picked up on Dan's sincerity and the genuine nature of his plea, so he decided to openly cooperate. "I don't know where he's located *exactly*. I know he's alive...or at least he was when I last saw him. He was near a manhole shaft but he wouldn't have been able to reach the exit rungs. I can go back there to get more information, but..."

Dan looked at G with an expectant look.

"...but I travel best in a dream state. So I have to be asleep. I haven't figured out a way to fall asleep at will, unless of course I'm knocked unconscious, which is the least preferred method, by the way," explained G with a hint of sarcasm, thinking back to the unpleasant encounter with the agent's fist.

"How do you respond to hypnosis?" asked the doctor.

"Not sure. Never tried it. Don't really believe in it, actually."

"You're a psych major and have never tried hypnosis?"

"Nope. Can't tell you whether or not I can be hypnotized," said G. "Some people simply cannot be hypnotized, you know?"

"While I'd love for you both to continue this conversation, I have an agent I need to help," said Dan. "Can we give it a try and see if you can be hypnotized, Mr. Weston?"

"Certainly," said G, shrugging his shoulders. "It couldn't hurt to try."

"OK, Mr. Keppler, if you would be kind enough to leave us so I can conduct the hypnosis?" asked the doctor.

"Absolutely, Doc. Mr. Weston, please find my agent and bring me a location."

G looked at Dan and nodded. He turned to Dr. Middleton, gave her a serious look of readiness, and took a breath.

"OK Mr. Weston—"

"Please...call me G," he said without breaking his serious gaze. "And whatever you do, don't touch me while I'm under...assuming you're successful with this hypnosis thing, that is," he added.

Dr. Middleton merely nodded, indicating her understanding, and began her hypnosis.

"OK G, I want you to focus on the sound of my voice. Allow all of your faculties to ride on the frequency and tone of my voice," said the doctor in a soothing calm manner. "Your eyes are getting heavy. Allow them to close and carry you through the dimensional portal to subconsciousness. You're very tired...drifting...drifting..."

Ox asked Pat to check in with the two scouts.

"Perry, this is Pat, how do you copy, over?" Pat paused for a few moments, awaiting a response, and tried again.

Dream Operative

"Perry, this is base camp. Come in, over!" The radio crackled with static as Pat and Ox listened for a response. Suddenly, the static yielded to a response from the two-man team.

"Roger, base. This is Perry. We hear you loud and clear...for now. But we're about to scale a ridge that may cause us to lose contact for a while. Over."

"Copy that, Perry," responded Pat. "Check in again once you've established contact with Mother. Over."

"WILCO," responded Perry.

It was the last they had heard from the scouts for the remainder of the day.

The ceiling fans pushed the thick air through the small café. The staff was busy serving a long line of customers. The door chime rang as Jeff walked through the crowded entrance and made his way through the maze of restaurant activity.

"Good morning and welcome to the Café," came the programmed response from most of the staff, without looking up to make eye contact while they remained busy filling orders.

Jeff found his way to a hallway leading to the restrooms, but instead of entering the men's room, he opened a door between the two restrooms marked only as "Private" and closed it behind him. He walked down a short, dimly lit flight of stairs to the basement of the business and came to yet another door. He removed a card from his wallet and waved it close to an obscure scanner. A subdued tone was his only indication that his key had deactivated the lock. Having gained entrance, he scanned the room for a familiar face.

"Agent Hines, good to see you again," called out a young Middle Eastern man, peeking from behind a computer terminal across the room.

Jeff nodded. "Where are the others?"

"You are early, my friend. They will be here in about fifteen minutes. You should let me show you what we are working on."

"The only thing I'm interested in now is the whereabouts of Mr. Weston," said Jeff.

"I ran a trace on the vehicles used to transport him from the hospital, where he and his friends were able to help him get away."

"What did you come up with?" said Jeff, peering over the shoulder of the young man.

"Local dude with deep roots in the city."

"OK, so can we get to him to *squeeze* him?" asked Jeff.

"Nobody's gonna *squeeze* this man anytime soon, my friend. When I say he has *deep roots*, they're *deep*. This man is entrenched with the South Side Mafia."

"Never heard of the South Side Mafia," said Jeff.

"That doesn't surprise me. Very few people know about 'em. Word has it, this man is the founder and CMFIC."

"CMFIC?"

"Chief Mother Fucker in Charge," said the young man, with a hint of a smile.

"This man have a name?"

"Only one name that keeps comin' up. Seems he goes by Mario. You know what they say; when you're known by one name, you *got* to be big. You know…Cher, Madonna, Michael…"

"I got it."

Jeff paced the room. He didn't want to start a turf war by pissing off a high roller Mafioso the likes of Mario, but he needed a lead on where he could find G. Finding Mario would take time he didn't have. His thoughts were interrupted when the door to the room opened and three men entered.

"Gentlemen! Greetings…*As-Salāmu 'Alaykum!*"

"*Alaykum as-salām*," responded Jeff, along with the young man, who was now bowing to the older men.

"Mr. Hines, thank you for taking the time to meet with us to prepare for the honorable Khalid Abdul-Hakim," said one of the men, reaching out both hands to greet Jeff.

"Of course. In the name of Allah and *the cause*," responded Jeff, as convincingly as he knew how.

"Do you have the envelope, Mr. Hines?"

Jeff removed a folded manila envelope from the inside of his shirt, handed it to one of the men, and waited while it was opened before him. The envelope contained four pages of text and a ScanDisk micro card—the kind that you'd find in most run-of-the-mill digital cameras.

"I assume you've examined the contents of the chip, Mr. Hines?"

Jeff returned his best stoic poker face. He wasn't sure whether it was OK for him to have seen the contents. The man tried his best to read Jeff, but he was outmatched. He simply handed the memory chip to the young man at the computer terminal.

"Examine it to make sure it contains what we're looking for," said the man.

"It's the real deal," responded the young man.

The man was satisfied and simply nodded affirmatively, then turned toward Jeff and reached his hand to the inside of his jacket.

"Whoa!" said Jeff, placing his own hand across his chest toward his weapon. "Nice and easy…I'm just a messenger."

"If you are just a *messenger*, then why do you assume to be so defensive, Mr. Hines?" said the man, slowly retrieving two envelopes from his pocket. "I wish only to close this transaction honorably."

Jeff breathed a sigh of relief. He had come close to blowing the entire transaction out of proportion and compromising the deal.

The man extended his right hand to shake hands with Jeff and extended his left hand that held the two envelopes.

"One envelope contains encrypted instructions and is to be delivered to the honorable Khalid Abdul-Hakim personally and out of sight from any knowing observers. The other contains a small token of our appreciation for you," said the man as he held onto Jeff's hand firmly.

"I understand," said Jeff, nodding.

26

She gripped his hand tightly as he made the transition from consciousness to a dream.

"I thought you'd *never* get here, G," said Angel.

Her voice was the first thing he detected as he became aware of his altered state of mind. He picked up a sense of urgency in her tone. He could feel the forces of speed acting on his supernatural body.

"Where are you taking me?"

"No time to explain. Use your mind to guide you the rest of the way. Remember, *nothing* is impossible in this dimension. Don't doubt yourself, because your abilities will be tested today," said Angel, letting go of G's hand.

"Don't leave me!" said G, suddenly finding himself surrounded by darkness and a thick cloud of dust.

He pushed his mind to make sense of his surroundings while trying to clear his senses. He ignored the dust and transformed his ability to see inside the dark room. The scene was vaguely familiar to him. He scanned the room. Everywhere he looked he saw debris. Stopping to listen closer, he picked up a faint sound of shallow breathing and a fading heartbeat. He tuned in on the breathing and was drawn to Mark, who was trapped under a pile of rubble. He immediately projected himself to Mark. Kneeling at Mark's side, he pulled some boards away to lighten the load from his chest, making it easier for him to breathe.

"Hang in there, brother," said G, encouragingly.

"You're back," said Mark, struggling to push the words from his mouth as he looked into the eyes of his savior. "I recognize your voice."

"Shhh, save your strength," said G, studying his surroundings.

Mark grabbed G's arm. A vision of Mark's recent past emotions blasted through G's mind as he witnessed the force of the explosion from Mark's point of view. G could feel his ears go numb from the blast. He caught glimpses of Mark's wife Heather and his two daughters and felt pain, loneliness, fear, and hope flood his senses in an alchemy of emotions. He also caught a glimpse of Hakim through Mark's eyes and realized he wasn't the only one who knew Mark's whereabouts. The seriousness of the situation had suddenly escalated.

"Danger..." whispered Mark, glancing up toward the broken platform.

G looked up at the platform and felt his adrenaline rising. He saw a door that was opened slightly at the threshold of the platform. As soon as his mind processed his concern, the door closed and locked. He stood to better determine how he would get to the platform to get a closer look. He heard Angel's words echo in his mind: *Remember, nothing is impossible in this dimension...*

G pushed the limits of his logic and envisioned the ability to project to a stable part of the platform and, before his mind could finish the thought, he found himself perched upon a corner of the platform, just outside the closed door. His heart began beating faster. He sensed a strangely familiar danger.

He turned to face the door and stared intently at its solid core. The door seemed to melt away as he could look right through it. What he saw startled him and disrupted his focus. Seeing the face of his familiar enemy spiked his adrenaline, causing him to take a step back where felt the platform give way. His pulse quickened and his breathing deepened. He heard the broken wood moan beneath his feet. Catching his breath, he struggled to regain his balance, footing and courage.

What do I do now, Angel? G thought.

Face your fear, G. You're the only thing standing in the way of life and death for those who need you.

G dug deep and summoned all the courage he could muster. He sensed a powerful surge of energy working against the door from the other side. The man he had seen so many times before in his dreams was trying to get the door open and was using his own supernatural forces against it.

G fought hard against the power and will of his enemy and worked to keep the door tightly secure with his own supernatural power. He opened his mind to study the man on the other side and could see the frustration

Dream Operative

and determination building. The man appeared to be unaware of G's presence, but G could clearly see that the he was determined to get through that door. An encounter was inevitable and would be a new experience for both men.

Holding the door closed was draining G's strength. He wouldn't be able to hold him off for long. It became a test of wills.

G closed his eyes to summon the deepest core of his power when, all of a sudden, he felt an electrical shock race through his body! The surge pushed him back onto the unstable platform. G felt the platform give way. Falling back uncontrollably, he felt himself slowly drifting into an alternate dream dimension. He looked back to see the door burst open so hard, it came loose from its hinges. But he was powerless to do anything about it.

G tried calling Angel, but he was unable to speak. Drifting, he could hear the sound of his heartbeat surround him. It slowly faded into a transition of another sound he couldn't quite distinguish. He began to see blurred visions and heard the sound of heavy breathing. Struggling to wrap his mind around the visions, he slowly began to understand the sound he was hearing. It was the heavy breathing a woman experiencing erotic pleasure.

The new surroundings began to take shape. He found himself in an unlit room, looking out onto a beautiful swimming pool. It was dark outside except for the dim, submerged pool lights. He could hear water moving and the heavy breathing he'd heard earlier. He walked past a small table with a mirror positioned just above it, located by an open sliding glass door. He stopped in front of the mirror and was intrigued by the absence of his reflection. He stepped into the threshold of the open doorway and looked out toward the pool. He saw a man and woman having sex in the shallow end of the pool.

G slowly stepped toward the couple and could hear her laughter and sensual satisfaction. The man was holding her naked body, her legs tightly wrapped around his waist as he rhythmically thrust himself into her hips. He could clearly make out the man's face, but he was unfamiliar. He couldn't make out the woman's face from his current angle. G was curious as to why he was there, so he continued to slowly walk toward the couple in search of an answer. He stepped into the shallow end of the pool and was within arm's distance of the couple when they slowly turned just enough for him to see the woman's face.

"Sibyl?"

As soon as G uttered the words, he was pulled from the dream with an overwhelming force. Suddenly, he began to see and hear various events surrounding Dr. Middleton's life. He saw her seated in a room interrogating various people, mostly men.

Who do you work for? Why are you here? Where's the device?

The questions echoed throughout the aspect plane of the dream sequence.

G saw various aspects of Dr. Middleton's life flash before him. He witnessed her interacting with children he assumed were her own. He also watched as she met with people he was vaguely familiar with, like Dan Keppler. He caught glimpses of her writing at her desk. He saw her at a restaurant, having lunch with the man he had seen in the pool. His curiosity gave him pause, so he paid closer attention to the details unfolding in his mind. Sibyl seemed to be romantically taken by the man. The look on her face revealed the vulnerability of a schoolgirl, infatuated with a new love. He, however, didn't seem as interested in love as much as he was in the envelope she discreetly handed him.

The dream sequence and visions faded as G felt his subconscious focus begin to drift. He became more aware of the entire sequence and remembered Mark's plight.

"Angel, take me back to Mark!" exclaimed G.

I can take you back but only for a moment, whispered Angel.

G was whisked away to his previous dream dimension, just long enough to find Mark safe from harm, but still in need of rescue. G couldn't detect his nemesis at all, but he wanted to be certain. So he projected himself to the doorway near the platform. He saw the broken door hanging loosely from its hinges. He walked through the doorway and descended the stairwell. He saw flashes of lights shining into the alcove below, so he approach cautiously. Looking up from the shadow of the stairwell, G saw flashes of light extending into the alcove. He projected his mind to the surface to get a good idea on a location he could bring back to Dan and Dr. Middleton. He saw a dark alleyway and four men looking at a map of some kind; one of the men was carrying a shoulder-mounted camera and was filming the others.

G felt an unexplainable wave of energy hitting him.

"Not yet, Angel!" cried G.

It's beyond my control, she whispered.

Dream Operative

Thunder rumbled in the distance as the wind picked up and the temperature dropped. The breeze was a welcome relief on Booker's skin as he peered out into the thick jungle canopy through the binoculars.

"Think it'll rain?" joked Hartman with a smile.

"It always rains in the jungle, my brother," responded Booker without putting down the binoculars.

The jungle became quiet as the indigenous inhabitants found shelter from the impending storm. The men could smell the rain as it approached. They did their best to protect anything that needed to remain dry. Their makeshift shelter provided some protection from the rain when it began to fall, but every hole in the roof made itself evident as it began to pour down.

"What's our exit strategy, Captain?"

"We must be on the same page, Hartman. I was thinking that if this rain does anything to swell that stream over there, we could build a raft and *float* outta here."

"And if it doesn't?"

"If it doesn't, then we *walk* out."

Hartman preferred the water option but knew it would expose the men to anyone in the jungle along the river. But it sure beat the alternative of having to walk out of the jungle...which could take months.

"If that stream leads to a river, we can quite possibly get past the cover of this thick canopy that's keeping us from getting a good radio signal," explained Booker. "We need to provide Mother with a good fix on our positions so we can formulate an extraction plan."

Hartman nodded.

The rain continued to pour down while thunder rumbled overhead.

G gasped for breath as he regained consciousness in the chair across from Dr. Middleton. He was sweating and breathing deeply from the experience of the dream.

He awoke to Dr. Middleton's hand on his shoulder. His eyes grew wide when he looked down at her hand and then intently into her eyes. Grabbing her wrist, he forcefully pulled her hand from his shoulder and let it go just as quickly.

"I thought I *told* you not to touch me!" G shouted.

"It...it was the only way I could bring you back. You seemed to be struggling. You were sweating and breathing heavily," said Dr. Middleton, defending her actions.

"I told you *not* to touch me! You may have cost the life of an agent with your sympathetic actions, Doctor!"

Dan returned to the room in an attempt to restore civility between the two psychologists.

"What's this about the life of an agent, G? Did you find Mark?"

"I'm not sure what his name is, but there is someone down there who needs to be rescued. He's in bad shape," explained G.

Dan became excited at the possibility that it could be Mark that G encountered. "So he *is* alive! What did he look like? Did you speak with him? Do you know where to find him?"

"That's a lot of questions from someone who doubted my abilities," said G defiantly.

Dan took a breath and gave G a serious look.

"Let me tell you something, G. You take me to my agent and there's *nothing* I won't do for you. You want to study this dream...ology stuff; I'll find a venue and a budget that'll make your eyes water. Take me to my agent. Tell me where he's located."

"I don't *know* exactly," said G, as he glared at Dr. Middleton.

"What do you mean, you don't know? You were there, weren't you?"

"Well, yes, but—"

"But what?" exclaimed Dan.

"I tried getting a good point of reference on where he's located, but it's all underground."

"OK, it's underground. That's a start. But we've already explored underground at the site of the explosion and there was no one found alive. Explain that to me," said Dan, trying to make sense of G's account.

"He's not *at* the site of the explosion."

"OK, you're losing me, kid. If he's not at the site then where the heck is he, man? He didn't just disappear, did he?"

"Not exactly. But he *is* in trouble."

"What do you mean, trouble? Is he hurt?"

"Yes," said G, looking at Dan seriously. "But there are people that are close by that may be able to help," he added.

Dream Operative

"What people? Who are they? Rescue? Civilians? Who?"

"Not sure. There are four men. They have some kind of map they're using. One of the men has a shoulder-mounted camera...like he's filming something. I took a look around and can only tell you that they're in an alleyway in between a lot of old red brick buildings. It's like the men are there for a reason," explained G. "I only caught glimpses. I'm sorry."

"No, G, *I'm* sorry. Let me try to make some sense out of this from what you've been able to tell me. Is there anything else you can remember that may be able to help me?"

"No."

"OK, I'll make a phone call to the site director," said Dan, glancing at Dr. Middleton on his way out the door.

"Oh, there is one more thing," said G.

"What's that?" said Dan and Dr. Middleton, almost simultaneously.

"He's not alone."

"So there are other survivors?" asked Dan.

"No. There's someone else who wants to do him harm," said G, looking at Dan with intense life-or-death seriousness.

"Who is it?"

"You wouldn't understand."

"Try me," Dan pressed.

"I don't know exactly. But I've seen him before," G explained.

"Where?" asked Dr. Middleton.

"In other dreams I've had."

"What do you make of that, Doctor?" asked Dan.

"Not certain at this point. This is new ground for me. For now, I recommend you give Tom a call to see if he can help in any way."

Dan nodded. "Give him whatever he needs," said Dan, referring to G. "And if you can get him to go back into his dreams, or whatever he does, send him back in to make sure Mark is safe."

"Hey, did you guys hear that?" asked Jay.

"Hear what?" said Russ.

"Coulda sworn I just heard something. Sounded like it was coming from—"

"There it is again! You guys hear that, or am I hallucinating? John, do you hear that?" asked Jay, as he looked for some kind of confirmation from the men.

"Negative, brother," replied his cameraman.

"I'll bite," said Russ, with a chuckle. "Where do you think it's coming from?"

"Look, you guys might think I'm frigging nuts, but I thought I heard some kind of commotion *beneath* us," said Jay.

"That doesn't sound crazy at all, dude," said Russ, looking at Tom while answering Jay. "OK, everyone be absolutely still and listen up for anything out of the ordinary. If you hear something, quietly move toward the sound."

The four men stood quietly, lights out, in the middle of the alleyway, listening intently for any sound that seemed to be out of the ordinary. All of sudden, Jay heard a loud bang. Hearing the sound, he slowly moved toward a manhole cover in the middle of the alleyway. Russ also made a move toward Jay, but the others remained motionless.

"So I'm not crazy?" whispered Jay to Russ.

"Nope, I heard it too," answered Russ. "OK, lights on! We're close to the source. I take it you guys didn't hear anything at all?" Russ said to the remaining two men in the group.

Tom and John were clueless but eager to help the two men. They scanned the street with their lights as the sun began its slow rise over the city. Tom's phone rang. The caller ID displayed *Dan Keppler*. "Tom Herring," he answered.

"Tom, Dan. We need to talk. You have any men on the outskirts of the blast site conducting any kind of search using a map of some kind?"

"Damn, Dan, I *figured* the Agency was good, but this is impressive. How do you know about the map? I mean, there are only four of us who know about it—"

"No time for that my friend. Just tell me how I get in touch with the men who have that map…the ones who're conducting a search," said Dan with urgency.

"You're talkin' to him, my friend," said Tom, still dumbfounded over Dan's intelligence.

27

I awoke peacefully, succumbed to the numbness of the dream I had just encountered. I'm trying to grasp the details as my mind peacefully climbs out of its slumber. I'm close to getting out of bed – I've been close for some thirty minutes now. My thoughts are racing to and fro as I try to align them into some sort of meaningful sequence to help me understand the realm I just departed. I watch the ceiling fan make its rounds as my mind relaxes to the rhythm of its motion. I can feel its gentle breeze against my skin. My mind fights for control as I catch glimpses of the lucid storyline taunting me.

Hakim's thoughts returned him to a gentle reality as he glanced at the clock and realized he had been asleep for four hours. He had suffered more from jet lag than he first realized. He randomly remembered parts of his dream and was able to slowly piece together the sequences that brought his journey back into focus. He grew frustrated as he realized the things he had left unfinished. He had always considered himself a perfectionist and a finisher, the best in the world. This time, both traits were compromised. He had not finished off the agent who had seen him, and he had been unable to manipulate a simple door opening. Questions lingered. How could the door have closed without him knowing it? Was he being challenged by someone? Was it the only one he had ever been challenged by in a dream dimension? Was it the man he had seen only once outside of a dream state? He prayed to be sent back to finish the job.

"Send me back to complete my mission, Allah," Hakim prayed quietly.

He rubbed his eyes and arose to the sound of the busy New York traffic in the streets below. His thoughts were interrupted by a knock at the door. He wasn't expecting anyone and felt his heart quicken as he shook the distracting thoughts to focus on what may lie beyond the threshold of the hotel doorway. He approached the door quietly and carefully and looked through the peephole.

"Who is it?"

"Guest services, sir. I have a message for you."

"Very well. Please slide it under the door. I am not dressed appropriately."

Hakim watched a small envelope reveal itself beneath the doorway as the young man dutifully did as he was asked and walked away. Hakim bent down to pick it up and carefully opened the note to read the words.

> PAY CLOSE ATTENTION TO THE COMPANY YOU KEEP. THINGS ARE NOT ALWAYS WHAT THEY SEEM. PROTECT YOURSELF WITH THE FULL ARMOR OF GOD.

Hakim held the note in his clenched hand, his mind attempting to decipher the warning. He slowly moved toward the window and drew back the curtains to look out onto the New York landscape, now soaked in neon lights and silhouettes moving about.

Although his eyes were fixated upon the city, his mind was weaving its way through the words on the note. Few people knew his whereabouts. Who would write such a note, and why? And what about the warning of the company he kept? He considered himself an excellent judge of character and could sense deceit from just about anyone. He was never wrong and played the game as if his life depended on it. In fact, his life *did* depend on it.

Hakim turned from the window. He removed a small travel case from his suitcase and placed blue-tinted contact lenses into his eyes. Then he placed a Harley-Davidson bandanna that he had purchased in Europe onto his head and put an earring into each ear lobe. The bandanna was the type with the fake ponytail sewn into the back to make it appear as if the wearer had long hair. After conducting a quick inspection of himself in the mirror, he headed for the door.

He thought about the door in his dream as he shut the hotel door behind him. Stopping at the elevator, he reached out to press the call button but stopped shy of making contact. His keen senses picked up a reflection in the oddest place—a flower arrangement set upon an ornate table near the elevator. He casually moved in to take a closer look and discovered a motion-sensitive camera had activated as he walked up to the elevator. He decided to take the stairs and made his way to a side exit on the ground level of the hotel.

Hakim walked through the crowded streets of New York in search of additional items to enhance his disguise. He knew the streets would be fairly crowded. He walked toward a small crowd he considered to be tourists. He bumped into several people waiting outside a local restaurant and repeated the routine once again a block later with people gathered outside a popular theatre.

Hakim walked another block where he found a fairly isolated place to sit and take a break. He removed his hands from his pockets and examined the treasures from his pick-pocketing adventure through the crowds. He counted the bills, stuffed them into his pockets, and examined all of the credit cards—seven in all. *Not a bad take for one city block*, he thought. He stood slowly and studied his surroundings. It was beginning to get cold outside. He needed a jacket.

Taking a side street, Hakim found a small shopping district two blocks away. He entered the first store he saw and purchased a leather jacket, a pair of jeans, boots, a pair of lightly tinted sunglasses, and a pack of smokes. He paid for the entire purchase with the credit card of some poor schmuck who hadn't discovered it missing yet. Hakim smiled when he signed for the purchase: *Sam Uncle*

He stepped out of the store and hailed a cab.

"Take me to the Blue Note, please."

Hakim stared out the window of the taxi as he was driven to the predesignated meeting place. He paid the driver and exited the cab. He glanced at a clock on the wall of a local business and stepped to the side of the entryway, where he lit a cigarette and waited. He wanted to take note of Jeff's arrival to ensure he was alone, and if he wasn't, to evaluate anyone accompanying him. Hakim had no intention of going into the Blue Note, because he would be at a disadvantage inside.

Hakim saw a taxi pull up to the front of the club. He didn't immediately recognize anyone, and no one paid him any attention. After all, he was a grungy-looking, long-haired biker dude smoking a cigarette. He watched the small group exit the cab, laughing together while they entered the club. He noticed two well-dressed men following the small group. He almost glanced away when he recognized one of the men—an FBI agent from a close encounter in Damascus some eighteen months earlier.

Hakim glanced over his shoulder and looked at the clock. He was patient and would wait as long as it took. Thirty minutes passed. While he was waiting, a man stopped to ask him for money and a cigarette. Hakim handed him a cigarette and lit it for him. The man thanked him and asked if he had any spare change. Hakim held out a credit card. The man hesitated and stared at him as if he were crazy.

"You may want to use it rather quickly," said Hakim, winking at the beggar.

The man reached out and took the card with raised eyebrows and thanked him. Hakim watched as he headed straight for a corner liquor store. "Desperate, pathetic Americans..." he said in a whisper.

Another taxi pulled up to the club. Hakim could clearly see Jeff in the back seat as the driver switched on the interior light for Jeff to pay the fare. Hakim tossed his cigarette into the street, breathed out a large plume of inhaled smoke, and approached the taxi. He opened the rear door and climbed in, nearly sitting on top of Jeff.

"Hey dude, what the hell?" exclaimed Jeff, revealing the edge of his pistol grip neatly tucked into his shoulder harness. The gesture didn't faze Hakim for one moment. He was used to dealing with such brave characters, many of whom were now dead because of—and in spite of—their bravery.

Hakim looked at Jeff, lowered his tinted glasses, and offered a short, calm, serious explanation in his raspy voice, his breath laced with cigarette odor. "Our meeting location has been changed. And don't even *think* you can get that thing out of its holster before I bury your nose into your skull. Driver, take us to Scores."

The driver looked at Jeff and waited for his concurrence. Jeff sat still, momentarily stunned by the expertise and prowess of Hakim's control.

"Driver!" demanded Hakim.

The driver reset the meter and pulled the taxicab into the wet street.

"You'll like Scores," said the driver in an attempt to ease the obvious tension. "You want me to arrange escorts for you gentlemen as well?"

"Nothing for me, thank you," said Jeff, snapping to. "But my new friend here likes *large* women. Do you have large women?" he wittingly added with a shit-eating grin, deciding he better play along or be consumed by this killer.

"Large girls will cost you extra," responded the driver with a gapped smile.

Hakim gave Jeff a look of disgust and angst.

"Never mind then," said Jeff, tilting his head slightly. "We'll wait to see how the girls at the club work for us."

The taxi sped off into the city on a course for the gentlemen's club.

"I take it I'm spending the rest of the night here, said G, looking to Dr. Middleton for confirmation. She returned a look that made it obvious he was correct.

"We're not finished," replied Dr. Middleton, closing her notebook and clicking her pen.

G stared right through her. She stood and walked to the door. "I need you to come with me, G."

"I'm sure you do," responded G with a sigh. "So where we headed?"

"I'm taking you to meet someone."

Dr. Middleton led G through a short corridor that led to an elevator. She pressed the call button, saying nothing, and walked through the doors as they opened. She held out her arm to hold the door open. G walked into the elevator and stood beside her. She placed a key card into a slot on the wall and pressed a button on the lower part of the panel that activated the doors to close.

G could feel the weight of his body lighten as the elevator began its descent. He closed his eyes for a moment to imagine being somewhere else. He thought about Athena. His moment was quickly interrupted by the slowing descent of the elevator. The doors opened to a long, well-lit, sterile corridor. G saw a door at the far end. He and Dr. Middleton stepped out of the elevator to begin their walk.

"So who exactly are you taking me to meet?"

She remained silent.

"Really, it's OK if you tell me, Sibyl," said G to illicit a response.

The two reached the door at the end of the hallway. G crossed his arms, leaned against the wall, and raised his eyebrows.

"I assume your secret decoder ring or government key card will give us access through this door?" said G sarcastically.

Dr. Middleton slid her keycard through a reader, placed her index finger on a scanner, and entered a six-digit code into a keypad. G could hear a loud "click" as the door lock bolt was released.

"This is as far as I go, G," she said, looking into his eyes and holding the door ajar for him to enter.

"Thought you were going to introduce me to someone."

"I think you'll know what to do from here."

G tried to make sense out of the coded message and manner in which it was delivered. So much had happened to him over the past forty-eight hours...so many *extraordinary* things. And now he found himself at the threshold — literally — of a life-changing moment.

His hesitation seemed oddly lengthy, yet he knew it was but a few moments of thought processing at true speeds known only to God himself.

What is it that lies beyond the threshold of the door? Who would be waiting for me? What would they want from me? Will this be the last I see of my true self and life as I knew it?

After all, he was trapped in the bowels of one of the tightest government agencies on the planet. He turned and walked through the door, hearing the locks engage behind him.

Russ and Jay crouched low to the street to try to recapture any hint of what they had heard earlier.

"You guys hear anything?" asked John.

"Shhh! If you'd be quiet, we might be able to do just that," retorted Jay.

"Tom, I have no idea why you're in that area, but boy, am I glad it's you out there. Listen very carefully. We have a missing man in your area *beneath* you in an underground system of some kind. I believe it may be one of my top agents. I need you and your guys to find a way to get below the surface to conduct a search. I'm hoping that map of yours will be useful. I have a satellite overhead that's got a fix on your position as we speak and I'm sending out a small team to secure the area. You have command of the area. No one gets in or out without your permission. Got it?"

"Got it, Dan, but—"

"Listen, Tom, I have no time to explain. Find my agent and report back to me as soon as you have something...anything!"

"Copy, Dan," said Tom.

"You guys were right. You did hear something," said Tom. "I'm just hoping it was something we can use."

Both men rose to their feet and looked at Tom expectantly.

"Whatcha got, Boss?" asked Russ.

"Find a way for us to get beneath the surface. There's some kind of underground system right below us, where NSA believes one of their own may be located. He may have found his way there through the very connector system Jay identified in those blueprints."

"Russ, the manhole," said Jay, running to the middle of the street, sliding to his knees to try to lift it himself.

"You're not gonna be able to get that off without some serious assistance," said Russ pulling out a handheld radio. "I'm gonna call some people in with the right tools."

Russ called one of his crewmembers and explained the situation. He asked for a paramedic truck and crew and asked that they respond quickly without sirens and lights. He knew the crew would have the necessary tools to help lift the manhole cover and provide the rope needed to descend into the area beneath the streets.

The three men waited patiently while Russ devised a plan using the blueprints. A vehicle arrived on scene the same time as the paramedics. It was a brown panel van marked with the logo of a local exterminator, *Buzz Pest Control*. Three men climbed out of the van and approached Tom and his team. "Which one of you is Tom Herring?"

"I'm Tom."

"Mr. Herring, I'm authorized to be here in the interest of national security," interrupted one of the men. "Who's the guy with the camera?"

"He's with a documentary agency. He's here to record how we do business," said Tom, careful only to reveal the cameraman's role.

"Not anymore," said the man, nodding to one of his men, who confiscated the camera and escorted John to the van.

John looked at Jay and the others. Jay motioned for him to play along and go quietly.

"Who are the other two men?"

"They're with me," Tom simply answered, being certain not to lie, only to slightly mislead. He passed on the opportunity to get back at Jay for holding out on him earlier.

"OK, we're keeping an eye on the perimeter and overseeing this operation. You're free to do your job."

"I should hope so," said Tom with a hint of sarcasm, turning to direct the paramedics to the manhole cover.

The paramedics brought out heavy-duty crow bars to pry the manhole loose from the street's grip and moved it away from the opening. Russ approached the opening first and shined his high-powered light into the darkness.

"Hello! Can anyone hear me?"

Everyone remained still, awaiting some kind of response.

"Turn your truck off," said Russ to one of the paramedics. "I can't hear shit over that diesel engine."

The paramedic shut down the engine and the area was suddenly still and quiet. Russ tried once more to determine if he could illicit some kind of response.

"Hello! Can anyone hear me?"

Nothing.

"OK, time for me to take a closer look. I assume you guys have a good rope on board you could loan me?"

"Yeah, we have a rope, but we're the only ones authorized to use it to conduct such an op—"

The young paramedic's answer was short-lived when Tom placed his hand onto the man's shoulder and assured him it would be OK for Russ to use their equipment.

"Let me get it anchored to the truck for your descent," responded the paramedic.

"I'm going with you," said Jay.

Russ looked at Tom for his approval and received a slight nod.

"Fine. But get some gloves, so you don't burn those delicate hands of yours," said Russ with a wink.

Jay bit his lip in response, because he knew he was already pushing the limit of his welcome, but he knew that if he played his cards right, he would walk away with one hell of an exclusive story. The absence of a camera hadn't deterred Jay, because he knew his new smart phone was fully charged, and he could capture video, although not as vivid, when the opportunity presented itself.

The men secured the rope and tossed the line into the hole and heard it hit the ground rather quickly. Russ shined his light into the hole. The light bounced off the reflection of the wet surface below.

The paramedics helped the two men secure personnel harnesses. Russ descended first. He reached the bottom and called up to clear Jay for his descent. Jay clumsily made his way down the rope to the bottom of the shaft.

"Man, I'm glad you made me wear these gloves. My hands are burning from that rope."

Russ instructed Jay to turn on his light. They scanned their lights in a complete circle. They saw two paths; one led to stairs that ascended to a door, the other to a dark corridor with a low-hanging ceiling. A faint trickling sound of water filled the musty air.

"Which way?" asked Jay.

28

G examined his surroundings. He found himself in a fairly small room that looked much like the sterile corridor he had just walked through with Dr. Middleton. He saw two small cameras mounted in the upper right and left corners near the ceiling and an open doorway in the right corner of the room.

"Please make your way to the first open door and take a seat at the table in the next room," instructed an obscure male voice from a well-hidden speaker system.

G assumed he was being watched from the cameras he saw earlier. He did as he was told and exited the room through the open doorway. He saw yet another open doorway when he rounded the corner into the hallway.

He walked into the room and took note of the interrogation-like setup: a small table with a chair on either side. The walls were bare, save for another two-way mirror flanked by a closed door he assumed led to an observation room. He was tired, so he played along.

The doorknob slowly turned. G raised his head as he watched a man enter the room and take a seat before him. He had an athletic build and exuded a confidence that commanded respect. He wasn't wearing an ID badge or any kind of accouterment that would provide a hint of who he was or what division he worked for.

"You've had a helluva few days," said the man, in a rhetorical opening line.

"I have," agreed G.

The man sat stoically for a moment, as if to size him up and provide time for G to figure out the discourse path. But G pressed him.

"So are we gonna continue staring at each other, or are you gonna to tell me who you are?"

"G, you are on the brink of having to make some choices…life-changing choices," responded the man.

"Look, Mister…whatever your name is…I'm not making *any* choices until I have a little more clarity," said G. "I've given everything I have to this Agency and to people I don't even know or have reason to trust. So you'll have to excuse me if I seem a little out of line," said G, his voice beginning to crack from the sheer amount of stress.

"I can imagine," said the man. "Then let's restart this with an introduction, shall we? I'm Damian…Damian Bush."

G squinted his eyes slightly and sat silently for a moment while his mind went into overdrive, trying to figure out where he'd heard the name. After all, he'd heard a lot of names recently. But Damian Bush was among the more unique names…Bingo!

"Todd's friend…or, uh…contact," stammered G, with his best recollection.

Damian nodded.

"You're the one who sent in the team to spring me from the airport. Man, those guys were rude," said G, as he recalled the entire airport ordeal. "So… you work for the NSA or some kind of clandestine government agency?" asked G.

"We'll get to *me* in due time," said Damian. "For now, I'd like to remain focused on getting you your answers. After all, I believe we owe you that much," he added.

G smiled and took a breath. For the first time in days, he believed he was in the company of someone empowered to tell him more of what he needed to know without worrying about security compromises or their precious jobs. There was something about Damian that he immediately liked. Despite his intimidating build and charming good looks, G felt a bond with the agent. But he knew well enough to know that things weren't always what they seemed. So he kept his full judgment in reserve…for now.

"All right, G…may I call you G?" asked Damian.

"Certainly," nodded G.

"OK, G, let me start by telling you what you may already know. The government is always looking for an edge or advantage in its quest to stay ahead of the rest of the world in terms of its ability to collect, exploit, and employ intelligence in its own best interests. We constantly recruit the best minds, hardware, software, and technology money can buy," explained Damian. "When the government learns about any new concept or ability that'll serve its purpose, they do everything they can to get their hands on it. The only real problem with this process is that other countries and entities are busy doing the same thing. Sometimes even the *same* country competes with itself. That's where conflict can develop and can sometimes escalate into clandestine, nonpublic *wars,* fighting over the same capability."

G sat listening to Damian and began to slowly put the pieces of his situation together.

"The government is consistently monitoring all kinds of sources in search of something new to give them an advantage. We consider *all* possibilities…even ones that first appear to be ludicrous, edgy, or utterly ridiculous. That's how we found you."

"Guess that's supposed to make me feel good?" asked G sarcastically.

"Your claims to have mastered the concept of dream manipulation were so far from being taken seriously that we had to investigate and validate them," said Damian, pausing to allow G to absorb the explanation. "How am I doing so far, G?"

"Not bad. Better than most," responded G. "It's refreshing that someone actually believes in my abilities."

"I can imagine," responded Damian. "But in the interest of full disclosure, we *are* still evaluating your abilities. We believe they hold promise and believe you to be gifted enough to warrant even further investigation and developmental assistance."

"Well that's the first thing you've said to cause me some concern," said G.

"How do you mean?"

"I simply mean you still have reservations."

"Of course we do. We'd be remiss if we didn't."

"So where does that leave us?"

"We're waiting to see if we find our agent, based on the assistance you provided to Dr. Middleton. Given a positive outcome—"

"By *positive,*" interrupted G, making air quotes, "I take it you mean *alive?*"

"That is our preferred outcome, G. But it's not the only one we're looking for. We just want to know you're as good as you claim."

"So you're planning on detaining me until then?"

"We prefer to see it more of an *accommodation* than a detainment, G. You're welcome to walk right out the front door of the NSA today, if you prefer. But our intelligence analysts give you about a twenty-four hour freedom expectancy without the proper protection protocols in place."

"What are the *protection protocols*?" asked G.

"More on that later. First, I have some questions of my own I'd like to ask of you. Can I do that?"

"Certainly."

"We'd like to help you develop your abilities. Would you be interested in a lucrative funding stream to do that?"

"What's the catch?"

"Good question. Why does there always seem to be a pesky catch with these things?"

"Because there typically is…"

"The catch…or *expectation,* would be that you remain loyal to the Agency and its allies, namely the US government. Seems simple enough doesn't it?"

"If there's one thing I've learned from everything I've been through, Damian, is that nothing is ever what it seems," said G.

"Well done, G. But in this case, we're seeking *you,* funding *you,* and providing *you* with resources. Things will be precisely what they seem, subject to the approval of our leadership here, of course," said Damian.

"Of course…so is this the way you guys make job offers?"

"It's not a job offer, G. It's a *lifestyle* offer."

There was a knock against the glass that captured the attention of both men.

"Sit tight, G. I'll be right back. Is there anything I can get for you while you wait?"

"No…thank you," said G as he tried wrapping his mind around everything that was unfolding before him.

Perry switched the handheld radio to the "off" position to conserve power. He looked up at the ridge towering above him and then at KK, while they studied a way to climb to its peak.

"What's your plan?" asked KK.

Dream Operative

"We take that first ridge there. It's the biggest hurdle, but we should be able to make up a lot of time once we scale it. Any other option that I can see from here will only increase our workload."

"Yeah, I can see that," said KK. "But we gotta use extreme caution, cuz one slip will put us on our asses on those jagged rocks below."

"Agree. Stay hydrated, and let's move out," said Perry.

Ox and the rest of his crew were busy creating a shelter from the sun and caring for Stokes by the river.

"How long you figure it should take our scouts to reach a height with a good strong signal?" asked Ox, to no one in particular.

Pat responded first. "I'm an experienced climber and if it were me, it would take about eighteen hours."

"So just what is it that you do besides climb mountains?" Ox asked Pat, figuring he had a captive audience.

"You mean besides keeping an eye on you?" said Pat jokingly. "Whatever the Agency tells me to do. Right now they have me gathering topographical geo-based data to be used in the big picture of Central American intelligence collection," responded Pat, in his best attempt to be vague enough for Ox to give up his inquiry.

Truth be told, Pat was indeed there to keep an eye on Ox and provide insight to his usefulness to the Agency in terms of continued support to national objectives. He had been assigned to work with Athena before she was given permission to be reassigned in support of getting G to the Agency.

After the day's events, Pat had more than a favorable impression of the man and his operation. All he had to do now was to keep from blowing his cover and getting left in the jungle if Ox discovered the real truth behind his presence on the mission. And Pat knew enough about Ox to know that he'd do just that, if he discovered Pat's true agenda.

Russ took a deep breath and slowly panned his light along the floor and the walls, looking for a clue that would provide the men with a direction.

"Let's split up," suggested Jay.

"Jay, think about it...you're not qualified to conduct search and rescue," said Russ. "If you go and get hurt, I'll be one man trying to rescue two. I don't like those odds. Give me a minute. I'm looking for anything that could help us."

Jay nodded. "So what are we looking for?"

"Something like this," said Russ as he pointed out a partial footprint. "Take a close look at this."

"OK! It's a footprint. We obviously *know* someone is here," responded Jay with a hint of sarcasm.

"Yes, we do," said Russ. "But what I'm more interested in is the direction of the print," he added. "We head this way."

Russ led the way toward the dark hallway leading to the stairs. "Watch your step, Jay."

Russ pointed his bright light in the direction of the doorway and could see that it was wide open. He scanned the floor before him to be sure of his footing. The two men approached the top of the stairs when Russ stopped suddenly and placed one arm behind him to stop Jay in his tracks.

"This doesn't look good at all," said Russ.

"What's up? What do you see?"

Russ crouched to his knees then to his stomach.

"Take a look. There's a platform ahead that's been destroyed," said Russ.

"Holy shit!" said Jay, panning his high beam over the dilapidated structure. "There's no way anyone would come this way."

"Let's be certain. Grab my feet and anchor me, so I don't fall into this mess. I'm gonna take a closer look," said Russ, extending his body over the threshold and partially onto the weak platform, boards creaking underneath him.

Russ slowly scanned his high-powered light through the dust and debris.

"Hello! Is anyone there? Can anyone hear me?" he called in a last attempt while listening intently for a response.

Russ began to pull himself back when he heard a shift in the debris below him. He reacted by quickly panning his light in the direction of the sound and called out once again, "Hello, is anyone there?"

He heard the shift in debris again and panned his light left and right over a small area, where he suddenly saw the movement of a board and the extension of a human hand!

"I've got him. Jay, I've got him!" shouted Russ.

Jay was so stunned by the announcement that he nearly let go of Russ.

"Dude, hang onto me! Don't let me fall," exclaimed Russ. "Hey buddy, hang in there. We're here to get you out," Russ shouted to Mark. "OK, Jay, pull me back in."

Russ rose to his feet and nearly pushed Jay out of the way as he rushed to the lower area and shouted up to Tom. He told Jay to talk to the guy while he went to get help.

"What should I say?"

"Just *talk* to him!" shouted Russ, running past him to the stairs.

"Tom, we found someone. Not sure who yet, but we have an injured man. I'm gonna need the paramedics, a backboard if you can fit one through that hole, and some more rope.

"Copy that, Russ," shouted Tom.

Russ could hear Tom barking instructions to the paramedics.

"Stand clear, Russ. I'm throwing down another line," shouted Tom.

Tom helped one of the paramedics descend through the manhole opening and managed to squeeze a backboard after him. Russ and the paramedic received the backboard and brought it to the threshold of the dilapidated platform. The men decided it would be best for the paramedic to be lowered to the victim and render first aid right away. The paramedic carefully made his way through the debris and cleared some broken boards away from the victim.

"Hey, buddy, we're here to get you out. Can you speak? What's your name?" asked the paramedic as he leaned in close to get the vitals.

"Mark...Mark Rubis," he responded in a weak whisper.

"OK, Mark, I'm gonna start an IV so we can take care of that thirst I know you must have right about now. Can you tell me where it hurts?"

"Can't breathe very well..."

"My friend, you have a collapsed lung," said the paramedic, shaking his head in disbelief. "So I need you to stay as calm as possible. Can you do that for me?"

Mark nodded. The paramedic looked at his eyes with a tiny flashlight and could see tears streaming down Mark's face.

"It's OK, Mark. You're in good hands, my friend. We're getting you outta here," encouraged the paramedic.

"Is he stable? How are his vitals? You got a name yet?" Russ shouted to the paramedic.

"Yes, he's gonna be fine. I have a man in his forties. He's got a collapsed lung and other unknown injuries. Possible broken ribs and a concussion as well. Says his name is Mark Rubis."

Russ looked at Jay and gave him a high five, then ran back to the landing to tell Tom.

"Yo, Tom."

"Yeah, Russ."

"We've located a Mark Rubis, forty-something-year-old male. He's got a collapsed lung, concussion, and possible broken—"

"Copy, Russ. That's all I need for now," interrupted Tom, as he dialed Dan.

"Dan here. Talk to me, Tom. Whatcha got?"

"Do you believe in second chances, Dan? Because this man just received one."

"What're the details? Confirm the name for me, Tom," responded Dan in a serious tone, expecting the best but fearing the worst.

"We have a Mark Rubis. Is that who you were hoping for?"

"Yes! Outstanding job, Tom. What's his condition?"

G's thoughts drifted to the dream he had about Dr. Middleton while sitting patiently, waiting for Damian to return. He kept thinking of the envelope exchange he'd witnessed and about the unprecedented access he now possessed.

This is a total mind job, G thought. *People are really starting to take me seriously — important people.*

Damian emerged from the observation room with a look of satisfaction and the hint of a smile. He stopped and stared at G for a moment. "Dude, you are *something* else. I don't know how you do it, but we're happy to have you here," said Damian.

"OK…" said G, with some hesitation and a question in his voice. "What is it *exactly* that you're referring to?"

"It seems your dream encounter led us to our agent. Our people never would've found him if it wasn't for your help. Mr. Keppler would be here to thank you himself, but he's busy notifying the agent's family."

The reality of it all began to sink in as G absorbed the news, all while seeing the collage of images from the dream that led him to Mark and his closest encounter with Hakim.

"So…he's alive and well?" asked G, thinking about how he was pulled from the dream with a threat still present.

"He's banged up and dehydrated, but he's gonna be just fine. Why? Were you expecting a different result?"

G felt a mixture of relief, emotion and euphoria as he realized Mark was unharmed and would soon be reunited with his family. "So, now what?" asked G.

"Now, you accept or reject our offer," answered Damian.

"I have so many questions still. Is that normal?"

"Yes. But as you've already seen, the answers come in many forms and typically in their own time. You can't force these things," explained Damian.

"OK, then, back to my first question: now what?"

"It's been a long day, G," said Damian. "Why don't we start by getting you set up in some accommodations here in the headquarters? It's not safe for you on the outside yet."

"Will I ever see the outside?"

"Of course," answered Damian. "You'll just see it in an entirely different way," he added with a wink and a nod.

Damian walked to the door, opened it, and turned to G, indicating for him to follow with a tilt of his head. G took a deep breath, knowing that following Damian was an acknowledgement that he was following him into a new life…a life altogether different from anything he had experienced to this point, save for the recent excitement for the competition of his abilities… and his very life. Looking back on it all, he realized he actually enjoyed the excitement.

Despite the many questions that still remained, G knew one thing. The Agency provided an excellent opportunity for him to perfect his passion. The allure of that alone was enough to convince him to accept the clandestine offer. He arose from his chair and willingly followed Damian.

G was led to an elevator that brought them up several levels. He had no idea how many levels, actually, because there were no traditional indicators on the elevator panel. All he knew was that Damian had a key card, similar to Dr. Middleton's, that provided him the access he required.

He was taken to what appeared to be a Distinguished Visitors suite. It had everything he would require for a short stay...except for windows and a phone.

"The television has been unlocked, there's food and drink in the refrigerator, fresh clothes in the closet—your size of course—and a lap top computer for you to write," explained Damian.

"A computer?" asked G, a bit surprised they would provide access.

"No Internet. Sorry."

"What if I need something? How will I...?" asked G, purposely leaving the end of his sentence unfinished.

"Just ask," responded Damian with a shrug of his shoulders.

G returned a look of confusion at first but quickly caught on. "OK, I get it. You guys are watching and listening to everything. Tell me...am I safe in the shower?"

"I don't know, are you?" said Damian, poker-faced. "Get some rest. We start early tomorrow," he added.

G watched as Damian closed the door on his way out. He stood there in the middle of the room, his mind temporarily blank from sheer exhaustion. *Now what?*

Dan was on the phone with Tom. He listened intently as Tom described the condition of missing agent. But Mark was more than an agent. He was Dan's friend.

"He's banged up, Dan, but he's in good spirits. We should have him on his way to the hospital very soon."

"I can't thank you enough, Tom. Please give me a call when he's en route to the hospital."

"You bet. Oh, there's one more thing, Dan."

"What's that, Tom?"

"Is he the only one remaining we're looking for?"

"Yes...why, have you found someone else?"

"No. It's probably just that he's incoherent, but...the reason I ask is that he keeps mumbling about someone else having been with him. I was thinking there may have been someone else we're supposed to be looking for, that's all."

The hair on the back of Dan's neck rose as Tom described what could only have been an encounter with G. But how could the two have recognized each other, if one was dreaming and the other…way too deep to analyze now. His priority was to alert Mark's wife that her husband was alive.

"Take a good look around before you pull the last rescuer, Tom. If there *is* anyone else down there, you should be able to spot them, as I suspect the two would've stuck close together. Otherwise, get your men out of there safely."

Dan hung up and immediately dialed the phone to connect with Heather.

"Hello?" said Heather, answering on the first ring.

"Heather, it's Dan. We found Mark. He's alive, and he's gonna be fine," said Dan quickly.

He paused to allow Heather to absorb the good news. He could hear her gasp for a breath as she began to cry out of sheer relief.

"Thank God…I prayed so hard," said Heather through her tears. "I didn't give up hope. And neither did you, Dan. Thank you so much."

"Not my style to give up, Heather. Now, let's talk about getting you on a plane to reunite with your husband."

29

The taxi pulled up to the Scores gentlemen's club.

"That'll be thirty-one fifty, including the first fare," said the driver.

"Pay the man," said Hakim. He opened the door and exited the vehicle.

Jeff shook his head at the audacity and handed the driver some money. "Keep the change," said Jeff. He exited the cab and slammed the door shut behind him.

Jeff approached Hakim, who was standing beside a marquis outside the entrance of the club. He had just lit another cigarette.

"You know those things will kill you," said Jeff sarcastically.

Hakim didn't respond.

"So why the venue change?" asked Jeff.

"No agents. I don't like agents, and they don't like me. And I really don't care much for you."

"No worries. I don't take it personally. Now that we have that out of the way," said Jeff. "What say we go inside and check out the entertainment?"

"I'd like to do that, but don't you think it would be wise to find a place for your weapon first?"

"This isn't my first time to the rodeo, cowboy," said Jeff with a wink and a shit-eating grin.

"I'm not exactly certain of the meaning of such Western dialogue, but I assume you think you have things well under control," said Hakim, gesturing for Jeff to lead the way.

The two men made their way into the club. It was illuminated with black lights that led to a hostess station. The low bass of the music, accompanied by a rhythmic techno beat, greeted them as they approached the hostess counter.

"Make sure he pays full price," said Jeff to a young lady behind a cashier window after flashing a law enforcement badge.

The young lady smiled and allowed Jeff to pass without batting an eye. Jeff looked over his shoulder to see Hakim reach into his jacket for his wallet. He paused to wait for Hakim to pay. He saw Hakim smile at the young lady, pull out a wad of cash for her to see, and handed her a fifty-dollar bill.

"Keep the change, Princess," said Hakim, with a flirty smile and a wink.

The young lady returned a big smile and leaned over to whisper into Hakim's ear. He smiled as he walked away.

The men were greeted at the door by a well-dressed bouncer...or *host*, as they're more commonly referred to in the business. The club lights were low, strobes filled the room, the music was thumping to a quick beat, and an exotic dancer performed on the main stage. The men barely gave her a glance as they followed the host.

The host knew that Jeff was some kind of law enforcement and that Hakim had money. He led them to a table near the stage.

"We prefer something a bit more private," said Hakim, speaking loud enough to be heard over the music.

"I can do that," said the host with a nod. "Would you like the VIP?" he added, referring to the higher-priced and more exclusive part of the club.

"What will that run us?" asked Jeff.

"I'm sorry, say again?" said the host, straining to hear over the music.

"Pay no attention to the rude manner in which my friend is acting," said Hakim. "We'll take the VIP. Please bring us a bottle of your best champagne, and keep the girls away for a while. We have some business to tend to first," added Hakim, handing him a hundred-dollar bill.

The host accepted the gratuity and showed the two men to an exclusive table. It was quieter than the main room, but the music could still be heard, and the percussion of the bass could still be felt inside the exclusive room.

A scantily clad waitress brought the men two fluted glasses. She was followed by the male host who had seated them. He uncorked the champagne and poured the first glass for each man and waited for Hakim to approve. He took a sip and told the host that it was acceptable.

"I'll check on you gentlemen shortly," the host told them.

Hakim motioned for the host to get close enough to be heard without shouting. "Please make sure we're not bothered until I call for you."

The host nodded, motioned for the waitress to follow, and left the two men. Hakim lit a cigarette.

"You ever had that feeling where you're not sure if you're awake or still dreaming?" asked Hakim.

Jeff tried analyzing the question but thought it better to just give an answer. "You mean déjà vu?" asked Jeff, saying the first thing that came to mind.

"No. Something much deeper," responded Hakim, looking for a more thoughtful response from Jeff. He took a drag from his cigarette and paused to allow the original question to sink in for Jeff.

"Where are you going with this?" asked Jeff.

"It's nothing. It's just something that hits me every now and then," said Hakim, purposely elusive while allowing smoke to escape from his nostrils. Hakim was beginning to feel a wave of euphoria he couldn't quite explain. Was it the cigarettes? After all, they made him feel somewhat lightheaded, because he smoked only when his disguise called for it. It could've been the expensive champagne. But he'd just had a single sip of that.

"Do you have the envelope?" asked Hakim, trying to break free from the euphoria and into the reality of business.

G decided to make the best of the situation and get some much-needed rest. He felt he could sleep like a baby, but he secretly wondered if he ever would again. He sat on the edge of the bed and contemplated grabbing a quick shower.

He studied his surroundings on the way to the bathroom. Opening the closet, he found a decent selection of fresh clothes to choose from. He pulled a pair of jeans from a hangar and examined the size.

Impressive, he thought. *My size exactly. Athena surely had a hand in this.*

He looked at the closet floor and saw four pair of shoes in various styles. He assumed they, too, would be perfectly sized. He made his way to the bathroom and turned on the shower. He remembered what Damian had insinuated about the fact that he was being watched. He took a quick look around and removed his clothes, tested the temperature of the shower, and stepped into one of the best showers of his life. Whether it was truly the best or just the fact that it was the first time he'd been able to relax and wash away the day's stress, was beside the point.

He turned off the faucet and drew open the shower door to reach for a towel. The bathroom had filled with steam, so he had to search through the fog for the towel. He sensed someone was there, but instead of becoming alarmed, he remained calm. He waited for the steam to settle. As it did, he could see the silhouette of a woman. The steam continued to fade until it revealed the woman of his dreams. It was Athena, and she was standing before him completely naked. She was tall, sensuous, and gorgeous.

Athena said nothing but smiled and slowly extended her hand. The touch of her hand electrified G as he pulled her close. He embraced the back of her head with his free hand and brought her lips toward his. Her mouth tasted like the sweetest nectar he had ever experienced. Her skin smelled fresh and was so smooth and soft. She led him to the bedroom, where she lay back onto the bed and gave him an inviting look. He stood before her at the foot of the bed and studied the lines and curves of her athletic body. The sensuality of the experience was more than he ever dreamed it could be. He lay down beside her and gently touched the side of her face. The sound of her breath echoed in his mind while he savored the essence of the moment with her.

"G...can you hear me, G?" came the voice in a soft whisper. He tried to discern its source. "I'm sorry for disturbing you, G."

He slowly blinked and opened his eyes to new surroundings.

"Where am I?"

"You're in the *collective*."

He recognized the voice. It was Angel. He was confused as to why she would pull him from his encounter with Athena but found it difficult to be angry with her.

"The *collective*?"

"Think of it as the gathering place to which all dreams intersect and share collective subconscious thought," said Angel.

"Why am I here? Why did you take me from—"

"That dream was over, G. I waited for it to end before I summoned you."

G was confused when she referred to his encounter with Athena as a dream. She could sense his discontent and frustration.

"So it wasn't real?"

Dream Operative

"Don't be disappointed. Because, as you already know, dreams are an alternate form of your reality...and of hers as well," said Angel with a sincere smile.

G broke his confusion with an emotional smile as he tried to comprehend it all. "Will she remember it?"

"She may indeed. After all, your souls have already bonded."

"So, she does have feelings for me then," said G with some encouragement.

"I need you to focus on the *now*, G. You're here because I have to show you something," said Angel. "But before we go, I need you to listen and absorb."

"Absorb what?"

"Whatever your mind allows; you'll know when it's time to move forward."

G closed his eyes and stood perfectly still, following the sincere wisdom of his guide. He allowed his mind to open to his surroundings and began to hear soft voices and random thoughts from the collective. Most were audible but indiscernible. He could literally feel his mind filter the nuances of its surroundings. He stood for a moment and then opened his eyes to look up at Angel. He was fully clothed and ready to travel. "I'm ready," he said with determination.

As soon as he uttered the words, G found himself in a new setting inside an exclusive club or lounge of some kind. He could see lights flashing and could feel a rhythmic beat, but the ambient sound was muted. He looked to Angel for answers. She motioned with her eyes in a direction for G to focus. Before him were two men, sitting at a table, engaged in private conversation.

G recognized his nemesis right away. He saw straight through his disguise. Like Hakim himself, G could recognize a man by the look of his eyes. His heart began to beat heavily and seemed to keep pace with the rhythm of the room as his adrenaline surged.

"Breathe," said Angel, reassuringly. "He cannot see you, but he *can* sense you."

"Why am I here?" asked G without breaking his gaze.

"You already know why. For now, pay close attention to the details as they unfold before you."

G watched as the two men sipped their champagne and engaged in dialogue. He could sense the seriousness of the meeting between them. He was watching Hakim so carefully, he had not bothered to notice the man beside him until he witnessed an exchange take place between them.

The man with Hakim handed him an envelope. G was surprised to see the exchange and tilted his head as the images of the man came flooding back to him. He remembered seeing him in the pool with Dr. Middleton and then in the restaurant with her, as she handed him the envelope. Was this the same envelope he was now handing over? He needed to see what that envelope contained.

"How can I see the contents of that envelope, Angel?"

"You already have, G. Reach deep within yourself and find the answer."

G closed his eyes and focused on the envelope as he had first seen it, in the restaurant between this man and Dr. Middleton. He still couldn't see the contents, so he put everything he had into focusing on the envelope and the contents within. He picked up a vision of Dr. Middleton at her desk. It was one of a few fleeting glimpses he had caught the night he saw her in the pool with this man.

He focused on the very short glimpse of Dr. Middleton at her desk. Then it happened...

For the first time ever, G was taken to a place he had not yet been. He found himself inside the mind of another human being. He could hear the random subconscious thoughts of Dr. Middleton and knew he was treading on sacred ground, having stumbled, albeit somewhat purposefully, into the very core of her existence.

G had no idea of the full impact of the position he now occupied. He could literally discover anything he wanted about this woman. After all, he was on the inside—the most intimate and guarded side a person has of themselves. He instinctively knew to be cautious and decided only to pay attention to that which he had come to find. He needed to know the contents of that envelope.

"OK, Sibyl, show me the money," said G, without thinking what he asked.

That command gave him insight to more than he bargained for when he discovered the good doctor's bank statements, offshore accounts, a high-speed boat, the shoreline of an exotic tropical island, lavish parties...the images came at him faster than he could process them. Even in a dream, he couldn't keep up with the speed at which his request had delivered answers.

"Slower...show me the envelope."

Dream Operative

The envelope appeared before him, as if she were looking at it on her desk. It was a new, legal-sized manila envelope.

"Show me the contents of the envelope."

G expected to see the contents spelled out before him on paper of some kind. What he saw instead was a another barrage of thoughts, ideas, visions, emotions, processes, people, and places displaying themselves before him, as if they were his own firsthand accounts. The sequence was lightning fast, but he was doing a decent job of processing it.

"Slower...in sequence," he calmly and quietly commanded.

The vision sequences slowed, and the elements fell into place to create an overall vision of Dr. Middleton's thoughts as they were framed by her mind and her hand and placed into the envelope—to be transferred from her hand to one of the most dangerous men on earth.

Something was missing in the entire sequence of what was taking place before him. There was something about the envelope exchange between Jeff and Hakim that didn't match what G was seeing inside the mind of Dr. Middleton. Nonetheless, he clung to the images that were processing through his mind at lightning speeds. He suspected he would be unable to remember the intricate details of the contents of the envelope, but he figured she may have the original hidden somewhere.

"Show me the original. Show me where it's kept."

Visions of a small table had emerged before him. He remembered seeing the table when he was in Dr. Middleton's house in his dream. There was a mirror positioned on the wall above the table. He saw hand carvings along the edge of the table and a small, inconspicuous handle that opened to a "hidden" drawer where she had placed a copy of the contents of the envelope. He now knew what only she knew—the location of her only copy.

He began to put the elements together from the visions of her mind when he looked up into the mirror above the table. Instead of seeing a reflection of himself, he saw Dr. Middleton. He stopped to stare into the mirror to examine the reflection through her eyes. The experience was surreal. She was suddenly startled when she saw the reflection of a man come up from behind her. It was the same man at the table now with Hakim.

The experience startled G as well. The surprise had broken his concentration enough to bring him out of the deepest parts of alter consciousness and back in front of the men at the club. He had enough information about the whereabouts of the envelope, however, and would follow up on that when he could. For now, he wanted to watch the transfer of the coveted envelope and follow the course of its journey.

Hakim placed the envelope into his jacket pocket and motioned to the host. "We're ready for some entertainment," he said, walking toward the door.

"Hey, where you going?" asked Jeff. "We're just getting started."

"Gotta pee," Hakim said calmly.

G kept his eye on the man he knew to be the bigger threat—the one who now possessed the envelope. He figured he'd be following him to the restroom and was not beyond doing so, but was instead taken to an obscure booth in a dark corner of the club, where Hakim met another man and a woman. G listened in on their short conversation.

"He's in the VIP," said Hakim.

"Do you have the envelope?" asked the man.

"Yes."

"What would you like us to do about him?" asked the woman.

"Eliminate him, he's of no more use to us," responded Hakim without emotion. Turning to walk away, Hakim stopped, staring directly into G's path and looked straight through him; almost as if he could actually see him. G stood still and returned the stare.

The couple stopped to see if Hakim would have further instructions because of his hesitation. Instead, he turned and walked out the front door, leaving Jeff with the expense of the evening and his fate in the hands of Hakim's hired couple.

G found himself faced with a decision. Would he attempt to follow Hakim to discover his hiding place in one of the largest cities on earth, or would he see if he could intervene somehow and save the life of an agent? As tough a decision as it was to make, he opted to stay. After all, he knew he'd run into Hakim again, even if only through sheer will and determination.

He watched the couple make their way into the VIP room. He was curious how they would play it with Jeff. The man stood by the doorway while the woman approached Jeff, now surrounded by three women, one of whom was straddling his lap, writhing to the music. The woman leaned in to whisper into Jeff's ear and motioned toward the man at the door.

"There's been a shooting outside. Your friend needs you to come with us at once," said the woman. It was a poor attempt, and Jeff saw right through it.

Dream Operative

Jeff pushed the dancer from his lap, reached for his weapon and found it was not there. He looked at the woman and then at the man and immediately became suspicious. He made his way outside the club and felt a light cold mist against his face as the sequence seemed to slow to a crawl.

G watched it all unfold as a van pulled up to the front of the club and screeched to a halt. He was powerless to help as he watched Jeff try to fight his way out of an ugly situation without his weapon. Jeff instinctively grabbed the woman and backed away from the van. The man she was with drew his weapon and fired. The woman was hit several times and mortally wounded as she fell limp in Jeff's arms. He dropped the woman's body before him, stood fully exposed with blood spattered on his clothes while he looked at the shooter in disbelief and shock. He was quickly subdued by three men, all dressed in dark clothing. They grabbed him and led him to the van and tossed him in. The man with the weapon jumped into the van last, leaving the woman's body lying in the street outside the club.

G ran to the woman's side and watched the life quickly fading from her. As he touched her he could see short image bursts of her life flash before him. He could also hear short captions of various voices, mostly her own. G looked into the woman's eyes, her pupils growing larger by the second, and became aware that she could actually see him. She tried to speak but no words came from her bleeding mouth. Instead, he heard only her fading thoughts.

Please understand there's a purpose to our actions...I am prepared to give my life for this cause...I didn't expect this to end so soon...like this. Oh, Billy...there's a clock here for a reason...get on with it...I'm so cold...

The fragments of her thoughts weren't enough to immediately make sense of. But G would place it all into memory all the same.

"It's time, G," said Angel in a soft whisper. "She's gone."

"Will I ever get used to this?" he asked, rising slowly to his feet, still starting at the lifeless woman.

"I hope not," she responded.

30

By morning, the rain had slowed to a steady mist. Hartman awoke to the sound of his team leader climbing down from the shelter platform.

"I'm gonna check the stream to see how much the rain has affected it," said Booker.

Hartman nodded as he sat up, grabbed a drink of water, and wiped the sleep from his eyes, then collected some gear. He slipped his boots on and heard the familiar "zip" sound as he cinched the laces. He checked his 9 mm sidearm, holstered it, and grabbed a machete.

Booker returned to the campsite with a look of encouragement and three full canteens.

"Stream's up about four inches," he said. "If it keeps raining, it should continue to rise."

"Awesome," said Hartman. "How do you want to work this?"

"We'll need wood that'll float. I'll search for that. We'll also need rope to tie it all together. You can find that from the bark of a Banyan tree," instructed Booker. "You can also gather some vines, but the bark is our best bet. Remember to be careful and watch your back—and your noise footprint. We don't want to alert any unfriendly company."

"Copy that, sir."

The jungle had an eerie calm during the steady rain. Both men saw it as a bittersweet circumstance, because the very rain they found difficult to work in would end up becoming their greatest ally when they were ready to set their raft afloat. And it was a much better alternative than working in the hot Central American sun.

By day's end, the men managed to gather all the supplies they needed to begin construction.

G awoke to an alarm placed by the side of his bed he hadn't noticed before. It displayed 0600 and was playing soothing jazz music. He heard a knock at the door. It was Damian.

"Get a shower and be ready to grab a bite to eat in thirty minutes. We have a meeting with Mr. Keppler at zero-seven-hundred."

G thought he had already grabbed a shower but realized that too was a dream, because he was still in some of the clothes he had worn the day before. Images of the dream consumed him as he went through the entire sequence of examining his closet to find the right clothes in the right sizes and half expected to see Athena once again when he emerged from the shower. But she wasn't there.

"OK, I'm ready when you are," said G, standing in the middle of his quarters to no one in particular.

Less than a minute later he heard another knock at his door.

"This way, G," said Damian, holding the door open and motioning for him to follow along. "How'd you sleep?"

"I'm still trying to figure that one out, D," said G, half sarcastically.

Damian led G to a small private area after grabbing a few things for breakfast. G sipped a hot cup of coffee to push the remaining drowsiness out of his system before meeting with Mr. Keppler.

"You ready, G?" asked Damian glancing at his watch.

"Certainly."

Damian led G to a large conference room blocked by a heavy metal door with a security warning placard pasted to the outside. Damian had to spin a combination dial to gain access. He led G inside a handsomely appointed conference room with a large oak table anchored as its centerpiece. If G didn't know any better, he'd have sworn the table was built inside the room because there was no way it would've fit through the door. It had at least twenty high-quality high-backed leather chairs surrounding it—the one at the head was built a bit better than the rest, sort of like the difference between coach and first class on an airliner. It had one word embroidered on the upper portion of the headrest: *Director*.

Dream Operative

He was surprised to see that there were others already seated at the table. He focused first on Athena, as he had not seen her for what seemed like days, even though it had been less than twenty-four hours. She looked good and offered a smile when their eyes met.

"Have a seat here, next to the director, G," instructed Damian.

G looked around the table and saw Dr. Middleton seated toward the front, nearest the director, across from his own position. She was busy writing some notes with her head down. Damian waited by the door for Dan to arrive.

"Ladies and gentlemen, the director," said Damian, as Dan walked through the door.

G watched as Damian closed the door behind Dan and activated some kind of device on the wall, wrote something quickly in a logbook, and took a seat beside G. Dan took his seat at the head of the table.

"Is the room secure?" asked Dan.

"The room *is* secure," answered Damian.

"Very well," said Dan. "I'd like to start off this meeting with good news. We found Mark Rubis last night. He's banged up a bit but very much alive. We couldn't have done it without the help of our guest, Mr. Weston. G, thank you for helping us find one of our very best," said Dan.

G nodded humbly.

"As most of you know, I rarely use this room to call a meeting unless the highest levels of security must be met. This is such an occasion. We have among us a man with a gift so rare that there may not be another one like him anywhere on the planet. Therefore, secrecy and protection is of the highest importance."

Dan looked at each person as he spoke. Then he looked at G once again.

"But before we proceed any further, I'd like to offer our guest an opportunity," said Dan. "Mr. Weston, we'd like you to join our team. You'll be given resources to develop and research your gift or theory or whatever it is you call it that you used to help us locate our agent. We see a mutual benefit in having you on our team. We'll be able to use your skills in the highest interest of national security; you will, of course, be free to exploit those skills to continue to improve and gain scientific knowledge and insight as you see fit. You're free to make a choice, but you should know that there are others who seek to use you — or eliminate you — for the very skills and abilities you possess. I don't suspect you'll find a better offer."

"So either way," said G, "my life as I knew it is pretty much over."

"We prefer to see it as *changed* rather than being over," said Dan.

The others in the room listened and watched the two men converse.

G sat expressionless as he thought about how it all came down to this moment. They say that we all face a pivotal moment in life. This was one such moment for G—one that would alter the very course of his life. The thought of working for the NSA was exciting on the surface. But what were the deeper implications? Would they *own* him? Would he have a life? Or would he become a prisoner to himself and his abilities? He looked at Dr. Middleton, who returned a cold stare. He looked at Athena, who returned a look of hope and encouragement. He glanced at Damian but couldn't get a good read from the experienced agent. Then he looked back at Dan, squarely in the eyes.

"I accept."

Perry and KK crested the ridge as the sun reached its highest peak. The two men were exhausted but eager to establish some kind of radio contact with anyone who could assist the team. Their preferred target was the remotely piloted aircraft overhead, somewhere in the skies above them.

The men worked together to set up a satellite antennae and solar array and plugged a radio into a small laptop computer. The ensemble was ready within five minutes.

"Any secure receiver...this is Dagger Two-Two, how copy, over?"

The two men listened for a response with anticipation. They breathed heavily from the climb and the thin mountain air. KK offered Perry a swig of water from his canteen. Perry declined and tried the radio again.

"This is Dagger Two-Two on secure frequency, does anyone copy?" said Perry. He heard the return of static on the radio, followed by a short radio transmission.

"Dagger Two-Two, this is Firefly. We read you loud and clear, over." The static-laden reply came from a drone operator out of Cannon AFB, New Mexico.

KK almost choked on his water upon hearing the reply. He wiped his mouth as a smile spread across his dirty, sunburned face. He listened intently while he watched his teammate interact with the drone operator.

Dream Operative

"Roger, Firefly. Dagger Two-Two is located at 8.1596 North latitude, 77.77 West longitude. Request an overhead look and authentication, over."

The Predator operator explained that they would experience a delay for *other priorities* and would provide authentication later. The men knew the routine was meant to ensure the radio call was coming from legitimate sources. So Perry tried to invoke a higher priority to stress the complexity and urgency of their situation.

"Dagger Two-Two copies. Be advised, Dagger Two-Two is a priority *code five* with injured and a disabled aircraft, over."

The two men listened to empty static for a few moments, which seemed to take forever. They assumed the drone operator was coordinating and authenticating their priority call. They were right.

"Uh, Dagger Two-Two, this is Firefly. We copy your request. We should have you onscreen in thirty minutes. Are you co-located with your disabled aircraft?"

"Firefly, Dagger Two-Two, that's a negative. The location of the aircraft and remaining team is located at 8.1006N – 77.7855W. They're located adjacent to a river alongside a mountain ridge."

"Firefly copies. Please state the number of personnel and disposition of the crew."

The men felt a sense of relief knowing they had made contact and that help was on the way. They relayed all the details of the crew and the one injured member and remained in place to keep the lines of communication open until help arrived.

"Looks like a hell of a storm approaching the valley," said KK, peering through his binoculars back toward the riverbed where Ox and the crew awaited.

"I'm sure Ox is prepared for it," said Perry, making some keyboard entries onto the laptop. "Just for shits-n-grins though, I'll check the satellite picture if I can find one," he added.

"Good call," said KK.

Dan wasted no time with G's indoctrination to the agency. He began the meeting with a situation report, or "SITREP" as it is more commonly referred to, inside secret circles.

"This will be an abbreviated briefing with our top priority updates," explained Dan. "Mark Rubis is recovering nicely and sends his regards to the group. I'd like to once again express the gratitude of the Agency to our newest member, Mr. Weston, for Mark's safe recovery," said Dan looking at G.

G nodded once again, this time with a look of determination and confidence.

"OK, listen up. We have reports of a CIA agent who may have been abducted last night in New York City," said Dan.

G felt the hair on the back of his neck bristle as he listened to Dan explain Jeff's situation. He was also wise enough to evaluate the look on Dr. Middleton's face as Dan broke the news to the group.

"We have reason to believe he may have been in the company of Khalid Abdul-Hakim, number one on the international terrorist manifest," said Dan, circulating three pictures of Hakim to the group. "These pictures are extremely rare and most assuredly do *not* represent what Mr. Hakim currently looks like. As you may or may not know," said Dan looking at G, "he is a master of disguises. This only adds to the difficulty factor when we try to track his movements."

G examined each of the pictures, paying close attention to the eyes of the most wanted man in the world. They were the very eyes of the man he had seen with Jeff in the club in his dream. A chill ran through his veins when he finally made the connection.

"I can find this man for you," said G, without realizing he was interrupting Dan.

"I'm sorry...what did you just say?" asked Dan.

G looked up from the pictures and noticed everyone at the table was staring at him intently. His comment had commanded the attention of the entire small, but powerful group.

"I...believe I can help you find this man," said G. "But if he's every bit as dangerous as you say he is, I'll need to know what you know...as *much* as you know. I'll need everything you have on him."

"It's not much, G," said Athena, speaking to him for the first time since his arrival at the super-secret Agency.

"Whatever..." responded G, quickly discounting her comment as insignificant. "I need *all* of it. Sightings, photos, habits, psych profiles," said G, looking directly at Dr. Middleton as if he were ordering her from a position of authority.

Dr. Middleton looked at Dan.

Dan shrugged his shoulders slightly. "Give him what he needs. I'm granting him an interim *Top Secret* security clearance and accompanying access codes effective immediately," said Dan. "Damian, Athena, work with G to ensure he gets whatever he needs."

G's mind absorbed the enormity of it all as he listened to Dan make good on his promise to clear a path for G to develop his gift, albeit with a huge expectation as his first task.

"G, I'm providing unprecedented access to someone with an *interim* security clearance," explained Dan. "As your new boss, I *order* you to exercise extreme prejudice when handling the data and information you'll have access to. You should know that I've *never* done this before, and I'm placing the reputation of this Agency, and my very position, in your hands."

G suddenly realized the gravity of his decision and, for the first time, felt nervous about his acceptance. Nonetheless, he nodded affirmatively and confidently as if to offer some kind of assurance. Dan appeared to be satisfied, at least for the time being, that G understood the magnitude of his responsibilities.

"Is there anything anyone would like to add before we move to the next item on our agenda?" asked Dan.

"I have one thing," said G, again with some hesitation.

"Go ahead, G, whatcha got?" asked Dan.

"I can confirm, with a high degree of certainty, that this Hakim dude was in fact the one with the agent. Your sources were correct when they said they spotted him with your agent in New York City."

"And you know this how?" asked Dan.

G looked at Dan and offered an abbreviated response.

"Dreamt it. Last night…or rather, early this morning. Most assuredly in real time, as it happened," explained G. "I'm not sure just why I dreamt it, but I did."

Dan sat back in his chair, somewhat lost in the very thought that this terrorist was in fact inside US borders. He was also trying to get used to the fact that his newest member of the team would offer such a concise and candid perspective. He glanced at Damian.

"Damian, get a confirmation from the team on the specifics. Corroborate the facts with the details that G provides and work up a report ASAP," ordered Dan.

"I'm on it, Boss."

"So this man is in fact in our very backyard. Isn't that just wonderful," said Dan sarcastically glancing at his notes. "Any idea where he is, precisely?"

"Not yet," responded G, as he slowly shook his head.

"What do you need from us to find him?"

"Like I said, I need everything you've got on him. The one thing I know about him is that he possesses a similar ability to mine—"

"You're kidding me." interrupted Dan.

"I wish I were," said G. "But I think I'm better than him. I believe he attributes his ability to that of a divine nature. Not that I don't believe in a higher power, mind you. I tend to take more of a scientific approach and catalogue everything I've learned."

"How does that give you an advantage?"

"It's difficult to explain. But the more I know about him, the more I can manipulate him, predict the way he'll react, any habits or patterns he has," explained G. "If I can break into the one thing he guards most, I'll be able to gain the advantage."

"And what is it exactly that he guards the most?" asked Dan.

"His mind."

"No offense, G, but we've had some of the best analysts study his habits and he continues to evade us...with his brilliant mind and manipulations," said Dr. Middleton.

"I understand," said G with a single nod. "But you've not had the advantage of analyzing that mind from the inside out. Give me a chance to see if I can see something the conscious mind cannot," added G. He briefly thought about the insight he had gained about the good doctor already.

"OK, folks, I have only one more item on the agenda for this group," said Dan. "Athena, would you like to brief this?"

"Yes, sir," responded Athena. "G, some of the following information may come as a surprise to you, but I promise everything will make sense."

31

Hartman found Booker at the edge of the swollen river. He was wearing a bandanna and a rain-soaked T-shirt, camouflage pants, and gloves.

Booker looked up to see his teammate, whose arms were full of vines and strips of bark. They would be used to lash the logs together that Booker had set aside as a floatation base for their makeshift raft.

"Awesome, brother!" said Booker, wiping his brow and examining the supplies.

"I gotta run back and grab the rest," said Hartman, turning to make another trip.

"Copy that. I'll get started tying these logs together, so we can be ready to launch at sunset."

The men kept working despite the steady rain. They were soaked, but the mosquitoes and flies weren't bothering them much, so they were happy they could get the work done without the nuisance. They also knew that the river would continue to rise because of the weather conditions and would eventually offer them the best hope of a water escape.

Booker had most of the logs tied together when Hartman returned with another load of vines.

"I'm glad you're back. I need you to hold this part of the raft up while I tie the mains together," said Booker.

Hartman assisted his teammate with the task while Booker secured the final logs together. They used the last of the vines to secure a makeshift rudder to the stern of the raft.

"Got any more strips of bark?" asked Booker.

"No, but that's an easy fix. Why?"

"I was thinking we could use a couple of strips to secure our gear and keep it from floating away. Just in case…"

"No problem. I left a few pieces where I just came from," said Hartman.

"Cool. It'll be dark soon. Help me push the raft to the edge of the bank, so we're ready to shove off. I'll grab the gear while you get the vines."

The men worked together to push the raft to the edge of the bank, but not so far into the water that the rising river would sweep away their coveted transportation. Booker collected the gear—rucksacks, weapons, and personal items—and returned to find the raft partially floating in the rising river. He had to wade into the water to keep it from floating away with the increasing current. He checked his watch, loaded the gear onto the raft, and waited.

Dusk had nearly given way to the approaching darkness when Booker began to wonder about his teammate. The rainfall had slowed a bit. He thought about looking over the ridge of the bank to see if he could see any signs of his teammate, but he couldn't leave the raft. He had nothing to secure it. The very rope he needed was the reason Hartman was gone in the first place. Suddenly, he heard something.

Athena briefed the group about a developing situation in Central America involving a special tactics team who was ambushed by a faction of a large Mexican drug cartel.

The team had collected intelligence on their operation and was preparing to be extracted when they were discovered by the cartel. A plane was sent in, and they were able to find the team.

"The good news is that *most* of the team was successfully extracted," explained Athena. "There were two who were left behind because of extenuating circumstances. We believe they are in danger, but we don't have a good fix on their location yet."

"What were the *extenuating* circumstances?" asked G. "And why couldn't the pilot wait for the entire team?"

Athena looked at Dan for his approval to continue.

Dan nodded.

"This is where this gets personal, G," explained Athena. "The pilot is a mutual friend of ours. I believe you may know him as *Ox*," explained Athena.

Dream Operative

"This *is* a small world," said G, slowly shaking his head. "Well, the Ox I know woulda waited on the entire team."

"Under typical circumstances, I would agree," said Athena. "But he and the crew were under fire and opted to save the majority at the expense of the few. Besides, the two who remained are highly trained at escape and evade tactics." Athena went on to explain the added complication of Hartman's apparent capture and explained what Booker's expected actions were.

"So we don't even have an update on whether or not we're dealing with a hostage situation?" asked G.

"You ask very good questions, G," said Dan. "This is precisely the kind of thing you can help us with."

G nodded as he thought about how his abilities could help.

"We also know that Ox's plane didn't have enough fuel to make it back to Howard Field in Panama. We know they went down near a riverbed at the base of a small mountain ridge southwest of Navagandi," explained Athena.

"Have we heard from anyone or received any radio calls?" asked Dan.

"Yes, sir. That's another piece of good news I recently received from SOCOM—the Special Operations Command," she added, clarifying the acronym for G. "The special tactics team riding along with Ox made contact with a Predator squadron out of Cannon Air Force Base, New Mexico. We should have an exact location on the team any time now."

"Keep me posted. OK folks," said Dan. "Any alibis?"

G looked around the table and tried processing the sheer amount of information he had been exposed to. His mind was swimming with details and questions. He had figured Ox was into some kind of government operation, but had no idea just how deep…until now.

"Doctor…I need you to help G settle in," instructed Dan. "G, I'm afraid it's gonna be another long day for you once again, my friend. We appreciate you taking on the responsibility and helping your country. Please work closely with the team here and let us know if there's anything we can do to accommodate you. Athena, please meet me in my office. That'll be all, team," said Dan, terminating the meeting.

Hakim worked his way through the city to put some distance between himself and the gentleman's club. He stopped at an old Irish Pub. Business was slow, and Hakim saw it as an opportunity to be alone. He found an isolated booth and ordered a cup of coffee.

The waiter placed a napkin on the table, set the coffee in front of Hakim, and left him alone. Hakim pulled the envelope from his coat pocket and tore off the edge. He tipped the envelope slightly and poured a small SD chip into the palm of his hand. Holding the chip between his forefinger and thumb, he smiled. Then he removed several pages containing text from the envelope. He unfolded the pages to skim the contents. The pages contained what at first appeared to be an encrypted message, until Hakim reached the beginning of the second paragraph...

You ignorant prick! Do you think I'm stupid? If you want the real chip and the real documents, you'll have to play this my way. I'm the only one who can help you. I'm the only one who has knowledge on where the original information is located. As I told you when we first met, you're in my country, so you do things my way. Don't even bother wasting your time with the chip. It's empty.

Hakim was livid. He had to force himself to slow down and think clearly. He took a sip from his coffee and remembered the instructions he had last given to the couple at the club.

"Eliminate him..."

The fatal instructions echoed in his raging mind as he sprang to his feet, threw a twenty on the table, and made his way to the street. He had no way of calling Jeff's captors but knew where they would take him. He hailed a taxi.

"Café Napoli. Hurry, please," demanded Hakim, throwing a handful of bills at the driver, which was pretty much all he had left in his pocket.

Jeff's head hit the floor of the van as he unsuccessfully tried to maintain his balance from being tossed in by the thugs.

The men were yelling at him as they turned him onto his stomach. One of the men put his knee into the middle of Jeff's back while waiting for the shooter close the sliding door behind him. The van sped off. They bound his hands and placed a hood over his head and rolled him onto his back. He felt a rather large sized boot pressing against his chest. He guessed it was to keep him from making any sudden moves or to prevent him from rolling over during sharp turns. He was uncomfortable nonetheless.

Dream Operative

Jeff listened as the men spoke to each other in Arabic. They had no idea he was an Arabic linguist and could understand them clearly. He knew he was not in a good position and that these guys were deadly serious about their jobs. His heart pounded as he listened to the conversation.

"Why did you shoot Basma?"

"She was careless. She let her guard down and got in the way. The bitch was beginning to become a liability anyway."

"The teacher will *not* be happy."

"Let me deal with him."

"What now? What do we do with *him*?"

"We take him to the office and eliminate him as we were told. I want to capture it on video, so we can exploit his death."

Jeff's mind raced. *Where is this "office" they're taking me to? And how can I manipulate the situation?*

The van slowed, then came to a stop. The driver turned off the engine. Jeff could hear the door slide open.

"Get up!" commanded one of the thugs. He felt two hands grip each of his arms and lift him to his feet. He was led out of the van and taken inside a building, where they helped guide him down a short flight of stairs.

Jeff picked up the scent of food. He tried to figure out where he was being taken so he could devise an escape plan...if only there was one. He heard a door open. Then he was shoved into a chair. His hands were tied to the chair behind his back. Zip ties. Impossible to break free.

Jeff felt the intensity of bright lights through the shroud covering his head. He squinted when the shroud was removed and the bright lights beamed against his face.

"What is your name?"

Jeff tried looking around the room but found it difficult to see beyond the bright lights and the dark background of the room. The cowards were hiding in the shadows, like the cockroaches he knew them to be. He could barely make out their silhouettes beyond the fringe of light.

"What is your name?" shouted an indiscriminate voice once again.

"My name? My name is Jeff."

"What is your *full* name?"

"Fuck off."

Without warning, a fist slammed into the right side of his face. His ears began ringing and his head was swimming as he tried to shake off the hit.

"Answer the question!"

Jeff could feel blood trickling from his mouth and could barely hear from his right ear any longer. He opened his mouth to readjust his jaw and spat blood onto the floor.

"What is your name?"

"My name is Jeff."

"Who do you work for, Jeff?"

Realizing his ensuing fate, Jeff raised his head, spit another wad of blood, smiled, and simply responded, "I work for the American people. The very people who hunt down pieces of shit like you and kill you."

He braced himself for another blow to the face, but it never came. Instead, he heard the slide of a handgun being cocked. He knew there was a bullet in the chamber of someone's assassination weapon. He blinked slowly, awaiting the inevitable. Time slowed...

"Very well then, Mr. Jeff," responded the voice. "If it is the American people you work for, then it is the American people you will die for. *Allahu Akbar!*"

Dr. Middleton waited to escort G to yet another secure area of the building he hadn't yet seen. Athena and Damian weren't permitted, because it was classified outside their "need to know."

"We're here when you need us, G," said Athena.

G thank them both and asked Athena if she had a moment. He spoke to her quietly but candidly in a corner of the room.

"Look, I have no idea who to trust here," he confided. "I'm not certain I even trust *you* anymore. I *want* to, but—"

Athena stopped him.

"You're right to take that attitude, G...for now," she said, glancing at Dr. Middleton over G's shoulder. She leaned in closer. "You'll figure out who you can trust around here. You'll also figure out who really gives a shit about you," she whispered.

She paused long enough to look into his eyes and do her best to communicate with him on a deeper level—a level she knew only he could discern.

He responded with a hint of a smile and a simple nod. He turned toward Dr. Middleton and followed her out of the room.

Dream Operative

The taxi screeched to a halt outside Café' Napoli. Hakim's feet hit the pavement as the cab was still coming to a full stop. He slammed the door behind him and ran into the building past the few remaining wait staff and cleaning crew.

Hakim quickly made his way down a short flight of stairs to a locked entrance door. He began to bang both fists furiously while shouting to be let in.

"Let me in at once! This is—"

Hakim's attempt was quickly diverted by the sound of a single gunshot. He knew by the sound that it was a small-caliber handgun. A 9 mm or a .38˜caliber, perhaps. Either way, a shot at close range to the head would be instantly fatal. He became disheartened and enraged and proceeded to bang on the door again. As he continued to furiously pound on the door, it opened. Despite the fact that he was face-to-face with an armed man nervously aiming a handgun at him, he pushed his way past him and ran into the room directly toward the bright lights.

"Teacher. We…did not assume you would be here," exclaimed the man operating the camera, still recording.

Hakim dropped to one knee beside Jeff's lifeless body, now toppled onto the floor from the impact of the bullet to the right side of his head, hands still bound to the back of the chair. Blood pooled as it continued to drain from the exit wound.

Hakim stared into Jeff's eyes, realizing that he took with him the very secrets of the contents of the envelope. The room became eerily quiet. Hakim was lost for a moment in the abyss of his thoughts. The silence somehow seemed appropriate in a twisted sort of way.

Hakim took a deep breath and let out a sigh. Slowly raising his head, he caught something out of the corner of his eye in a dark corner of the room. As quickly as he turned his head, the object had disappeared. He detected a presence he couldn't explain and quickly rose to his feet, stared into the corner, and yelled out in defiance, "Show yourself! I know you're there. I don't know who you are, but I am coming for you. And I am coming for *her*."

The men in the room looked at each other with curiosity, each witnessing the oddity displayed by their teacher and master. Who was he speaking to? Had he gone temporarily mad? They shone one of the bright lights into the corner to see if there was indeed someone there. It was empty, but they were spooked nonetheless.

"Clean this mess. And turn that damn camera off!" commanded Hakim, turning to walk out of the room.

One of the men followed him out of the building but couldn't keep up. Hakim had vanished as quickly as he had appeared and was nowhere to be found.

"He's expecting you," said Janet, as Athena walked in to see Dan. "Thank you, Janet."

Dan looked up for a moment. "Come on in. Please close the door behind you and have a seat," he said, with the calm tone of a mentor and friend.

Athena closed the door and sat in one of two high-back leather chairs positioned informally off to the side of Dan's massive, executive-style redwood desk. Dan moved from behind the desk and took a seat beside her in the adjacent chair and crossed one leg over the other. He paused.

"I am so far out on a limb bringing G into the fold, Valerie," said Dan, confiding in her, using her real name.

Athena tried to figure out where his dialogue was headed.

"I know we routinely step outside the lines in this business, but I just hired someone whom virtually *none* of us understands or knows, beyond the simple fact that he may be able to help us in ways we can't begin to comprehend. To be honest, I was ready to release him until we found Mark using the very details he provided."

"What do you need from me?" Athena calmly asked.

"You've developed a relationship with him. He's a bit overwhelmed right now, but I really think he trusts you. What I need from you is to watch him, shape him, and condition him."

Athena listened patiently and nodded without emotion as she began to understand the responsibility that was being handed to her.

"Look, I realize you're used to being more of a freelance operative, but I hope you'd be willing to take this on. If I'm being presumptuous, please tell me."

"No. You're right, he does trust me. What are my limitations?"

"Standard protocol, Val...your methodologies are your business. Just keep them from becoming *my* business. And don't get emotionally involved."

Dream Operative

Athena glanced away for a second and quickly realized the psychology behind that behavior may have revealed a possible distracting vulnerability. She reconnected her attention and assumed the full focus of her position as a *deadly ghost*, as is sometimes a common reference to agents with her skills and abilities.

"I won't allow anything to compromise Agency objectives, Dan," said Athena, returning a look of serious confidence to her boss.

"I know," said Dan. "Keep me posted on this periodically, Valerie. And thank you for your service. That'll be all," said Dan, rising to his feet, indicating the meeting was over.

Perry pulled up the satellite weather picture on his laptop. This part of the country was known for short but intense thunderstorms that seemingly came out of nowhere.

"Looks like there's an intense rain cell building just off the western coastline. Not sure if it'll move onshore, though. We should keep an eye on it," he said.

The two men remained atop the ridge, patiently awaiting word from the Predator crew to assist with an accurate fix on their location. KK broke the silence with a question.

"You think Captain Booker made contact with Hartman?"

"Yes, I do," responded Perry, as confidently as any young Marine would be expected to respond.

"We should've stayed," said KK, the younger of the two men.

"We did the right thing, brother. They'll be OK...even if I have to go back in alone and get 'em out myself," said Perry, thinking about his leader and teammate.

The conversation was interrupted with a crackle of the radio frequency and a call from the Predator.

"Dagger Two-Two, this is Firefly, how copy, over?"

"Firefly, Dagger Two-Two, loud and clear."

"Roger, Dagger Two-Two, Firefly is overhead your reported position. You are requested to illuminate your IR strobe, so we can obtain an accurate location of your position, over."

Perry instructed KK to activate an infrared strobe that would be visible to the sensor operator searching for the signal with encrypted sophisticated detection equipment.

"Dagger Two-Two, Firefly has a visual on your position. Be advised, you are located eighty-three miles east-southeast of Howard Field. We are dispatching search and rescue assets for pickup. ETA is approximately one hour, over."

"Dagger Two-Two copies. Thanks, Firefly." answered Perry, giving a high five to his teammate.

32

Hartman ran over the ridge and slid down the river bank, tree bark strips in arms.

"We gotta scoot, brother. We have company," said Hartman, as quietly but urgently as possible.

"Copy that. Climb aboard, and I'll shove us off," said Booker, pushing the raft deeper into the current of the river.

Hartman offered a hand as the water reached Booker's waist. While he was climbing onto the raft, the men heard two explosions in the distance-one right after the other.

"Perimeter detonations," said Hartman, as if Booker needed the confirmation.

"They *were* close," said Booker. "No wonder you were in such a hurry."

The men looked back into the darkening twilight. No threats were detected. Maybe the explosions wounded the intruders. They were hopeful. Either way, the noise would wake up the jungle and anyone else in the area.

The raft hit the edge of an embankment and surprised the men. Hartman nearly fell off. They were focusing so much on their escape and the distraction of the explosions, they nearly forgot about navigating the river. Darkness had descended upon the jungle and would make good cover for the escape, as long as they could effectively navigate the river.

"Grab a set of NVGs and hand 'em to me, so I can see what the hell I'm doing," said Booker.

Hartman grabbed a rucksack and eventually found a set of NVGs for Booker and handed them to his teammate. He found a second pair, put them on, and activated the switch. Suddenly, the intimidating darkness turned into a familiar green tint of comforting detail.

"Thank God for NVGs," said Hartman quietly, grabbing a makeshift oar Booker had thought to craft while waiting on his return.

The men maneuvered the raft toward a small bend in the river and did their best to remain as quiet as possible. The only sounds they heard were the rush of the current and the awakening jungle nightlife. Hartman secured the gear with the bark strips that were left on the deck then looked up to check on his teammate. Booker was busy steering the makeshift craft. Suddenly, he saw a handful of men appear on the crest of the embankment they had just left. Hartman communicated to Booker using hand gestures — *crouch low, check six, remain quiet.*

Booker slowly lowered to a crouched position, glanced over his shoulder, and saw several men searching the shoreline as he and Hartman rounded the first bend in the river. They were now safely out of sight and were completely covered by the total darkness of the night.

Hartman scanned the river banks for any signs of life…friendly or otherwise. The rainfall began to taper off as the men drifted along with the slow-moving current.

G heard the door close behind him and stepped and stepped into Dr. Middleton's clinical executive office suite.

"Nice digs, Sibyl," said G.

He got no response. Then again, he didn't really expect one.

The room was handsomely appointed. The walls were a warm, deep red color, framed in mahogany trim and matching crown molding. He assumed Dr. Middleton had a personal hand in decorating the room. There were no distracting personal mementos hanging on the walls. No diplomas or certificates or licenses. An expensive leather psychologist's couch was positioned against a wall. Above it hung an original oil painting of a nature scene, framed in an antique gold hand-carved frame that gave the painting an elegant contrast against the dark wall color. The scene depicted a cobblestone path to nowhere, adorned with large oak trees and hanging Spanish moss and reminded G of an earlier time in his life when he lived in the rural south near his grandfather. The picture held his attention as he began to extract a personal meaning from its composition.

Dream Operative

"What does the picture tell you, G?" asked Dr. Middleton, breaking into the solace of G's moment.

He didn't answer. He wasn't interested in playing mind games with the doctor. Instead, he continued to study the layout of the room. Adjacent to the couch was a matching leather wingback chair, which he assumed was for the counselor or shrink.

There was a desk on the adjacent wall. On the desk were three computer monitors and several wires protruding from the lower part of the desk. There was no real attempt to conceal them. A closer look revealed that the wires were electrode sensors, the kind with the sticky adhesive pads on the ends. An assistant of Dr. Middleton was seated behind the monitors, busily tapping on a keyboard.

"I'd like to see if we can provide the conditions to help you slip into a dream state, G."

"I'm not tired," answered G, as if to challenge the good doctor.

"We have ways to help you relax," responded Dr. Middleton confidently.

"You have an answer for everything don't you, Sibyl?"

"The Agency wants me to help you, so I'm here to help."

"And I'm certain you're here for the love of God and country too," said G sarcastically. "So what are all the wires, and who the hell is *he,* anyway?"

"He's here to collect neural data," said Dr. Middleton, inviting G to examine the computer displays. "See for yourself."

"So...you hook me up to the electrodes, and he collects brain wave activity while I'm dreaming?"

"Among other things."

"Such as?"

"Your vitals—pulse, breathing rate, external physical reactions."

"Remember *not* to touch me...under *any* circumstances."

Dr. Middleton nodded. "I understand, G."

G took a deep breath, looked suspiciously at her assistant, and let out an accepting sigh. "OK, when do we start, and what's my mission?"

"We need to help you relax," she said. "How do you react to Loritab?"

"Wonderfully. Even better with a rum and coke," said G, with a shit-eating grin.

"Your mission today is primarily designed for us to collect baseline data. Try to note where your dreams take you and how they're different from any other dreams you typically have," explained Dr. Middleton, as she handed him a 750 mg tablet of Loritab and a glass of water.

G listened to her instructions as he examined the pill, popped it into his mouth, swallowed it, and chased it with the water.

"Should you decide to wander off—and I fully expect you will—you'll be on your own. Try to remember as much as you can, so we can correlate the data when you return to consciousness. I need to remind you that because your sleep will be drug-induced, you may not have the control over the timing of your return to consciousness that you're used to having. If your vitals spike, and you should go into any kind of physical arrest—"

"I won't."

"*If* you do, I will not only touch you, I will *treat* you. It's my obligation as a doctor.'

"You mean *someone* around here actually follows a set of ethics and has a *conscience*? Amazing. Just give me a chance to control the exit myself, and do your best *not* to touch me."

Dr. Middleton returned a glance of professional indifference and led G to the couch. She grabbed the electrodes and brought them toward G.

"Unbutton your shirt, please."

He gave her a quick look of distrust but conceded nonetheless.

She strategically placed electrodes on his chest, wrist, neck, and both temples.

"Are you comfortable?"

"You want my honest opinion?" he said, sarcastically. "I'm good," he conceded, as he looked up to study the painting above him.

"G?"

"Yeah?"

"If you do decide to take this opportunity to explore..." said Dr. Middleton, with a bit of hesitation.

"Sibyl...I'll find him. And I'll find the bastard that's behind all this," said G, his eyelids beginning to lower. "That is...*if* I should wander..."

"Then what?"

The question hit G like a ton of bricks. *Then what?* Great question, actually. Two words; each backed with a rather powerful force behind them. More powerful when asked by a sensible person rather than from one blindly in pursuit of evil or danger.

"I have to get close enough to read him," said G, his mind continuing to relax.

"Remember, if you get close enough to see his thoughts…he can see yours."

Damn, she's good, G thought. *But she's right. I have to find a way in without being detected…if there is such a way.*

G placed his gaze back upon the painting. He fell asleep, wondering where the path to nowhere led.

Dr. Middleton offered a slight nod and glanced at her assistant as he began quietly tapping on the keyboard. She glanced at her watch and made a note of the time.

Hakim locked the door behind him and paused as he turned around to the emptiness of his hotel room. He scanned the room.

The room looked different. It was cleaner, and the bed had been made. He had forgotten to tell the front desk that he didn't want maid service. Another uncharacteristic mistake.

His mind was still swimming as he examined his personal belongings. Everything seemed to be in order. He sat on the edge of the bed and ran his fingers through his hair and got caught up once again in his thoughts. Frustration and disappointment set in.

He fell back against the firm mattress and looked up at the ornate ceiling. Dead ends often disguised themselves, and Hakim was determined to see through this seemingly problematic situation. Thinking…Analyzing… Reconstructing…

He thought about the contents of the envelope and how Jeff had been able to predict Hakim's double-cross. Of course, he had paid the ultimate price in the end.

Hakim continued to replay the entire evening in his mind and thought about how things had ended with the execution of his informant.

His mind snapped to when he remembered the vision he had encountered in a dark corner of the room. His thoughts centered on trying to figure out just what…or *who* he saw. He detested knowing anyone could follow him, much less keep up with him for this long. The fact that he now seemed to have a formidable foe bothered him. He gave little credence to the fact that his foe operated primarily on a secondary dimension. The fact remained that the secondary dimension was affecting his primary dimension—and the ability to operate freely in *either* dimension. He was determined to find, confront, and eliminate him once and for all. His first dilemma, however, was to figure out, if he could, who Jeff's connection was. He knew if he could find Jeff's connection, that person would lead him to the *real* envelope and the information he so desperately needed to conduct the type of operation he had planned.

He became so fixated on the day's events that it sapped what energy remained. Exhaustion overcame him. He fell asleep hanging onto the thought of what options remained for him…and the man with the now-familiar eyes.

The wind whipped at the makeshift canopy covering the starboard wing of the Casa as the storm approached.

The plane was positioned adjacent to the incoming direction of the storm, so Ox and the crew would have to tie down the wings as best they could to prevent the tiny craft from overturning with any sudden strong gust of wind.

"Make sure Stokes is comfortable," said Ox, looking at Ronaldo, who was closest to the injured member. "And make sure he's dry and warm. This storm won't last long, but it may have a sucker punch embedded in it."

Ronaldo nodded and made his way into the aircraft to check on Stokes, while Pat and the others tied down the wings.

Ox puffed on a cigar while peering toward the mountain through a pair of binoculars.

"Whatcha lookin' for?" asked Pat.

"Signs of our recon team."

"I'm sure they're all right."

"I'm not worried whether they're all right. Hell, they're trained to be all right. Seeing our radios are pretty much useless here…I'm just lookin' for a signal."

"I hope they managed to make contact with someone," responded Pat.

Ox was secretly hoping for the same thing. He suspected the approaching storm prevented the men from signaling with any kind of reflective device—per typical radio-out protocol. But something would've been better than nothing.

The sun set over the adjacent mountain ridge. The only light left in the darkening sky was an occasional burst of lightning.

Dream Operative

"I'll go make sure the gear is secure," said Pat. He left Ox peering at the impending storm.

G heard what he thought was the sound of cicadas as he became aware of his drift into alter-consciousness. He breathed in aroma of flowers and fresh-cut grass while his eyes discovered psychedelic surroundings that transformed themselves to bright white.

He felt the firm ground meet his feet. As much as he tried, he could only see the nothingness of bright white. It was if he were looking at a blank painter's canvas. He looked down and saw that he was standing on a cobblestone road. Slowly turning around, he was amazed by what he saw. Laid out before him was the very painting he had studied in Dr. Middleton's office—except now, he was a part of it. Everything was even more vivid than he remembered from the painting. He quickly turned around again and saw that his dream had completed the painting for him, with a thickly wooded cypress forest where, a moment before, had been the nothingness of the blank painter's canvas.

The road at his feet was the beginning of a path that drifted between two of the most beautiful oak trees he had ever seen. Childhood memories flooded his mind as he studied the beauty of Spanish moss hanging from the trees, beautifully draped as if personally decorated by the angels themselves. Birds sang in the distance, backed up by that familiar sound of cicadas, providing a backdrop of constant white noise to accompany the occasional sound of crickets calling to each other.

I thought I'd find you here, said Angel.

G smiled when he heard her voice, but he had not yet caught a glimpse of her.

I didn't think I could do it, actually, said G, answering her in his mind. *It was more of an effort to see if I could,* he added.

Your abilities continue to improve. Impressive, indeed.

It's even more awesome on the inside, said G, as he gazed at his surroundings. He closed his eyes for a moment to focus on the aroma of grass and flowers and of the sounds speaking to his soul.

"Where is this place?" he asked audibly, opening his eyes to see Angel standing before him.

"You tell me," she answered.

G smiled. "It's a place I come to for strength. It always has been."

"You were surprised to see it in a painting?"

"Of course—why wouldn't I be?"

"Because you placed it there," she said with a smile.

"Where does the path take me?"

"Where do you wish to go?"

"It's not really where I *wish* to go this time, Angel. It's more a matter of where I *need* to go."

"Then this path will take you there."

Angel tilted her head slightly as she subconsciously connected with G. *You're concerned — why?*

I question my ability to confront the unknown, he responded.

The unknown will always be present. It's the one thing you will never defeat.

G absorbed the wisdom coming from his friend and guide.

There is one thing that will help mitigate the unknown, she said.

What's that?

Courage.

Seems too simple.

Far from it, answered Angel. *But if you face your fear and trust your instincts and abilities, courage will emanate from within and become a welcome accomplice.*

G continued to listen to her wisdom echoing in his mind, all the while contemplating the path ahead…leading to somewhere.

"C'mon, there's someplace you need to be," she said, grabbing his hand to lead him down the path.

33

The fuselage of the clandestine aircraft did a good job of shielding the crew from the steady wind and driving rain. Ox was able to see that his airplane wasn't exactly watertight, because he was standing in the aft section right under a seam that was leaking steadily. The rain continued to come down steadily, but the wind wasn't as bad as expected.

Most of the crew had worn earplugs to reduce the sound of the rain coming down against the aluminum exterior of the aircraft. Everyone except Pat was sleeping or doing a good job of faking it, as far as Ox could tell. Pat looked up briefly to acknowledge him and picked up a book to read.

Ox took a last look around to make sure the crew and craft were in good shape and placed earplugs into his ears as well. He never realized how loud it could get in this section of the aircraft, because he was always in the cockpit wearing headphones. He found a moderately comfortable place in a dry corner and decided to get some sleep. His slumber took him directly to REM sleep and ultimately to a rare dream state.

―⁂―

Angel brought G to a small musty room that seemed oddly familiar to him. He heard voices shouting in what sounded like an Arabic dialect.

His focus was somewhat obscured when bright lights appeared before him. Angel pulled him toward a darkened corner of the small room.

G watched familiar men drag Jeff into the room and sit him in a chair in the center of the floor. He was interrogated and beaten when he resisted. G winced at the blow to Jeff's head and face as he watched blood spew from his mouth at one point.

"I have to stop this," said G.

"You can't," responded Angel without emotion.

"I can. You even said so. You said *anything is possible* here. Why isn't it possible for me to stop this?"

"Because it has already happened."

G's face registered a look of confusion and frustration. He reluctantly turned to watch as one of the men chambered a round in a handgun, placed it against Jeff's right temple, and pulled the trigger.

"No!" shouted G.

But no one heard him.

G felt his body go cold as he watched the assassination unfold before him in an eerie slow motion. The bullet blew through the left side of Jeff's head and splattered blood and brain matter against an adjacent wall. His body, still bound to the chair, toppled to the floor. G was shocked at what he had witnessed. "Why did you bring me here?" he angrily demanded.

Angel remained silent.

G heard someone banging violently on a door. A few moments later he watched as Hakim entered the room, shouting. He ran to Jeff and knelt down in the pool of blood emanating from his fatal wound. Hakim looked into Jeff's eyes in a sinister sort of way, as if he were trying to silently communicate with a dead man. He was lost in his own thoughts, and for a moment, his guard was down.

G saw opportunity and vulnerability reveal itself. He attempted to read Hakim's thoughts. As he made a first-time mental connection with Hakim, he remembered the cautious words of wisdom from Dr. Middleton.

Just remember, if you get close enough to see his thoughts...he can see yours.

G's mind became a jumble of chaotic thoughts, emotions, and visual glimpses of everything ranging from passion to lust, people, places, disguises, killings, rape, laughter, sobbing, tactics, disguises, theft, sirens, music, love...hate, deceit. The images and thoughts sped through G's mind at blistering speeds.

Hakim stood quickly and looked in G's direction. G felt the compromise of discovery as he simultaneously felt Angel's hand grasp his.

"We should leave," she said.

"Wait," said G, pushing hard against the will of Hakim. But it was more than he could withstand.

"OK...I'm ready, Angel. Get us outta here."

Dream Operative

G did the best he could to break the focus of his mind from Hakim and escape to anywhere. But he felt the pull of Hakim's power making a connection with him. He did the best he could to resist. It was more difficult than he had anticipated. G fought as hard as he could against Hakim's attempt pull him back.

G could hear Hakim shouting as he and Angel were able to break free and escape the encounter...and the grasp of Hakim's psychological warfare.

"Show yourself! I know you're there. I don't know who you are, but I am coming for you. And I am coming for *her*." shouted Hakim.

Dr. Middleton watched as G slept, occasionally checking his vitals with her assistant. His heart rate had spiked, and his brain wave activity was some of the most active she had ever witnessed.

"This is incredible," said her assistant, carefully watching the computer readouts. "Look at these synapse responses."

Dr. Middleton was impressed, but she was concerned about where G had wandered off to as she watched his body twitch and react to his dreams. She imagined what it must be like to have such abilities. She was slowly becoming a believer. She approached G close enough to observe his rapid eye movement and took a few notes, all while being extremely careful not to touch him.

"Where did you run off to now, G?" she rhetorically asked in a whisper.

She glanced at her watch. Thirty-five minutes had elapsed since he fell asleep.

Hakim reacted to the sound of gunfire—a single shot at close range. His experienced reflexes put his body posture in a low defensive crouch position as he searched for the origin of the shot.

He was in a dark room but could make out a faint light coming from a wall ahead of him. He moved slowly toward the light.

Peering around a corner, Hakim could see a silhouette about ten feet in front of him. The light behind the shape was bright. He slowly and cautiously approached the dark figure with the intent of confronting him and subduing him, if possible. He got within a couple of feet when the figure simply vanished. He blinked hard in an effort to be certain of what he *thought* he saw.

The light grew brighter and revealed a man before him lying in a pool of blood, bound to a chair. He knelt down to take a closer look at the body. It was Jeff. His face haunted Hakim's mind, even though he had seen many corpses before.

Hakim remained motionless and attempted to read Jeff's final thoughts, but it was no use. His thoughts had escaped with his life. Hakim suspected those final thoughts now belonged to the man he had seen just briefly a moment before. He stood and closed his eyes and put the full focus of his mind on finding the whereabouts of his dream nemesis.

Peace and tranquility had replaced the emotional turmoil G had experienced when he found himself surrounded once again by the Spanish moss covered oaks. Angel was nearby, but G wasn't able to see her.

"Are you here, Angel?"

Always.

"What did he mean when he said he's coming for *her*? Could he *see* you?"

It wasn't me he was referring to, responded Angel confidently.

G looked confused. "Then who?"

Sibyl...he must have somehow made a connection with her through Jeff sometime during their brief encounters.

"Is she in danger?"

No, not in any immediate sense that I can tell.

"I have to warn her," said G. "Can I go back now?"

Soon. Your spiritual mind is ready but your physical body is not.

"Damn drugs...what now?"

Up to you. Where would you like to go?

"I'd like to go to a hotel," said G, with a smirk.

With G's last push past Hakim's mind, he was able to catch a glimpse of a hotel room. He hoped it was a mental image of Hakim's current residence.

"So you *did* see that. You *are* getting stronger," said Angel aloud.

G had captured enough of a glimpse to focus and allow his mind to take him to the origin of the mental image. With any luck, he would end up in the very place Hakim was currently staying and not in some distant foreign land. Either way, he was ready.

He stood, lowered his head slightly, drew in a deep breath, and focused on the visual he had stolen from Hakim. He was accustomed to traveling this way but had always had a much clearer image of his destination. This time was different. This time he knew there could be danger awaiting him. He closed his eyes and felt his mind and body surge.

G's vision cleared to reveal the very hotel room he had taken from Hakim's mind. The room was a split-plan suite, the kind with the bedroom on one side, a small living room on the other, and a separate bathroom off to the side.

He stood in place and slowly scanned his surroundings to absorb the detail. He moved to the window to confirm his location. He pulled the curtain back and looked out. He could recognize a New York street when he saw one. This hotel was located somewhere in the middle of the city. He looked at the stationary near the phone.

Chelsea Hotel, 222 West 23rd Street, between Seventh and Eighth Avenues, near the Jacob K. Javits Center, Empire State Building, Midtown, Greenwich Village, and other NYC attractions.

G looked for signs that Hakim still occupied the room. He had to be certain he could report his whereabouts. Nothing immediately out-of-the-ordinary in this room.

He cautiously ventured toward the bedroom. Slowly peering in past the threshold, his heart nearly pounded out of his chest when he witnessed a man in the bed before him. Could it be the man he frequently encountered in this dimension? Only one way to find out.

His mind raced as he tried to mentally evaluate the situation and interrogate the sleeping man's mind. He moved closer to the bed to see if he could catch a glimpse of his face. He was very much aware of his own heartbeat as it tried to keep pace with the adrenaline rush unlike anything he'd ever experienced. The man appeared to be sleeping soundly.

G focused intently to find a way into his mind to be sure it was indeed Hakim, but he got nowhere. He mentally called out to Angel for answers but she too was out of reach. G looked back at the door to the bedroom. Something wasn't right. He was in over his head and decided to back out. He slowly made his way back into the first room while looking back to ensure the man in the bed didn't wake.

He slowly turned his attention from the man while stepping back into the first room and came face-to-face with the *man* himself, not more than ten feet away. It was Hakim, his worst nightmare…literally. He was pointing a small-caliber handgun directly into G's face. He glanced over his shoulder into the bedroom and saw the sleeping man still lying in the bed. The irony of it all was strangely euphoric.

"I predicted you would follow me here," he said in calm, low tone. "I let my guard down, and you took advantage of it. Good move."

G stood still and said nothing; his mind began to race with options.

"Who are you?" asked Hakim.

G said nothing. Instead, he peered into the eyes of the man and attempted to manipulate his mind.

Feeling the grip G had on his mind, Hakim gave a warning. "Do you believe you can *die* in this dimension?" He chambered a round.

G clearly heard the click of the handgun and perceived Hakim's determination to shoot. But he knew Hakim wanted answers before he wanted another empty assassination. G released the psychological grip he had on Hakim.

"Tell me who you are before I kill you," said Hakim.

"You're gonna *try* to kill me anyway," said G.

G's heart was still pounding; his mind racing as he evaluated the man standing before him…and on the question of whether or not he *could* actually die in this dimension.

"I don't *try* anything. And I'm not known for my patience," warned Hakim.

A man burst through the door aiming a Colt .45 double-action revolver. Hakim turned to defend himself but the man got off the first shot. He missed and rolled to the ground behind a short wall. Hakim fired three rounds through the wall. G took advantage of the distraction and leapt toward Hakim in a near-perfect open-field, American football–style tackle.

Hakim lost the grip he had on his handgun. G had enough of a field of view to watch, in slow motion, as the weapon hit the floor. The two men tumbled to the ground when G realized what he had done. Now what? He was a research student—not technically schooled in fighting, save for the few years he had as a scrawny kid in the art of Kung Fu in a local dojo three blocks from home.

Dream Operative

The men were evenly matched when it came to weight and body type, but G suspected his fighting skills were no match against the world's worst terrorist. So it was not a fair fight in any form or fashion. G knew he'd have to fight without remorse or any sense of fairness. He'd have to hurt his opponent or even kill him. The alternative to was to accept the same fate should he fail.

The men struggled. G placed his forearm across Hakim's neck, but he easily broke free and was in control fast. G would've actually been impressed, had he not been the one fighting for his life. Hakim drew back his right fist. G was prepared to take the blow and wondered where it would take him. The philosophical questions loomed in his mind as he looked up at Hakim.

Can I be knocked out here? If so, where will I go — to yet another dimension perhaps? Can I die here? What will happen to my physical body?

Hakim's punch was interrupted when he and G glanced at the gun lying on the floor some ten feet away. They both watched as a size-thirteen boot stepped on the gun. They both looked up to see a man smiling while taking steady aim directly at Hakim. It was Ox!

34

"His vitals are all over the place!" exclaimed Dr. Middleton's assistant, pointing to the monitors.

"I can see that without looking at the numbers," she said. "Seems he's a very active sleeper."

"Maybe a lighter dose next time?" offered the assistant.

She sat near him watching, wondering, and waiting for him to find a place to return.

"Let me know when his levels return anywhere near normal. Something tells me he's not in a good place."

KK and Perry were up before the sun had crested the eastern horizon.

The men watched the warm orange hue trace the lower landscape as the black and blue sky began to give way to its arrival. The stars began to fade as the black stardust sky turned to blue. The radio came to life at the same time. It was a beautiful thing, actually.

"Dagger Two-Two, this is Firefly, how copy, over?"

"Firefly, this is Dagger Two-Two, loud and clear," answered Perry.

"Dagger Two-Two, be advised, we have a Chinook helo en route to your location. ETA, twenty minutes."

"Dagger Two-Two copies; we're searching for the Chinook."

"Send a green laser signal to Ox and the gang," said Perry. "They'll know to get ready for pickup."

Smoke billowed from a glowing red ember at the tip of a thick cigar as he curiously cocked his head sideways for an instant. The hand holding the Colt .45 military-issue handgun was rock steady and determined.

"Get up kid," commanded Ox, in a rather deep voice, pushing an aromatic puff of smoke from the corner of his mouth.

G grinned slightly and took advantage of the moment by surprising Hakim with a right cross to the jaw with his elbow. Hakim rolled away quickly and backed into a nearby corner of the room.

Ox looked at G without saying much more. Ox's face reflected a look of confusion, followed by a knowing smile.

"It sure is good to see *you* here, Ox," said G, pushing the wrinkles out of his shirt and running his fingers through his tussled hair.

He no sooner finished his comment when Ox disappeared. He was suddenly alone again with one of the most dangerous men on the planet—perhaps *the* most dangerous.

Time slowed as G felt a crushing body blow from behind that nearly snapped his neck. It seemed Hakim had a better perspective of Ox's sudden disappearance than he had and was a lot quicker reacting to the opportunity for advantage. G knew, all too late, that he had made two serious mistakes.

Mistake one: Never turn your back on your enemy if he's not dead.

Mistake two: Never count on things to remain static, especially in a dream.

As G was literally swept from his feet and in midair, he realized he was no physical match for Hakim. He was superior in most things physical and, as G was quickly learning, most things tactical as well. He had remembered a comment he made to Dr. Middleton about how he had to use his mind if he was going to seize the advantage.

Despite the chaos of the moment, G caught a glimpse of Hakim's gun lying on the floor, just before the two men came crashing down. He extended his arm, opened his hand and pushed his mind to envision the gun in his grasp. What happened next stunned even G himself. The weapon literally lifted from the floor and flew into G's grasp. It happened so fast, Hakim hadn't even noticed.

Time returned to normal speed as G braced for the inevitable impact of the floor and the weight of Hakim's body. He gripped the handgun so tightly that it went off as they hit the floor. The blast shocked both men but was especially surprising to Hakim, who wasn't aware that G was able to get to the gun.

"Ox, wake up," called Pat from outside the aircraft.

Ox rubbed his eyes and exited the aircraft to talk with Pat. "What's up?"

"I was hoping you could tell me," said Pat, pointing to the green laser coming from the top of a ridge.

"That, my friend, is a good thing," answered Ox, with a yawn. "It means our ride is on the way. Help me roust the crew for an evacuation."

Ox checked his sidearm and paused for a moment, catching a brief glimpse of the dream he had encountered, but not quite enough to fully realize the impact he had in saving G's life. He shrugged it off, as most do, and returned to the Casa to prepare the crew for evacuation. Ox was more than ready to get his passengers to safety so he could finish his mission, get his pay, and return to the island lifestyle. He'd had enough excitement for one day.

His ears were ringing from the sound of close gunfire. His heart was racing from his fight-or-flight response. His head was processing options at light speed as he gained control of the weapon in his hand.

G rolled to his right and frantically took aim at…nothing. He suddenly found himself alone. He wasn't exactly certain whether he should be thankful or afraid. He backed into a corner of the room and braced himself for another surprise.

Nothing.

He heard movement and rose to a crouching position, still nervously holding the handgun straight out in front of himself. His eyes darted about the dim room. The noise he heard was that of Hakim in a sleep state, lying on the bed in his hotel room. The blast must have pushed Hakim from this dimension back into his physical body.

G decided he wouldn't stick around long enough to see if Hakim would wake up or reappear.

"Angel, take me home."

"You have got to wake him. His vitals are spiking off the charts," exclaimed Dr. Middleton's assistant.

"Then expand the damn charts. This one is different," quipped Dr. Middleton, second-guessing her own response and better judgment.

The assistant shook his head in disbelief while he watched G's vitals dance all over the place.

"Wait," he said, suddenly. "They seem to be subsiding…significantly," he added while trying to make scientific sense of it all.

Sibyl watched as G's breathing became more rhythmic and peaceful, his chest rising and falling comfortably, his eyes no longer indicating REM sleep. She took a seat at his side and patiently waited for him to return to consciousness. She glanced at her watch. Two hours and nine minutes had elapsed.

The makeshift raft was making good time with the increasing speed of the river current. Booker and Hartman were able to cover a lot of ground during the night without being detected.

"See if you can get a good signal on the radio and figure out where we are," said Booker.

"These high mountain ridges surrounding us are making it damn near impossible to get a good lock on the satellites," said Hartman.

"Keep trying. We have to figure out where we are. We get a satellite connection, and we can send a message. It'll be daybreak soon, and we'll have to stop."

"Looks like the river is widening up ahead," said Hartman.

"Ordinarily that would be a good thing, my brother…if it were still dark. Keep your eyes peeled for unfriendly and keep checking the SATCOM."

"WILCO."

G drew a deep breath as he slowly opened his eyes. The first thing he saw was the oaks with the Spanish moss, yet this time he was looking at them from the conscious side of life, into the painting.

He blinked purposefully to push the remaining drowsiness from his mind and slowly raised himself to a sitting position on the couch. He began pulling wires from his temples.

Dream Operative

"Get these things off me, Sibyl," he said, struggling to find all the connections.

"It's good to see your charming personality has returned along with your consciousness, G," she said, patiently awaiting the details of his encounter.

G closed his eyes and lowered his head slightly to recapture some of the details of his dream.

Sibyl remained respectfully quiet, as did her assistant. This was breakthrough science for both of them. At least, that's what they had hoped. They weren't about to break his concentration with any interruptions whatsoever. The assistant had the video recorder strategically positioned to record G's account of the experience as soon as he was ready to talk.

G opened his eyes, slowly raised his head, extended an open hand and looked directly at Sibyl, now seated directly in front of him at eye level. She instinctively placed her hand into his and returned the gaze while trying to read him. She wasn't prepared for the news.

"Your boyfriend is dead, Sibyl. I'm sorry," said G in a whisper.

"He's not my boyfriend," she said with glassy eyes.

"Then why are you crying?"

"Oh, G...I..." Dr. Middleton struggled to maintain her composure to find the words.

"There's something you need to know, Sibyl. He knows about you."

"Who? Why me? What are you talking about?" she said, trying to make sense of it all.

"I'm hoping *you* can tell me that," G said in a calm whisper.

Dan Keppler received a secure call from the operations center supervisor. "Sir, we have a couple of situations developing you may be interested in. Should I come to your office, or would you care to stop by to watch it play out on the grid?"

"I'll stop by," said Dan, ending the call abruptly. He called out to Janet. "I'm headed to the ops center, Janet. Be gone about thirty minutes, if that."

"OK, Boss."

Dan entered an elevator just around the bend of a short hallway near his office. He swiped a secure card and rode the elevator to the ops center floor. He was greeted by an analyst who escorted him to the floor supervisor.

"Sir, the director..." announced the analyst.

"Thank you, that'll be all," said the supervisor.

"What are we looking at, Dave?"

"Central America, Boss. You're no doubt aware of Ox Waddy's forced landing at the edge of a ridge near Yaviza, south of Howard, Panama."

Dan nodded, watching the large-screen monitors on the walls of the ops center. One of the screens depicted a satellite view of the Central American landscape. Dan could hear muted radio chatter playing out in the background.

"Big picture first, Boss," said Dave. "Ox and most of his passengers are located here," he added, placing his cursor over Ox's position. "We have a Predator overhead, providing real-time video feed and IR location assistance from two special ops scouts positioned on a high ridge about two hundred kilometers, here," said Dave pointing to a position on the map just east of Ox and the crippled aircraft.

Dan continued to follow along without questions. "Go on."

"We have a Chinook inbound that will evacuate Ox and the passengers—"

"Dave, you may be able to get every one of the passengers out, but there's no way Ox is leaving his precious aircraft behind without trying to fly it outta there. I hope your Chinook is bringing fuel. If not, he'll probably highjack it long enough to siphon enough from the tank of the helo."

"We figured that, sir. That's why we're bringing in enough fuel for him to get to Howard...if he can manage to find the room to fly it out of the tough spot he's in."

"I hate to say this, Dave, but Ox will either do it or die trying. Do everything you can to accommodate him and keep me posted."

"Will do," said Dave. "Oh, sir, you have a call."

"Thank you," said Dan. He picked up the secure line. "Dan Keppler."

"Sir, this is Janet. You have an urgent call from Dr. Middleton. Shall I push it through?"

"Yes, thank you, Janet."

Dan heard two short clicks, followed by a tone.

"What do you have for me, Sibyl?"

"Yes, sir, our *traveler* just returned. He had a direct encounter, and we have the current whereabouts of KAH. This is time-critical."

"You're damn right it is," retorted Dan. "Give me a location, and then get his ass to the ops floor ASAP."

"New York City...we're on our way," Answered Dr. Middleton.

Dream Operative

"Dave, I need only essential personnel on the floor. We have a *Tier One* sighting that requires immediate action. Alert the New York station chief and activate the *wet boy*. Make sure there's a controller and a cleaner in the area, and for God's sake, make sure they remember the eleventh commandment."

Dan's instructions were crystal clear to the ops floor supervisor, who took immediate action to dismiss a couple of new analysts, a handful of computer terminal hackers, and a maintenance crew working in the equipment room in the back. He also understood Dan's lingo.

Roughly translated, Dan had laid out a coordinated plan, written and rehearsed by the best operatives in case they ever discovered the whereabouts of Khalid Abdul-Hakim anywhere on the planet.

The station chief would activate a *wet boy*, or government assassin, to make their way to the *mark*, this time, Hakim, and eliminate him. A *controller* is a trusted operative who would ensure the kill and activate the necessary *cleaners* to eliminate any and all traces of evidence. The eleventh *commandment*, simply stated, is *Thou shall not get caught.*

"We have to tell someone. We should tell Dan. He'll know what to do," said Dr. Middleton.

G nodded in agreement.

"So, just so I have this straight," said Dr. Middleton. "You claim to have had a direct encounter with Khalid Abdul-Hakim himself?"

"That's right," responded G matter-of-factly.

"I'm assuming you can lead us to him, then?"

"If we hurry. He's not known for sticking around once he's discovered...which is rare in and of itself. I figure you have two choices..."

"What's that?"

"Either find him or, as I said, he'll find you...specifically you, Sibyl," said G, as serious as he knew how.

"I'll call Dan," she said.

Sibyl returned a short time later.

"Let's take a walk, G."

"Where we headed?"

"To the ops floor to see Dan. I think you'll find it interesting. Besides, they need you to help them find KAH."

"Who is KAH?" said G. Then it dawned on him that the Agency loved to acronyze everything they could. He wasn't certain whether it was a move of efficiency or one of vanity. Either way, it often made things more difficult to follow. This one was a bit easier, however, as he knew they were talking about a person, specifically Khalid Abdul-Hakim.

35

The sunrise was spectacular; it was a welcome sight to Ox and the crew after having to endure rain throughout most of the night.

"I've got a visual!" shouted Ronaldo, perched atop the Casa, searching for the inbound helicopter. Soon after his announcement, Ox could hear the familiar sound of helicopter blades cutting through the thick jungle air.

"OK, warriors, make sure everything is secure. The prop wash generated by that thing can surprise you," warned Ox.

The sun made its way over the ridge in its fullness as the Chinook arrived on scene and found a safe distance to set down, about fifty yards from the Casa. The flight engineer emerged first and grounded the craft. The blades slowed to a stall as the aircraft commander shut her down. Three more crew members, one of whom appeared to be a medic, emerged from the aft end.

"Sir, I'm Major Tom Bikerston. I'm here at the request of the US government—"

"Pleased to meet you, Tom, but you can spare me the pleasantries," interrupted Ox, as he politely shook the major's hand. "We appreciate you men taking time out of your day for the inconvenient stop."

"No problem, sir. That's what we're here for," said Tom, with a wink and a smile.

Ox knew better. They were *here* for some of the very reasons he was.

"Got any fuel on board you can spare?"

"We figured you'd ask, sir, so we brought as much as we could manually haul. We're not normally equipped for such a mission."

"All I need is enough to make it to Howard for a total refuel," responded Ox with confidence.

Equipment and personnel were loaded onto the Chinook in minimum time. Ronaldo stood beside Ox, looking at the massive helicopter blades beginning to turn as the helicopter applied power.

"You sure you don't need me to stay back with you?" asked Pat.

"Nothing you can do that'll help," said Ox. "No offense, but you'll be added weight we don't need for the interesting departure we anticipate outta this place. We'll catch up at Howard."

Pat nodded and turned toward the helicopter, its blades now turning at much higher speeds.

"Hey, don't forget our two scouts perched up on the ridge." shouted Ox, as he pointed skyward.

Pat returned a thumbs-up and climbed aboard the workhorse. Ox and Ronaldo watched as the helo made its way to the ridge in a hover for less than a minute and then departed to the north.

G and Sibyl entered one of the most secure rooms at NSA Headquarters — the operations center. Providing one of the absolute best tools for situational analysis and operations known to the free world, its technology is the best anywhere and is continually updated.

Dan shook G's hand firmly when he and Dr. Middleton arrived to the Operations Center. He didn't waste time on pleasantries.

"G, I need to know what you know. Don't spare any details," instructed Dan. "I understand you had an encounter with someone significant this morning. Is that correct?"

"Yes."

"Come with me, please."

Dan led G to a computer terminal. Dr. Middleton stood, silently observing the operation, behind the two men.

"Was it this man?" asked Dan, showing G an electronic picture of Hakim.

"That's him," G answered. "It's not exactly how he looks now, but that's him."

"How can you be certain?"

"It's just something I know. Besides, as I said, the eyes don't lie. They reveal a man."

"Can you tell us where he is?"

"I can tell you where he was about twelve minutes ago," answered G, checking his watch.

"Understand," answered Dan. "Then we have to move fast. Step over here with me. That'll be all, Doctor," said Dan, dismissing the Dr. Middleton and leading G to the operations center supervisor pit.

"G, this is Dave Daniels. He's the ops center supervisor. I need you to tell him, exactly, Hakim's last known location."

"Chelsea Hotel, Manhattan," answered G succinctly.

Dan looked at G and then back to Dave. Dave looked at a computer analyst, who quickly typed some lines of code or instructions, G wasn't certain which.

"Think really hard, G. What room is he in?"

"I never saw a room number."

"G, I need more than a hotel. Don't get me wrong, I appreciate the location, but I need a room number. Think. Is there anything that would help jog that mind of yours into a bit more detail?"

"Tenth floor," answered G.

"Now we're getting somewhere," said Dan.

The computer analyst was typing away as fast as he could. Dave grabbed a headset and connected with the New York station chief. "Tenth floor… negative, no room number yet."

Dave activated a camera and drew Dan and G's attention to an infrared image of a building peppered with heat signatures from several obscure and unknown possible "marks." The monitor flickered, indicating a change to a tighter field of view, now depicting a single floor.

"G, that monitor depicts several people who are on the tenth floor of the Chelsea hotel. Look closely and tell me if you see anything at all that draws your attention to anyone who could be our man," said Dave.

Dan was impressed with Dave's assertion and the manner in which he caught on to G's abilities to *see* the situation differently. G studied the display while Dan and Dave hoped he'd be able to recognize something or someone familiar. Without a room number, they were forced to wait on Hakim to reveal himself, which he was known *not* to do quite well.

"Do you have any *normal* cameras on the tenth floor I can see?" asked G.

Dave pressed a button and asked to be hacked in to any security cameras stationed on the tenth floor. He directed G's attention to a screen expected to reveal a picture at any moment. The men waited for the video feed. It flashed on screen as a man walked by but not long enough for any of them to get a good look. Dan and Dave passed it off as another hotel patron.

"That's him!" shouted G.

Dave got on the radio and directed a *shadow* to the man's location for confirmation. He also demanded to be connected to any other security cameras available.

"Which camera was that? If we know which camera that was, we can grab an overhead view and follow the IR signature on that person," said Dave.

"Are you certain it was Hakim, G?" asked Dan.

"Yes."

Dan shook his head. "Seal the frigging building, Dave. No one leaves."

"Sir, this is supposed to be a covert op—"

"We cannot afford to allow the world's most wanted man to slip through our fingers," answered Dan emphatically.

"If he wants to slip through, he'll slip through," said G calmly.

Both men looked at G.

"We'll see about that," said Dan. "We get the picture we're looking for yet, Dave?"

"Screen three, boss," answered Dave.

The screen revealed another IR signature view; this one was expanded to reveal a tighter zoom, which was now focused on an unknown *mark*. The *mark* entered the tenth-floor elevator. Before the door closed, another man stopped the doors and squeezed his way in. Dave listened to his headset.

"Our *shadow* is in the elevator with him."

The men watched the scene play out. The elevator seemed to take forever to reach the first floor. G could see another camera depicting the lobby with several people milling about. Something had to happen quickly if it was going to happen.

The elevator passed the fourth floor when the action took place. The *mark* looked at his wrist, presumably his watch. The shadow reacted to his movement, drawing a weapon. He was too slow. Hakim barely moved when the shadow dropped to the floor. Hakim stepped over him, pressed a button, and made his way out of the elevator.

"What just happened?" demanded Dave. "Get me a camera on whatever floor they just stopped...now!"

Two screens came to life and revealed empty hallways. The IR signature camera zoomed out in an attempt to find the *mark*, but he had simply vanished once again. A look back at the elevator camera revealed a pool of blood oozing from the *shadow*. A radio call announced that the shadow was dead. Knife wound to the throat.

Dave looked at Dan for further instructions. They were already operating on the edge.

"Knock it off and get a cleaner in to take care of the shadow. Erase this fiasco and get the hell out. G, come with me," said Dan.

The mouth of the river had emptied into a lake large and wide enough to allow Hartman to receive a satellite signal on the handheld SATCOM.

"Got a signal," announced Hartman, in a whisper.

"Awesome. Because we have to get ashore and find a place to hide out. We're sitting ducks out here," said Booker. "Push a location burst, then stow that thing and help me get this raft outta sight."

Hartman sent a secure transmission burst via satellite to an operations center that would help the US government find them.

The men maneuvered the makeshift raft to a secluded embankment and placed most of their gear on dry land to wait out the daylight or hear from home. They hoped for the latter to occur first.

"Make sure your earpiece is snug, so you can hear Mother calling when she sees our signal," instructed Booker.

"Will do, sir."

"Sir, before you go..." Dave hollered across the ops center floor.

Dan stopped and turned to look at Dave.

"Got a moment for a quick update on the other situation?" he said as cautiously as he could, considering G's presence and unsure of his need-to-know clearance.

"Central America?"

Dave nodded.

"Certainly, speak openly and give me the short version," he said. "G, I need you to listen to this as well."

"We just learned that the Chinook has picked up all passengers with the exception of Ox and his copilot, pretty much as you suspected. So that situation is developing nicely in the right direction."

"Good. At least we have one situation moving in the right direction. What else you got?"

"We received a location burst from what we can assume is our remaining two SOF team members in an E&E, uh, *escape and evade*," said Dave, correcting the acronym for G's sake. "We're authenticating the signal and should have confirmation shortly."

"I know you're all over it, Dave. Please keep me posted with a SITREP as the situation warrants."

"Let's go, G; we've gotta take care of the big fish who *thinks* he got away."

Ronaldo secured the last of the empty fuel cans in the aft section of the Casa and strapped himself into the right seat. He barely got seated and buckled in before Ox started barking commands.

"Ignition on number one."

"Check," confirmed Ronaldo, with a touch of the ignition switch.

"Oil pressure looks good...rpm is good...checking fuel...fuel levels are low, but we know that."

"Check, check, copy," responded Ronaldo.

"Ignition on number two," announced Ox.

"Check."

The tiny craft vibrated and shook from the thirsty, turbine-powered engines pushing air over the leading edge of the wings. The only thing keeping it in place was both men standing on the brakes.

"Flaps...rudder..."

"Check, check."

"OK, let's make the best of this," said Ox, turning the yoke as far left as it would go in his best attempt to turn the aircraft around in place.

Both men heard the crunch of gravel giving way to the tiny craft as Ox applied power and released the brakes. The aircraft shook and shuddered but barely moved.

Dream Operative

"Straighten out the yoke a bit, Ox. You've got it turned too tight."

"Good call," said Ox, loosening the turn radius enough for the aircraft to break loose from its position.

Both men adjusted the throttles and the yoke as they maneuvered the craft to a 180-degree turn and the best angle for takeoff.

"I figure we've got just over three hundred feet to get her airborne," said Ox with all the confidence in the world.

"That puts us about a hundred feet shy, Ox," exclaimed Ronaldo, hoping to get some kind of reaction out of him. Instead, he got nothing. The distance remaining wasn't the real issue. It was the steep climb they were facing immediately after that, assuming they were able to get the craft airborne to begin with.

"Power up, kid. Here goes our best shot."

More like our only shot, Ronaldo thought.

"Release brakes…now," commanded Ox. The reliable aircraft leapt forward from the grip of the loose gravel. "Fifty knots…sixty…" Ox continued to call out the speed while Ronaldo watched the distance remaining shrink fast ahead of them. They needed to clear a jagged ridge ahead that rose about twenty feet. If they didn't, they would hit it head on and risk destruction and possibly death.

"Seventy knots. Pull back, and let's convince her to fly."

Both men yanked hard on the yoke while Ronaldo banked the yoke slightly right to avoid the highest part of the ridge. The Casa performed marvelously in the morning air, the relatively light payload helping to clear the ridge with plenty to spare.

Ox grinned and surprised Ronaldo with a firm slap on the left shoulder. "She's one *hell* of an airplane, eh, Sport? Probably helped we didn't have much weight this time," he laughed. "Set a course for Howard. I'm ready to land on a real runway and get some fuel and that cheeseburger you were asking for."

Ronaldo breathed a sigh of relief and checked the instruments for the best course and heading. He pushed the aircraft to climb high and fast. He looked back to see the tough spot they were in. Given the lay of the terrain, there was no way they would have been able to fly everyone out using the Casa.

Dan led G to his office and shut the door.

"Tell me we didn't just allow the world's most dangerous man to slip right through our fingertips. Hell, we're not even sure why he's here," said Dan, with obvious frustration.

"If there's one thing I've learned in this business so far, sir, it's that things aren't always what they seem," said G, realizing how many times the mantra kept haunting him.

"And that's supposed to comfort me, G? Do you see something I don't? Because what I don't see is my terrorist either dead or in custody. What am I missing?"

"You may be missing the obvious. Hakim is a master of deception and he's not finished getting what he wants by being in the US in the first place."

Dan sat back in his chair to contemplate G's words while realizing how quickly G was adjusting to critical thinking of the Agency.

"What is it he wants?"

"Before we get to that, I'd like to tell you what I want," said G boldly.

Dan returned a look that would've intimidated most any seasoned agent, but G was entirely too new to have learned how to be intimidated by the boss. And Dan knew G held the keys to help him bring down Hakim, his number one priority. Even so, Dan pushed back enough to test G's mettle.

"That's *not* what I asked you. So now you think you're in a position to bargain with me? After everything I've provided for you and have *promised* to provide for you? You *bargain* with me over something this serious? You're on thin ice, mister. Tread carefully," Dan warned.

"I'm not asking for anything that won't help me bring down your terrorist."

"Well, it better make sense, and it better damn well be connected with the mission. What is it you *want*?"

"I can't get this man from inside the fence. I have to get away from the Agency...outside of the building. He'll find out sooner or later, if he doesn't already know, that you've got me under wraps here...or somewhere near here. That'll provide him a reasonable level of comfort to know he's mobile and I'm not," explained G.

"Where do you plan on going?"

"Wherever I need to go that puts me in a position to kill him. But there's one stop I'll need to make before that."

"OK, I can arrange that, given a plan I can endorse," answered Dan quickly. "Not certain what the stop en route is about but I'm certain you'll explain that one to me."

"I'm not finished," said G.

"Of course you're not," Dan answered sarcastically with a raised eyebrow and a look of impatience as he waited for the rest of G's desires.

"I want Athena to accompany me. I need resources—cash and protection. Best I can figure, she knows this case best and is definitely equipped to help protect me."

"Athena is subject to my approval when you give me your plan. The rest of your demands are a given when she's on a mission. Now tell me what it is *he* wants, and how are you planning to find him?"

"The sooner you approve this operation, the sooner I can make my stopover. Once I complete that stopover, I'll have what *he* wants. Then it'll only be a matter of time before he finds me," explained G.

"You still haven't told me what *he* wants," pressed Dan.

36

Howard Field came into view relatively quickly as Ronaldo maneuvered the Casa high enough to see over the mountain ridge. A quick course adjustment followed by a seventeen-minute flight, led the craft to a five-mile final approach, followed by a most welcome chirp of the tires making contact with the runway and an uneventful landing on a hard surface. Ox and Ronaldo could see the Chinook rescue helicopter parked nearest the airfield operations building, and they were directed by the tower to park next to it.

Ronaldo lowered the aft hatch of the Casa. Pat and some of the crew met them on the tarmac. A fuel truck pulled up to the starboard side.

"Fill her up and check under the hood," said Ox with a wink, pulling a fresh cigar from his shirt pocket.

"You can't smoke here, sir," said the nervous fuels specialist.

"No worries," said Ronaldo, giving Ox a disapproving look. "He won't light up."

"What's shakin', Pat?" said Ox, looking to make small talk.

"I need to get to my equipment," responded Pat, in a bit of a rush.

"Oh, that," said Ox. "Well, we sorta had to find ways to lighten our load, so we tossed your precious equipment. But I know where it is, if you'd like us to drop you over the spot..."

"Don't have time for bullshit, Ox," said Pat, pushing his way into the back of the Casa.

"Guess I shouldn't get between a man and his *equipment*," Ox said to Ronaldo, who was only half listening to him anyway.

"Hey, can you unload these empty fuel cans when you're finished refueling us?" Ox asked.

"Will do," responded the fuels specialist.

Ox walked into the Casa to check on Pat.

"Sorry about the bullshit. What's got you so wrapped up?"

"I'm told that Booker transmitted an echo location burst early this morning. I'm trying to get a fix on their location."

The information was enough to command Ox's attention. "So your equipment can detect that kind of thing, huh?"

"It can do that and much more, as we've already seen," said Pat, continuing to bang on the keys. "Oh, this isn't good."

"What's that?" Ox asked.

"It seems Booker and Hartman are digging themselves *deeper* into hostile territory, instead of navigating away from it."

"If they're using the river as their mode of transportation, then I can see why," said Ox, looking at a map displayed on one of the small monitors.

"I hope they stop and do the math before they press into that lake."

"Can we get a message to them?" asked Ox.

"I can do anything you want, but we're no longer on this mission," said Pat.

"Says who?"

Pat showed Ox message traffic that terminated their mission with the extraction of the crew, despite the fact that Pat sent a secure message indicating two from the original mission had remained behind. The message further stated that the men were now the responsibility of the Department of State and under the Department of State direction and authority.

"How the hell did that happen?" said Ox out loud.

"Could've happened when we crash—I mean, when we went unaccounted for."

"We didn't crash. But I know what you mean. No harm, no foul, Pat. Do me a favor and get a good fix on them, and if you can indeed determine the two men are together, that's even better. Meantime, let me make a phone call."

Booker and Hartman secured the raft and stowed their gear onshore to prepare for the long day ahead.

"Keep your eyes and ears open, and be careful to avoid exposure. Until we get a good idea of where we are and what's around us, we've got to assume there will be unfriendly who won't like the fact that we're here," instructed Booker.

Hartman nodded and made his way to a nearby tree surrounded by thick jungle to conduct a close recon of the area. Booker stowed the gear, pulled out a small laptop and began to triangulate their position and send another message to "Mother".

Hartman returned after a few minutes. "No signs of movement or human life of any kind so far. This place is eerily empty."

Booker nodded. He began to decipher the information pouring into his micro laptop. "Oh, this isn't good," he announced.

"What's up?"

"Seems we've jumped from the frying pan into the fire and have taken ourselves to the very doorstep of one of Colombia's most dangerous cartel regions."

"Any way out?" asked Hartman. "Besides swimming back upstream?"

"Well, let's see if Mother has any suggestions before we go swimming with the alligators and piranhas," Booker said. He typed a message to the operations center. "I sent our coordinates and asked for a suggestion on an expeditious route. I don't see them sending in a helicopter, although that's the only way I see us getting out of our current position, judging from the lay of the surrounding terrain."

G was reluctant to disclose Hakim's motivation to Dan, but he felt he knew Dan well enough to know he'd be receptive to the sensitivity of the information.

"OK...not sure how this will affect your decision making within the Agency, but—" said G, but they were interrupted by Janet over the intercom.

"Sir, Athena is here to see you. Shall I have her wait?"

Dan looked at G for a nod, as if he was looking for an approval before answering. G nodded.

"Send her in, Janet."

Athena entered the room and closed the door behind her. G's emotions were still involved. He evaluated her from head to toe as she walked into the room and sat near him. She looked great. Better than ever, actually. He kept his composure and waited for Dan to resume the conversation.

"Have a seat. G was getting to the heart of a matter that bears some explaining before I brief you on your next assignment," explained Dan.

Ox managed to get a secure line to Dave, who was on duty as the Ops Center supervisor.

"Look, Ox, you know the drill. The decision was made several layers above even *my* pay grade. There's very few who can override the directive."

"Who would that be, Dave? Dan? If so, patch me through," Ox demanded.

"He's currently working a higher priority mission. You know how these things go, mate."

Ox let out a disappointed sigh. "Unfortunately, I *do* know how such things go, my brother. At least let me have some fidelity on the particulars, so I can analyze whether we can assist. We're halfway there, for God's sake. I can be back in the air at sunset," Ox pleaded.

"Yeah, I copy that. And where you gonna set that ol' bird down to conduct the exfil?"

"That bad, huh?" said Ox, not willing to fully reveal the insight he already had.

"Yeah, dude, they're in deep."

"That's where I need you to work with my ghost and tell me where to go," Ox retorted, referring to Pat as *his* ghost.

Dave thought about the many ways in which he could respond to such an opening but thought better of it, considering the seriousness of the situation.

"Tell you what, Ox, as soon as I can get a moment with the boss, I'll see if I can convince him that you're the one who can get those guys out...but only because I know you can."

"We have the resources, Dave. Everyone on the team can shoot; I have an excellent copilot, special tactics, and a ghost who's proven to be worth his salt."

"Yeah, I know all about your team. What I don't know is if you have the right aircraft to complete the mission. Besides, you don't always have to *shoot* your way in and out of an op, my friend. Those days are far and few between, fortunately."

"Find an airstrip for me, and I'll make it happen," said Ox.

Dream Operative

"Only thing I can promise is to find the boss and trust him to give me insight into his plan. I'll be in touch. Out here." Dave terminated the call without warning.

"When do we leave?" asked Pat, watching Ox terminate the connection.

"We don't. We sit tight...at least until the sun begins to set. Then I make another phone call, if I don't have info by then."

"It seems you may have had a mole inside your organization," said G, beginning his explanation to Dan.

"It wouldn't be the first time; so it doesn't surprise me, and so far, you're not convincing me of a damn thing," said Dan from behind his desk with his arms folded and his head slowly moving from side-to-side.

Athena listened while watching the two men.

"There's an envelope I need access to," explained G.

"So access it," retorted Dan.

"I have, but—"

"Wait," said Athena. "You said 'had'."

Both men looked at her with uncertainty as to where she was headed with her comment.

"You said we may have *had* a mole. What do you mean?"

"Your mole is dead, but there's something he left behind that Hakim wants. I know where it is. I'm just not certain yet exactly *what* it is."

"Let me get this straight, G," said Dan. "Are you *insinuating* our mole was Jeff Hines?"

"Yes."

"Now, that *does* come as a surprise. Who was he working for?"

"Freelance—pretty much serving his own greed."

"*Money?*"

"Mostly. That, and power. You know, greed in its purest form," explained G.

"Well, *someone* had to be paying him or getting ready to pay him," said Dan rhetorically.

"I can only assume Hakim made him an offer that got his attention and eventually took his life."

"So Hakim is after this *envelope* you say Jeff left behind, and you think you know where it is? Tell me, why did Hakim have Jeff killed before he took possession of the envelope?"

"Because Jeff played him and handed him a decoy. Hakim was just too stupid to open the damn thing before he had Jeff eliminated."

Dan winced. "So we have one pissed-off terrorist on our hands."

"Exactly why I need to get to that envelope before he does," explained G.

"So *Hakim* knows where it is? And we're sitting here debating?" said Dan with raised eyebrows.

"Not exactly. But he knows *who* can lead him to it."

"Who, you?"

"Dr. Middleton. She and Jeff had an intimate relationship that he took advantage of—"

"OK, this is really getting deep. How many twists and turns does this shit sandwich have?" asked Dan. "So she's holding some kind of sensitive documents for someone she *knew* to be corrupt?"

"I'm not convinced she actually knows what she's got or was ever an accomplice," explained G.

"And you know this how?" asked Dan.

"Because I pressed her, and I…" G hesitated.

"Go on."

"I didn't find any evidence of corruption when I examined her thoughts," said G reluctantly, as he waited for a reaction from Dan and Athena.

Dan sighed. "You're *really* asking me to stretch my imagination here, G, you know that?" said Dan sternly as he glanced at Athena for some kind of support. Athena remained stoic, neutrally committed to the cause of finding the *mark*…with whatever means possible.

"I understand. But allow me prove it to you by being able to find what we're *all* seeking."

Dan drew a deep breath and slowly exhaled while trying to wrap his mind around a completely celestial concept of reality…which seldom makes sense among laymen. "OK, so tell me whether or not I'm following your logic," said Dan, trying to make sense of where G was going with his plan. "You gain *physical* access to this envelope—"

"—and the contents," interrupted G.

"—and its contents," added Dan for emphasis, "And what? Hakim loses focus on Dr. Middleton and targets you? Then what?"

"Then he finds his way to me."

"How does he *discover* you have what he's looking for?"

Dream Operative

"That's where you come in," explained G. "I need your permission to access *some* of the contents of whatever is in that envelope to be convincing enough that I have the real thing."

"I'd be happy to grant partial access, but why not *full* access?" asked Dan.

"Insurance and assurance," explained G. "If he senses that I have *some* of the info, he'll assume I have *all* of it. If there's any way he gains a mental advantage over me, I have a reasonable assurance he won't kill me right away, and he'll hesitate long enough for me to kill him."

"Are you capable of killing him?" asked Dan without emotion and all the seriousness of a seasoned professional.

"I never would've imagined I could ever do such a thing," explained G, "until he nearly killed me...or so I felt. But it's almost as if this dude has no remorse written into his DNA. There's so much hatred for the Western way of life in this man. Only way someone like him can change is through elimination. He's gotta be stopped."

"Where's this mysterious envelope?" asked Dan.

"In a place I can only assume is the home of Dr. Middleton," answered G.

"I've been to her home," said Dan. "Describe it."

G painted a descriptive visual for Dan. It didn't take him long to confirm that it sounded as if G was describing Dr. Middleton's home in an upscale Arlington development. He was now faced with authorizing G and Athena to break in and enter the premises or enlist Dr. Middleton's willing assistance. After carefully considering the risks, Dan decided to keep the circle of trust as tight as possible and opted to authorize a covert breach operation.

"G, I cannot begin to explain the sensitivities of this kind of operation. I don't need to remind Athena at all, but for your sake, I'll put it as bluntly as I know how, so you understand the full ramifications of being discovered," explained Dan.

G glanced at Athena, who was now looking directly at him while Dan advised him of the basics of a clandestine operation.

"In the unlikely event you *are* discovered, Athena will do everything she can to neutralize the threat and help you escape and evade capture, arrest, or personal injury. You have one simple mission: get in, collect, and get out...quickly and without a trail."

G nodded. "I understand."

"I hope so," said Dan. "Athena is in *absolute* command. She has my full authorization to shoot you on site and leave you at the scene if you decide to act on your own. This will *not* be the time to do that, should you be so inclined. Do you still understand and agree to these terms?"

"Yes."

"Good. What is your plan once you obtain what it is you're looking for?"

G looked at Athena, hesitated slightly, and surprised them both with his answer.

37

Hartman suggested Booker get some rest while he stood first watch. He laid out a fifty-yard perimeter he would remain within to conduct close recon. He assured Booker he'd wake him with any discovery and set off slowly toward the east.

It was still relatively early in the day, but the sun was already beating down through the jungle canopy. He was careful to watch his step and stop along the way to listen to what his surroundings were telling him.

Through the rising mist from the jungle floor he could see spiders collecting and consuming their nightly meals in their webs, an occasional monkey jumping through the trees, and birds busy picking off bugs not yet hidden by the jungle's intense canopy.

He pondered how such a beautiful place could hold so much potential danger for him and his teammate. He crouched low, closed his eyes, and listened intently to all the sounds, carefully allowing his mind to paint a picture the sounds were telling him.

He had learned a technique early in training that helped him separate the sounds that were distinct among the many. He turned it into a personal game. He'd listen to what most would consider "noise" and attempt to separate it and discover the true origin. The technique paid off especially well while trying to decipher distinct conversation between two people at parties. Especially if the two people were girls he was interested in.

As the sounds of the jungle competed with his concentration on sound separation, he focused on the largest sound he could hear—the wind. He opened his eyes and looked to the tree tops to get an estimate of the wind's direction and speed and found that the wind wasn't blowing at all. In fact, what he'd assumed was the wind wasn't the wind at all.

"Just goes to show you," he whispered, "things aren't always what they seem."

He remained in a crouched position while he walked some twenty more yards, where he slowly peered through the brush to discover a paved road some one-hundred yards out just beyond a clearing. He found the origin of the sound was actually that of car tires speeding along a long stretch of the roadway. He marked his spot and returned to Booker to report the discovery.

"I'll need two tickets to San Jose, Costa Rica," said G.

Athena cocked her head to the right slightly, sort of like a puppy does when it's trying to understand its owner's intent or instruction. Dan sat back in his chair and began putting the pieces together. He gave the slightest hint of a smirk.

"So, once you're convinced he's aware you have what he wants, your plan is to draw him out of the country?" asked Dan to be certain.

"I figure we take the trash as far away from home as possible before we incinerate it," said G, doing his best to offer his version of an analogy.

"I like it. Make it happen," said Dan, looking first at G, then to Athena. "I don't need to remind you how to go about ensuring he gets what he needs. Just remember our discussion."

Athena nodded.

Dan stood and walked them both to the door.

"So, I'm free to go now?" said G, in a last-minute attempt to be as clear as possible.

"As free as she allows you to be," said Dan. "But you better hurry before I start actually thinking about what it is I've authorized," he finished with an encouraging smile. "Seriously…" He wanted to wish them luck. But luck isn't what an agent wants any part of during an operation. Instead, Dan offered a firm handshake to them both.

"Sir," Janet called out to Dan. "Dave Daniels has been trying to get ahold of you since you've been in conference. He's got an updated SITREP for you from the ops center."

"Thanks Janet. I'll stop by there in a few minutes to see what he's got."

Dream Operative

"Now what, G?" asked Athena, as they made their way to his temporary quarters.

"I need access to Dr. Middleton's home, so *now* you take me there."

"When exactly do you suggest we make the breach?" asked Athena.

"What part of the word *now* didn't make sense, Athena?" asked G. "I don't know…find out if she goes home for lunch. I don't need her walking in on us while we're there."

"That's easy," said Athena. "I know she prefers to eat lunch in the Agency after a thirty-to-forty-five-minute workout. I see her in the gym from time to time whenever I'm here."

"Awesome," said G. "Then we leave right away. You got a car?"

"I have access to a couple."

G grabbed his backpack and slung it over his shoulder. "Then I'm ready when you're ready."

The two made their way to the parking garage where Athena led him past several parked cars and through an adjacent, dimly lit passageway. She pushed a button on the wall, and elevator doors opened for them to enter. She pushed a lower-level button that took them a couple of floors below street level. The doors opened to garage full of nondescript vehicles G could only assume were privately owned.

"Ever seen that commercial on TV where they let you choose *any* car?" asked Athena.

G stopped in his tracks and gave her a look of disbelief. "Don't tell me we get to choose *any car*," said G, almost in disbelief.

"Oh, no, I was just asking," laughed Athena. "Did you honestly think for one second that you'd get to do that here?" She started laughing harder as she realized how gullible G could be.

"Hey, *you* insinuated—"

She stopped suddenly, turned around, and walked up to him and whispered into his ear. "Look at me and tell me this isn't exciting you just one little bit." She stared into his eyes looking for some kind of response. The look alone was irresistible. He wanted to kiss her right there, but he realized they were both probably on some camera display somewhere in the Agency. Hell, they could be plastered all over the ops center's giant monitors, for all he knew.

"Of *course* it's exciting…and at times, frightening as hell."

"Well, I get a rush from the very thought of it all," said Athena, raising her eyebrows. "Besides, we get to choose *any* car we want," she said, with a sexy wink. "What are you feeling?"

"OK, so you *weren't* kidding about the car thing. Awesome. I'm feeling we should choose something someone wouldn't remember if their lives depended on it…because ours may," said G.

"Then we should opt for the blue Impala or Malibu," said Athena, approaching the Malibu.

"That'll work," said G, tossing his bag into the backseat from the passenger side.

"Oh, no you don't," said Athena, "you're driving. I'll get us there, but you're driving. Too many people will remember a female driver before they'll remember a male driver."

"You're right," said G reluctantly, making his way to the driver's side, knowing how much he despised driving in the city.

"Whatcha got, Dave?" asked Dan, as he approached the operations center supervisor.

Dave peered over his glasses to bring up two monitors; one depicted a map of the Central American landscape, the other was full of text and numerical data.

"We've established communications with your remaining two operators who were separated from the exfil op attempted by Ox a couple of days ago. I'm certain you recall they were separated when they came under fire," explained Dave.

"Yeah, I know the details. So what's the latest?"

"Well, the two men are positioned here, northwest of Medellín, Colombia."

"How the hell did they get so far off course from their assigned area of responsibility?"

"Their messages indicate that part of their E&E route was taken by raft. The move may have in fact saved their lives, as they were being pursued after having killed a couple of their captors."

Dan nodded while analyzing the situation.

"They're in deep shit either way. And we need to get 'em out," explained Dave.

"What assets do we have available? What are the LIMFACS? Do we have any locals nearby we can count on to assist?"

"The limitation factors are pretty much confined to their inability to move very far from where they are without being detected. And neither one speaks the language. No immediate assistance available from anyone local. We do have one very eager Ox Waddy, who would like to complete the operation. He and his team are the closest assets we have available. They're sitting at Howard Field, awaiting permission to lean forward at sunset."

Dan took a closer look at the map monitor. "Damn, that's way too close to the San Pablo airport. They'll easily be picked on ATC radar. Any suitable LZs further away our team can hump to that'll put them in a safer position?"

"Not without exposing them to the general population."

Dan carefully weighed the factors and quickly realized he had a puzzle on his hands. And this puzzle was complicated by a limited timeline factor. He needed to get the men out, and he needed to do so before they were discovered by their pursuers.

"Does Ox have a Spanish linguist on his team?"

Dave nodded. "One of the best we've got right now…new kid by the name of Ronaldo Torres. He's his new copilot."

"That may work, for starters," said Dan. "Send Ox the data. If he can convince me of a plan to get them out without guns blazing, I'll consider it. Meantime, see what else you can come up with that'll help us. We've got to move on this by sunset and get those men out."

"Do me a favor and pull into the small strip mall at the next light," said Athena.

G gave her a questioning look and wanted to ask why, but he was almost afraid of the answer he'd get, so he decided to simply comply with her request.

"Park here and wait, please."

G continued to do as he was asked. He quickly realized he didn't particularly enjoy being outside the information loop, so he decided he'd play it differently upon Athena's return. He'd start by keeping her posted on the details his mind played out in terms of his own plan. He drew a deep breath through his nose and detected the sweet, subtle scent of cologne she left lingering in the car. He closed his eyes for what seemed to be a few seconds and was startled by a knock at the passenger window. He had unknowingly locked her out, and she had returned faster than he had expected.

"Good call on locking the doors, G, but I gotta be able to get back in, sweetie," she said smiling.

G focused on two factors. One, she called him "sweetie." He could focus on that fact for days alone. Two, she returned with a small bouquet of flowers.

"For me? You shouldn't have," he said with a smile.

Athena gave him a sarcastic look. "Don't flatter yourself, G. They're a prop in case we need them. If we don't, then you can consider them yours. I have to admit, you're not the type I pegged for a flower lover."

G gave her a quick glance. "Which way?" he asked.

A nondescript rental car made its way down the I-95 toward the nation's capital. Behind, the wheel was a man driven as much by instinct and intuition as by the clear vision of his objective.

Hakim had taken on a new identity and successfully made his way out of New York, where things had become too hot for him. He was en route to find Dr. Middleton, the *real* envelope, or both.

Hakim knew he wouldn't be the only one seeking the whereabouts of the envelope but assumed his nemesis had to convince his *hosts* to allow him to retrieve it. Even then, Hakim would have the advantage of time and proximity, but he'd have to drive as fast as he could without drawing the attention of law enforcement. Luckily, the traffic was moving at a pretty good pace, as it often does on the I-95. Most were moving along quite briskly at their typical eighty-five miles per hour rush. Good enough for Hakim to make decent time.

Hakim was feeling something else he had rarely, if ever, felt—frustration. G had distracted Hakim's objectives enough for him to question his own strengths and weaknesses. The long drive gave him plenty of time for reflection as he made his way toward his objective.

His drive took on a secondary, intuitive focus as he became enamored and consumed by the whereabouts of the envelope. He could literally feel things change as G inched closer to the envelope. Hakim considered his

Dream Operative

options as he passed a rest stop sign indicating a place to pause between Baltimore and the DC Beltway. Something new was taking place, and there was only one way to truly find out.

Rest area ahead, 5 miles...

―⁂―

Nervousness set in as G entered the affluent neighborhood of Dr. Middleton. Athena had never been to her residence before, but unfamiliarity was never a deterrent when she had an objective to accomplish.

"Take a left," she said, examining the GPS app on her smartphone.

G nodded and slowly made the turn.

"Nice homes in this place," Athena said softly, slightly distracted from the commands of her GPS phone. She noticed G taking another left turn without her input. She checked her phone and didn't say anything, because it was a correct turn. She fell quiet and watched, as he seemed to know where he was going all of a sudden.

G's mind raced as he began to see numbers flashing through his mind: 3...no, 8...2...9...9...8299. There, on the left. He turned the car into the driveway, turned off the engine, and looked at Athena, who was staring at him with her mouth open, clearly impressed with his "abilities."

"This is it," he said, simply and matter-of-factly.

"Yeah, I...know," she said, with a look of reverence and awe.

G opened his door and slowly made his way to the front door of the house, his mind flashing familiar images from his dream.

Athena grabbed the small bouquet of flowers and quickly followed G. She reached out and rang the doorbell with the knuckle of her right hand to avoid leaving any fingerprints. G picked up on it immediately and understood the technique.

"Hold these," said Athena, pushing the flowers into his chest. She grabbed a small tool kit from her purse and examined the door lock and deadbolt mechanism.

"Don't you think we should look for a key?"

"Too much time," responded Athena, working the lock mechanism.

G placed the flowers at his feet, tilted a nearby potted plant positioned on the front porch, reached his hand below it, and discovered a key. "We really should just use a key," he offered once again, showing her what he had found.

She shook her head. "How did...do I even dare ask?"

"I figure she's got kids or grandkids. They need something easy and obvious to get in. Just trying to think more like *you people*," he said.

They opened the door and quickly made their way inside. Both G and Athena heard a beeping sound.

"Alarm." said Athena. "I'll take care of it—"

"Eight, two, nine, nine," said G.

Athena returned a questioning look.

"Do it," G commanded.

Athena entered the numbers. The alarm accepted the code and went dim.

"OK, that one I *will* ask about. How did you know the code? Is that something you actually saw in one of your *alter dimensional encounters*?" she asked sarcastically.

"Nope," he responded, shaking his head. "Same logic I used for the key. The kids need something simple. And I'd bet she would, too. Big-brain people have an easier time remembering things that have a relationship or a pattern attached to them."

He's a damn natural, Athena thought, as she processed G's simple logic.

G stopped in his tracks just short of the dining room and closed his eyes. His heart pounded with adrenaline. As he drew a deep breath, his senses filled with all of the nuances he had experienced the night of his dream. The room was darker then, but everything was in the same place he had seen it in his dream.

Athena watched as G slowly made his way through the living room with his eyes closed. Cocking his head slightly to the right, he stopped in front a small table with a mirror positioned on the wall just above it. He opened his eyes and could clearly see the image of his reflection.

G knelt to one knee and studied the hand carvings that were meticulously etched into the table. He discovered a small handle and gently pulled to open an inconspicuous drawer. He reached inside the drawer and pulled out a small, folded manila envelope. He slowly turned his head, made eye contact with Athena, and winked. He placed the envelope into his pocket, closed the drawer and rose to his feet.

Time slowed...

As he rose to his feet, G pushed the envelope deeper into his pocket and turned toward Athena to make their exit. Just before turning away from the mirror, he caught a glimpse of Hakim facing him from the other side of the mirror, pointing a gun at him. He reacted with a leap toward Athena just as Hakim fired the weapon. The last thing he saw was the muzzle flash from Hakim's weapon.

Time returned to normal as he embraced Athena and brought her to the floor.

"What the hell?" exclaimed Athena, shocked by the move.

""We gotta go…*now!*" warned G.

"Whoa, big guy…if I didn't know any better, I'd say you just saw a ghost."

"Worse," explained G. "Much worse. He knows I'm here, and he's close. We need to go *now*," he repeated.

38

At the rest area, Hakim awoke from a short power nap, where a dream had provided the discovery he needed—that G now possessed what *he* wanted…what he had traveled so far for…the very envelope he had sought to obtain, even killed for. His only hope was that G wouldn't be able to discover what he really had until Hakim had a chance to kill him.

But where was G headed now? Would he retreat to the safety of his captors and government allies? Hakim was free to get to him, regardless of where he went. If he couldn't get to him physically, he'd get to him in a dream and discover the contents of that envelope.

Before pulling away from the rest area, Hakim paused to consider his options. He could chase his intuition, or he could slow down enough to try to discover G's plan. He allowed the car to idle while he focused on G with all he had. He thought of G's unshakable demeanor, his drive, his mind, and his eyes. He prayed to be connected to it all, as G was fast disappearing into one of the most densely-populated areas of the country: Arlington, Virginia. His thoughts carried him to a shallow slumber and the introduction of yet another dream.

The vision of Hakim's dream began to materialize as he caught glimpses of random objects. Things that made little sense to him began to take shape as he began to see things G allowed to occupy his mind. Hakim squinted, trying to come to grips with random numbers that flashed through his mind. He saw the numbers 8, 2, and 9. He figured them as part of a combination of some kind, so he stored them in his memory. Objects began to take shape as he focused; a key hidden under a small potted plant, a hallway, a small table...and a mirror. There was something about the mirror that demanded his attention.

He had recently discovered he could use a mirror as a portal from which to provide clear glimpses between dimensions, so he projected himself to a vantage point to provide a better view into exactly what G was up to. He reached the mirror and actually startled himself when he came face-to-face with his dream nemesis some two feet away. He was so surprised, he barely had time to instinctively draw his weapon and aimed it directly at G. His heart pounded as he tried to observe all he could before being discovered. He had arrived in time only to see G place something into his pocket and glance back into the mirror at him. He had no time to react to G's quickness but fired one single shot anyway.

Time slowed...

The bullet left Hakim's weapon and penetrated the mirror but never made it past his own dimension. It merely penetrated the mirror and was silently absorbed by the confines of the dimension, as if he were shooting into a pane of water instead of glass.

G was suddenly nowhere to be found.

"Let's go!" shouted G, grabbing Athena's hand and leading her to the car. "Find the quickest route to the airport, Athena, and do it now," said G. his mind flooded with the image of the bullet coming, slow motion, from Hakim's weapon.

Athena's instincts and training taught her to know when to react and when to question. This was no time to question. She queried her smart phone for a route to Reagan National and provided turn-by-turn instructions to G as they made their way toward the airport.

Hakim studied his surroundings, suddenly realizing he was in the exact same room as G, only in an exact opposite-reflected dimension. He closed his eyes to concentrate on anything G may have thought of or allowed to penetrate his mind before he left the room. He needed to know where G was headed, because he knew that he had what Hakim wanted—the elusive envelope.

Dream Operative

Time returned to its typical pace when Hakim discovered something significant. There was something about the subtlety of a scent that lingered in the room. The slight presence of a sinister smile crossed his face as he continued to interrogate the room. He shifted his focus throughout the room in search of a clue, any clue, that would lead him to confirm his suspicions. His eye caught a glimmer of something shiny in a rug at his feet. He bent down and picked up the tiny object and held it in his open palm, but he couldn't immediately determine what it was.

The room began to warp and dissolve around Hakim. His dream was in transition. Items began to fall from shelves. Curtains flowed upward as if gravity were being manipulated. The wall on one side of the room gave way and dissolved to nothingness. Hakim rose to his feet, his eyes darting about in search of the source of the alteration. He placed the object he had found into his pocket. Overcome by the rapid changes, he decided it was time to leave and look for another way to follow G.

<hr />

"I've got a plan to get our remaining team out of Colombia, if you're ready for the details," said Dave to his Boss.

"Certainly...be right there," responded Dan, eager to hear Dave's plan for the exfiltration of the remaining two special tactics operators.

Dan looked at his watch and confirmed the hour was getting late in terms of approving a same-day operation, but he was not prepared for the delicacy and expense of what he was about to hear.

Dan arrived at the ops center floor and was led to a planning room with maps spread out on a conference table, electronic charts displayed on several CRT screens, and a couple of analysts wearing headsets, typing away at keyboards.

"What's the plan, Dave?"

"Let me hit you with the heaviest part of this first, then you tell me if you're prepared to proceed," answered Dave.

Dan waited a moment and nodded.

"This is gonna cost a million dollars cash before we calculate the actual residual expenses," said Dave, as straightforward as he knew how, knowing Dan preferred the obvious facts up front anyway.

Dan sat and waited for another moment and nodded, indicating to Dave that he was listening.

Dave explained the operation in detail. Dan asked all the typical risk analysis and exit strategy questions. It seemed Dave had come up with one of the best plans to rescue the remaining warriors with the least potential for violence and risk to incite an international incident.

"I assume Ox has already been briefed on this?" Dan asked.

"Affirmative."

"And you can assure me he's surrounded by the best we've got?"

"Affirmative, most of which were requested by Ox himself."

Dan looked at his watch. "We need to get this underway, then."

"Sir, you'll excuse me, but I put the plan into motion an hour ago, assuming you'd approve it with minor changes," said Dave. "Ox's translator and one of our operatives are on their way to secure the money from the US Consulate in Panama as we speak. Of course they'll require your *final* authorization before they'll make the actual transfer. I assured them we'd have it from you by then."

"OK, is it safe to assume someone has briefed Booker and Hartman on the plan?"

"We put 'em on alert, pending your approval."

"Then put 'em in motion," said Dan, indicating his approval. "They have a lot of ground to cover and some hurdles to overcome as well. So they'll need time to execute their part of the plan."

"Will do," answered Dave, as he glanced over and nodded to one of the analysts.

"Incoming message," said Hartman, looking at a flash notice on his handheld device. "It's an OPORD," he added as he watched the message complete its download.

"An operations order requires us to act immediately, so be prepared to move," instructed Booker.

"Copy," responded Hartman, waiting for the complete download.

"I have the file," he reported, after a minute and a half.

Both men carefully reviewed the order to ensure they fully understood the plan.

Dream Operative

Op Order Name:	OPERATION BUY-OUT
Op Order Number:	TS-EO-0070-SA
Op Dates:	XX Jun XX
Report Date:	Immediate

TOP SECRET

From: Director of Operations, NSA (Disavowed)
To: CIA/DOD/SOCOM/NAVSPECWARCM/USASOC/AFSOC/RAWHIDE STS

A. Management/Supervisor Intent: Recover/extract two ST/SOF mbrs
B. General Concept: Clandestine air op using drug-buy as cover. Crew preselected.

EXECUTIVE SUMMARY

A. General Situation: 2 US Spec Tactics team mbrs being pursued by unfriendly forces of a known drug cartel. Have already escaped and evaded capture and imminent death. Require immediate extraction. Helo air impractical. Heavily protected/fortified.
B. Terrain/Weather: Urban/VFR.
C. Criminal Element: Known drug cartel/situation volatile & dangerous.

I. MISSION

Gulfstream 4 (G4) NSA/CIA operatives (5) will fly to Juan Pablo II Airport, Colombia, under the cloak of darkness and the registry of Panama to extract two ST mbrs. Operatives will pre-coord after-hours arrival with Colombian contacts in an effort to conduct a large-scale ($1mil) drug buy. ST mbrs will use all available means to breach airport perimeter and make their way aboard the G4 in the cargo hold area prior to unscheduled departure. Aircraft is equipped to transfer mbrs in-flight from cargo hold to aft cabin once airborne. Global Hawk UAS will monitor op from overhead. Do not shut down engines! No jet restart capability.

II. SITUATION

Asymmetrical w/the US at a disadvantage. Small arms are expected to be aboard the G4 but not to extremes. The success of the mission is highly dependent upon skilled drug transaction negotiations and the ability to discern when to close the deal/depart, NOT in the effective exchange of gunfire. Effective timing and use of diplomacy is of the utmost essence of this operation. ST mbrs will be solely responsible to find a way to board the aircraft while parked.

III. EXECUTION: Upon receipt; Immediate.

C. Specific Responsibilities
1. ST mbrs—Maneuver and board G4 cargo bay undetected without engaging unfriendly forces or civilians. Lethal force authorized only in the event of undeniable potential mission compromise.
2. G4 Crew—Fly to Howard Field, Panama under US registry. Change registry to Panamanian, then fly to destination and RTB Howard Field, Panama. Reapply US registry and return to CONUS.
3. Operatives—Execute drug buy using all known training and tactics sufficient to permit the boarding time required by ST mbrs. Delay only when/if necessary.
D. Coordinating Instructions: Coord with ST mbrs as appropriate: ETA, tail number, expected parking location while on the ground at extraction pt. End of Message—EOM.

"So, we make our way to the airport and practically climb aboard our ride home and cloud surf outta here, eh?" said Hartman, with a hint of sarcasm.

"Well, you and I know that's a bit of an oversimplification, but that's pretty much it in a nutshell," responded Booker.

"What are the risks?"

"In this country? The risks are pretty much all the unknowns divided by the *hell* we'll experience if we're left here for much longer."

"So, failure is not an option…is that what you're sayin'?"

"That's *exactly* what I'm saying," said Booker.

"Understood," said Hartman. "Awaiting your orders then, sir."

"Right…put on your night gear, all black…take only what we need. We'll be expected to act quickly when that plane lands, so make sure your socks are dry and your boots are tight. Bring your sidearm with one full clip, silencer, your knife, zip ties, NVGs, and your GPS handheld device with earpiece. Everything else stays for the lucky shopper who happens to find it. I have a compass in case we need it, but I think we can find our way to the perimeter of that airport."

"You want me to set a proximity charge to destroy the gear or in case we need the distraction?" asked Hartman.

"Negative. Something like that would be a dead giveaway of our presence. For now, no one is really certain we're here. We wanna keep 'em guessing," said Booker.

"Actually I was thinking more along the lines of wanting them *eliminated* instead of guessing. Because, personally speaking, I'd rather them to be *dead* than getting any ideas about chasing us down. But that's just me," said Hartman, with a sarcastic look.

Booker shook his head. "Let's move."

Hakim awoke to the sound of laughter coming from a family outside his car. They were on their way back to their vehicle after having stopped for a break from the road.

Hakim was seated upright in the driver's seat of his vehicle, gripping the steering wheel with both hands nearest the six o'clock position of the steering wheel. His hands were sweaty and were turned palms-up in a firm grip. His breathing was heavy but not labored.

Dream Operative

He sat motionless for a few minutes, maybe longer, as he began to go over every detail he could remember about his dream. The adrenaline was still moving through his veins at a quick pace while glimpses of his encounter with G flashed through his mind. He managed to capture enough of the dream sequence to put most of the pieces together and was even able to decipher some of G's lingering thoughts. He learned enough to know that G was on his way to the airport, en route to someplace in Central America. He winced at the thought of how well G's prowess, abilities, and movements had improved.

It was time for Hakim to make a move of his own. He knew G had successfully found and captured what had eluded Hakim since arriving in country—the envelope. Its contents promised to reveal something of significant value to the Jihad and had the potential to cause grave harm to the United States if left in the hands of someone willing to exploit it against America.

Hakim reached into the back seat for a small leather bag and made his way to the public restroom. He focused on G's moves and the remnants of the thoughts he remembered from the dream. The possibility had occurred to Hakim that G had purposely allowed a random thought or two to linger that would provide a trail clue to his next destination. However, Hakim scoffed at the possibility that he could be that smart, given how surprised G was at Hakim's *guest appearance* in his dream. He had discovered enough to know that he was headed to a nearby airport. Hakim stopped outside the men's restroom and studied a map on the wall. He stared at the map and watched as it began to warp in front of his very eyes. Was he still dreaming? He sat down on a bench positioned against a wall opposite the map.

The map continued to move and warp. He focused on G and quietly waited for the map to draw his attention toward a destination. There…in the lower part of the map…his mind was drawn toward the Reagan National Airport. Hakim knew he needed to act quickly to keep up with G, but he also knew it was time for an identity shift.

Hakim made his way into the restroom. He found a handicapped stall equipped with its own sink, toilet, and mirror where he recreated himself once again. He began the transformation by shaving his head and most of the heavy stubble of his beard. He left enough facial hair to form a neatly trimmed goatee. He changed into a pair of blue jeans, black leather belt, and a subdued polo shirt. He emerged from the stall hidden under another one of his many disguises and casually made his way back to the car.

Hakim walked between his car and a late model GMC Yukon that had arrived after he had entered the restroom. He glanced inside the vehicle and noticed a baseball cap with a fishing logo embroidered in the center. He casually looked around to see if anyone was looking and tried the door. It was unlocked. He reached in, quickly grabbed the old worn cap, and placed it on his head. Before leaving the vehicle, he opened the glove box and found a pair of sunglasses with dark lenses. *Perfect,* he thought. *If he cannot see my eyes, he will be slow to react, if he reacts at all.*

39

The Gulfstream IV pulled in front of the small terminal at Howard Field and shut off its bright landing lights. The pilot kept the engines on the sleek jet running and awaited further instructions from air traffic control.

The tower directed the aircraft to a small hangar, where the doors were immediately closed behind the taxiing aircraft. The pilot shut down the engines, and within a few minutes, the forward door opened, and a short set of stairs extended to the floor.

Ox and Pat approached the aircraft first and waited at the base of the stairs for the aircraft commander and any operatives assigned to the trip. The first person to stick his head out of the cabin door was none other than Todd "T-Rock" Jordan himself. Preceded by his well-known smile, he took one look at Ox and the hangar surroundings and offered a friendly greeting in his own typical style.

"Yo, is this the Vegas connection? Cuz it sure doesn't look the same, best I can recall," said Todd with a chuckle. "Of course, I was pretty drunk when I last left Sin City."

Last time he and Ox were together, best either of them could recollect, was some four years back on R&R in Vegas. Neither one retained a crystal clear memory of the quick weekend. Aside from the sheer amount of cigars, alcohol, and women they celebrated with, the penthouse of the Rio had provided the perfect outlet to celebrate a rather nasty but successful mission in Afghanistan. Best they could remember, they were asked to leave the hotel after *over-celebrating* the success of a covert op they had completed together that resulted in the exposure and eventual capture of an Al Qaeda leader and several other undesirables in the region.

Ox returned a slight hint of a smile and greeted the younger Jordan with a firm man-hug as he took his final step off the aircraft. "Still smoking those shitty Cubans, I see," said Todd, examining a cigar he expertly lifted from Ox's pocket.

"Still pretty good at taking things that clearly don't belong to you, *I* see," said Ox in return.

"I still can't pull that trick on you, can I? Yo, Ox, this is our pilot, Monty," said Todd, as Monty emerged from the aircraft. The two shook hands. "He's good people and one helluva pilot."

"And this is Pat," said Ox, turning toward Pat. "He's shown himself to be a real asset over the last several hours. He'll work with your folks to get the correct registry applied to the aircraft."

"Pat, how long you figure it'll take to make the changes?" asked Ox.

"Two hours, tops."

"OK, you have an hour-and-a-half," said Ox, with a wink. "Ronaldo should be back with the loot by then, and we should all be ready to put this mission into play."

Pat nodded and introduced himself to the small labor team. Their mission was to remove US registry markings connecting the aircraft with the US government and to reapply a foreign registry that would deceptively connect the aircraft with the Panamanian government.

Ox led Todd and Monty to a private room to brief the mission, including the flight plan, time on the ground, expected risks, and rules of engagement, or ROE.

Ox was in the middle of briefing the OP ORD when Ronaldo walked into the room with Perry. Each of them was carrying two large black bags. Ox looked at Ronaldo and asked, "You're back early. Any issues?"

Dream Operative

Ronaldo shook his head slightly and answered with a simple "Negative" as he glanced at Todd and Monty.

"TJ, this is my co-pilot, Ronaldo. He'll be up front with Monty on this mission. And this is SFC Perry, USMC Force Recon," said Ox proudly.

Todd took aim directly at Ronaldo in his typical straightforward style. "*¿Cómo es su español?*" (How's your Spanish?), asked Jordan.

"*Bueno, esto depende en cual dialecto usted pregunta sobre y quién pregunta*" (Well, that depends on which dialect you're asking about and who's asking.), answered Ronaldo in his typical tough guy style.

Todd started laughing out loud while Ox looked on unimpressed. "Are you two finished sparring?"

"I just had to make sure the brother could speak the language before I go putting my life in his hands, cuz these boys we're dealing wit' ain't no joke." said Todd with a smile. "Besides, I already know Monty can't speak a lick of Spanish." He chuckled.

"Then what good is he?" asked Ronaldo. "No offense," he added, looking at Monty.

"He's the only one I trust flying that technological wonder parked in your garage," said Todd, intentionally pushing back on Ronaldo to assert his dominance. "As I understand it, *your* role will be to answer the radio calls…in Spanish…and *help* Monty fly us into and out of the AOR, or area of responsibility," he added, looking to Ox for confirmation.

"*Everyone* has a role to play," said Ox, in atypical political fashion.

Ronaldo didn't enjoy being tested, much less pushed around by someone he'd just met. But he knew all too well he was the new *kid on the block* and would have to prove himself over time.

"We're ready," announced Pat without warning, walking into the room.

G checked his watch as he and Athena approached the ticket counter. It was 5:40 P.M. He checked the board to see that their flight was scheduled to depart at 7:20 p.m. "on time."

Athena produced a passport for each of them and informed the ticket agent they had business class reservations. The agent glanced at the passports and printed two boarding passes then directed them to airport security screening on the mid-level of the terminal.

"I'd love to know how you got ahold of my passport, but I'd probably just get a vague response from you," G said, with a hint of sarcasm and a smile.

Athena returned the smile, and the two made their way through airport security without any issues. G stood nervously by a large window at the departure gate looking out at the busy ramp as the sun set on another typical DC day. Meanwhile, Athena sat patiently in a waiting room chair nearby, all the while keeping an eye on G and a visual scan on the immediate area.

G was lost in thought until he saw Athena's reflection in the darkening window in front of him. He turned and took a seat beside her and instinctively put his arm around her as he took his seat. She responded by laying her head on his shoulder, offering a natural response of affection as an answer to his gesture.

G glanced at his watch: 6:17 p.m. They would board in a few minutes, assuming schedules were still running on time.

"OK, let's roll," announced Ox to the group. "Pat, make sure you send the new tail number to mother, so she can relay it to Rawhide."

"Done," said Pat with confidence, pleased that he had successfully predicted the boss's orders.

Ox was the last to board the G4 as Monty and Ronaldo started the engines. He glanced over to see Perry anxiously standing near the jet. Ox stopped for a moment, then walked toward the young scout and looked him squarely in the eyes. "I can't take you with us on this one, young man, but trust me when I tell you that I'll bring 'em back, come hell or high water."

"Roger that, sir." said Perry with all the respect and discipline expected of his profession.

"Make sure we make it out of the hangar safely, would ya?" said Ox, winking at the young man and turned and boarded the jet. As he closed the cabin door, he could hear Perry shouting commands to the crew to get the hangar doors opened quickly for the G4's nighttime departure.

Ronaldo responded smartly to Monty's cockpit commands. The engines whispered to a smooth start. The crew was waiting for Ox to board when Monty announced, "Checklist complete, copilot," expecting the same response from Ronaldo.

Dream Operative

"Not quite," responded Ronaldo, pulling a Beretta Cougar 8000, a small-caliber sidearm, from a rib holster. He checked the chamber to ensure he had a full clip of ammo and the crimson laser illuminated. Ronaldo preferred the light thirteen-round version and never saw a need to be in any situation that required him to have more than a few rounds. He felt it was enough to get him out of most *situations*.

"*Now* checklist complete, pilot," said Ronaldo, with a wink and a smile. He snapped the clip into place, quickly flipped the safety switch, and holstered the weapon.

"Nice," replied Monty. "Real nice."

Hakim found a parking space in the short-term lot at the Reagan National Airport. He chose that lot because it was the closest to the terminal and had no intention of returning to claim the vehicle he had fraudulently rented in New York with stolen credentials.

Hakim sat in the vehicle and looked out at the terminal, focusing on G and the envelope. He closed his eyes and contemplated the fact that G may have been playing him…baiting him, in fact, into thinking he had what he wanted. He need to be sure. After all, he was getting ready to make the bold move of exiting the country. Passing through the Customs gate of any country proved to be Hakim's greatest vulnerability risk. He always took the move seriously.

Hakim lowered his head and pushed all distractions from his mind as he accessed the memories stored in the deepest corners of his mind. His thoughts were random at first, but he had learned to yield to them, to bring out thoughts gathered during his alter-conscious experiences. He and G each employed their own *style* once they transcended conscious dimensions and were each getting better at manipulating their journeys and accessing memory synapses.

Random images flashed before Hakim's subconscious mind as he slipped deeper into his thoughts. His heart kept pace with the rhythm of his encounter with G as he remembered the destruction levied upon the room just before he left that dream. Hakim pushed past the encounter and tried to track G's movements through his thoughts and was able to catch a glimpse of random landscapes he encountered on his way to the airport. He watched as G obtained his airline ticket and kept catching a glimpse of a woman he had little knowledge of. He was clearly not traveling alone. Hakim considered it a weakness he could quite possibly exploit when the time was right.

He pushed deeper into G's mind but came up with little to nothing plausible. G was good and clearly knew to guard his thoughts, knowing Hakim would attempt to use them against him. Hakim kept seeing the letters "S...J...O" flash across his mind. Discounting them as random at first, he paused slightly to allow them to sink into his own mind as a possible clue to something...anything that would help lead him to G.

He emerged from his semiconscious state of mind, took a deep breath, and got out of the rental car while trying to reason with the images his mind played for him. Walking away from the car, he activated the locks with the remote key fob and tossed the device into the nearest trash receptacle and made his way into the airport.

Hakim stopped to study the departure destination screens to pick up a clue as to where G may be headed. He waited for his mind to help him reveal the destination, as it had when he studied the map at the highway rest area. His eyes scanned the board as if he were looking for a specific word in one of those cheap word puzzle games. And then he spotted it: SJO.

―――⚬⚬⚬―――

Booker and Hartman reached the perimeter of the airport close to midnight. Dressed in full black and assisted by the latest in night vision technology, they had successfully made it through several populated areas undetected.

The only thing that separated them from the tarmac was an eight-foot chain-link fence. The airport did not appear to be heavily guarded. But the men wouldn't take that for granted.

"Keep an eye out for unfriendly," commanded Booker, in slightly more than a whisper. "I'm gonna get to work on breaching this fence so we can get onto the tarmac when our ride arrives."

"Copy," answered Hartman. "Uh, stand by one..." he began, as he checked an in-coming message on the hand-held device. "Incoming message from Mother. She says; our ride is a white G4, Panamanian tail number HP809LD. Scheduled arrival time is zero-two-forty-one local. Max ground time will be twenty minutes. Then they depart *with or without* us," reported Hartman. He and Booker simultaneously checked their watches.

"Copy," said Booker, going back to work on the fence with his wire cutters, more determined than ever to breach the fence and create an opening for the two operators to get through.

"Should I send an acknowledgement?"

"Negative. We maintain complete silence from here on out," answered Booker. "They'll assume we have the message and will arrive to the party on time."

40

"**N**ovember eight-zero-niner Lima Delta, cleared for takeoff," announced the tower to the G4.

"Sit tight ladies, we've just been cleared for takeoff," announced Ronaldo over the intercom. He and Monty pushed the power throttles forward, bringing the engines to a very respectable roar.

The aircraft surged down the runway with amazing power and quickly leapt into the night air. It carried the clandestine team of Ox, Pat, Todd, Ronaldo, and Monty, along with over one million dollars in US-backed drug money, toward a destination they knew to be extremely dangerous and potentially hostile if things even *smelled* wrong to the cartel.

Within minutes, Ronaldo broadcast the first stratum of altitude calls to the crew. "Passing ten thousand," he announced indiscriminately over the intercom.

Todd picked up the handset of a telephone next to his plush leather seat and dialed the phone while he looked at Ox.

"*Hola, ¿cómo estás?*" (Hello, how are you doing?)

"*Sí, estamos en el aire.*" (Yes, we are airborne.)

"I know my Spanish sucks, so I'll say it in English then…you understand English, yes? Good. We are *airborne* and en route to the destination," reported Todd, as he listened for an acknowledgment. "Yes, we have the money as agreed. Confirm same destination? Ah, good…Muy bien. Yes, about one hour and forty-two minutes. Yes, very fast plane. Identification? H…P…eight-zero-niner…LD…sí, yes, *Lima-Delta*. OK, OK…see you soon. Adiós, good-bye."

"We good to go?" asked Ox.

"Good to go, brother," answered Todd, turning his head to look out the window.

Ox could see through Todd's cool facade and knew the situation to be enough to test the agent's cool under pressure. It was enough to test them *all*, because it wasn't a simple mission. It was a complex operation set up to extract two of their own. Everything hinged on all of the independent pieces coming together to work as a whole. It would have to work better than well.

"So what's the word, TJ?" asked Ox.

"Level at flight level two-zero-zero," reported Ronaldo over the intercom, as he and Monty set in the autopilot coordinates.

"Thanks, kid," answered Ox. "Pat, conduct a sweep on that equipment of yours and ensure Mother has overhead support engaged."

Pat nodded affirmatively while he tapped on his keyboards.

"Listen up, ladies," said Ox, as he gained the attention of the team. "TJ is gonna go over our roles one last time. Memorize what he says and prepare to play your part. I don't need to remind you how important it is that we all gel together on this for the sake of our objective."

"*Aight*, listen up," said Todd. "I have a drug-buy greased with a small faction of the Medellín Cartel. We're in with a minimum buy of a million bones. A lot of play has gone into this plan, so we can't fuck it up by gettin' all nervous. We *will* be tested, it's their nature. So that's your warning. They've been doing this a *long* time. They expect us to have weapons, but *nobody* better be thinkin' about pullin' their piece," explained Todd.

"Here's the roles. Ox, you're the silent boss. The less you say, the more they're gonna respect you. Your job is to sit in the shadows and make a lot of hand gestures telling the rest of us what to do. Don't worry, we'll pretty much be ignoring you anyway, but they'll think you're the one in charge. And get rid of those cheap cigars. If you've got any real Cubans, use 'em, cuz they can spot little things like that a mile away. Any questions?"

"No questions," responded Ox. It had been a long time since he had been on the receiving end of orders and instructions, but he took it all in stride.

"Ronaldo, you up comms?" asked Todd.

"Affirmative."

"*Aight*, cool. Your role is to effectively translate for me. I'm playing the front man, but they already know I'm from another planet and don't speak the language very well, so I'll need someone to keep the dialogue straight between us. Don't lose your cool if they get squirrely on us, because I already warned you to expect it. They *will* challenge you, but your role is peacekeeper and translator, dig?"

"Dig...uh, I mean, copy."

"Yo, Pat," said Todd, as he glanced at Pat, keeping the intercom microphone engaged for all to hear. "Your role is pretty much to be the geek on this trip. I need you to use your hardware to pretend you're the accountant, mathematician, and bookkeeper. So drum up whatever scientific screens you can to be convincing. They may want to take a look at whatever you're working on, but they can be baffled pretty easily by a few complicated algorithms and charts. Keep Mother posted as best you can on our progress. If shit goes south, your role will be to send an emergency message burst and destroy your gear. Any questions?"

"Negative."

"*Aight,* cool. Yo, Monty, your role is to be the driver. Keep the jet running, no matter *what* they tell you. Put us in a position on the ramp for a smooth, quick departure," said Todd.

"OK, ladies, they *will* chock us, so before we move we have to ensure several things happen—mainly that we conduct the transaction without tipping them off on why we're really there. Then we have to make sure we allow enough time for our party guests to join us, and *then* we have to make sure our gear chocks are removed. If everything goes well, they'll do that *for* us. If not, one of us will have to dislodge the chocks before we can roll. Who do we suggest do that?"

"Pat, get a message to Mother and have one of the ST bubbas ensure the wheels are free if we need the assistance," said Ox.

"On it," responded Pat, as he typed out a short message to the ops center.

Ox looked at Todd to see if his plan on getting the wheels free was acceptable. Todd returned a nod, indicating he agreed with the plan of action.

"OK, I'll say this one more time so everyone's clear. If shit goes south, a lot will depend on who has the advantage. If we're not in a position to fly out quickly, then we're the ones at a disadvantage. We're gonna be outnumbered and outgunned. We know that going in, so no one needs to be a hero or a badass. Everyone copy?"

Todd looked around to see everyone nod in agreement.

Hakim checked the flight schedule for "SJO." The only scheduled departure remaining was 7:20 p.m. He scanned his surroundings and felt he was close to G. He glanced at his watch—6:17 p.m. —then made his way to the Delta ticket counter and inquired on seat availability.

"You're in luck, sir," said the ticket agent. "There are four seats available. But they're toward the back of the plane."

"Very well," said Hakim with a nod.

"OK, sir, I'll just need to see a passport."

Hakim placed his hand in his pocket to retrieve his passport. In doing so, he noticed something he hadn't noticed before. Along with the Canadian passport and credit card he handed to the ticket agent, he noticed he had a tiny metal object of some kind in his hand. A closer look revealed the back of an earring post. His mind raced as he thought about just how that object managed to find its way into his pocket. How could he have physically transferred an object from a dream state to the conscious or physical dimension?

"There you go, sir, you're all set. Seat forty-one C. If you'd like, you can check with the gate agent to see if there are any better seats available before departure."

"Thank you," said Hakim, accepting the ticket and placing the tiny metal object back into his pocket.

Athena gently placed her hand on G's and reminded him to breathe.

"You're way too tense, G. Take a deep breath and relax. We've got a good five-hour flight," she said, encouraging him to take her advice.

"You're right," said G, trying to force himself to relax in the business class seat of the Boeing 767. But his thoughts kept drifting to the encounter with Hakim. He kept wondering whether or not he'd given Hakim too much information too quickly. The last thing he would want is for the terrorist to be on the same flight with him and Athena to Costa Rica.

G looked over his shoulder and could see passengers boarding the coach section of the aircraft. He took special notice of one of the passengers boarding, but he didn't get a good look. All he knew is that the man made him a little uneasy...enough for the hair on G's neck to bristle. He turned back around in his seat and thought of the odds of Hakim catching up with him and actually finding his particular flight. He convinced himself that he was overreacting and took a deep breath and closed his eyes to wait for the boarding process to be completed.

Hakim arrived at the gate area to find that most of the first and business-class flyers had already boarded the flight. He cautiously made his way through the remaining crowd gathered at the gate, all the while carefully studying the people around him.

He approached the gate agent and lowered his dark sunglasses enough to make eye contact and offered a smile.

"Tell me, young lady, would you happen to have a better seat selection than the one I now possess?" asked Hakim, handing his boarding pass to the agent.

"Let me see sir," said the agent as she examined the computer terminal. "We are pretty booked, but I do have some openings…are you willing to sit in an exit row?"

"Certainly," responded Hakim, knowing he'd have more room to maneuver should he need it. The seat would allow him to stand straight up without having to climb over anyone as well.

"There you go, then…thirty G," said the agent, handing him a new boarding pass.

He smiled and pushed his dark glasses back into place and slowly moved away from the ticket counter back into the crowd. Hakim's dark lenses helped him to continue to scan his surroundings without being obvious.

Hearing the call for boarding, Hakim made his way onto the Boeing 767-400. The boarding doors were located aft of the business class section, so if G was seated in that section, Hakim would have to confirm it later by taking a casual stroll through the forward cabin. Meantime, he examined every occupied seat on his way through the aisle toward his assigned seat. He could feel G's presence but couldn't quite understand why he had not yet physically seen him.

The flight attendants secured the doors while G sat quietly and contemplated the day's events. He had become so fixated on the encounter with Hakim, he had nearly forgotten the fact that he now had the envelope that, before this time, was only a figment of his dreams.

The 767 was pushed back onto the taxiway by the ramp attendants. Time slowed as G placed his hand into his coat pocket to convince himself he truly had possession of the envelope.

Come and get it, you son of a bitch, he thought, as he focused on calling out Hakim.

G felt the forces of power on his body as the 767 began its takeoff roll down the runway and break free from the grip of the earth, climbing into the night sky. The plane veered left, then right, then left again in search of its preferred route toward the Central American destination of Costa Rica. He pulled the envelope from his pocket and looked at Athena, who returned a knowing look of anticipation.

"Would either of you like something to drink?" asked the flight attendant with a smile.

G stuffed the envelope back into his pocket and looked at Athena.

"Nothing for me," said Athena.

"No thanks," said G. "Check on us in a few minutes please," he added.

"Certainly. My name is Barbara. Just push the call button when you're ready, and I'll be happy to serve you."

"So what's in the envelope?" asked Athena quietly, leaning in closer to G.

G removed the envelope from his pocket and slowly breached the seal. He pulled three small index cards from the envelope. Each card was marked "Top Secret/FOUO," *for official use only.* He glanced at Athena and looked back at the cards.

"It looks like some sort of code," whispered G. "Do you recognize or understand it?" he asked Athena, showing one of the cards to her.

"Nope, and aside from my own curiosity, I'm *happy* I don't understand it," she said.

G examined the cards longer and more critically, as if they would suddenly make sense to him. He placed the cards back into the envelope, pressed the seal tightly and returned it to his pocket. His mind raced as it naturally tried to solve the deceptive code. G extended his arm and pressed the call button. Barbara soon returned with a sincere smile painted across her face.

"Hi, Barbara, can I get a Bloody Mary?" asked G, exchanging smiles with the flight attendant.

Dream Operative

"Certainly." answered Barbara. "How 'bout you dear, would you like anything?" she asked Athena.

"No, thank you."

Booker had nearly completed cutting an opening in the fence large enough to crawl through when Hartman noticed headlights approaching.

"We have company approaching, sir."

"Take cover," answered Booker, loosely securing the opening to keep the breach hidden.

Booker ducked and rolled into a nearby shallow ditch near the fence line just before the beam of headlights reached his position. He and Hartman waited and watched as a truck slowly passed.

The men quickly slipped through the breach and made it safely onto the airport property. Booker tied a couple of wires to the fence to keep anyone from spotting the breach from a distance.

Hakim found his seat as the flight attendants secured the aircraft doors and made their customary scripted announcements. Most passengers ignore the announcements. Hakim used the time to visually scan his surroundings and analyze those around him.

The man seated next to him seemed to be an ordinary traveler — probably someone with business ties to Costa Rica. Not overly dressed, but he didn't fit the image of a tourist, either. Most other passengers seemed to fit one of two categories: tourists or residents, judging from the way they were dressed or the state of mind they seemed to exude. He exchanged pleasantries with the man next to him, with a simple nod and a short greeting, and picked up a magazine to ward off any threat of conversation.

Once airborne, Hakim reclined his seat and watched the earth outside grow smaller as the 767 climbed its way toward its assigned cruising altitude. His thoughts were caught up in determined focus to find and track down the one man who consistently thwarted his every move.

Hakim closed his eyes for a moment, forcing his mind to drift into alter-consciousness. He had to be certain that the path he was on would lead him to G. He was uncertain how much of a lead G had on him toward his destination but was determined to catch him and pry the envelope from his dead hands. The ambient noise from the jet engines became a catalyst of white noise he would use to ride into a dream as he drifted off to sleep.

Hakim crossed the threshold of reality into alter consciousness, finding himself alone in an aisle in the back of a small, dimly lit performance theatre. The stage of the theatre was empty and was illuminated by a single soft spotlight splashed gently upon a deep blue backdrop curtain. The rows of seats were empty. Hakim was drawn to the stage and stepped forward courageously to satisfy his curiosity.

Passing the seventh row, his attention was drawn to a man seated alone on the far end of the aisle. He stopped and stared but couldn't recognize him from the distance. Hakim projected himself to a safe position from the man, directly behind and slightly to his right. He watched as the man slowly reached into his coat pocket. Hakim reacted by reaching for his weapon... but he wasn't armed. He watched carefully as the man pulled a small envelope from his pocket. He recognized the envelope but not the man.

He watched closely while the man opened the envelope and studied the contents: three small cards, each laden with code. The code gave Hakim hope, because he was able to determine its authenticity from the manner in which it was marked: *"Top Secret/FOUO."* He tried catching more of a glimpse but was unable to completely see the cards. It was enough to convince him that the man clearly had what he was looking for.

Hakim heard a voice call out from nowhere, *Come and get it, you son-of-a-bitch!*

Hakim reached out to place his hand on the man's shoulder. Just before making contact, he disappeared.

"Why are you here?"

The question and the voice startled Hakim when he looked up to the stage. There, illuminated in the soft spotlight, was G, holding an envelope tauntingly, looking Hakim squarely in the eyes.

"I've come to retrieve that which is rightfully mine," answered Hakim.

"Well, then...like I said, come and get it, you son of a bitch!" answered G, defiantly.

Hakim was angered. He immediately projected himself onto the stage and appeared in the very spot G had occupied. He was ready to kill for the envelope, but he found only himself standing alone in the spotlight.

"We'll finish this soon," said a voice from nowhere, trailing off as the stage spotlight dimmed and Hakim's dream went dark.

41

"We're about one-hundred yards from what appears to be an airport maintenance building," reported Hartman, looking through the night vision binoculars. "If we can get to that building, we can get a better perspective on how to manipulate things when our ride arrives."

The men were about to cross a nearby perimeter road when they heard an aircraft pass overhead. It seemed to pass so low they could touch it. The runway lights were turned on to their lowest setting, illuminating the entire airport environment, including their position.

"Stay low," said Booker quietly.

The two remained stationary and watched while a small single-engine Cessna landed. They heard the chirp of the landing gear making first contact with the runway and watched until it taxied off the runway onto a taxiway. The airport went dark soon after the aircraft exited the runway.

Booker silently signaled to Hartman to move out but to keep his eyes open for the unexpected. Booker followed closely behind, after providing armed cover for his teammate. The men moved across the field in alternating covering maneuvers until they reached the building.

The men had come from the far side of the airport and made their way across a taxiway, an active runway, and a tarmac before they reached the maintenance building. The hangar, where their aircraft would most likely park for the transaction, was located across the airfield, approximately three hundred yards from the maintenance building.

Booker arrived at the building first and positioned himself adjacent to an exterior wall with a window just above and to the left of his head. The inside of the building was dimly lit. Hartman watched through his night vision device as Booker carefully peered through the bottom edge of the window and quickly dropped back to his knees. He signaled to Hartman that he saw two men inside who appeared to be unarmed. Then he signaled Hartman to move in and join him.

Hakim was convinced not only that G had the envelope, but that he was very close to a confrontation that would provide an opportunity for Hakim to take it from him. An announcement from the flight attendants startled Hakim as he opened his eyes to the vaguely familiar surroundings of the cabin interior.

"Ladies and gentlemen, we've reached our cruising altitude of twenty-four thousand feet. We will be offering our first in-flight service to you shortly. Your choices of beverage include…"

Hakim unbuckled his seatbelt and casually made his way to the back of the airplane. He was careful to ensure his dark glasses stayed in place, in case he happened to come across the one who would surely notice him.

He carefully scanned each seat occupant on his way to the back of the plane but didn't immediately recognize anyone or detect any real threat. He stepped into the bathroom and waited for a few moments. He washed his face and looked into the mirror, staring at his own reflection for several moments.

G arose from his seat and made his way past Athena, who had fallen asleep. He stood and stretched and decided to take a stroll through the cabin. He walked to the coach section of the aircraft and looked down the long aisle of passengers of the nearly full flight. He slowly walked past the first set of restrooms and was greeted by his friendly flight attendant, Barbara.

"Hello," said Barbara with a smile. "Out for a stroll?"

G returned a glance and a smile but quickly returned his focus to the passengers and the path ahead. Something wasn't right. He could feel it in the pit of his stomach. He continued to slowly walk down the aisle toward the back of the aircraft, examining the face of each passenger along the way. Nothing looked out of the ordinary, but he was nonetheless burdened with concern for some reason.

G found his way to the back of the plane, where he saw two flight attendants preparing their service carts. He was going to use the restroom but noticed the occupancy sign illuminated, so he continued his stroll and proceeded to return to his seat from the adjacent aisle. He was at a bit of a disadvantage now, because he would have to observe passengers from the back of their seats. He had to be careful not to be so obvious for fear his behavior would spook the passengers or the flight attendants.

Hakim opened the door of the latrine and decided to take the same route as G back to his seat. He unknowingly began his walk down the long aisle from several rows behind G. He glanced down the long aisle and saw one or two people in the aisle ahead, along with the flight attendants preparing their service carts for the first round of passenger service. He passed four rows of seats and detected a weapon protruding from one of the passengers' jackets. He made a mental note of the seat number, noting it as a possible air marshal.

Hakim's evaluation was so focused on passengers seated in the rows that he had given little thought to those in the aisle ahead of him.

G ran into Barbara once again when passing the latrines between the business class and coach cabins. She was speaking with a passenger about the weather in Costa Rica when she offered another smile his way.

G stepped into the latrine and secured the door behind him. The light illuminated as soon as he locked the door. He took a deep breath and looked at himself in the mirror while he reflected on the twists and turns his life had taken in such a short amount of time. He closed his eyes for a moment and immediately heard a familiar voice. Keeping his eyes closed, he concentrated in an effort to hear the voice clearer. It was a whisper, but it was clear.

Be very careful, G. Many lives are in the balance; they hang on the very decisions you will soon be forced to make.

It was Angel. He hadn't heard her voice since...the last time he had been in a dream state. He opened his eyes and again met his own reflection, which displayed his confused look. Angel's voice was no longer evident.

Hartman reached the edge of the building and took a position in an adjacent dark corner to the right of Booker, his weapon drawn. It was a black .40-caliber Smith & Wesson, equipped with a silencer and laser sight attached to the barrel.

He disengaged the laser to keep from being discovered by the tiny crimson beam, but he was ready to take out anyone who got in the way of their exit plan. He crouched low and held onto the handgun with both hands as he checked the back of the building for anyone or anything unexpected. He signaled to Booker that he detected no threat in the immediate area.

Both men froze in position when they heard a loud noise overhead. Looking up they couldn't see much but knew enough about the sound of aircraft to know it came from the likes of a small private jet. What they didn't know was whether or not it was the jet they were there to meet. Both men checked their watches: 0420 local time.

The men in the building began to move about. One man emerged from the building and got into a small truck and started the engine. The other man was shouting something to the driver in Spanish. He didn't immediately join the first man. Instead he made his way around the building and proceeded to urinate indiscriminately in the dark. Booker was close enough to take him out but not close enough to get pissed on.

The man finished urinating and joined the driver. The truck sped off toward a position on the tarmac, presumably to meet the landing aircraft.

Hartman remained in a crouched position and joined Booker at his side.

"You get pissed on?" whispered Hartman.

"Negative."

"I thought for sure you were getting ready to take that dude out."

"I've been through worse," quipped Booker.

"Put your *night eyes* on that aircraft that just landed and give me a tail number," instructed Booker. "And keep your head on a swivel for anyone headed this way. I'm gonna go inside to see if there's anything we can use to get ourselves close enough to the aircraft to get on board."

"Will do."

Booker drew his weapon—a silenced 9 mm semi-automatic Berretta, fourteen rounds, with a crimson laser sighting. Unlike Hartman, Booker had his laser engaged, so he could be sure not to miss what he was aiming at… should he find himself in a position to use it.

He cleared each of three rooms carefully, then holstered his weapon when he confirmed he was alone. The room was dusty and not well kept. There was a television on in one corner of the room. The audio was muted, and the picture reception was poor.

You're a long way from Kansas and high-definition TV, Booker thought.

He rifled through some drawers and eventually came upon a set of open wall lockers, where he found several sets of dark blue coveralls. They weren't the cleanest clothes he'd ever discovered, but they would work well enough to help him and Hartman blend in. He opened the next locker and found four ball cap–style hats. He held up a set of coveralls against his body for a quick size check, placed one of the caps on his head, and left the building.

"You get a tail number on that jet?" asked Booker in a whisper.

He and Hartman watched it roll almost to the end of the ten-thousand-foot runway and begin a 180-degree turn to taxi back toward a hangar.

"Still trying. Stand by," said Hartman, continuing to watch for the aircraft to place itself in a better position.

"Got 'em…Hotel-Papa-eight-zero-nine-Lima-Delta," said Hartman.

"That's our ride. Get yourself in the building and find a pair of coveralls that fit and grab a cap in the lockers on the south side of the building. Make it quick. We move out as soon as you're ready."

"I'm on it."

Booker watched the G4 taxi for a distance down the runway to midfield, and then it turned onto the ramp area adjacent to a well-lit hangar. The aircraft was positioned for an expeditious departure, with a short taxi route back to the active runway. Booker glanced at the building and began to wonder why it was taking Hartman so long to exit the building. He saw a vehicle approaching the building. There was no way to warn his teammate.

"I'm sorry, sir, only business class passengers are permitted in this section," said Barbara as she approached Hakim.

"My apologies," said Hakim, turning toward Barbara and doing his best to charm the experienced flight attendant. "I'm merely trying to stretch my legs with a short walk," he added glancing around the cabin to scan the passengers.

"We certainly don't mind you walking around, sir, but as I stated, this section is reserved for business class passengers only," said Barbara, gesturing for Hakim to make his way back to the aft section of the plane.

Hakim smiled and nodded, reluctantly making his way toward the higher-numbered seats and coach section. He slowly sauntered toward the restroom area, where a small group of people had gathered to stretch their legs.

G opened the door and stepped into a small group of people gathered outside the lavatory. Time slowed to a crawl as he picked his way through the people to find a path back to the first-class section to his seat.

Making his way past the last passenger between him and the aisle, G slowly focused his sights down the aisle and saw one man between him and Athena. The man was wearing a bandanna and had sunglasses perched just above his eyes, resting on the ridge of his eyebrows and was walking toward G down the aisle. G looked closer at the man as he was reaching up to lower the dark lenses over his eyes.

Hakim looked down the aisle and discovered the man he'd been searching for. A sinister smile slowly appeared on his face as he lowered his glasses. He stepped purposefully toward G.

The maintenance men laughed and joked with each other in their native language as they exited the vehicle in front of the small building. Booker watched from the fringe of the building. He calculated the costs as he thought of the implications of an encounter.

Avoid confrontation and civilian casualties, Booker thought, while watching the two men step into the building. Any commotion would certainly compromise the mission and severely alter or ruin their exit strategy. He peered through the window and watched the men, now seated in front a television, still chatting and joking, their backs to the door, giving Booker an advantage of a surprise entry, if he should need one.

Booker made his way to the vehicle in front of the building. It was a fully loaded fuel truck. He looked through his NVG binoculars across the flight line and could see activity around the parked G4. The escape clock had begun to tick. Twenty minutes max...

Todd glanced out the window as the G4 came to a slow, deliberate stop. Two SUVs pulled alongside the starboard side of the aircraft.

"Guess it's our move," said Todd, checking his watch and unbuckling his seatbelt. "Put on your game faces, ladies. Time check, zero-four-twenty-five local, *hack,*" announced Todd to the group, then turned to open the main cabin door. Each man checked his watch.

As the aircraft door opened, several armed men emerged from the awaiting vehicles and assumed tactical positions. One of the men approached the plane and waited for Todd to lower the stairs, then purposefully climbed

Dream Operative

aboard, weapon drawn. He carried a small-caliber hand gun, finger on the trigger. He was clearly a front man—expendable, but brave and a bit cocky. He could afford to be, because there was no way Todd and the gang could get away with taking one man out without risking certain death and mission failure. They were on enemy turf, and vulnerable. It was clearly time to act the part and play the game.

The front man entered the plane and asked for the leader. Ronaldo stepped into the cabin, noticed the weapon and offered a local greeting in a Colombian dialect of Spanish. He told the front man that Ox was the boss and pointed toward Ox with a slight tilt of his head. The man demanded that Ox accompany him off the plane and into an awaiting vehicle. Ronaldo translated for Ox and awaited a reply. Ox slowly shook his head and pointed toward Todd with a nod without uttering a word.

Pat sat stoically in his seat with an open laptop in front of him. He had pre-activated a request for overhead support before they landed and received confirmation that an armed, unmanned aircraft was monitoring everything, including every word, from far overhead.

The front man was confused and insulted that Ox refused to deplane and join the cartel boss waiting in the vehicle outside. Ronaldo assured the man that Todd was a much better choice for such transactions and could speak for the boss. He convinced the man by pointing to the bags of cash.

The man reluctantly accepted the fact that Todd would be the intermediary for the transaction and asked to see the contents of one of the cash bags. Ronaldo unlocked the zipper and opened it, revealing several bundles of Panamanian paper currency. The man smiled, nodded, and told Ronaldo to carry the bags outside; then he motioned for Todd to exit the aircraft. Ronaldo relayed the translation to Todd.

"Tell this crazy son of a bitch that I don't like the way he looks," said Todd, revealing a huge smile while looking straight into the eyes of the front man.

Ronaldo returned a look of surprise and shock to Todd.

The front man chuckled in an attempt to decipher Todd's humor more than his message.

Before Ronaldo could translate, Todd changed his course of dialogue. "Never mind, I'm just testing him to see if he understands English. Apparently the dumbass clearly doesn't understand a fucking word I said," Todd chuckled.

The front man simply responded, "Fuck?" and began to laugh.

Everyone laughed. Even Ox revealed the hint of a smile.

"Now you can tell him no one is going anywhere, including him, until I see a fuel truck pull up to this jet," said Todd, with a smile as he revealed his own weapon, still holstered at his waist.

The front man's smile quickly disappeared from his face when he detected the threat. He raised his weapon and pointed it at Todd. Todd remained calm, stood his ground and stared straight into the man's eyes, the smile now gone from his face.

"Whoa!" shouted Ronaldo, attempting to control the situation. He quickly translated Todd's demands and convinced the man to call for a fuel truck and assured him that it was a reasonable request.

The man lowered his weapon, poked his head out of the cabin door, and shouted something in Spanish.

Todd looked at Ronaldo to see if he could determine how well his request was taken.

Ronaldo gave an inconspicuous thumbs-up. The deal was in motion.

42

Booker crouched below the window to consider his options. He needed a distraction, but he didn't want to harm the men. They seemed to be innocent civilians just doing their job. But then again, they were in the heart of one of the world's biggest drug distribution centers. Booker heard a phone ring inside the building. He slowly peered into the window.

"Hola...sí...sí," said the man who answered the phone. He said something else Booker didn't understand at all and hung up the phone. The man spoke to his partner, and they began to walk toward the door.

Booker peered around the front corner of the small shack to observe the men as they departed the building. One man emerged alone, took about five steps, and turned around. He shouted something else to his partner who was still inside.

No answer.

Booker's mind raced. *Can't allow him back in that building.* He stood and casually made his way toward the man outside the building.

"Hola," said Booker, in his best Spanish accent.

The man answered "Hola," followed by more Spanish dialogue and allowed Booker to get within striking distance. Booker hit him hard with a right cross to the jaw, sending the man toward the pavement. He jumped forward to catch the man and break his fall but didn't quite get a good enough grasp. The man was out cold before his body slumped to the pavement. Booker dragged his unconscious body to a position outside the front door and waited. He figured either Hartman or the second man would emerge soon.

The phone rang again. No one answered.

Booker figured whoever was calling, needed fuel. And he could bet his life it was for the ride home he and Hartman so desperately needed. In fact, it was his very life that was on the line at that moment. Booker heard someone approach the door, so he crouched into the shadows and readied himself for another encounter.

"Hola?" he heard.

Booker listened as the greeting came again. "Hola?"

Booker stood and approached the door. "That's one of the worst Spanish accents I've ever heard," he said with a smile, staring at Hartman in mock disapproval.

"Well, it certainly beats your bird calls," quipped Hartman.

G froze in his tracks when he recognized Hakim. His mind racing, he began to realize the full impact of his dilemma. He glanced around the cabin. People were oblivious to the potential chaos and mayhem that could ensue if either of them EITHER chose to take care of "business" right then and there.

G glanced quickly toward Athena, who was stirring in her seat, unaware of the encounter unfolding behind her. He glanced quickly to his right and left to evaluate his surroundings and to react to his strategic instincts. *Think...what are your options?* His heart raced.

Hakim continued to stare with a sinister grin painted on his face, now frozen in his tracks, mentally evaluating G.

He could feel Hakim's attempt to penetrate his thoughts to get ahead of his reaction. G resisted. The two were standing in the aisle separated by six rows of seats, engaged in a mental game of chicken. Who would flinch first?

"Sir, now I've asked you nicely to return to the aft cabin—" interrupted Barbara.

The flight attendant gently touched Hakim on the shoulder to convince him to move. The gesture interrupted Hakim's focus long enough for him to provide a window of opportunity for G. As Hakim turned to address Barbara, G slipped out of sight back into the crowd, his heart racing as he tried to come up with a plan on how to deal with the terrorist in such a confined space at such a high altitude without scaring the hell out of the passengers and creating chaos at twenty-four thousand feet.

Dream Operative

Hakim turned to acknowledge the flight attendant and quickly glanced down the aisle once again to find that G had disappeared. His rage got the best of him, and he turned around and directed it at the flight attendant. "I told you I would return to my seat!" he shouted.

Some of the passengers started to stir and take notice of the tense situation developing. G could hear Hakim's voice from the shielded position he had taken beyond the latrine area some nine rows from the commotion.

"Sir, remain calm and return to your seat," said Barbara, in a calm but firm manner, the smile now erased from her face.

Two other flight attendants made their way into the business class section of the plane to try to help calm the situation. This only served to infuriate Hakim. He could see the situation deteriorating around him.

G glanced around a wall to see Hakim standing in the aisle with his back turned as he addressed Barbara. Hakim was standing right next to Athena and the empty seat G once occupied before the encounter. Athena was now awake and aware of the commotion developing next to her. G wasn't too concerned, because if anyone could handle such a situation, it would be Athena. He did think of her, however. And that opened a huge mental image for Hakim to sense and seize upon.

G looked down the aisle into the coach cabin. A flight attendant was speaking with a passenger and pointing toward the front of the plane. He figured the flight attendant was alerting an air marshal, who would be way too eager to be a hero and would only serve to make things worse. G had to figure a way to calm the situation, and he had to do it quick.

G boldly stepped into the aisle. Hakim's back was to him. Time slowed as he took his first few steps toward the terrorist. Hakim noticed Barbara glance around him. The glance indicated to Hakim that someone was approaching from behind. Hakim quickly turned to see G making his way toward him with a determined stride and a look of confidence.

Hakim smiled.

Athena turned in her seat to see G approaching.

Hakim knew he had to find a way to break G's concentration and determination, so he reached down and grabbed Athena by the hair and pulled her into the aisle.

"Your heart makes you a weak warrior and has made you vulnerable," declared Hakim.

G froze in his tracks.

Barbara stepped back.

G shouted, "No."

Some passengers gasped, some screamed. Confusion and panic set in among the passengers.

Athena looked at G.

G didn't break his gaze into Hakim's eyes.

Barbara got on the phone to alert the crew.

The seat belt lights illuminated.

A man grabbed G's shoulder from behind and forced him to the floor. It was the air marshal. He had his weapon drawn and pointed straight toward Hakim.

G was faced with a dilemma. Should he allow the air marshal to do his job, or should he intervene?

The plane began a rapid descent.

G looked at Athena.

Hakim looked at G. "The envelope. I just want the envelope."

"Ladies and gentlemen, the pilot has illuminated the seat belt sign…"

The entire cabin went black. G listened intently as an eerie calm descended upon the passengers. He tried to evaluate everything as he continued to contemplate his role in a solution that would keep them all alive.

G heard the echo of the same announcement from the flight attendant as his surroundings drifted to nothingness.

"Ladies and gentlemen, the pilot has illuminated the seat belt sign indicating our approach to the San Jose airport. Please return to your seats and prepare for our arrival…"

Hartman was relieved to see his teammate waiting for him as he exited the building. They were both wearing what could only be described as poorly-fitting company jumpsuits; Booker's fit his frame slightly better.

"I see you managed to find a uniform," said Booker.

"Yeah, it isn't quite my color, but I'm hoping it'll work long enough for us to get past the guards and onto that jet," responded Hartman. "Speaking of which, what's the plan?"

"The plan is for us to kill two birds with one stone," said Booker. "We're taking fuel to the jet."

"It sounds like that's about the limit of your plan, Captain. I only have one question."

"What's that?"

"How do you fuel a jet?"

"Well, lucky for us, I was an enlisted fuels specialist before I crossed over. Just follow my lead. And remember; don't ask questions, because your questions will probably come out in English — dead giveaway."

"So what's taking so long with the fuel?" asked Todd, looking to Ronaldo to engage the locals for an answer.

Ronaldo translated Todd's question but didn't get an immediate response. The men outside the airplane seemed visibly frustrated as they waited for the fuel truck to arrive.

The front man turned to Ronaldo and assured him the truck should be arriving very soon. Ronaldo was about to translate when he heard shouting from one of the men outside the airplane.

"*El camión de combustible está aquí. Vamos a cerrar este acuerdo.*"

Ronaldo translated, "The fuel truck is here. Let's close this deal."

"Cool," said Todd. "Tell him you're comin' wit' me...to translate. But I want your head on a swivel. Your number one priority is to look for our guys. Your number two priority is to pick up on anything that'll get us killed."

"Like what?"

"Like nervous energy...or anyone looking for a *free* deal. They're already nervous, so we're one factor away from a flash point. Be ready."

Pat looked outside his window and saw a fuel truck approaching. "Fuel truck pulling up on my side," he said.

"Copy," said Todd. "Keep your eye on 'em. I don't need anybody fuckin' with the jet. If they do anything aside from fuelin' the jet, give me a shout-out, and I'll put a slug inside somebody. I ain't dyin' or doin' time in this shithole."

Pat nodded.

Ronaldo and Todd grabbed the bags. "Let's move," said Todd.

The front man shouted to the men waiting outside, and the three men stepped outside the cabin of the aircraft. As they stepped onto the tarmac, one of the men opened the rear door to an SUV parked a few feet away. The men got inside, and the door closed behind them.

"G? Wake up, G," said Athena in a soft tone. She was careful not to touch him, as she heard of the times people had made that mistake before.

G slowly opened his eyes to see Athena sitting comfortably in her seat next to him, smiling.

"Have a good nap?" she asked innocently.

G squinted slightly while trying to wrap his conscious mind around his latest dream. His hand was wrapped around a full glass containing the Bloody Mary he had ordered just before he fell asleep. G squinted his eyes as he questioned himself. *Was it really a dream?* The visions suddenly flooded his mind as his heart began to send adrenaline throughout his body. He took a deep breath. Concern suddenly appeared on his face.

"What is it, G? What's wrong?"

"How long have I been asleep?"

"For most of the flight...why?"

G looked up to see the seatbelt signs illuminated. He opened his window shade and looked outside. They were descending.

"We're pretty close to landing," she said.

G reached into his pocket to ensure he still had the envelope. It was right where he had last placed it. His mind continued to replay the images of the dream.

"What's wrong, G?" asked Athena. "You look like you've seen another ghost."

G gave her a look she was starting to become familiar with. It was the one that told her that her comment had some merit.

"He's on board with us, isn't he?" asked Athena solemnly.

G sat frozen in his thoughts, trying to figure out a strategic move for them to keep from being seen by Hakim. But had they already been detected? He continued to wrestle with the implications of his dream encounter with the terrorist. It was becoming apparent to him that his plan to lure Hakim out of the country may have worked better than even he had given himself credit for.

Looking at Athena, he asked, "Tell me if you have the backs to both your earrings."

Athena checked behind both ears and hesitated slightly before easily removing one of her earrings, because its post back had slipped off somewhere. She looked at G with concern and wondered how he would know to have her check such a thing in the first place.

Perhaps, for the first time, he and Athena were truly communicating without having to say a word.

Booker slowly approached the right side of the jet with the fuel truck; purposely parking away from the SUVs positioned on the opposite side.

"Push your cap down lower to conceal your face," instructed Booker. "The last thing we need is someone recognizing either one of us before we get the jet fueled."

The two men exited the vehicle and went to work. Hartman followed Booker's lead on getting the jet grounded and the fuel hose connected.

Pat watched the men from his seat through the small window of the jet. Booker looked up long enough to make eye contact with Pat and offered an inconspicuous wink and a thumbs-up held close to his chest. Pat's eyebrows rose in surprise. He returned a nod and quickly turned to Ronaldo, who was the last to leave the jet, following closely behind Todd.

"Yo, Ronaldo," called Pat.

Ronaldo hesitated and looked at Pat.

"It looks like we're getting the very best fuel they've got," he added with a wink and tilt of his head to ensure Ronaldo received the intent of his encrypted message.

"Copy," said Ronaldo. "I'll let the boss know."

As Ronaldo reached the tarmac, he glanced under the jet toward the opposite side and saw the two men busy at work.

Todd hesitated for a moment to allow Ronaldo to catch up with him before they were summoned inside one of the SUVs.

"What's up?" asked Todd, detecting the look on Ronaldo's face.

"Just checking to make sure the fuel is the kind we're looking for."

"Well, is it?"

"Absolutely," Ronaldo said with a smile.

"Cool. Then let's get this shit over with and get the hell up outta here," said Todd, as he and Ronaldo stepped into the darkened back seat of the SUV.

43

Barbara and a fellow flight attendant stood by the cabin door, saying good-bye to passengers as they deplaned. Athena stood to retrieve her carry-on when G grabbed her hand and slowly shook his head as an indication that he wanted to wait longer before exiting.

Athena slowed her pace but remained standing to keep an eye on the exiting passengers.

"See anyone suspicious?" asked G. "Dude in a cap...wearing sunglasses, maybe?"

"They all look suspicious in some form or fashion," she said quietly. "Wait..."

"What have you got?"

"The *only* passenger, as far as I've seen, wearing sunglasses while he's still on the plane," said Athena. "How did you...never mind."

"Let me know when he's off the plane," said G.

"He just stepped past the flight attendants."

"Let's move," said G. He grabbed her hand and his backpack and led her toward the exit.

G stopped at the cabin door to yield to a couple of passengers and noticed they were the air marshals he had seen in his dream. It confirmed his suspicions—Hakim had been onboard with them. He needed to find Hakim before he slipped out of sight into the crowd inside the terminal.

Booker kept a close eye on the men positioned outside the SUVs as he and Hartman finished refueling the jet. He evaluated the conditions while thinking of ways he and Hartman could board the plane undetected.

"We need a diversion," whispered Booker to his teammate.

"Thought we were gonna slip into the cargo bay," questioned Hartman.

"Me too, until I remembered that's where they'll be loading the plane. No way we're gonna be able to get close to those doors without being shot."

"What are you thinking?" asked Hartman.

"Not quite sure."

"You open for a suggestion?"

"Of course," said Booker.

"How big of a diversion you need?"

Booker looked at Hartman, who was wearing the smug smile he was fast becoming known for. "What's your suggestion?"

"I just happen to have a little C4 left in my rucksack."

"Perfect," answered Booker. "We wait for our guys to exit that vehicle. I expect one vehicle to lag behind to make sure the jet moves before they escort it to the runway."

The men disconnected the fuel lines and secured the jet. Booker removed the wheel chocks from the fuel truck while Hartman retrieved the explosives and fuse from his rucksack and placed it between the truck cab and the fuel bladder. He carefully placed a remote detonator fuse into the small patch of clay and slowly backed away.

Booker climbed in the cab and started the truck while Hartman stood in front of the truck to direct him to move backward away from the jet. Booker watched the men and the SUVs for movement from his position in the cab of the truck. Hartman kept his eye on Booker and his back toward the jet.

Booker gave a nod to Hartman when he saw Ronaldo emerge from the back seat of the SUV. Ronaldo walked toward an open cargo door where two men were finishing loading crates onto the jet. Ronaldo spoke to them in Spanish and laughed. He kept walking toward the fuel truck and spoke in Spanish to Hartman, who didn't respond.

Hartman was unaware the voice was Ronaldo's, so he stood still and ignored him.

"Hey, brother, I'm talking to you," he said in plain English.

Hartman slowly turned around as Ronaldo approached him.

"Don't respond. Just nod your head," instructed Ronaldo.

Dream Operative

Booker watched from the cab of the truck. He easily recognized Ronaldo and could only assume Hartman was providing details of the diversion plan with the young copilot.

"What's the plan?" asked Ronaldo.

"Diversion...fuel truck explosion," answered Hartman quietly.

"I assume you plan on making sure we're out of the way when you blow it. So, how do you guys plan to board?"

"We're gonna put the truck in motion and allow it to get away from us. We'll need you to delay the stair pull until you see the explosion," explained Hartman. "We'll be in the shadows when we set off the fireworks, so give us ten seconds, and we'll climb aboard."

Ronaldo pretended to laugh as he examined his surroundings and calculated the distance and timing he needed to make it to the runway. It would be enough to get there in the minimum time he needed under normal circumstances. But if they were under fire, things could get a lot more interesting, to say the least.

"You'll get your ten seconds. We'll give you more if we can...but no promises. This is gonna spook the locals, so we have to make it work," warned Ronaldo, casually turning away. "We pull the stairs at ten seconds and start our taxi," he added for clarity.

Athena and G reached the crowded terminal and quickly noticed they were two insignificant travelers among a sea of hundreds of other people. Everywhere they looked, they saw someone occupying the space surrounding them.

"Check the bathroom, G," said Athena. "He's got to be changing his look. I mean, *I* would if I were him."

G's frustration kept him from concentrating. He kept looking into the sea of people hoping to catch a glimpse of Hakim. Athena squeezed his hand and looked into his eyes.

"Check the men's room," she said again with a nod and a softer tone that captured his attention.

Without much of a reaction, G let go of her hand and headed for the men's room.

Todd and Ronaldo were escorted to the base of the stairs of the jet by the same man who led them off.

"Yo, we can make it from here. Tell this chump we don't need an escort all the way to the top, unless he wants a ride to Central America. For that I wouldn't blame him, but he'll have to leave all this," said Todd, as he sarcastically looked at his dingy surroundings.

Ronaldo offered a politically correct translation to the escort, who allowed them to continue up the stairs alone.

"Our guys safely on board?" asked Ox.

"Not quite yet," said Ronaldo as he and Todd boarded the plane.

"Pull the stairs and let's get on up outta this place," said Todd.

"Not quite yet," said Ronaldo again, looking at Todd, who looked at Ox, who looked at Pat.

"Don't look at me. I don't have a clue as to what the fuck the plan is," said Pat.

"OK, brainiac," said Todd, looking at Ronaldo. "What is the plan? Cuz it's not like we have a whole lotta time left to come up wit' one."

The plane suddenly shuddered by the percussion of an explosion. Ronaldo began barking orders.

"Monty, time to go. Spool up the engines and start your taxi. Don't stop for shit. Normal taxi power...not too fast. I'll be in the cockpit beside you in ten seconds."

Ox stepped forward toward the cockpit. "I'll help Monty up front. You handle things back here and get those men on board," he said to Ronaldo.

The sound of the jet engines spooling up to taxi power could be heard over the confusion setting in on the ramp and was louder than normal inside the fuselage, considering the door was still open.

"I need everyone's eyes peeled for our two hitchhikers. We pull these stairs at ten seconds."

"That's your plan?" shouted Todd. "What the—"

"Wait, I see 'em." said Pat, leaning forward to look out the starboard window.

Ronaldo crouched low and shouted to Hartman as he approached the stairs. Sparks were starting to come from the dragging stairway as Hartman grabbed the handrail and stepped on the first stair.

Ronaldo reached out a hand and continued to look for threats as he searched for Booker. He didn't want to leave with just one member. He leaned out as far as he could. Pat grabbed the back of Ronaldo's pants to keep him from falling out of the jet, and anchored himself to a handrail.

Hartman looked up to see Ronaldo reaching out, encouraging him to continue. Hartman purposely paused to check on his teammate, who was following closely behind him.

"C'mon man, keep climbing. We've got to get outta here." shouted Ronaldo, partly to get his attention and partly because of the noise and confusion.

Hartman turned to see his partner crouched under the fuselage of the taxiing jet, keeping pace with its increasing speed when shots began to ring out from the dark. They were under fire.

G walked into the dingy bathroom. He pushed open the door to six toilet stalls.

All empty.

He stepped into the last stall, sat on the toilet and pulled the envelope from his pocket. He needed to know more about the contents. He attempted to put the data into a place in his mind that Hakim couldn't compromise. Storing them in his memory would be better and more secure than walking around in a third-world country with such sensitive, top secret documents that could potentially fall into the hands of Khalid Abdul-Hakim — or anyone else, for that matter. But how could he do that? Where, in his mind, could he store such a thing? He sat there examining the outside of the envelope, contemplating his dilemma. He took a deep breath and opened the envelope.

He examined the index cards closely and forced his mind to capture the data as he transferred the characters to memory. As much as he tried, he couldn't get a read on a translation of the code his eyes absorbed. Despite that, he filed away each line to memory. When he was certain he had the contents firmly parked in his mind, he placed the cards into his pants pocket and the empty envelope back into his shirt pocket.

He opened the door and stepped out of the stall, examined his reflection in the soiled mirror, washed his hands in lukewarm water, and left the restroom. He found Athena outside, patiently waiting.

"Everything OK, G?"

"Yeah, I think so. Any action worth mentioning out here?"

"No. What now?"

"Now we find a place to stay and get some rest...if we can."

"What about the *mark*?"

"Not too concerned about him, unless he's watching us right now and manages to surprise us. And I don't believe he is," said G with some hesitation, casually looking about the room as inconspicuously as possible. "Besides, I have a gut feeling he'll find us," he added.

"There's a taxi station this way," said Athena, grabbing G's hand again. She had come to trust his "gut feelings" as she learned more about him. He enjoyed the touch of her hand entwined with his.

"Airport hotel, please," instructed Athena to the taxi driver.

"Of course," responded the driver.

44

"Son-of-a-bitch," shouted Ronaldo in reaction to gunshots. "Dude, you better grab my hand *now* and get your happy ass on board this jet, or I swear to God I will leave you right here."

"Not without my wingman," shouted Hartman, crouching and extending his free hand to his teammate.

More shots rang out. A bullet hit the jet just above Ronaldo's position.

"Dammit," shouted Ronaldo, realizing how close that one landed.

"We gotta pull the stairs." shouted Monty from the front.

"Yo, I hear that, but we got people hanging out the frigging door, so you're gonna have to bear with us for a second," shouted Todd.

Hartman felt the wind pick up with the taxi speed of the jet.

"C'mon boss, you need to commit real soon," said Hartman, crouching lower with an extended hand to Booker.

A black SUV emerged from the darkness and pulled alongside the jet.

Ox moved forward past the chaos into the cockpit to help Monty.

Ronaldo looked up to see guns pointed straight at him and Hartman form the SUV. He made eye contact with one of the men who was specifically taking aim to shoot him. It was the same man who had served as escort for the drug buy.

Time slowed...

More gunfire erupted.

Ronaldo shut his eyes and prepared to take a bullet. He just hoped it wouldn't be fatal.

The gunfire got louder and closer. He waited...and waited. The next thing he felt was a firm grasp to his extended hand.

Ronaldo opened his eyes to see Hartman staring at him with determination. Booker close behind him, now firmly planted on the stairs with his weapon drawn, aiming out toward the ramp.

Time shifted past normal speed to what seemed like hyper speed. The wind was blowing harder from the increase in taxi speed, sparks were flying off the extended stairway, and the engine noise was deafening.

Ronaldo heard a gunshot at close range. It came from the barrel of Todd's weapon when he had taken a preemptive shot from an awkward straddle position above Ronaldo from the open doorway. He hit the driver squarely in the left temple, sending the SUV veering off into the darkness and clearing the way, at least for the moment, for things to reach a momentary and eerie quiet.

"I never really liked that dude anyway," said Todd, stepping back into the jet to make room for the newest passengers.

"What's the status of operation buy-out?" asked Dan.

"I'd like to say things are smooth, but that would be a half-truth," reported Dave. "Got fresh overhead video for you from the Predator—less than five minutes old."

Dan watched as things got a little dicey and asked to see a live feed.

Dave directed him to a different screen that showed the Gulfstream jet still on the ground in Colombia. He could clearly see something on fire some distance away from the aircraft, now positioned near the runway.

"Why are they still on the ground? What's the status?"

"Unknown. We do know shots were fired," reported Dave.

Dan looked at Dave, expecting him to have more information than that.

"We're doing what we can to keep this as quiet as possible, despite the excitement and current conditions. We're also trying to get a read from the crew on why they're still on the ground. But, as you can imagine, they're very busy right now."

Dan sat quietly as he watched the monitors. "Well, I'm not going anywhere until they get airborne and we get a status update," he said. "I assume our Predator is armed?"

"Affirmative," Dave said, nodding, and went to work.

Athena placed her bag on the floor and sat on the edge of the bed. G locked the hotel door and sat in a chair next to her. They were both tired.

"Let's get some sleep," said G, removing his shoes. "You take the bed," he added as he reclined the chair.

"I was hoping you'd join me," responded Athena with an inviting overture.

G drew a deep breath as he considered the offer. As inviting and irresistible as it was, he had to decline. He knew Hakim would be seeking him and his secrets. If he gave in to the desire and allure of Athena, he'd risk exposure to himself and to Athena.

"There's nothing I'd like more," said G, looking deep into her eyes. "But I have to stay centered on why we're here."

Athena agreed, despite her disappointment in his response. She removed her shoes and unbuttoned her blouse and made her way to the bathroom. G could see through an opening in the door she purposefully left open to give him a glimpse of what he turned down.

He studied her as she removed her blouse. He watched as she brushed her hair and then unsnapped her bra and took her time removing it before slipping into a T-shirt. G studied her long slender legs as she slid off her jeans and carefully folded them. She emerged from the bathroom dressed in a T-shirt that barely covered the crest of her perfectly shaped ass.

She leaned over and kissed G on the forehead and smiled. Then she whispered in his ear. "Be careful tonight, G. I can feel it, too."

G returned the smile and closed his eyes.

Ronaldo reeled Hartman aboard the jet with the help of Todd and Pat.

"Rescue one,'" shouted Ronaldo, loud enough for everyone to hear the progress report.

"Copy, rescue one," responded Ox, as they approached the threshold of the runway.

Ronaldo looked down to see Booker making his way toward the door. A single set of headlights appeared in the distance and was headed their way. He reached down to offer a hand to Booker and helped him aboard the jet.

"Rescue two...rescue two," shouted Ronaldo.

"Get 'em strapped in, so we can leave this party," said Ox, as he and Monty powered the jet onto the runway.

Todd pulled the stairs and closed the door, but it wouldn't lock.

"Yo, Ronaldo, gimme a hand, bro," said Todd, struggling with the lock lever.

"Are we all strapped in?" asked Ox over the intercom.

The jet came under fire once again from the approaching vehicle.

"Get her airborne, Ox. We're fine back here. Just get her airborne," shouted Ronaldo as he and Todd struggled to get the door locked. They both knew an unlocked door would prevent them from being able to pressurize and climb to a safe altitude.

An SUV drove onto an adjacent taxiway positioned about half-way down the runway. Ox saw the vehicle turn off its headlights as he looked down the runway to ensure it was clear before taking off.

"Yo, Pat, you busy?" asked Ox over the intercom.

"Never too busy for you, boss. Whatcha got?"

"I need to squash a bug," answered Ox in his usual clandestine slang.

Pat knew what he needed and quickly banged the keys on his laptop.

"Type and position?" asked Pat.

"SUV 'bout half-way down the runway on the right side."

Having direct communications with the Predator, Pat was ready to execute on Ox's command.

"Copy," said Pat. "Ready on your call."

Pat and the crew could hear the engines spooling up as Ox and Monty held the jet in place until they had the power to take off. The jet leapt forward when they released the brakes while the engines loudly announced their departure.

"Now!" said Ox.

Pat hit the command key. Ox and Monty watched from the cockpit windows when the vehicle exploded, illuminating the darkness with an orange fireball.

"Good job, Pat," said Ox.

Ox and Monty pulled back on the yoke as the jet screamed by the carnage of the burning vehicle. The G4 quickly climbed away from the chaos and danger of the Colombian landscape.

Todd and Ronaldo struggled to maintain their balance as Ox and Monty maneuvered the jet through the night sky.

"This bitch is pissin' me off," announced Todd. "She ain't never let me down, bro, but I've never given anyone a sleigh ride on the stairs before, either."

"Oh shit, check this out," said Ronaldo, pointing to a piece of metal lodged into the door seal.

"All we gotta do now is figure out a way to remove that and we should be good to go," said Todd. "Any suggestions?"

"You're gonna have to open the door," said Booker.

Todd and Ronaldo looked at Booker then at each other.

"Seems like a simple fix, if you can get that door open," Booker said reassuringly.

Ronaldo alerted the crew. Ox and Monty leveled off and slowed the jet so the men could open the door while Booker removed a small metal flange that had been bent during the departure chaos.

Todd pulled the door, pushed the lock lever down, and sealed the door. Ronaldo made his way to the cockpit and offered a thumbs-up.

"Good to go, gentlemen. Let's go home," said Ronaldo with a smile. "You want me to take the right seat back, Ox?"

"No way kid. I'm having too good a time up here. Have a cocktail and enjoy the flight," he said with a rare smile, flipping a switch to pressurize the aircraft.

As Ronaldo returned to the cabin, he felt the increasing forces of the climb and the pressurization take effect on his inner ears.

G looked over at Athena while she drifted off to sleep. A smile appeared on his face at the thought of knowing she was close by. He could smell her perfume in the air when he shut his eyes and drifted into REM sleep almost immediately thereafter.

G felt the weight of his body lighten. He looked back at himself as he drifted from his resting place in the recliner. He gave in to the flow of his dream and accelerated toward a destination.

Angel…are you there, Angel? he subconsciously asked.

Yes, she whispered.

I hear the sound of water, he said.

Your source of self, she answered, still in a whisper.

G could see his surroundings unfold before him. He was standing in ankle-deep water at the edge of a tranquil ocean. The sun had set, and the full moon illuminated a blue hue across the sky in one of the most spectacular displays of color he had ever witnessed.

The colors…

Your source of wisdom, she calmly answered.

He knelt to one knee. *I'm humbled by it all, Angel.*

"Your source of strength," she said, as he felt the warm touch of her hand on his shoulder.

He looked up to see Angel standing before him. She had taken on a beauty he had not yet seen since the encounter with the snake. Her hair flowed in suspension. The aura surrounding her was familiar. In an instant, he learned this was the visual manifestation of the culmination of her spiritual strengths…as if she were preparing for battle. There truly was none like her in the real world.

"We have to go now," she said forcefully. "Collect yourself and focus on the power of your strengths."

G rose to his feet and stole another look at the sky, now changing into a darker version of the beautiful blue hues he'd seen moments ago.

"Where are you taking me?"

"*I* am not the one taking *you* anywhere," she said. "Your mind is made up on where you need to go. You have merely to decide…and you will go there."

G closed his eyes and focused on finding Hakim. He felt another surge on his body, his mind driving him in the direction of a familiar place. As his surroundings came into view, he could see that he had come full circle back to the same hotel he and Athena had chosen in San Jose.

His heart quickened when he realized the close proximity of Hakim.

He watched the picture unfold before him while visually scanning the lobby. His vision carried him down the very hallway that led to his room. His journey paused just outside the threshold of the door to his hotel room. He grew concerned while trying to come to grips with the meaning behind this dream. He slowly looked to his right and then his left. He turned around and examined the door behind him and felt the hair on the back of his neck bristle as his adrenaline surged. He decided to enter when he heard a noise in the room behind him—his room.

"Athena…"

45

G reached out to turn the doorknob. Before his hand made contact, the door opened for him. He stepped into the room, and there, standing before him, was Hakim.

I've been waiting for you, Hakim said subconsciously. *Give me what I want, and I'll kill you quickly.*

G stood his ground and looked at Hakim with defiance.

Hakim slowly closed his eyes, tilted his head back slightly, and smiled as he drew a breath in through his nose.

"I see you continue to gain strength," he said. "I can feel it. But I can *smell* your fear. You have locked away secrets in your mind, but I too have gained strength," he said, opening his eyes and quickly thrusting his arms toward G.

G felt a powerful energy overwhelming him, lifting him from his feet and forcing him into the wall behind him. He raised his head to see Hakim approach G's earthly body, resting in the recliner where he had begun his dream. G rose to one knee and slowly lifted his head to peer back into Hakim's eyes.

"There's no mirror separating the dimensions of reality and alter consciousness this time," said Hakim. "That simply means I can kill your real body and watch you suffer to your death in this dimension."

"If that's the case," said G, with determination and grit, "then I can do the same."

"Admittedly so," answered Hakim with a smirk. "But you'd have to know where my *real* body is resting."

G studied Hakim's movements and thoughts while watching Hakim slowly move about the room.

"I see you have a companion," said Hakim, stopping to look at Athena sleeping in the lone hotel bed. "You know, a woman can make a man very weak."

G continued to analyze the man and absorb the nuances of his tactics and intentions while he continued to talk.

"Perhaps I should demonstrate the strength of my abilities by killing your friend first," he said, moving toward Athena.

G slowly rose to his feet.

"A woman may weaken a man," said G, defiantly. "But your mouth weakens you," he added, raising his hand and silencing Hakim's ability to speak.

Unable to physically speak, Hakim turned his attention from Athena and lunged at G. Both men fell to the ground in a struggle for dominance.

G fell back onto the floor and used the momentum to push Hakim up and away from him, flipping him onto his back. As Hakim rose to his feet, G ran toward him and threw his entire weight into Hakim's ribcage, sending both men crashing through the hotel door and into the hallway.

Hakim managed to get to his feet first and hit G with a right uppercut to his jaw as he arose from the floor. The punch set G back on his heels as his mind began to swim away.

Hakim pulled a revolver from his waist and aimed it directly at G. *Tell me what I need to know*, demanded Hakim telepathically.

"Or what?" scoffed G. "You gonna shoot me?"

Hakim fired his weapon.

Time slowed…

G reacted by projecting himself immediately behind Hakim and punching him squarely in his kidneys with a force that both surprised and impressed him.

Hakim fell to his knees and loosened his grip on the revolver.

G grabbed the weapon with his right hand and grabbed Hakim's shirt collar with his left. He kicked in the door across the hall and dragged Hakim into the room.

Hakim's heart raced when he realized G knew *exactly* where his earthly body rested.

Dream Operative

How did you...? exclaimed Hakim, suddenly at a loss for words to complete the thought.

"See anyone familiar, asshole?" asked G, bringing Hakim face-to-face with his sleeping, earthly body.

Please, Hakim pleaded.

"You want to know what was in that envelope, asshole?" shouted G. "Authority for me to kill you!" He raised the gun, pointed it at Hakim's temple, and squeezed the trigger, sending a bullet into the head of Hakim's earthly body.

Time slowed once again. Hakim watched in shock as the bullet penetrated his own earthly body. Intense pain seared through Hakim's head. He closed his eyes and fell limp in G's grasp.

G stood silently, breathing deeply, Hakim's collar tightly wrapped in the firm grasp of his left hand, a smoking pistol in his right.

It's over, whispered Angel.

G let go of the weapon and allowed it to fall to the floor, caught in the slow motion of altered time and space.

G felt overwhelmed as the emotion of it all came rushing to him.

The gun continued its fall.

Who am I? he questioned, as the gun silently bounced on the wood floor.

What have I become?

Is this really a dream?

Is he really dead?

What is reality?

They left the hotel early the next morning.

"How'd you sleep last night?" asked Athena, as G hailed a taxi.

"Had a rough start...but eventually ended up sleeping pretty damn well, actually," he answered with a smile.

Athena raised her eyebrows and looked at G as the taxi pulled up.

He held open the door for her and smiled again.

"Where to, sir?" asked the driver.

"San Jose Airport, my friend," said G, as he closed the door.

Athena gave him a look of curiosity.

"You wanna tell me the plan, G?"

"We're goin' home."

"Home?"

"Well, sort of," said G. "I thought we'd head back to Belize for a bit."

"Thought we had a job to do," questioned Athena.

"Job is finished," said G, as the taxi pulled away from the hotel. He motioned for Athena to take notice of the ambulance and police vehicles approaching the hotel as they drove away into the city.

"I won't even ask. At least not now, anyway," said Athena, shaking her head slowly. "Have I ever told you how amazing you are?"

G smiled.

He sat alone on the quiet Belize shoreline, just beyond a line of palm trees between the beach and the BOHICA biminis bar.

G was lost in thought as the recent events of his life rushed through his mind like the waves crashing before him. His attempt to make sense of it all only added to the enormity of the responsibility of his newfound gift.

"You up for some company?"

G slowly turned his head to see Athena standing there with the warm, familiar smile she was known for. She was as stunning as ever.

"Absolutely," he replied.

She sat next to him on the sand, laid her head on his shoulder, and looked out over the ocean.

"I can see why you enjoy it here as much as you do," she said. "It really is so peaceful."

He said nothing and evaluated the remaining thoughts that flashed through his mind. He simply looked out over the water at the setting sun.

"Moments like these can really bring you back to reality," she commented softly.

"Actually, Athena, I much rather prefer the dream state."

She smiled.

G turned to look at her. "So what's next for me?"

She paused for a second, then looked into his eyes. "Ironic you should ask...then again, irony seems to follow you, now doesn't it?"

G smiled.

ABOUT THE AUTHOR

Gary Westfal is a freelance writer, artist, and educator, currently employed full-time in government service to the United States as a member of the Air Force Special Operations Command. His specialty is airfield and airspace operations supporting joint special operations forces worldwide.

He received his BS in Professional Aeronautics and his Masters of Aeronautical Science degree from Embry-Riddle Aeronautical University, where he currently teaches as a part-time adjunct professor. This is his first novel.

Gary's writing credits have come from professional editorials stemming from his in-depth knowledge of aeronautically related material connecting to processes within his profession as an operator, program analyst, and educator for the US Air Force Special Operations Command and that of his teaching experience. He is a licensed FAA air traffic controller.

Gary Westfal

He is the creator and chief contributor to a bi-weekly blog, *Introspection* (**http://gwestfal.blogspot.com/**), which provides thought-provoking topics that seek to challenge readers to think deeper, and offers a fresh perspective on personal empowerment and human interest topics.

A recent review of his manuscript by Writer's Digest 2nd Draft referred to the first hundred pages of Dream Operative as "Expertly woven with a well-written narrative, supported by a colorful cast of characters that provides a great deal of suspense, action, and a thrilling climax."

Made in the USA
Lexington, KY
19 February 2013